MIDNIGHT AT MARBLE ARCH

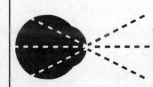

This Large Print Book carries the
Seal of Approval of N.A.V.H.

A CHARLOTTE AND THOMAS PITT
NOVEL

MIDNIGHT AT
MARBLE ARCH

ANNE PERRY

THORNDIKE PRESS
A part of Gale, Cengage Learning

GALE
CENGAGE Learning®

Detroit • New York • San Francisco • New Haven, Conn • Waterville, Maine • London

LIBRARY OF CONGRESS CATALOGING-IN-PUBLICATION DATA

Perry, Anne.
    Midnight at Marble Arch : a Charlotte and Thomas Pitt novel / by Anne Perry.
        pages ; cm. — (Thorndike Press large print basic)
        ISBN-13: 978-1-4104-5709-7 (hardcover)
        ISBN-10: 1-4104-5709-5 (hardcover)
        1. Pitt, Charlotte (Fictitious character)—Fiction. 2. Pitt, Thomas (Fictitious character)—Fiction. 3. Police—England—London—Fiction. 4. Police spouses—Fiction. 5. Great Britain—History—Victoria, 1837–1901—Fiction. 6. Large type books. I. Title.
PR6066.E693M53 2013
823'.914—dc23   2013003390

Published in 2013 by arrangement with The Ballantine Publishing Group, a division of Random House, Inc.

Printed in the United States of America
1 2 3 4 5 6 7 17 16 15 14 13

To Susanna Porter

CHAPTER 1

Pitt stood at the top of the stairs and looked across the glittering ballroom of the Spanish Embassy in the heart of London. The light from the chandeliers sparkled on necklaces, bracelets, and earrings. Between the somber black and white suits of the men, the women's gowns blossomed in every color of the early summer: delicate pastels for the young, burning pinks and golds for those in the height of their beauty, and wines, mulberries, and lavenders for the more advanced.

Beside him was Charlotte, her hand resting lightly on his arm. She had no diamonds to wear, but he knew that she had long ago ceased to mind that. It was 1896 and she was now forty years old. The flush of youth had gone, but the richness of maturity became her even more. The happiness that glowed in her face was lovelier than flawless skin or sculpted features, which were mere gifts of chance.

Her hand tightened on his arm for a moment as they started down the stairs. Then they moved into the throng of people, smiling, acknowledging this one and that, trying to remember names. Pitt had recently been promoted to head of Britain's Special Branch, and it was a heavier weight of responsibility than he had ever carried before. There was no one senior to him in whom he could confide, or to whom he could defer a difficult decision.

He spoke now to ministers, ambassadors, people of influence far greater than their casual laughter in this room might suggest. Pitt had been born in the most modest of circumstances, and gatherings like this were still not easy for him. As a policeman, he had entered homes through the kitchen door, like any other servant, whereas now he was socially acceptable because of the power his position gave him and because he was privy to a range of secrets about almost everyone in the room.

Beside him Charlotte moved easily, and he watched her grace with pleasure. She had been born into Society and knew its foibles and its weaknesses, even if she was too disastrously candid to steer her way through them, unless it was absolutely necessary, as it was now.

She murmured some polite comment to the woman next to her, trying to look interested in the reply. Then she allowed herself to be introduced to Isaura Castelbranco, the wife of the Portuguese Ambassador to Britain.

"How do you do, Mrs. Pitt?" Isaura replied with warmth. She was a shorter woman than Charlotte, barely of average height, but the dignity of her bearing made her stand apart from the ordinary. Her features were gentle, almost vulnerable, and her eyes were so dark as to seem black against her pale skin.

"I hope you are finding our summer weather agreeable?" Charlotte remarked, for the sake of something to say. No one cared about the subject: it was the tone of voice, the smile in the eyes, that mattered.

"It is very pleasant not to be too hot," Isaura answered immediately. "I am looking forward to the Regatta. It is at Henley, I believe?"

"Indeed it is," Charlotte agreed. "I admit, I haven't been for years, but I would love to do so again."

Pitt knew that was not really true. Charlotte found the chatter and the pretentiousness of lavish Society events a little tedious, but he could see in her face that she liked this woman with her quiet manner.

They spoke for several minutes more before courtesy required that they offer their attention to the others who swirled around under the lights, or drifted to the various side rooms, or down the stairs to the hallway below.

They separated with a smile as Pitt was drawn into conversation with a junior minister from the Foreign Office. Charlotte managed to catch the attention of her great-aunt, Lady Vespasia Cumming-Gould. Actually she was great-aunt by marriage to Charlotte's sister Emily, but over the years that distinction had ceased even to be remembered, let alone matter.

"You seem to be enjoying yourself," Vespasia said softly, amusement lighting her remarkable silver-gray eyes. In her prime she had reputedly been the most beautiful woman in Europe, certainly the wittiest. Did they but know it, she was also one who had fought at the barricades in Rome, during the turbulent revolution that had swept Europe in '48.

"I haven't forgotten all my manners," Charlotte replied with her usual frankness. "I fear I am reaching an age when I cannot afford to wear an expression of boredom. It is terribly unflattering."

Vespasia was quite openly amused, her smile warm. "It never does to look as if you are waiting for something," she agreed. "Which is good. Women who are waiting are so tiresome. Who have you met?"

"The wife of the Portuguese ambassador," Charlotte replied. "I liked her immediately. There is something unusual in her face. I'm sorry I shall probably never see her again."

"Isaura Castelbranco," Vespasia said thoughtfully. "I know little of her, thank heaven. I know too much about so many other people. A little mystery lends such charm, like the softness of the late afternoon or the silence between the notes of music."

Charlotte was turning the thought over in her mind before replying when there was a sudden commotion a dozen yards away from them. Like those around her, she turned toward it. A very elegant young man with a sweep of fair hair took a step backward, raising his hands defensively, a look of disbelief on his face.

In front of him a girl in a gown of white lace stood alone, the skin of her bosom, neck and cheeks flushed red. She was very young, perhaps no more than sixteen, but of a Mediterranean darkness, and already the woman she would become was clear in the curves of her body.

Everyone around the two fell silent, either in embarrassment or possibly out of confusion, as if they had little idea what was happening.

"Really, you are quite unreasonable," the young man said defensively, his voice light, trying to brush off the incident. "You misunderstood me."

The girl was not soothed at all. She looked angry, even a little frightened.

"No, sir," she said in slightly accented English. "I did not misunderstand. Some things are the same in all languages."

He still did not seem to be perturbed, only elaborately patient, as with someone who was being unintentionally obtuse. "I assure you, I meant it merely as a compliment. You must be used to such things?"

She drew in her breath to answer, but obviously could not find the words she wished.

He smiled, now openly amused at her, perhaps just a little mocking. He was good-looking in an unusual way. He had a strong and prominent nose and thin lips, but fine dark eyes.

"You'll have to get used to admiration." His look swept up and down her with just a fraction too much candor. "You'll receive a great deal of it, I can promise you."

The girl was shaking now. Even from where she stood, Charlotte could see that she had no idea how to deal with such inappropriate appreciation of her beauty. She was too young to have learned the necessary composure. It seemed her mother was not close enough to have overheard the exchange, and the young man, whom she now recognized as Neville Forsbrook, was very confident. His father was one of London's foremost bankers and the family had wealth and status, and all the privilege that came with it. He was not used to being denied anything, most especially by a girl who was not even British.

Charlotte took a step forward, and felt Vespasia's hand on her arm, restraining her.

The color had drained out of the girl's face, leaving her ashen. "Leave me alone!" Her voice was shrill and a little too loud. "Don't touch me!"

Neville Forsbrook laughed quite openly now. "My dear young lady, you are being ridiculous, and making something of a spectacle of yourself. I'm sure that is not what you wish." He was smiling, and he took a step toward her, one hand out in front of him, as if to soothe.

The girl swung her hand wildly in an arc,

13

catching his arm with hers and knocking it aside roughly. She swiveled around to escape, lost her balance and almost fell against another young woman, who promptly screamed and flung herself into the arms of a startled young man close to her.

The girl managed to untangle herself and fled, sobbing now. Neville Forsbrook remained where he was with a half smile on his face, which quickly changed to a look of bewilderment. He shrugged and spread his hands, elegant and strong, but the shadow of a smile remained. Was it out of embarrassment, or was there still the faintest hint of mockery there? Charlotte wasn't sure.

Someone stepped forward and began a polite conversation about nothing in particular. Others joined in gratefully. After a few moments the hum of voices resumed, the rustle of skirts, distant music, the slight sound of feet moving on the polished floor. It was as if nothing had happened.

"That was very ugly," Charlotte said to Vespasia as soon as she was certain they were not overheard. "What an insensitive young man."

"He must feel foolish," Vespasia replied with a touch of sympathy.

"What on earth was that all about?" a

dark-haired woman near them asked confusedly.

The elderly man with her shook his head. "Young ladies tend to be rather excitable, my dear. I wouldn't worry about it. It's just some misunderstanding, no doubt."

"Who is she, anyway?" the woman asked him, glancing at Charlotte also, in case she could shed light on it.

"Angeles Castelbranco. Pretty young thing," the elderly man remarked, not really to anyone. "Going to be a beautiful woman."

"That's hardly relevant, James!" his wife snapped. "She doesn't know how to behave! Imagine her doing that at a dinner party!"

"Quite bad enough here, thank you," another woman joined in. The brilliance of her diamonds and the sheen on her lush green silks could not disguise the bitterness of her expression.

Charlotte was stung to the girl's defense. "I'm sure you are right," she said, meeting the woman's eyes boldly. "You must know far more about it than we do. All we saw was what appeared to be a rather self-assured young man quite clearly embarrassing a foreign ambassador's daughter. I have no idea what preceded it, or how it might more kindly have been handled."

Charlotte felt Vespasia's hand fall very lightly on her arm again, but she ignored it. She kept the fixed, inquiring smile on her face and did not lower her gaze.

The woman in green colored angrily. "You give me too much credit, Mrs. . . . I'm afraid I do not know your name . . ." She left the denial hanging in the air, not so much a question as a dismissal. "But of course I am well acquainted with Sir Pelham Forsbrook, and therefore his son, Neville, who has been kind enough to show a very flattering interest in my youngest daughter."

Pitt now rejoined them with a glance at Vespasia, but Charlotte did not introduce either him or herself to the woman in green. "Let us hope it is more graciously expressed than his unflattering interest in Miss Castelbranco," she continued in a tone so sweet as to be sickly. "But of course you will make sure of that. You are not in a foreign country and uncertain how to deal with ambiguous remarks from young men directed toward your daughter."

"I do not know any young men who make ambiguous remarks!" the woman snapped back, her eyebrows arched high.

"How pleasant for you," Charlotte murmured.

The elderly man coughed, and raised his

handkerchief to conceal his mouth, his eyes dancing.

Pitt turned his head away as if he had heard some sudden noise to attract his attention, and accidentally pulled Charlotte with him, although in truth she was perfectly ready to leave. That had been her parting shot. From here on it could only get worse. She gave a dazzling smile to Vespasia, and saw an answering sparkle in her eyes.

"What on earth are you doing?" Pitt demanded softly as soon as they were out of earshot.

"Telling her she's a fool," Charlotte replied. She had thought her meaning was obvious.

"I know that!" he retorted. "And so does she. You have just made an enemy."

"I'm sorry," she apologized. "That may be unfortunate, but being her friend would have been even more so. She's a social climber of the worst sort."

"How do you know? Who is she?" he asked.

"I know because I've just seen how she acts. And I have no idea who she is, nor do I care." She knew she might regret saying that, but just at the moment she was too angry to curb her temper. "I am going to speak to Senhora Castelbranco and make

17

sure her daughter is all right."

"Charlotte . . ."

She broke free, turned for a moment and gave him the same dazzling smile she had offered Vespasia, then moved into the crowd toward where she had last seen the Portuguese ambassador's wife.

It took her ten minutes more to find her. Senhora Castelbranco was standing near one of the doorways, her daughter with her. The girl was the same height as her mother, and even prettier than she had appeared at a distance. Her eyes were dazzling, and her skin softly honey-colored with a faint flush across her cheeks. She watched Charlotte approach them with an alarm that she could not hide, even though she was clearly trying to.

Charlotte smiled at her briefly, then turned to her mother. "I'm so sorry that wretched young man was rude. It must be impossibly difficult for you to do anything, in your diplomatic position. It really was inexcusable of him." She turned to the girl, then realized she was uncertain how fluent her English might be. "I hope you are all right?" she said a little awkwardly. "I apologize. We should have made sure you were not placed in such an ugly situation."

Angeles smiled, but her eyes filled with

tears. "Oh, I am quite all right, madam, I assure you. I . . . I am not hurt. I . . ." She gulped. "I just did not know how to answer him."

Isaura put a protective arm around her daughter's shoulder. "She is well, of course. Just a little embarrassed. In our own language she would've known what to say." She gave a little shrug. "In English one is not always sure if one is being amusing, or perhaps insulting. It is better not to speak than risk saying something one cannot later withdraw."

"Of course," Charlotte said, although she felt uneasy. It seemed like Angeles had actually been far more distressed than they were admitting. "The more awkward the situation, the harder it is to find the words in another language," she agreed. "That is why he should have known better than to behave as he did. I am so sorry."

Isaura smiled at her, her dark eyes unreadable. "You are very kind, but I assure you there is no harm done beyond a few moments' unpleasantness. That is unavoidable in life. It happens to all of us at some time or another. The Season is full of events. I hope we will meet again."

It was gracious, but it was also a dismissal, as if they wished to be left alone for a while, perhaps even to leave.

"I hope so too," Charlotte agreed, and excused herself. Her feeling of unease was, if anything, greater.

As she returned to where she had left Pitt, she passed several groups of people talking. One of half a dozen included the woman in green, of whom she had undoubtedly made an enemy.

"Very excitable temperament," she was saying. "Unreliable, I'm afraid. But we have no choice except to deal with them, I suppose."

"No choice at all, so my husband informs me," another assured her. "It seems we have a treaty with Portugal that is over five hundred years old, and for some reason or another, we consider it important."

"One of the great colonial powers, I'm told," a third woman said with a lift of her fair eyebrows, as if the fact was scarcely credible. "I thought it was just a rather agreeable little country off the west side of Spain." She gave a tinkling laugh.

Charlotte was unreasonably irritated, given that she knew very little more of Portuguese colonial history than the woman who had spoken.

"Frankly, my dear, I think she had possibly taken rather too much wine and was

20

the worse for it," the woman in green said confidentially. "When I was sixteen we never drank more than lemonade."

The second woman leaned forward conspiratorially. "And too young to be engaged, don't you think?"

"She is engaged? Good heavens, yes." Her voice was emphatic. "Should wait another year, at the very least. She is far too immature, as she has just most unfortunately demonstrated. To whom is she engaged?"

"That's the thing," the third woman said, shrugging elegantly. "Very good marriage, I believe. Tiago de Freitas. Excellent family. Enormous amount of money, I think from Brazil. Could it be Brazil?"

"Well, there's gold there, and Brazil is Portuguese," a fourth woman told them, smoothing the silk of her skirt. "So it could well be so. And Angola in the southwest of Africa is Portuguese, and so is Mozambique in southeast Africa, and they say there's gold there too."

"Then how did we come to let the Portuguese have it?" the woman in green asked irritably. "Somebody wasn't paying attention!"

"Perhaps they've quarreled?" one of them suggested.

"Who? The Portuguese?" the woman in

green demanded. "Or do you mean the Africans?"

"I meant Angeles Castelbranco and Tiago de Freitas," came the impatient reply. "That would account for her being a bit hysterical."

"It doesn't excuse bad manners," the woman in green said sharply, lifting her rather pronounced chin, and thereby making more of the diamonds at her throat. "If one is indisposed, one should say so and remain at home."

At that rate, you should never set foot out of the door, Charlotte thought bitterly. *And we should all be the happier for it.* But she could not say so. She was an eavesdropper, not part of the conversation. She moved on quickly before they became aware that she had been standing in the same spot for several moments, for no apparent reason except to overhear.

She found Pitt speaking with a group of people she didn't know. In case it might be important, she did not interrupt. When there was a break in the discussion, he excused himself temporarily and came over to her.

"Did you find the ambassador's wife?" he asked, his brow slightly furrowed with concern.

"Yes," she said quietly. "Thomas, I'm afraid she's still very upset. It was a miserable thing to do to a young girl from a foreign country. At the very least, he made public fun of her. She's only sixteen, just two years older than Jemima." In the moment of saying her own daughter's name she felt a tug of fear, conscious of how terribly vulnerable Jemima was. She was partway between child and woman, her body seeming to change every week, to leave behind the comfort of girlhood but not yet gain the grace and confidence of an adult.

Pitt looked startled. Clearly he had not even imagined Jemima in a ball gown with her hair coiled up on her head and young men seeing so much more than the child she was.

Charlotte smiled at him. "You should look more carefully, Thomas. Jemima's still a little self-conscious, but she has curves, and more than one young man has looked at her a second and third time — including her dance teacher and the rector's son."

Pitt stiffened.

She put her hand on his arm, gently. "There's no need to be alarmed. I'm watching. She's still two years younger than Angeles Castelbranco, and at this age two years is a lot. But she's full of moods. One

23

minute she's so happy she can't stop singing, an hour later she's in tears or has lost her temper. She quarrels with poor Daniel, who doesn't know what's the matter with her, and then she's so reticent she doesn't want to come out of her bedroom."

"I had noticed," Pitt said drily. "Are you sure it's normal?"

"Consider yourself lucky," she replied with a slight grimace. "My father had three daughters. As soon as Sarah was all right, I started, and then when I was more or less sane again, it was Emily's turn."

"I suppose I should be grateful Daniel's a boy," he said ruefully.

She gave a little laugh. "He'll have his own set of problems," she replied. "It's just that you'll understand them better — and I won't."

He looked at her with sudden, intense gentleness. "She'll be all right, won't she?"

"Jemima? Of course." She refused to think otherwise.

He put his hand over hers and held it. "And Angeles Castelbranco?"

"I expect so, although she looked terribly fragile to me just now. But I expect it's all the same thing. Sixteen is so very young. I shudder when I remember myself at that age. I thought I knew so much, which shows

24

how desperately little I really did know."

"I wouldn't tell Jemima that, if I were you," he advised.

She gave him a wry look. "I hadn't planned on it, Thomas."

Two hours later the idea had crossed Pitt's mind a few times that he and Charlotte could finally excuse themselves and go home, satisfied that duty had been fulfilled. He caught sight of her at the far side of the room, talking to Vespasia. Watching them, he could not help smiling. Charlotte's dark, chestnut-colored hair was almost untouched by gray; Vespasia's was totally silver. To him, Charlotte was increasingly lovely, and he never tired of looking at her. He knew she did not have the staggering beauty that was still there in Vespasia's face — the grace of her bones, the delicacy — but he could see so much of each in Charlotte's poise and vitality. Standing together now, they spoke as if they were oblivious to the rest of the room.

He became aware of someone near him, and turned to see Victor Narraway a few feet over, looking in the same direction. His face was unreadable, his eyes so dark they seemed black, his thick hair heavily streaked with silver. Less than a year ago he had been

Pitt's superior in Special Branch, a man with access to a host of secrets and the iron will to use them as need and conscience dictated. He also had a steadiness of nerve Pitt thought he himself might never achieve.

Betrayal from within the department had cost Narraway his position and Pitt had been set in his place, his enemies sure he would not have the steel in his soul to succeed. They had been wrong, at least so far. But Victor Narraway had remained out of office, removed to the House of Lords, where his abilities were wasted. There were always committees, and political intrigues of one sort or another, but nothing that offered the immense power he had once wielded. That in itself might not matter to him, but to be unable to use his extraordinary talents was a loss he surely found hard to bear.

"Looking for the cue to go home?" Narraway asked with a slight smile, reading Pitt as easily as he always had.

"It's not far off midnight. I don't think we really need to stay much longer," Pitt agreed, returning the slightly rueful smile. "It'll probably take half an hour to make all the appropriate goodbyes."

"And Charlotte, another half hour after that," Narraway added, glancing across the room toward Charlotte and Vespasia.

Pitt shrugged, not needing to answer. The remark was made with affection — or probably more than that, as he well knew.

Before his train of thought could go any further, they were joined by a slender man well into his forties. His dark hair was threaded with gray at the temples but there was a youthful energy in his unusual face. He was not exactly handsome — his nose was not straight and his mouth was a little generous — but the vitality in him commanded not only attention but an instinctive liking.

"Good evening, m'lord," he said to Narraway. Then without hesitation, he turned to Pitt, holding out his hand. "Rawdon Quixwood," he introduced himself.

"Thomas Pitt," Pitt responded.

"Yes, I know." Quixwood's smile widened. "Perhaps I am not supposed to, but seeing you standing here talking so comfortably with Lord Narraway, the conclusion is obvious."

"Either that, or he has no idea who I am," Narraway said drily. "Or who I was." There was no bitterness in his voice, or even in his eyes, but Pitt knew how the dismissal had hurt and guessed how heavily Narraway's new idleness weighed on him. A joke passed off lightly, a touch of self-mockery, did not hide the wound. But perhaps if Pitt had been so easily deceived he would not belong in the leadership of Special Branch now. All his adult life in the police had made understanding people as second nature to him as dressing a certain way, or exercising courtesy or discretion. Seeing through the masks of privacy worn by friends was a different matter. He would have preferred not to.

"If he did not know who you were, my lord, he would be a total outsider," Quixwood responded pleasantly. "And I saw him speaking with Lady Vespasia half an hour ago, which excludes that as a possibility."

"She speaks to outsiders," Narraway pointed out. "In fact, I have come to the conclusion that at times she prefers them."

"With excellent judgment," Quixwood agreed. "But they do not speak to her. She is somewhat intimidating."

Narraway laughed, and there was genuine enjoyment in the sound.

Pitt was going to add his own opinion when a movement beyond Narraway caught his eye. He saw a young man approaching them, his face pale and tense with anxiety. His gaze was fixed on Pitt with a kind of desperation.

"Excuse me," Pitt said briefly, and moved

past Narraway to go toward the man.

"Sir . . ." the man began awkwardly. "Is . . . is that Mr. Quixwood you were speaking to? Mr. Rawdon Quixwood?"

"Yes, it is." Pitt wondered what on earth was the matter. The younger man's distress was palpable. "Is there something wrong?" he prompted.

"Yes, sir. My name's Jenner, sir. Police. Are you a friend of Mr. Quixwood's?"

"No, I'm afraid not. I've only just met him. I'm Commander Pitt, of Special Branch. What is it you want?" He was aware that by now at least one of the other two would have noticed the awkward conversation and Jenner's obvious unhappiness. They might be refraining from interruption on the assumption it was Special Branch business.

Jenner took a deep breath. "I'm sorry, sir, but Mr. Quixwood's wife has been found dead at their home. It's worse than just that, sir." He gulped, and swallowed with difficulty. "It looks pretty plain that she's been murdered. I need to tell Mr. Quixwood, and take him there. If he has any friends who could . . . be there to help him . . ." He trailed off, not knowing what else to say.

After all his experience with violent and unexpected death, Pitt should have been

29

used to hearing of it and been familiar with the grief it would cause. But, if anything, it seemed to grow more difficult with each case.

"Wait here, Jenner. I'll tell him. I daresay Lord Narraway will go with him, if Quixwood wishes."

"Yes, sir. Thank you, sir." Jenner was clearly relieved.

Pitt turned back to Narraway and Quixwood, who had continued talking together, deliberately not paying him attention.

"Never off duty, eh?" Quixwood said with much sympathy.

Pitt felt the knot of pity tighten inside him. "It isn't actually me he was looking for," he said quickly. He put his hand on Narraway's arm in a kind of warning. "I'm afraid there has been a tragedy." He looked directly at Quixwood, who stared back at him with nothing more than polite bemusement in his eyes.

Narraway stiffened, hearing the catch in Pitt's voice. He glanced at him, then at Quixwood.

"I'm sorry," Pitt said gently. "He's from the police. Mr. Quixwood, they have found your wife's body in your home. He has come to take you there, and anyone you may wish to accompany you at this time."

Quixwood stared at him as if the words made no sense. He seemed to sway a little before making a deliberate effort to compose himself. "Catherine?" He turned slowly to Narraway, then back to Pitt. "Found . . . ? Why the police, for God's sake? What's happened?"

Pitt wanted to reach out and take the man's arm to steady him. However, on so brief an acquaintance, such a gesture would have been intrusive, unless Quixwood was actually on the brink of falling. "I'm very sorry; it looks as if there was some kind of violence."

Quixwood looked at Narraway. "Violence? Will . . . will you come with me?" He passed his hand across his brow. "This is absurd! Who would hurt Catherine?"

"Of course I'll come," Narraway said immediately. "Make my excuses, Pitt, and Quixwood's. Don't give the reason. Just an emergency." He took Quixwood's arm and led him toward where Jenner was waiting, and together the three of them left.

The ride by hansom cab was one of the most distressing Narraway could recall. He sat next to Quixwood, with the young policeman, Jenner, on the far side. Half a dozen times Quixwood drew in his breath to speak, but in the end there was nothing to say.

Narraway was only half aware of the brightly lit streets and the warm, summer night. They passed other carriages, one so closely that he glimpsed the faces of the man and woman inside, the brief fire of the diamonds at her neck.

They turned a corner and were obliged to slow down. Light spilled out of open doors and there was a sound of laughter and distant music from inside. People were starting to leave their various parties, too busy talking to one another, calling good-byes, to pay attention to the traffic. The world continued as if death did not exist and murder was impossible.

Could it really have been murder, or was Jenner misinformed? He looked quite young and very upset.

Narraway did not know Quixwood well. Theirs was a social acquaintance, a matter of being pleasant on a number of occasions where both were required to attend a gathering, and now and then a drink at a gentlemen's club or dinner at some government function. Narraway had been head of Special Branch; Quixwood was involved in one of the major merchant banks, handling enormous amounts of money. Their paths had never crossed professionally. Narraway could not even remember meeting Quixwood's wife.

They were coming from the Spanish Embassy in Queen's Gate, Kensington, traveling east toward Belgravia. Quixwood lived on Lyall Street, just off Eaton Square. They had less than two hundred yards to go. Quixwood was sitting forward, staring at the familiar façades as they slowed down and came to a stop just short of a house where police were blocking the way.

Narraway alighted immediately and paid the driver, telling him not to wait. Jenner came out from the same side, with Quixwood beside him. Narraway followed them across the pavement and up the steps, through the classically pillared front door, into the vestibule. Every room was lit and there were servants standing around, white-faced. He saw a butler and a footman, and another man, who was probably a valet. There were no women in sight.

A man came out of the inner hallway and stopped. He looked to be in his forties, hair mostly gray, his face weary and crumpled with distress. He glanced at Jenner, then looked at Narraway and Quixwood.

"Which of you is Mr. Quixwood?" he said quietly, his voice cracking a little as though his throat was tight.

"I am," Quixwood answered. "Rawdon Quixwood."

"Inspector Knox, sir," the man answered. "I'm very sorry indeed."

Quixwood started to say something, then lost the words.

Knox looked at Narraway, clearly trying to work out who he was and why he had come.

"Victor Narraway. I happened to be with Mr. Quixwood when the police found him. I'll be of any help I can."

"Thank you, Mr. Narraway. Good of you, sir." Knox turned back to Quixwood again. "I'm sorry to distress you, sir, but I need you to take a very quick look at the lady and confirm that it is your wife. The butler said that it is, but we'd prefer it if you . . . you were to . . ."

"Of course," Quixwood replied. "Is she . . . ?"

"In the inner hall, sir. We've covered her with a sheet. Just look at her face, if you don't mind."

Quixwood nodded and walked a little unsteadily through the double doors. He glanced to his left and stopped, swaying a little, putting out his hand as if reaching for something.

34

Narraway went after him in half a dozen strides, ready to brace him if he were to stagger.

The body of Catherine Quixwood was lying sprawled, slightly on its side, mostly facedown, on the wooden parquet floor, all of her concealed by the bedsheet thrown over her, except her face. Her long, dark hair was loose, some of it fallen over her brow, but it did not hide the bloody bruises on her cheek and jaw, or the split lip stained scarlet by the blood that had oozed from her mouth. In spite of that it was possible to see that she had been a beautiful woman.

Narraway felt a knot of shock and sorrow that he had not expected. He had not known her when she was alive, and she was far from the first person he had seen who had been killed violently. Without thinking, he reached out and grasped Quixwood's arm, holding him hard. The other man was totally unresisting, as if he were paralyzed.

Narraway pushed him very gently. "You don't need to stay here. Just tell Knox if it is her, and then go into the withdrawing room or your study."

Quixwood turned to face him. His skin was ashen. "Yes, yes, of course you're right. Thank you." He looked beyond him to Knox. "That is my wife. That is Catherine.

35

Can I . . . I mean . . . do you have to leave her there like that? On the floor? For God's sake." He took a deep breath. "I'm sorry. I suppose you do."

Knox's face was pinched with grief. "Mr. Narraway, sir, perhaps if you would take Mr. Quixwood into the study." He indicated the direction with his hand. "I'll ask the butler to bring brandy for both of you."

"Of course." Narraway guided Quixwood to the door Knox had indicated.

The room would have been pleasant and comfortable at any other time. The season being early summer, there was no fire lit in the large hearth, and the curtains were open onto the garden. The lamps were already lit. Possibly Knox and his men had searched the house.

Quixwood sank into one of the large leather-covered armchairs, burying his face in his hands.

Almost immediately a footman appeared with a silver tray holding a decanter of brandy and two balloon glasses. Narraway thanked him. He poured one and gave it to Quixwood, who took it and swallowed a mouthful with a wince, as if it had burned his throat.

Narraway did not take one himself. He looked at Quixwood, who was almost collapsed in the chair.

"Would you like me to ask this man Knox what happened, as far as they can tell?" he offered.

"Would you?" Quixwood asked with a flash of gratitude. "I . . . I don't think I can bear it. I mean . . . to look at her . . . like that."

"Of course." Narraway went to the door. "I'll be back as soon as I can. Is there anyone you would like me to telephone? Family? A friend?"

"No," Quixwood answered numbly. "Not yet. I have no immediate family and Catherine . . ." He took a shaky breath. "Catherine's sister lives in India. I'll have to write to her."

Narraway nodded and went out into the hallway, closing the door softly behind him.

Knox was standing beyond the body, closer to the outside doors. He turned as Narraway's movement caught his eye.

"Sir?" he said politely. "I think, if you don't mind, it would be better if you could keep Mr. Quixwood in there, with the door closed, for the next half hour or so. The police surgeon is on his way." He glanced at the body, which was now entirely covered by the sheet. "Mr. Quixwood shouldn't have to see that, you understand?"

"Do you have any idea what happened yet?" Narraway asked.

"Not really," Knox replied, his politeness distancing Narraway as a friend of the victim's husband, not someone who could be of any use, apart from comforting the widower.

"I might be able to help," Narraway said simply. "I'm Lord Narraway, by the way. Until very recently I was head of Special Branch. I am not unacquainted with violence or, regrettably, with murder."

Knox blinked. "I'm sorry, my lord. I didn't mean to —"

Narraway brushed it aside. He was still not used to his title. "I might be of some assistance. Did she disturb a burglar? Who was it that found her? Where were the rest of the servants that they heard nothing? Isn't it rather early in the night for someone to break in? Rather risky?"

"I'm afraid it isn't that simple, my lord," Knox said unhappily. "I'm waiting on Dr. Brinsley. It's taking awhile because I had to send someone for him. Didn't want just anyone for this."

Narraway felt a twinge of anxiety, like a cold hand on his flesh.

"Because of Mr. Quixwood's position?"

he asked, knowing as he said it that it was not so.

"No, sir," Knox replied, taking a step back toward the body. After placing himself to block any possible view from the study doorway, he lifted the sheet right off.

Catherine Quixwood lay on her front, but half curled over, one arm flung wide, the other underneath her. She was wearing a light summer skirt of flowered silk and a muslin blouse, or what remained of it. It had been ripped open at the front, exposing what could be seen of her bosom. There were deep gouges in her flesh, as if someone had dragged their fingernails across the skin, bruising and tearing it. Blood had seeped out of the scratch marks. Her skirt was so badly torn and raised up around her hips that its original shape was impossible to tell. Her naked thighs were bruised, and from the blood and other fluids it was painfully obvious that she had been raped as well as beaten.

"God Almighty!" Narraway breathed. He looked up at Knox and saw the pity in his face, perhaps more undisguised than it should have been.

"I need Dr. Brinsley to tell me what actually killed her, sir. I've got to handle this one exactly right, but as discreetly as possible, for the poor lady's sake." He looked again toward the study door. "And for his too, of course."

"Cover her up again," Narraway requested quietly, feeling a little sick. "Yes . . . as discreetly as possible, please."

CHAPTER 2

"You're part of Special Branch, sir?" Knox asked, reassuring himself.

"Not now," Narraway replied. "I have no standing anymore, but that means no obligations either. If I can help, and at the same time keep this as quiet as possible, I would like to. Have you any idea at all how it happened?"

"Not yet, sir," Knox said unhappily. "We haven't found any signs of a break-in, but we're still looking. Funny thing is, none o' the servants say they opened the door to anyone. Least, not the butler or the footman. Haven't spoken to all the maids yet, but can't see a maid opening the door at that time o' night."

"If a maid had let this man in, surely she would have been attacked also?" Narraway observed. "Or at least be aware of something going on? Could Mrs. Quixwood have . . ." He stopped, realizing the idea was ugly and unwarranted.

Knox was looking at him curiously. "You mean, was the man expected?" He said what Narraway had been thinking. "Someone Mrs. Quixwood knew?"

Narraway shook his head. "But who would do this sort of thing to a woman he knows? It's bestial!"

Knox's face tightened, the lines of misery deepening around his mouth. "Rape isn't always by strangers, sir. God knows what happened here. But I swear in His name, I mean to find out. If you can help, then I'll accept it gladly, long as you keep quiet about it. Can't do with every amateur who fancies himself a detective thinking he can move in on police business. But you're hardly that." He sighed. "We'll have to tell Mr. Quixwood what happened, but he doesn't need to see her. Better not to, if he'll be advised. Don't want that to be the way he remembers her." He passed his hand over his brow, pushing his hair back. "If it were my wife, or one o' my daughters, I don't know how I'd stay sane."

Narraway nodded. He wasn't going to get it out of his mind easily.

They were interrupted by the arrival of Brinsley, the police surgeon. He was at first glance an ordinary-looking man, with drooping shoulders and a tired face, which was not surprising after midnight on what had probably become a long day for him even before this.

"Sorry," he apologized to Knox. "Out on another call. Man dead in an alley. Appears to be natural causes, but you can't tell till you look." He turned toward the sheet on the floor. "What've we got here?" Without waiting for an answer, he bent down and with surprising gentleness pulled the covering away. He winced and his face filled with sadness. He said something, but it was under his breath and Narraway did not catch it.

In case Quixwood should come out into the hall, possibly wondering what was happening, or to look for him, Narraway excused himself and went back into the study, closing the door behind him.

Quixwood was sitting in the big armchair exactly as he had been before. Aware of movement, he looked up as Narraway entered. He started to speak, and then stopped.

Narraway sat down opposite him. "Knox seems like a decent and competent man," he said.

"But . . . does that mean you won't help . . ." Quixwood left the half-spoken request hanging in the air.

"Yes, of course I will," Narraway answered, surprised by his own vehemence. The face of the woman lying on the floor only a few yards from them had moved him more than he expected. There was something desperately vulnerable about her.

"Thank you," Quixwood said quietly.

Narraway wanted to talk to him, distract his attention from what was going on out in the hallway, and above all make absolutely certain Quixwood did not go there while the surgeon was working. His examination of the body would be intimate and intrusive; it would have to be. The violation would be so terribly obvious that seeing it would be almost as bad as witnessing the rape itself. But what was there to say that was not facile and rather absurd in the circumstances? No conversation could seem natural.

It was Quixwood who broke the silence. "Did they find where he broke in? I don't know how that happened. The doors and windows all lock. We've never been robbed." He was speaking too quickly, as if saying it aloud could change the truth. "The house must have been full of servants at that time. Who found her? Did she cry out?" He swallowed hard. "Did she have time to . . . I mean, did she know?"

That was a question Narraway had been dreading. But Quixwood would have to hear it sometime. If Narraway lied to him now he would not be believed in the future. Yet if he told him anything even close to the truth, Quixwood would want to go out and look. Such a need would be instinctive, hoping it was not as bad as his imagination painted.

"No," he said aloud. "They haven't found any broken locks or forced windows so far. But they haven't finished looking yet. There might be a pane of glass cut somewhere. It wouldn't be easy to see in the dark, and there's little wind to cause a draft." He went on to describe the burglar's skill of pasting paper over window glass, cutting it soundlessly and then pulling out a circular piece large enough to let a hand pass through to undo the latch. "Star-glazing, they call it," he finished.

"Do you know that from working in Special Branch?" Quixwood asked curiously, as if it puzzled him.

"No, I learned it from a friend of mine who used to be in the regular police." Narraway went on reciting other tricks Pitt had mentioned at one time or another: small details about forgers of many different sorts, about pickpockets, card sharps, fencers of all the different qualities of stolen goods. Neither of them cared about it but Quixwood listened politely. It was better than thinking about what was going on in the hall only feet away.

Narraway was just about out of explanations of the criminal underworld of which Pitt had educated him, when at last there was a knock on the door. At Quixwood's answer, Knox came in, closing it behind him.

"Excuse me, my lord," he said to Narraway, then turned to Quixwood. "The surgeon's left, sir, and taken Mrs. Quixwood's body with him. Would you mind if I ask you one or two questions, just to get things straight? Then . . . I don't know if you wish to stay here, or perhaps you'd rather find somewhere else for the night? Do you have any friends you'd like to be with?"

"What? Oh . . . I'll . . . just stay here, I think." Quixwood looked bemused, as if he had not even considered what he was going to do.

"Wouldn't you rather go to your club?" Narraway suggested. "It would be more comfortable for you."

Quixwood stared at him. "Yes, yes, I suppose so. In a little while." He turned to Knox. "What happened to her? Surely you

46

must know now?" His face was white, his eyes hollow.

Knox sat down in the chair opposite Quixwood and Narraway. He leaned forward a little.

Narraway could not help wondering how often the inspector had done this, and if anything ever prepared him for it, or made it any easier. He thought probably not.

"I'd rather not have to tell you this, sir," Knox began. "But you're going to know it one way or another; I'm sorry, Mrs. Quixwood was raped, and then killed. We're not quite sure how she died; the surgeon will tell us that when he's had time to make an examination in his offices."

Quixwood stared at him, eyes wide, his hands shaking. "Did . . . did you say 'raped'?"

"Yes, sir. I'm sorry," Knox said unhappily.

"Did she suffer?" Quixwood's voice was hardly audible.

"Probably not for very long," Knox said. His tone was gentle, but he would not lie.

Quixwood rubbed his hand over his face, pushing his hair back, hard. His skin was ashen. There was no blood in it, and the darkness of his hair and brows looked almost blue. "How did it happen, Inspector? How did anyone get in here to do that?

Where were the servants, for God's sake?"

"We're looking into that, sir," Knox answered.

"Who found her?" Quixwood persisted.

Knox was patient, knowing the answers were needed, no matter what they were.

"The butler, Mr. Luckett. It seems he frequently goes for a short walk along the street and over the square before retiring. He found her when he checked the front door last thing before going to bed himself, sir."

"Oh . . ." Quixwood looked at the floor. "Poor Catherine," he murmured.

"I presume he locked the front door, then left for his walk through the side door and up the area steps?" Narraway asked Knox.

"Yes, sir. And returned the same way, bolting the door after him for the night."

"And saw no one?" Narraway asked.

"No, sir, so he says."

"It'll be the truth," Quixwood interjected. "Been with us for years. He's a good man." His eyes widened. "For God's sake, you can't think he had anything to do with this?"

"No, sir," Knox said calmly. "It's just practice to check everything we can, from every angle."

"Does Luckett know what time he returned to the house?" Narraway asked Knox.

"Yes, sir, just after half-past ten. He sent the footman for the police immediately."

"No telephone?" Narraway looked surprised.

"He was probably too flustered to think of it," Quixwood cut in. "Wouldn't know the police station number anyway, or think to ask the exchange for it."

"I understand," Knox agreed. "Fall back on habit when we're shaken up badly. Find the first policeman on the beat. Turned out to be a good idea, as it happens. He ran into Constable Tibenham a couple of hundred yards away, other side of Eaton Square. He came here at once and used the telephone to call me. I got here just after quarter-past eleven. Sent for you at the Spanish Embassy. You got back here, I made it half-past midnight. It's now about twenty minutes past one."

He shook his head. "I'm sorry, Mr. Quixwood, but I need to speak to at least some of the servants before I let them go to bed. Got to get it when it's fresh in their minds. Could forget something if I wait until morning."

Quixwood looked down at the carpet again. "I understand. Do you . . . do you

49

need me?"

"Not to stay for the interviews, sir. Not necessary you should know anything as you'd rather not. Just a few things I need to ask you."

Quixwood seemed confused. "What?"

"This was a party at the Spanish Embassy you were attending, sir?" Knox asked.

"Yes. What of it?"

"It was a social sort of thing? Ladies there as well as gentlemen?"

Quixwood blinked.

"Oh! Oh, I see what you mean. Yes. Catherine didn't go because she wasn't feeling very well. Bad headache. She has . . . she had them sometimes."

"But she was invited?"

"Of course. She said she preferred to go to bed early. Those parties can drag on a long time."

"I see."

Quixwood frowned. "What are you saying, Inspector? There was nothing so remarkable in that. My wife didn't go to lots of the social parties I have to attend. Great deal of noise and chatter, most of it with very little meaning. I wouldn't go myself if it weren't part of my profession to make new acquaintances, contacts and so on."

"What time did you leave the house to go

to the Spanish Embassy, sir?"

"About half-past eight or so, arrived a little before nine. I didn't need to be early."

"Take a hansom, sir?"

"No, I have my own carriage." He looked momentarily stunned. "Dear heaven, I forgot all about that! It'll still be at the embassy, waiting for me." He half rose out of his chair.

"No," Narraway responded at once. "I gave your apologies. Commander Pitt would know to have your driver informed."

Quixwood shot him a quick glance of gratitude, then turned back to Knox. "So when did it happen?"

"Probably about ten o'clock, sir, or thereabouts. After half-past nine, when the maid was in the hallway and spoke to Mrs. Quixwood, and before half-past ten, when Mr. Luckett came back and found her."

Quixwood frowned. "Does that help?"

"Yes, sir, it probably does," Knox agreed, nodding slightly. "It's very early yet in the investigation. We'll know more when we've spoken to the servants and had a proper look around in the daylight. There may even have been people — neighbors — out walking who saw something. Now, if you'll excuse me, sir, I need to go speak to the servants."

"Yes, yes, of course," Quixwood said hastily. "Please do what you must. I shall just sit here a little longer." He looked at Narraway. "I quite understand if you want to leave. It must have been a damned awful night for you, but I would be more grateful than I can say if you'd just . . . just keep an eye on things . . . do what you can . . ." His voice trailed off as if he was embarrassed.

"Anything that Inspector Knox will allow me," Narraway said, looking toward the inspector, who nodded at once.

"Come with me then, by all means, my lord," Knox said. "I'm having the servants meet with me in the housekeeper's room. They're a bit shaken up, so I thought it best to question everyone there. Cup of tea. Familiar surroundings."

Narraway saw the wisdom of it. "Good idea. Yes, I'd like to come," he accepted. "Thank you."

He gave Quixwood's shoulder a squeeze then followed Knox — past the crime scene, which was now occupied solely by a woman on her hands and knees with a bucket of water and a brush in her hand, scrubbing to clear the streaks of blood off the parquet floor where Catherine Quixwood had lain.

There were no other visible signs of disturbance. Presumably whatever had been knocked down or broken was already attended to. Narraway was grateful. At least when Quixwood himself emerged there would be no violent reminders of what had happened here.

In the housekeeper's room, a very homey and surprisingly spacious parlor, they found the housekeeper, Mrs. Millbridge. She was a plump, middle-aged woman in a black stuff dress, her hair obviously hastily repinned. With her was a young maid, red-eyed and dabbing a wet handkerchief to her nose. On a small table there was a tray of tea with several clean cups, a jug of milk, and a bowl of sugar. Knox looked at it longingly, but it seemed he did not think it suitable to indulge himself.

Narraway felt the same need and exercised the same discipline. To do less would seem a little childish; also it would put a distance between them and mark him as something of an amateur.

The maid was the one who had last seen Catherine Quixwood alive. Knox spoke to her in soothing tones, but there was nothing she could add beyond being quite certain of the time. The long-cased clock in the hallway had just chimed, and it was always right, so Mr. Luckett assured her.

Knox thanked her and let her go. Then he

asked a footman to fetch Luckett himself from wherever he might be.

"Trying to keep the staff calm, sir," the servant told him. "And see that everything's tidied up and all the windows and doors are fast. I expect they are, but the women'll rest better if they know he's checked, personal like."

Knox nodded his head. "Then ask him to come as soon as he's done. In the meantime I'll speak with Mrs. Millbridge here."

"Yes, sir; thank you, sir," the footman said gratefully, and went out, closing the door behind him.

Knox turned to the motherly woman. "Mrs. Quixwood stayed at home alone this evening. Why was that, do you know? And please give me the truth, ma'am. Being polite and discreet may not actually be the best loyalty you can give right now. I'm not going to tell other people anything I don't have to. I have a wife and three daughters myself. I love them dearly, but I know they can have their funny ways — like all of us." He shook his head. "Daughters, especially. I think I know them, then I swear they do some strange thing as has me completely lost."

Mrs. Millbridge smiled very slightly,

perhaps as much as she dared in the circumstances.

"Mrs. Quixwood wasn't all that fond of parties," she said quietly. "She liked music and the theater well enough. Loved some of the more serious plays, or the witty ones, like Mr. Wilde's used to be." She blinked, aware that since Oscar Wilde's disgrace perhaps one shouldn't admit to enjoying his work.

Knox was momentarily at a loss.

"So do I," Narraway put in quickly. "His wit stays in the mind to be enjoyed over and over again."

Mrs. Millbridge shot him a glance of gratitude, then turned her attention back to Knox.

"Did Mr. Quixwood often go to parties by himself?" he asked.

"I suppose, yes." She looked anxious again, afraid that she might unintentionally have said the wrong thing.

Knox smiled at her encouragingly, the lines of weariness on his face momentarily disappearing. "So anyone watching the house, maybe with a mind to burgling it, might have noticed that she would be alone, after the servants had retired for the night?"

She nodded, her face pale, perhaps picturing someone waiting in the dark outside, watching for that moment. She gave a very slight shiver and her body remained rigid.

"On those nights, she wouldn't have visitors?" Knox went on. "Not have a lady friend come over, for example?"

"No," Mrs. Millbridge answered. "Nobody that I know of."

"And would you know, ma'am?"

"Well . . . if she had someone visit her, she would want tea, at the very least, and perhaps a light supper," she pointed out. "There would be someone to fetch that, and then wait to let the visitor out and lock up. That means at least one maid and one footman."

"Indeed," Knox said calmly. "And if she were to leave the house herself, then I suppose there would have to be a footman available to let her back in again. Not to mention perhaps a coachman to take her wherever she was going?"

"Of course." Mrs. Millbridge nodded her head.

Narraway thought of the other alternative, that a man had visited her and she had let him in and out herself. Any refreshment he had taken would be a glass of whisky or brandy from the decanter in the study. However, he did not say so. The inspector would surely have thought of it also.

Knox left the subject of visitors. "What did Mrs. Quixwood like to do with her time?"

Mrs. Millbridge looked puzzled, and the anxiety was back again. She did not answer. Narraway wondered immediately what it was she feared. He watched Knox's face, but had no idea what lay behind the furrowed brow and the sad downturn of the inspector's mouth.

"Did she enjoy the garden, perhaps?" Knox suggested. "Maybe even direct the gardener about what to plant, and where?"

"Oh, I see," Mrs. Millbridge said with relief. "Yes, she was interested in flowers and things. Often arranged them herself, she did. In the house, I mean." For a moment there was life in her face again, as if she had allowed herself to forget why they were here. "Went to lectures at the Royal Horticultural Society now and then," she added. "Geographical Society too. Liked to read about other places, even far-off ones, such as India and Egypt. She read about the people who used to live there thousands of years ago." She shook her head in wonderment at such a fancy. "And the Greeks and Romans too."

"She sounds like a very interesting lady," Knox observed.

Mrs. Millbridge gulped and the tears spilled down her cheeks. Suddenly her grief was painfully apparent. She looked old and crumpled and very vulnerable.

"I'm sorry," Knox apologized gently. "Maybe we can leave anything else for another time. You must be tired." He glanced at the clock on the mantelpiece. "It's nearly two."

"It's all right," she insisted, lifting her chin and looking at him with a degree of defiance, her dignity returned. Perhaps it was what he had intended.

"I'm sure," he agreed. "But you'll have your hands full in the morning. The maids are all going to look to you. You'll have to be like a mother for them." He was telling her what she knew, but the reminder of her importance was obviously steadying. "They won't have known anything like this before," he went on. "We're going to have to see Mrs. Quixwood's lady's maid tomorrow anyway. I realize it's very late and she's surely too upset to speak to us tonight. But when we do . . . well, even with the extra time, she's still going to be in considerable distress. It's only to be expected. And she'll need someone's support, someone's strength. A person she knows and trusts."

"Yes." Mrs. Millbridge stood up. "Yes, of

course. Flaxley was devoted to Mrs. Quix-wood." She smoothed her skirt down. "You're right, sir." She glanced at Narraway, but she had no idea who he was. For her, Knox was in charge. "Thank you, sir. Good night."

"Good night, Mrs. Millbridge," Knox answered.

When she had retired to her bedroom, Knox at last took some tea, which was now cold. He said nothing, but it was clear in his face the strain this questioning placed on him. Narraway was overwhelmingly grateful that his professional years had not put him again and again in this position. Not seeing the confusion and the grief so closely, but dealing instead with the greater issues of danger to the country. Having to distance himself from the individual human loss had insulated him from the hard and intimate reality of it. The responsibility he had carried was heavy, sometimes almost unbearably so, but it still did not have this immediacy. It called for courage, strength of nerve and accuracy of judgment; it did not need this endurance for other people's pain. He looked at Knox with a new regard, even an admiration.

The butler, Luckett, knocked on the door and came in. He looked exhausted, his face deeply lined, his eyes red-rimmed. Still, he stood at attention in front of Knox.

"Please sit down, Mr. Luckett." Knox waved at the chair where Mrs. Millbridge had been. "I'm sorry, the tea's cold."

"Would you like some fresh tea, sir?" Luckett asked, without making a move toward the chair.

"What? Oh, no, thank you," Knox replied. "I meant for you."

"I'm quite well, thank you, sir," Luckett said. He followed Knox's gesture and sat down. "The house is in order, sir, and I have checked that all the doors and windows are locked. We're safe for the night."

"Did you find where anyone had broken in? Or any open windows, where someone could have pushed them wider and climbed through?" Knox asked.

"No, sir. Nothing out of place, and all the windows were locked when I checked them. I don't know how he got in."

"Then it looks for now as if he must have been let in," Knox said.

"Yes, sir," Luckett agreed obediently, but his face was tight with unhappiness.

"Have you known Mrs. Quixwood to have visitors late in the evening, and see them in and out herself, on any other occasion?" Knox asked.

Luckett was acutely uncomfortable at the question and all that it implied. "No, sir, I haven't," he said a little stiffly.

"But it is possible?" Knox pressed.

"I suppose it is." Luckett could not argue.

"Was the front door locked when you found Mrs. Quixwood's body tonight?" Knox asked.

Luckett stiffened, and for seconds he did not answer.

Knox did not ask again but sat staring at Luckett with tired, sad eyes.

Luckett cleared his throat. "It was closed, sir. But the bolts were not sent home," he said, looking back at Knox levelly.

"I see. And the other doors, from the side, or the scullery?"

"Locked, sir, and bolted," Luckett said without hesitation.

"So whoever it was, he came in the front, and left the same way," Knox concluded. "Interesting. At least we have learned something. When you went for your walk in Eaton Square, how did you go out, Mr. Luckett?"

Luckett froze, understanding flooding into his eyes, his face.

"I went out through the side door to the area," Luckett said very quickly. "I have a key. I lock the door as I leave — but, of course, I can't fasten the inside bolts. Then I come back through the same door. It was after that, when I went to check the front door a last time . . . that was when I saw Mrs. Quixwood."

"Do you normally do it that way?" Knox asked. "Walk, then come through and check the front door?"

"Yes, sir."

"So the side door bolts would be undone while you were out?"

"Yes, sir, but the door itself was locked," Luckett said with certainty. "I had to use my key to open it. There was no doubt, sir. No doubt at all. I heard the latch pull back, I felt it!"

Knox inclined his head in agreement. "Thank you, Mr. Luckett. Perhaps we'll speak again tomorrow. I think it would be a good idea if you went to your bed now. This isn't going to be easy for you for quite some time. You'll be needed."

Luckett rose to his feet with something of an effort. Suddenly he seemed stiff, and moved with obvious pain. He was an old man whose world had imploded in one short evening, and the only guard he had against it was his dignity. "Yes, sir," he said gratefully. "Good night, sir."

When he had gone Narraway wondered

who was going to lock up the house after he and Knox left. He turned to Knox to ask, just as there was a loud ringing on the bell board outside the housekeeper's door.

Knox looked up. "Front door?" he asked of no one in particular. "Who the devil can that be at two o'clock in the morning?" He hauled himself up out of his chair and led the way from the servants' quarters to the front hallway. As he stood there, Narraway almost on his heels, the bell rang again. In the hall it was only a dim chime.

When they reached the front entryway, there was a constable standing to attention on the outside step. Narraway could see his shadow through the hall window, and another person a little farther away.

Knox opened the door and the constable turned to face him.

"Gentleman of the press, sir," the constable said in a voice so devoid of expression as to be an expression in itself.

Knox stepped out and approached the other man. "When there's something to say, we'll tell you." His voice was cold and had an edge of suppressed anger in it. "It's past two in the morning, man. What the devil are you doing knocking on people's doors at this time of night? Have you no decency at all? I've half a mind to find out where you live and wait until you've had a tragedy in your family, and then send a constable around to bang on your front door in the middle of the night!"

The man looked momentarily taken aback. "I heard —" he began.

"I told you," Knox grated the words between his teeth, "we'll tell you when there's anything to say! You damn carrion birds smell death in the air and come circling around to see what profit there is in it for you."

Narraway saw a fury in Knox that took him aback — and then the instant after, he realized how deeply the inspector was offended, not for himself but for those inside the house, who were shocked and frightened by events they could not even have imagined only hours ago. There was a raw edge of pity in the man as if he could feel the wound himself. Narraway was about to go out and add his own weight to the condemnation when he heard a step on the polished floor behind him and turned to see Quixwood standing there. He looked appalling. His face was creased and almost bloodless, his eyes red-rimmed, his hair disheveled. His shoulders drooped as if he were exhausted from carrying some huge, invisible weight.

"It's all right," he said hoarsely. "We will

have to speak to the press sometime. I would as soon do it now, and then not face them again. But I thank you for your protection, Inspector . . . I'm sorry, I forget your name." He ran his fingers through his hair as if it might somehow clear his mind.

"Knox, sir," Knox said gently, then: "Are you sure you want to talk to him? You don't have to, you know."

Quixwood nodded very slightly and walked past Narraway to the open front door. He went out onto the step, acknowledged the constable, then looked at the man from the press.

"Perhaps I should say 'good morning' at this hour," he began bleakly. "You have no doubt come because you heard we are in the middle of tragedy so overwhelming we hardly know how to act. I was summoned here before midnight because my wife was found assaulted and beaten to death in the hallway of her own home. At the moment we have no idea who did this hellish thing, or why."

He took a deep, shuddering breath. "We don't seem to have been robbed, but on further search we may find we have. The servants were in their quarters at the back of the house — except for the butler, who was out for his brief walk — and they heard nothing. The butler was the one who discovered my wife's body, when he returned. I have nothing more to say at the moment. I am sure the inspector will inform you when there is anything that is of public interest rather than private grief. Good night." He turned toward the door.

"Sir!" the man called out.

Quixwood looked back very slowly, his face like a mask in the light from the lamp above the door. He said nothing.

The man lost his nerve. "Thank you," he acknowledged.

Quixwood did not reply, but walked inside and allowed Knox to close the door behind him, leaving the constable outside.

Quixwood faced Narraway. "Thank you. I am enormously grateful for your support." His eyes searched Narraway's face. "I would appreciate it if you would do what you can to help the inspector keep speculation as . . . as low as possible. The circumstances are —" he swallowed "— are open to more than one interpretation. But I loved Catherine and I will not allow her memory to be soiled by the vulgar and prurient, who value nothing and know no honor. Please . . ." His voice cracked.

"Of course," Narraway said quickly. "As I said, anything Knox will allow me to do, I will. There may be avenues I can explore that he can't. I may not be head of Special Branch anymore, but still have some influence in higher offices."

Quixwood gave the ghost of a smile. "Thank you."

Narraway took one of the cabs that the police had kept and went home to get a few hours' sleep before facing the next day and trying to see the case with clearer vision. He had a hot bath to wash away some of the weariness and the tension that gripped him, then went to bed.

He slept deeply, out of exhaustion, but woke before eight, haunted by dreams of the dead woman and the terror and searing pain she must have felt as the most intimate parts of her body were torn. His head was pounding and his mouth was dry. The emptiness in his own life since losing his position as head of Special Branch seemed ridiculously trivial now, something he was ashamed to own, compared with what had happened to Catherine Quixwood.

He washed, shaved, and dressed, then went down to have a quick breakfast of scrambled eggs, toast, and tea before going out into the warm early summer day and finding a hansom to take him to Dr. Brinsley.

The morgue was a place Narraway loathed. It was too much a bitter reminder of mortality. The smell of it turned his stomach. He could always taste it for hours afterward.

Today the heat and dust, the smell of horse manure in the street outside, was suddenly sweet compared with what he knew he would face as soon as the doors closed behind him.

He found Brinsley almost immediately. The man's long-nosed, wry-humored face told Narraway that the news was ugly and probably complicated.

"Morning, my lord," Brinsley said with a grimace. "Not seen Inspector Knox, I take it?"

"No, not yet," Narraway replied. "Are you able to tell me anything?"

"Come into the office," Brinsley invited him. "Smells a little better, at least." Without waiting, he walked along the corridor, turned right, and led the way into a small room piled high with books and papers on every available surface. He closed the door behind them.

Narraway waited. He did not want to sit; it implied remaining here for longer than he wished to.

Brinsley noticed and understood. The recognition of it flickered in his eyes.

"She was raped and pretty badly beaten. The damn animal even bit her breast," he said with anger harsh in his voice. "But I don't think that was what killed her, at least not directly."

Narraway was startled, momentarily disbelieving.

Brinsley sighed. "I think she died of opium poisoning."

Narraway felt a bitter chill run right through him. The smell of the place seemed to have crept into his nose and mouth. "Before she was raped, or after?" His voice sounded hoarse. "Do you know?"

"After," Brinsley said. "Knox found the laudanum bottle and the glass from which she'd which she'd drunk in the hall cabinet. There was blood on the glass."

"Her attacker forced her to drink it?" Narraway knew the question was foolish even as he asked it.

Brinsley's face was filled with pity, for Catherine, but possibly for Narraway as well. "Far more likely she was stunned, close to despair," he answered. "Either didn't realize how much she'd taken or, more probably, meant to drink that much. The attack was very brutal. God knows what she must have felt. Many women never get over rape. Can't bear the shame and the horror of it."

"Shame?" Narraway snapped.

Brinsley sighed. "It's a crime of violence, of humiliation. They feel as if they have been soiled beyond anything they can live with. Too many times the men they think love them don't want them after that." He swallowed with difficulty. "Husbands find they can't take it, can't live with it. They can't get rid of the thought that somehow the woman must have allowed it."

"She was beaten to —" Narraway started, his voice rising to a shout.

"I know!" Brinsley cut him off sharply. "I know. I'm telling you what happens. I'm not justifying it, or explaining it. It does strange things to some men, makes them feel impotent, that they couldn't defend their own woman. I'm sorry, but it looks as if she drank it herself. God help her." He swallowed, his face pinched with pain. "Find this one, will you? Get rid of him somehow."

"We will." Narraway felt his throat tighten and a helpless anger scald through him. "I will."

CHAPTER 3

Pitt was distracted at the breakfast table. He ate absentmindedly, his attention absorbed by whatever he was reading in the newspaper. He looked up briefly to bid goodbye to Jemima and Daniel, then returned to his article. He even allowed his tea to go cold in the cup.

Charlotte stood up and took the teapot to the stove, pushed the kettle over onto the hob, and waited a few moments until it reached a boil again. With the teapot refreshed, and carrying a clean cup, she returned to the table and sat down.

"More tea?" she asked.

Pitt looked up, then glanced at his cup beside him, puzzled.

"It's cold," she said helpfully.

"Oh." He gave a brief smile, half-apologetic. "I'm sorry."

"From your expression, it's not good news," she observed.

"Speculation on the Jameson trial," he replied, folding the paper and putting it down. "Most people seem to be missing the point."

She had read enough about it to know what he was referring to. Leander Starr Jameson had returned to Britain from Africa, accused of having led an extraordinarily ill-conceived invasion from British-held Bechuanaland across the border into the independent Transvaal in an attempt to incite rebellion there and overthrow the Boer government, essentially of Dutch origin.

"He's guilty, isn't he?" she asked, uncertain now if perhaps she had misunderstood what she had read. "Won't we have to find him so?"

"Yes," Pitt agreed, sipping his new hot tea. "It'll be a question of what sentence is passed and how much the public lionizes him. Apparently he's a remarkably attractive man; not in the ordinary sense of being handsome or charming, but possessing a certain magnetism that captivates people. They see him as the ideal hero."

She looked at Pitt's face, the somber expression in his eyes that belied the ease of his voice.

"There's more than that," she said gravely.

"It matters, doesn't it?"

"Yes," he answered softly. "Mr. Kipling believes him a hero for our time: brave, loyal, resourceful, seizing opportunity by the throat, a born leader, in fact."

Charlotte swallowed. "But he isn't?"

"Mr. Churchill says he is a dangerous fool who will, in the near future, cause war between Britain and the Boers in South Africa," he replied.

She was horrified. "War! Could it?" She put her cup down with a slightly trembling hand. "Really? Isn't Mr. Churchill being . . . I mean, just drawing attention to himself? Emily says he does that a bit."

Pitt did not answer immediately.

"Thomas?" she demanded.

"I don't know. I have a fear that Churchill could be right." His gaze did not waver from hers. "Not just because of the Jameson Raid — there are other things as well. The gold found there is going to attract a lot of adventurers and profiteers."

"Will it affect us?" she asked him. "Special Branch? You?"

He smiled. "I can't absolutely ignore it."

She nodded, started to say something else, then decided it would be wiser not to go on asking him questions no one could yet answer. She stood up.

"Charlotte," he said gently.

She turned, waiting.

"One thing at a time." He smiled.

She put out a hand and touched his. It was not necessary to say anything.

She had been looking forward to the garden party that afternoon, largely because she was going with Vespasia, who would call to pick her up. It was only lately, since Pitt's promotion, that Charlotte had been able to afford new gowns suitable for such occasions, rather than borrowing something from either Vespasia, which would fit her very well but be a little different from her own taste, or her sister Emily, who was slimmer and a couple of inches shorter. Not to mention the fact that Charlotte's coloring was more vivid than Vespasia's exquisite silver or Emily's delicately fair hair and alabaster skin.

Charlotte always enjoyed Vespasia's company. The older woman never spoke trivially, and she was informed about all manner of things, from the most important to the merely amusing. Charlotte was filling the time reading a book in the parlor when Vespasia arrived and was shown in by Minnie Maude, their maid. Although Minnie Maude had been with Charlotte over a year now, she was still overawed when announcing, "Lady Vespasia Cumming-Gould, ma'am."

Charlotte rose to her feet immediately.

"You are early. How very nice," she said warmly. "Would you like a cup of tea before we leave?"

"Thank you," Vespasia accepted. She sat gracefully in the other large chair and arranged her sweeping skirts, immediately at home in the modest room with its comfortable, well-used furniture, bookshelves, and family photographs.

Charlotte nodded to Minnie Maude. "The Earl Grey, please, and cucumber sandwiches," she requested. She knew without having to ask what it was that Vespasia would like.

As soon as the door was closed Charlotte regarded Vespasia more closely and noticed a certain tension in her.

"What is it?" she asked quietly. "Has something happened?"

"I believe so," Vespasia replied. "At least, beyond question, something has happened, but I believe it is more serious than it is pretending to be." She smiled very briefly, as if in apology for the darkness she was about to introduce. "I heard from a friend of mine that Angeles Castelbranco has

75

broken off her engagement to Tiago de Frei-tas."

Charlotte was puzzled. "Is that so serious? She is very young. Perhaps that is why she was so highly strung the other evening? She is not yet ready to think of marriage? She's only two years older than Jemima. She's still a child!"

"My dear, there is a lot of difference between fourteen and sixteen," Vespasia responded.

"Two years!" Charlotte could not possibly imagine Jemima thinking of marriage in two years. Any thought of her leaving home was years away.

Now Vespasia's smile was gentle but bright with amusement. "You will be surprised what a change those two years will bring. The first time she will fall in love with a real man, not a dream, is not nearly as far away as you think."

"Well, perhaps Angeles is in love, but not yet ready to think of marrying," Charlotte suggested. "It is fun to be in love without the thought of settling down in a new home, with new responsibilities — and before you know it, children of your own. She has barely begun to taste life. It would be very natural to wish for another year or two at least before that."

"Indeed. But one may remain engaged for several years," Vespasia pointed out.

Charlotte frowned. "Then what is it you think may have happened? A quarrel? Or she imagines herself in love with someone else?" A more painful thought occurred to her. "Or she has heard something distressing about her fiancé?"

"I doubt that," Vespasia answered.

Minnie Maude knocked on the door and came in with a tray of tea and very thin cucumber sandwiches, which Charlotte had recently taught her to cut.

The maid glanced at Charlotte to see if she approved.

"Thank you," Charlotte accepted with a little nod of her head. Minnie Maude had replaced Gracie, the maid the Pitts had had since their marriage. Gracie herself had at last married Sergeant Tellman and set up her own house, of which she was immensely proud. Her place would be impossible to fill, but Minnie Maude was gradually making the role her own. Now a wide smile split her face for a moment before she recalled her decorum again, dropped a curtsy, and withdrew, closing the door behind her.

Charlotte looked at Vespasia.

Vespasia regarded the sandwiches. "Excellent," she murmured. "Minnie Maude is coming on very well." She took one and put it on her plate while Charlotte poured the tea.

"What do you fear has happened to Angeles Castelbranco?" Charlotte asked a few moments later.

"The marriage was an arranged one, naturally," Vespasia replied. "The de Freitas family is wealthy and highly respected. For Angeles it is a good match. Tiago is six or seven years older than her and, as far as I hear, nothing ill is known of him."

"How much is that worth?" Charlotte asked skeptically, surprised how protective she felt of a girl she had seen only once. Did that mean she was bound to become overprotective of Jemima as well? She could remember her mother being so, and she had hated it.

Vespasia was watching her with wry amusement and perhaps also with recollections of her own daughters. "A good deal," she replied. "Plus Isaura Castelbranco was young once, and I am sure has not forgotten the romance she dreamed of for herself; I doubt she would arrange for her daughter to marry someone unworthy."

"Then why are you worried?" Charlotte asked, suddenly grave again. "What is it you fear?"

Vespasia was silent for several moments. She sipped her tea and ate another of Minnie Maude's cucumber sandwiches.

Charlotte waited, recalling the party at the Spanish Embassy and the look in Angeles's face. Had it truly been as fearful as she pictured it now, or was she putting her own feelings onto it?

"What is it you think has happened?" she asked more urgently.

"I don't know," Vespasia admitted. "It is a big thing indeed to break an engagement in a family like that. If she does not give a powerful reason, then other reasons will be suggested, largely unflattering in nature. It has been said, so far, that it is she who broke it off, but sometimes a young man will allow that, as a gallantry, when in fact it is he who has done so."

Charlotte was startled. "What are you saying? That she has . . . has lost her virginity? She's sixteen, not a thirty-year-old courtesan. How could you suggest such a thing?"

"I didn't," Vespasia pointed out gently. "You did. Which perfectly makes my point. People will look for reasons, and if they are not given them they will create their own. Breaking a betrothal is not something one does lightly."

Charlotte looked down at the carpet.

"She's so young. And she looked so vulnerable at that party. The room was crowded with people, and yet she was alone."

Vespasia finished her tea and set the cup down. "I hope I am mistaken." She rose to her feet. "Shall we leave?"

For some time at the party Charlotte accompanied Vespasia as they met friends or acquaintances and exchanged the usual polite remarks. She had wanted to come, to be in the swirl of conversation, feeling the exhilaration of meeting new people, but after half an hour or so she realized how little she truly knew, could know, of the men and women around her; their clothes, their manners, and their speech covered up far more of the truth than they revealed.

Looking at a woman in a bright dress, she wondered if it was exuberance that prompted her to wear it or bravado hiding some uncertainty, fear, or grief. And the woman in the plain-cut, subdued shade of blue — was that modesty, a supreme confidence that needed no display, or simply the only gown she had not already worn in this same company? So much could be interpreted half a dozen different ways.

It was about ten minutes later that Charlotte encountered Isaura Castelbranco and with pleasure found an opportunity to engage her in conversation. It seemed very easy to ask what region of Portugal she grew up in and to hear a description of the beautiful valley that had been her home until her marriage.

"Port wine?" Charlotte said with an interest she did not have to feign. "I often wondered how they make it because it is quite different from anything else, even sherry."

"It is wine from the grapes in the Douro Valley," Isaura replied, enthusiasm lighting her eyes. "But that is not really what makes it special. It is fortified with a brandy spirit, and aged in barrels of a particular wood. It takes a great deal of skill, and some of the process is kept secret."

She smiled and there was pride in it. "We have made it for centuries, and the arts are passed down the generations within a family. Not that mine is one of them," she added hastily. "We just lived in the region. My husband's family is, however. His father and brothers were disappointed when he studied politics and chose the diplomatic service, but I think he has never regretted it. Although, of course, we still feel that tug of nostalgia when we go back to the vineyards, the sun on the vines, the labor of picking, the excitement of the first taste of the vintage.

"As a girl I used to daydream about the gentlemen whose tables it would be passed around. I pictured who they would be, what great events of state might be discussed with a glass of port in one hand." She laughed a little self-consciously. "I would think of daring adventures planned, explorations, discoveries recounted, theories put forward on a hundred new ideas, reforms to change the laws of nations. Silly, maybe, but . . ."

"Not silly at all!" Charlotte said quietly. "Much better than half the daydreams I had, I promise you. It is something to be proud of."

Isaura laughed. "Some of my in-laws' port was in the glasses of great Portuguese navigators, traders in exotic silks and spices, but much of it was also on English dining tables after the ladies had withdrawn. In my mind every great Englishman drank port, while he planned to settle America or Australia, find the Northwest Passage to the Pacific, discover how the circulation of blood works, or write about the origin of species." She flushed slightly at her own audacity.

"I think you have a marvelous imagination," Charlotte said warmly. "I shall never look at a good bottle of port again without my own being inspired. Thank you for enriching me so happily."

Before Isaura could respond, they were joined by three ladies in highly fashionable gowns and hats that drew the attention, and certainly the envy, of every woman who caught even a glimpse of them. With regret, Charlotte reverted to the conversation of gossip and trivia.

"Marvelous," one woman enthused. "You can't imagine how It looked, my dear. I'll never forget it . . ."

"Do you suppose she'll marry him?" another asked with intense curiosity. "What a match that would be!"

"I shudder to think." A third gave the slightest indication with a twitch of one elegant shoulder. "Anyway, I'm quite sure she has her eye on Sir Pelham Forsbrook."

Charlotte's attention was caught by that last name. He was the father of Neville Forsbrook, who had so cruelly taunted Angeles. She glanced sideways at Isaura and saw the distress in her face before she could conceal it with a feigned smile of interest.

"Is Sir Pelham thinking of marrying again?" Charlotte asked, with no idea of the circumstances, except that, with a son he owned to, he had to have been married once.

"*She* is thinking of it, my dear," the first woman said with a smile very slightly condescending. "Pelham is worth a fortune. All kinds of investments in Africa, I believe. Probably gold, I should think. Didn't they find masses of it in Johannesburg last year? And he's a very charming man, sort of dark and interesting, a powerful face."

One of the others giggled slightly. "I do believe you are attracted to him yourself, Marguerite."

"Nonsense!" Marguerite said a trifle too quickly. "Eleanor was a friend of mine. I wouldn't dream of it. Such a tragedy. I haven't got it out of my mind yet."

Charlotte made a mental note to ask Vespasia what had happened to Eleanor, who was presumably Forsbrook's late wife. For the moment, she turned to Isaura and said how delighted she had been to meet her again, and excused herself from the conversation.

She was still wondering about the Forsbrook family when she noticed a group of young women, perhaps seventeen or eighteen years old, laughing and talking together. They were all pretty, with the unlined features and the blemishless complexions of the young, but one of the girls in particular caught Charlotte's attention.

Her hair and eyes were both startlingly dark and quite beautiful against the peach tones of her high-necked gown. Also, she had an air of intensity that instantly made her stand out; she seemed far more serious than the others, with a look of being occupied in some private concern. Charlotte watched her for several moments as one of the other girls spoke to her and she had to ask for the words to be repeated before she replied. Even then her answer was vague, drawing a taunt, and then giggles from two of the others.

There was something familiar in her unease, and then Charlotte realized that she was Angeles Castelbranco. Her dress was utterly different from the ball gown she had worn at the embassy, but the resemblance to her mother should have been sufficient for Charlotte to recognize her again, even at a slight distance and from an angle.

There was more laughter. A young man passed close to them and smiled. Discreetly he regarded all of them but clearly it was Angeles who took his eye. Beside her the others looked pallid, even ordinary, though today her dress was extremely modest and she made no attempt to hold his glance.

The young man smiled at her.

She gave a very slight smile back at him, then immediately lowered her eyes.

He hesitated, uncertain whether he dared speak to her when she had given him no encouragement.

One of the other girls smiled at him. He inclined his head in a small bow, then walked on. Two of the girls giggled.

Angeles looked unhappy, even uncomfortable. She excused herself and moved away toward where Isaura was still involved in conversation.

Charlotte found Vespasia again. Together they strolled over toward a magnificent bed of mixed flowers, bright with pink and blue spires of lupin and dozens of gaudy oriental poppies in a profusion of scarlets, crimsons, and peaches.

Charlotte described to Vespasia how she had seen Angeles act, the other girls and the young man.

"And it troubles you?" Vespasia asked quietly.

"I'm not sure why," Charlotte admitted. "She looked so ill at ease, as if she had a deep unhappiness she was trying to overcome, but could not. I suppose I have forgotten what it was like to be sixteen. It is an alarmingly long time ago. But I think I was awkward, rather than unhappy."

"You were not engaged to be married," Vespasia pointed out.

"No, but I would've liked to have been!" Charlotte said ruefully. "I thought about it nearly all the time. I looked at every young man, wondering if he could be the one, and how it would happen, and whether I could learn to love him or not." She recalled with embarrassment some of the wilder thoughts that had passed through her mind then.

"Of course," Vespasia agreed. "We all did. The grand romances of the imagination were . . ." she smiled at her own memories, ". . . like reflections in the water — bright, a little distorted and gone with the next ripple of wind." Then her amusement vanished. "Did you sense something more seriously wrong with her?"

"Perhaps not. It was an arranged marriage, you said earlier? Sixteen is very young to feel that your fate is already decided, and by someone other than yourself."

"It is a common practice," Vespasia pointed out. "And I daresay our parents' choice for us was no more reckless than our own would have been. I remember falling in love at least half a dozen times with men it would have been disastrous for me to have married."

Charlotte drew in her breath to ask if the choice Vespasia had made in the end had been so much better. Then she realized how appallingly intrusive that would be. From the little she knew of Vespasia's life, her marriage had been tolerable, but not a great deal more than that. The great love she had known had been elsewhere, brief and ending in all but memory when she returned from Italy to England. What Vespasia had felt Charlotte did not know and did not wish to. There are many things that should remain private.

Charlotte watched a bumblebee meander lazily through the blossoms.

"I thought I would die when Dominic Corde married my elder sister, Sarah," she said candidly, turning the conversation back to her own feelings. "I cherished an impossible infatuation with him for years. I don't think he ever knew, thank heaven."

"Perhaps Angeles Castelbranco likes someone rather better than she liked her fiancé, and finds it difficult to reconcile herself to keeping her promise," Vespasia said, smiling a little in the sun and watching the same bee as it settled in the heart of a scarlet poppy. "Life can tend to lurch from one wild emotion to another at that age. Of course, with a lot of laughter, excitement, and soaring hopes in between. I don't think I could bear all that anguish again."

Charlotte looked at her quickly. Vespasia was Still beautiful, but — in spite of her poise, her wit, and all her accomplishments — perhaps she was also still vulnerable. Certainly she was very much alone. Charlotte had never thought of it before, but it struck her now with the force of a blow. Had Vespasia ever known the safety of heart that Charlotte took so much for granted?

She changed the subject quickly, before her face betrayed her thoughts.

"Perhaps we are being too fanciful about Angeles," she remarked. "I expect there is no grand passion for someone else and no betrayal by her fiancé with another woman. I am more bored with Society than I had remembered, and I can see that the devil has made more work for idle minds than he ever does for idle hands. Sometimes I wish Thomas were back in the regular police instead of in Special Branch, where all his cases are secret. I can't help anymore because he can't even tell me what they are about."

"Be careful what you wish for," Vespasia warned gently. "It may not be so pleasant if you are granted it."

Charlotte glanced at her and, seeing the

gravity in her eyes, changed her mind about responding. Instead she said, "By the way, I was listening to a piece of gossip just now, and they mentioned Pelham Forsbrook possibly marrying again. They hinted at some tragedy regarding his first wife. I had no idea what they were referring to."

Vespasia's face filled with a sudden sadness. "Eleanor," she said quickly. "I knew her only slightly, but she was charming and funny and very kind. I'm afraid she was killed in a traffic accident. Something startled the horse and it bolted. One of the wheels was caught and the whole carriage was overturned. Poor Eleanor was crushed. I think she died instantly, but it was an appalling thing to happen."

Charlotte was taken aback. "I'm sorry. Was it long ago?"

"About four years. I don't think Pelham has ever considered marrying again but, of course, I could be mistaken. I never knew him well." She smiled, dismissing the subject. "I should like you to meet Lady Buell. She is ninety if she's a day, and has been everywhere and met everyone. You will find her most entertaining."

An hour later Charlotte was looking for somewhere to set down her empty cup. She went into the big marquee, which had been erected for the unlikely event of rain, or for those who wished more adequate shelter from the sun than even the most excellent parasol could offer.

She placed her cup down and was moving toward the entrance again when she saw Angeles Castelbranco four or five yards away, on the other side of a table set with samovars for tea, which partially concealed her from view.

Angeles was holding her cup and saucer and was also facing the door when a young man came in. He was tall and fair-haired, and when he smiled at Angeles he was good-looking enough to be considered handsome.

"Good afternoon," he said warmly. "Geoffrey Andersley. May I pour more tea for you, Miss . . . ?" He hesitated, waiting for Angeles to introduce herself.

She took a step backward, holding on to her cup and saucer.

He reached for it and his fingers brushed her hand.

She dropped the cup instantly and it fell to the grass.

"I'm sorry," he apologized, as if it had been his fault. He bent to pick it up, moving closer to her to reach it.

Angeles jerked backward as though he had in some way threatened her.

He looked embarrassed as he rose to his feet again and straightened up.

"I say, I'm sorry. I didn't mean to startle you."

She shook her head, her face flushed with color, her breathing heavy, as if she had been running. She began to speak and then stopped.

"Are you all right?" he asked anxiously. "Would you like to sit down?" He held out a hand as if to steady her.

She flinched and backed farther away, knocking against a table set with glasses and clean cups and saucers. They clattered against one another and half a dozen tall champagne flutes fell over.

Angeles swung around, distressed by her own clumsiness. Now her face was scarlet.

"I'm perfectly all right, Mr. . . . Mr. Andersley. If you will allow me to pass, I would like to go outside and get a little air."

"Of course," he agreed, but he did not move.

"Let me pass!" she repeated, her voice rising, wobbling a little, out of control.

He took a small step closer to her, his face creased with concern. "Are you sure you are all right?"

Charlotte decided to intervene, even though it was possibly tactless and certainly none of her concern.

"Excuse me." She came out from behind the samovars and moved toward Angeles.

Angeles saw her and her face filled with relief.

"Perhaps you don't remember me, Miss Castelbranco," Charlotte said smoothly. "We met the other evening. I am Mrs. Pitt. I should so like you to meet my great-aunt, Lady Vespasia Cumming-Gould. Would you care to come with me?"

"Oh, yes!" Angeles said immediately. "Yes. I would be delighted." She stepped closer to Charlotte.

Charlotte looked at Andersley and smiled. "Thank you for your courtesy. I hope you have a pleasant afternoon."

"Mrs. Pitt." He bowed and stepped back to allow them both to pass, giving them room for their wide skirts. Even so, Angeles was obliged to pass within a yard of him. Her face was pale as she did so, and she moved hastily and without looking at him.

Outside in the sun Charlotte kept up the pretense while they walked side by side the hundred yards or so to where Vespasia had just left another conversation. She was standing in the sun, her face lifted a little to its light, looking more like the Italians with whom she had stood at the barracks in '48 than the English aristocrat she was now. Charlotte wondered what memories were in her mind or her heart.

Charlotte and Angeles approached Vespasia. They went through with the charade, the polite smiles, the affected interest, the trivial exchange of words, until convention was satisfied. Then Angeles excused herself and Vespasia looked at Charlotte.

"I think perhaps you had better explain," she invited.

Charlotte told her briefly what she had observed, adding no comment, watching Vespasia's face for her reaction.

"Oh dear." Vespasia's eyes were sad, her face in an expression of profound gravity.

Charlotte waited, fear beginning to grow inside her. She had been clinging to a hope that she was being unnecessarily alarmed, and now it was melting away.

"What is it you think?" she said at last.

Still Vespasia hesitated. "I think that Angeles Castelbranco has had a terrible experience," she said at last.

It was exactly what Charlotte had thought also, though she had hoped she was being melodramatic. "How terrible?" she asked.

"More than just . . . a forced kiss, perhaps a

torn gown?"

Vespasia's mouth pulled tight in deep unhappiness. "She appears a healthy young woman. I'm sure she could slap someone hard enough to make her refusal known very plainly. And from what you say, she was not acquainted with this young man Andersley."

"No. He introduced himself. It seemed they had not met until that point."

"But she was so frightened that she backed away from him even though he did not actually touch her?"

"Yes. She didn't look just unwilling, or even as if it were merely distasteful. She looked terrified." Charlotte pictured Angeles's face again. Her expression had been unmistakable. "You believe she was far more seriously assaulted, don't you?"

"I think that is probably so," Vespasia agreed, her voice low and strained with pity.

"What are we going to do?" Charlotte's mind raced over the possibilities, beginning with talking to Pitt.

"Nothing," Vespasia replied.

"Nothing! But if she was actually raped that's one of the worst possible crimes." Charlotte was outraged. It was totally out of character for Vespasia, of all people, to be so callous. "She must be helped," she said hotly. "And above all, whoever did it must be punished, put in prison." The thought of the man getting away with such a thing was intolerable.

Vespasia put her hand very gently on Charlotte's arm. "And if Angeles names a young man and says that he raped her, what do you suppose will happen?"

Charlotte tried to imagine it. The anguish would be profound. Isaura Castelbranco would be distraught for her daughter. Charlotte felt cold throughout her body at the thought of such a thing happening to Jemima. It was almost impossible to hold in the mind, it was so appalling. But if it ever happened, she would injure somebody in the most terrible revenge she could imagine. She would destroy him!

And it would change nothing. All the pain she could inflict would do nothing to help Jemima.

"Exactly," Vespasia agreed gently, as if she had followed Charlotte's train of thought. "It is an injury no punishment is ever going to heal. To blame anyone else, even if you could prove her total innocence —"

"Of course she's innocent!" Charlotte interrupted. "She's sixteen! She's a child!"

"For goodness' sake, my dear, were you innocent at sixteen?"

"Of course I was! I was innocent until —"

"I'm not questioning your chastity," Vespasia said a little more tartly. "I took that for granted. I am speaking of innocence in the sense of offering no temptation to a man with more appetite than decency, and no belief that he needs to exercise self-control."

Charlotte remembered her passion for Dominic Corde, and how far she might have gone, quite willingly, had he given her the chance. She felt blood surge to her face. She did not know whether to be furious or humiliated.

"It is not so simple, is it?" Vespasia observed. "And if this wretched young man should accuse her of being just as willing as he was, how does she convince people that she was not? I saw no cuts or bruises to prove her reluctance, did you?"

Charlotte was amazed. She stared at Vespasia with complete disbelief. For once she was at a loss for words.

"People can be very cruel," Vespasia continued, her voice very quiet. "Which, if you think about it, my dear, you know as well as I do. Perhaps I have a few years' advantage on you, but it makes little difference. Think what she will face: the whispers, the disapproval, the sniggers from young men, the alarm from other young women, the prurient interest. There will be questions from those who imagine it might secretly have been rather fun, because they have no idea that it has nothing to do with romance or passion, but rather the desire to humiliate and conquer."

Charlotte looked at Vespasia's face and saw that the pain on it was even greater than the anger.

"You knew someone it happened to, didn't you?" The words were spoken before she gave them thought. Immediately she regretted them.

Vespasia's mouth pulled tight in remembered grief and she blinked several times.

"I did, long ago. More than one. Some things are bearable only if no one else knows of them. Then at least you do not imagine that every remark you don't quite hear is about you, every joke you don't understand is an oblique reference to your shame." She winced. "You do not believe that every party to which you are not invited is because you are no longer considered eligible. Above all, you do not suppose that you are soiled forever and that no man will want to touch you, except for his own amusement; that you will never marry and never have children."

"But that's —" Charlotte stopped as the

full impact of what Vespasia had said overwhelmed her. "But it's not her fault," she said quietly, her own voice choking now. "Do we really have to just . . . just pretend it didn't happen, and let him walk away, untouched? For heaven's sake, won't he do it again?" She was so angry, so horrified she could hardly get her breath. The act itself almost paled compared with the misery that must follow, the lifelong guilt and loneliness.

"Almost certainly," Vespasia agreed. "But it is not our decision to make. If you were her mother, would you want any stranger, or even a friend, to make the choice and use your daughter in order to prosecute this man, on the chance that you might win — if proving to the whole world that your daughter had been raped would be regarded as winning? Would you do that to Jemima?"

Vespasia knew the answer as she asked. Charlotte saw it in her eyes.

"No. I . . . I would find some way of taking revenge myself," she admitted.

The ghost of a smile touched Vespasia's mouth. "And would you tell Thomas?"

"Of course."

"Are you sure? What do you think he would do?"

"I don't know, but he'd certainly do something!"

"Of course he would, in fury and pain, without thinking of his own safety or comfort," Vespasia said.

"Naturally! He'd be thinking of Jemima!" Charlotte protested.

Vespasia shook her head very gently. "Charlotte, my dear, you would have to protect Thomas just as much as you would Jemima. If he accused some young man from a good family —" she lifted her head slightly and indicated an elegant, wealthy young man moving easily from one group to another, laughing, flirting very slightly "— what do you imagine would happen to him?"

Charlotte stared at the young man, and then at Vespasia. She felt suffocated, even though they were standing in the open air and there was a very slight breeze tugging at parasols and ruffling the flower heads. She tried to remember her own days before her marriage, when she had moved in Society, the rules she had known implicitly, the fun, the laughter . . . and the cruelty.

Vespasia supplied the answer for her. "The oldest defense has always been to blame the victim. They would tell him his daughter was a whore in the making, and although they pitied him, if he made any more trouble he would find himself without a job. He, and you, would no longer be welcome in Society. And Jemima would feel even guiltier because she was inadvertently the cause of your ruin."

"That's monstrous." Charlotte's voice trembled.

"Of course it is." Vespasia put her hand on Charlotte's arm. Her touch was warm and very gentle. "It is one of the very worst of the private tragedies we have to bear in silence and with as much dignity and grace as we can. Kindness is perhaps the only gift we can offer. And perhaps we will then have a little more gratitude for the griefs we do not personally have to bear."

Charlotte nodded, too full of emotion at that moment to answer.

But that night, when Pitt was sitting downstairs in the parlor, absorbed in reading papers he had brought with him from his office, she went upstairs alone and soundlessly opened Jemima's bedroom door.

Jemima was asleep, lying on her back, arms spread wide, smiling a little. She looked very young and desperately vulnerable. She thankfully could not even imagine the kind of pain that Charlotte and Vespasia had been talking about, the kind that had already begun for Angeles Castelbranco — if, of course, their assumptions were correct.

Perhaps two years ago Isaura had stood in Angeles's bedroom doorway and watched her sleep. Had she been full of dreams for her daughter's future happiness, or had fear touched her as it did Charlotte now?

She stayed there only a few moments longer. She did not want Jemima to waken and see her.

Quietly she closed the door and walked along the passage a few steps to Daniel's room. The man who had raped Angeles was somebody's son. Did his parents have any idea what he had become?

She opened that door also, very softly, and looked in on Daniel. He was curled over, facing the window where the curtains were wide open and the last of the summer evening light still glowed. His dark eyelashes shadowed across his smooth, unblemished cheek. It was an impossible thought, but in another seven years he would be a man.

Suddenly she felt frightened, aware of how precious everything was, of the happiness, the safety, the hope she took for granted; even the little things like the daily certainty of kindness, someone to touch, to love, to talk to; of being surrounded by people who mattered to her.

Charlotte felt tears slip down her cheeks and a tightness in her chest. The enormity of life, the joy and the pain, the caring so deeply — it was almost too much.

She closed the door in case she disturbed Daniel, and walked very slowly along the passage. She hesitated at the top of the stairs. She did not want to go down yet. Pitt would wonder what on earth was the matter with her, and she was not ready to try to explain.

CHAPTER 4

Narraway had dreaded this encounter with Quixwood, yet he felt compelled to come here to the club where he had, very understandably, taken up residence. The servants would have cleared away all possible evidence, but it had been only a couple of days since Catherine's death. The sight of her sprawled across the floor would remain printed on Quixwood's memory, perhaps for the rest of his life. The very pattern of the furniture, the way the light fell across the wooden parquet — everything would remind him of it.

Perhaps in time he would have the hall changed entirely, move all the furniture, hang the pictures in another room. Or would it make no difference?

The club steward conducted Narraway through the outer lounge with its comfortable, leather-covered chairs and walls decorated with portraits of famous past members. They approached the silent library where Quixwood was sitting. There was a leather-bound volume open in his lap, but his eyes were unfocused and he seemed to be looking far beyond its pages.

"Lord Narraway to see you, sir," the steward said gently.

Quixwood looked up, a sudden light of pleasure in his face.

"Ah, good of you to come." He rose to his feet, closing the book and holding out his hand. "Everyone else is avoiding me. I suppose they think I want to be alone, which is not true. Or — more likely — they have no idea what to say to me." He smiled bleakly. "For which I can hardly blame them." He gestured toward the other chair, a few feet from him.

The steward withdrew, closing the door behind him. There was a bell to summon him should either of them wish for anything.

Narraway grasped Quixwood's hand for a moment, then sat down. "Sympathy hardly seems enough," he agreed. "Whatever one says, it still sounds as if you have no idea what the person is suffering and that all you want to do is discharge your duty."

"So are you here to tell me that this is the worst, and that time will heal the pain?" Quixwood said wryly.

Narraway raised his eyebrows. "It would seem a little redundant."

"Yes. And it's a lie anyway, isn't it?"

"I don't know," Narraway admitted. "I hope not. But I can't imagine you want to hear that now. Though, I'm afraid you probably aren't going to like what I have come to say either. Nevertheless I am going to say it."

Quixwood looked surprised. "What, for heaven's sake?"

"Have you heard anything further from Inspector Knox?"

Quixwood shrugged. "No, not beyond a polite message to say that he is pursuing every piece of evidence he can find. But I had assumed as much." He leaned forward earnestly. "Tell me, Narraway, what was your impression of him? Please be honest. I need the truth, something I can rely on so I'll stop lying awake wondering what is being kept from me, albeit with the best motives. Can you understand that?"

"Yes," Narraway replied without hesitation. "Left to imagination we suffer not one ill but all of them."

Quixwood searched Narraway's face feature by feature. "Do you do that too? Have you ever lost anyone to something so . . . so vile, so bestial?" he asked finally.

Narraway made a tiny gesture of denial. "You know, at least by title, what my job has been. Do you think I have never experienced disillusion, horror, and then a sense of total helplessness? But this is nothing to do with my situation, Quixwood; it's about you and your loss."

Quixwood lowered his eyes. "I'm sorry. That was a stupid remark. I didn't mean to be offensive. I feel so inadequate. Everything is slipping out of control and I can't stop it."

Narraway felt an overwhelming pity for the man.

"I think Knox is a good man, both personally and at his job. He'll find whatever there is that anyone can know." He said it with certainty.

"But you'll still help him?" Quixwood asked quickly.

"As long as you wish me to. But I come here to warn you that we might discover details you would prefer not to learn. All facts are open to different interpretations, and your wife is not here to explain anything." Was he being so delicate as to be incomprehensible?

Quixwood frowned. "You don't need to tiptoe around it. You are trying to warn me that I may find out things about Catherine

I would prefer not to know? Of course. I'm not entirely stupid or blind. I loved Catherine very much, but she was a complicated woman. She made friends with people I never would have. She tended to see good in them, or at least some value, that I didn't." He looked away. "She was always seeking something. I never knew what.

"I want justice for her," Quixwood continued with sudden vehemence. "She deserves that, even if I learn a few things that perhaps are not comfortable for me. I didn't save her from this. I wasn't there. Allow me at least to do what I can now. I am not so squeamish or self-regarding that I need to hide from the truth."

"I'm sorry," Narraway apologized sincerely. "I meant that when they have sufficient evidence to charge the man, whoever he is, don't look beyond that. Leave the details to Knox. Don't press him to tell you more than will be made public at the trial anyway."

"The trial . . ." Quixwood's face tightened and his hands, resting easily on his lap till this point, now clenched. "I admit I hadn't thought of that. Will they need to say any more than that she was killed?"

"I don't know. I imagine the man will put up a defense."

"Surely they won't allow —"

"If they find him guilty he may be hanged," Narraway pointed out. "He must be allowed to fight for his life."

Quixwood looked down at the floor. "Do you think . . . Catherine fought for her life?"

Narraway said nothing to that. Quixwood would know his wife's courage better than he. "I'll do everything I can," Narraway promised again. "To hang a man is a sickening thing, but this is one case where I would have few qualms about it."

"Thank you." Quixwood took a deep breath. "Thank you," he said again.

Narraway went first to the local police station to find Knox and was informed that he was at Lyall Street, so he followed him there. He approached Quixwood's house with an odd mixture of familiarity and complete strangeness. The only time he had been here before was at night, in Quixwood's company, and with the terrible knowledge of Catherine's death. The shock of seeing her body had sharpened his senses so he could remember every detail of the corpse with awful clarity. And yet he could recall only foggy impressions of anything else.

Now, in the daylight, it looked as ordinary

as any other wealthy and elegant house in the better parts of London. An open carriage passed by, then another in the opposite direction, coming toward him. The second was a landau, bodywork dark, brass gleaming in the sun. The liveried coachman sat bolt upright, the reins held tightly in his gloved hands.

In the back two women sat talking to each other, pink and yellow embroidered muslins fluttering in the breeze. One of them laughed. It was jarring, a waking nightmare, to think of Catherine lying obscenely flung like a broken doll on the floor of one of these quiet, sedate houses with their exquisite façades, life proceeding on outside as if her death was of no importance.

Narraway's hansom came to a halt. He alighted, paid the driver, and walked toward the front door. Flickering in his mind was the memory of Pitt telling him how, in his early days, he used to be sent to the servants' entrance. No one wished to have the police enter through the front part of the house, as though they were equal to the owners. Now Narraway was doing what had essentially been Pitt's job, and he planned to use every privilege and artifice he could to obtain information, whether it was intended to be shared with him or not.

The door was opened by a footman whose face was appropriately polite and blank, as if everything in the household was normal.

"Yes, sir? May I help you?" He clearly did not recognize Narraway from the night of the murder. Narraway recalled him, but it was his profession to remember faces.

"Good morning." He produced a card out of the silver case in his pocket. "If you would be so good as to ask Inspector Knox if he can spare me a few moments?"

The footman was about to refuse him when training took over from instinct and he looked at the card. The name was unfamiliar but the title impressed him.

"Certainly my lord. If you would care to follow me to the morning room, I shall inform the inspector."

It was a full ten minutes before Knox appeared, walking straight in without knocking, and closing the door behind him. He looked tired; his shoulders drooped and his tie was slightly askew. There were lines of anxiety etched deep in his face.

"Morning, sir," he said with a sigh. "Sorry, but I really don't have any news that'll help Mr. Quixwood. Only bits and pieces, and nothing's for certain yet."

Narraway remained standing rather stiffly by the mantel shelf.

"Regardless of its apparent lack of meaning, what have you found?" he asked. "You must know how the assailant got in by now, and have an excellent idea of what, if anything, is missing. Have you found any witnesses, if not nearby, then within a block of here? Has any missing jewelry or artifacts, or whatever, turned up at a pawnshop or with a receiver of such things? Have there been any similar crimes reported? Other break-ins or attacks on women?"

Knox looked down at the ground, his lips pursed in sadness rather than thought.

"There's no sign of a break-in anywhere, Lord Narraway," he answered. "We've searched every door and window. We've looked at the downpipes, ledges, everywhere a man could climb, and a few where he couldn't. We even had a lad up in the chimney to look." He saw Narraway's expression of irritation. "Some of the houses in this part have big chimneys. You'd be surprised how a skinny little lad can come down one o' these an' open a door."

Narraway acknowledged his error. "Yes, of course. I didn't think of that. I assume you are not saying the attacker was here all the time? One of the servants? Please God, you are not saying that! We'll have every household in London in a panic."

"No, sir." Knox gave a twisted little smile. "The servants are all very well accounted for."

Narraway felt a chill. "Then you are saying there's no doubt she let him in herself? That seems the only alternative left."

Knox looked even more crumpled.

"Yes, sir, I am. Nothing was damaged, nothing torn or broken except what you already saw in the room where we found her. This leaves us with the conclusion that he was someone with whom she was comfortable, at least enough so that she let him in herself."

Narraway started. "But it's possible she was tricked somehow? Maybe he pretended he was a friend, a messenger from her husband, or the husband of a friend. Perhaps he gave a false name?"

Knox did all he could to keep his face expressionless, but failed. "No, my lord, I'm saying he was someone she knew, and she felt no apprehension about allowing him into the house without having a servant present. Someone she opened the door to herself rather than waiting until one of the servants answered the bell. She might have even expected him."

Narraway breathed in and out deeply, slowly. He had done all he could to avoid facing this, even in his mind. His chest and stomach were tight. "You mean he was her lover?"

Knox chewed his lip, profoundly unhappy. "I'm sorry, sir, but that does seem probable. I'll be most obliged if you can think up a more agreeable alternative."

Narraway forced himself to picture again the inner hallway where they had found Catherine. She had fought hard for her life, but only there, not closer to the front door. She had allowed her attacker inside the house, beyond the vestibule.

"How did none of the servants hear her?" he demanded. "She must have cried out. A woman doesn't submit to rape without a sound. Didn't she scream, at the very least?"

"The servants had been excused for the night," Knox replied. "The baize door to their quarters is pretty heavy. Sound-proof, if you take my meaning? If she'd wanted anything she'd have rung one of the bells and someone would have come, but a shout, especially from the front of the house, no one would have heard."

Narraway imagined it. The baize door gave such privacy, locked you off from intrusion — or help. Perhaps one stifled cry, then a hand over your mouth, and only a muffled choking after that. If a servant heard anything at all, she would take it for a quarrel, and the last thing she would want would be to intrude on such a scene.

What were they used to, the well-trained servants in this outwardly respectable house? Did they recognize a mistress's dismissal for the evening as a tacit command not to return?

He looked at Knox.

"Sorry, sir," Knox said quietly. "This man may have stolen things, but the servants don't recognize anything gone. And there's very definitely been no break-in. The bolts across the front doors were undone. The butler and the footman have both sworn, without any hesitation, that the doors where she was found were closed only with the type of latch that shuts itself."

"But the butler was alone when he found her; he wasn't with the footman," Narraway pointed out. It was a foolish observation. He knew it as he said the words, just as he knew what Knox would say in reply.

"Yes, sir," Knox answered wearily. "He found her then he called the footman. Couldn't really call one of the women. I'm sorry, but I don't think there's a way around it, my lord. We can conclude only that she knew him and let him in."

"Then we'd better find out who he was,"

Narraway said grimly. "Any ideas?"

"Not yet. The servants are either very loyal or else they truly don't know." Again unhappiness filled Knox's tired face. Narraway wondered if he was thinking of his own family. He had said he had a wife and daughters. His voice had altered when he spoke of them: there was a gentleness, even a pride in it. Narraway had liked him for that.

"Have you looked at Mrs. Quixwood's diary?" Narraway asked. "Or spoken to her maid?"

"Yes. The diary doesn't tell me anything," Knox replied. "She was busy, lots of engagements, but very few names mentioned, none of them outside of what you'd expect." He frowned. "Do you want to see it? Maybe . . ." He left the idea hanging in the air, on the edge of asking Narraway something, but clearly not quite certain if he wanted to, or how to word it.

"Yes," Narraway answered. "I'd like to look. I may know some of the names, at least."

Knox frowned. "Do you think . . . I mean . . ." His expression was bleak. "A secret acquaintance? If it's true, then it's going to be very hard to prove."

"Rape?" Narraway said the word with distaste. "If that ends up being the case, then I'll settle for proving it's murder."

Knox smiled at him, as if they had reached some kind of understanding. "I suppose you'd like to speak to the lady's maid as well. Read the diary first. It won't take you long. Then I'll send for her."

Narraway thanked him and went into the garden room to wait while a constable fetched Catherine's diary.

The room was sunny and warm in the morning light, a curious sense of peace in it, in such a troubled house. It was surprisingly feminine, greens and whites, white woodwork around the windows. The curtains were patterned, but only with leaves, echoing the potted plants, none of them with flowers. It was at the same time both bright and restful.

He was just sitting down on one of the rattan chairs when the constable brought the diary. He thanked him and settled down to read it.

He started in January. At first it was not very interesting, just the usual brief comments on the weather as it affected her daily life. "Very cold, streets slippery with ice." "Ground quite hard, all very clear and glittering. Very beautiful." "So wet today I really would rather not go out — I'll get drenched no matter how careful I am."

Then as the days lengthened and the weather became milder she commented on the first buds in the trees, the snowdrops, the birds. She saw a starling with twigs in its beak and wrote a short paragraph on the faith of building a nest when the days were still so dark. "How can such a small creature, who knows nothing, be so sure of a good future? Or is it only a blind and exquisite courage?"

The comments on the weather continued, with notes as to the flowers that had pleased her. Her botanical interest was written with acute observation, but mostly it was the beauty of the plants that moved her.

Narraway put the book down and wondered what Catherine Quixwood had thought as she had written those words. Was the loneliness he felt within the pages, the sense of confusion, hers or his own? Unwillingly he pictured her again, but lying on the floor. There had been such possibility of passion in her face, such turbulence, even in death. Or was he imagining that too?

He picked up the diary again and resumed reading it, paying more attention to where she had been and, when she had noted it, with whom.

As the weather grew more clement she had attended lectures at the Royal Geographical Society. After one on Egypt she had made a note of its excellence. Reading on, he saw that she had then gone to an exhibition of paintings of the Nile by various watercolorists, and then to the library to find books on Egyptian history.

In May she had gone to a lecture on astronomy. This time it was not the night sky that drew her most enthusiastic comments, but the sublime order of the stars in their courses, from the most random comet or meteor to the most immense galaxies. There was too little room on the page for all she wanted to say to remind herself of her emotions, and her writing eventually became so small he could not read it.

Then she went back to the library and searched for other books on astronomy, and more lectures she might attend. In the following weeks she even went by train to both Birmingham and Manchester to learn more.

But, as Knox had said, there were very few names in the diary. Those that were present all seemed exactly the acquaintances one might have expected: other married women in Society of her own age and station, a couple of distant cousins, one unmarried and apparently of considerable means. Catherine seemed to enjoy her company when it was available. There were also two aunts mentioned, the vicar and his wife and business associates of Quixwood's and their wives.

He read the entry from the day before she was killed, then closed the book. There was nothing further. He asked Knox if he might now speak to the lady's maid, although he did not hold much hope of learning anything from her that would be of value.

Flaxley was a tall, spare woman, her brown hair liberally threaded with gray. The marks of grief were all too evident in her face. She came in and sat down opposite Narraway at his invitation, then folded her hands in her lap and waited for him to speak. Her back was ramrod straight, probably from a lifetime of self-discipline; every emotion within her seemed to have been drained away. She looked exhausted.

Narraway was deeply moved by her loyalty. He wondered for a fleeting moment how many people had inspired such sense of loss, even among their own families.

"I'm sorry to disturb you, Miss Flaxley," he said quietly. He decided to be completely honest with her. "But the more I learn of Mrs. Quixwood, the more determined I am to do what I can to see that the man who attacked her is punished." He chose very deliberately not to use the word "rape."

There was no need to distress Flaxley further.

He saw the flicker of surprise in her eyes.

"I am certain that if you had any idea how to achieve this," he went on, "with as little unpleasant speculation as possible, you would already have told Inspector Knox. I have been reading Mrs. Quixwood's appointment diary, and I feel I know her better than I did before."

"Her appointment diary," Flaxley repeated. She did not ask if he believed that Catherine could possibly have had any idea what would happen to her, but it was implicit in the lift of her voice and the contempt in her eyes.

"Do you believe Mrs. Quixwood would have opened the front door to a man she did not both know and trust?" he asked her.

"No, of course —" She stopped. Clearly she had not even considered the matter. "Was her . . . attacker not a thief?"

"I don't know what he was, Miss Flaxley, but it's clear he did not break into the house, which leaves only one other possibility — that she let him in. Indeed, that initially she had no fear of him. Therefore he was someone she already knew, quite well enough not to call a servant to attend her."

She stared at him, her eyes filling with horror, her hands knotted in her lap so tightly that the knuckles shone white. He noticed with surprise how delicately boned they were. In their own way, they were quite beautiful.

"I will not smear her reputation." There was anger in her voice, and warning. "But tell me, what can I do to help?"

He admired her for it. He hoped that she would be able to keep that resolve and it pained him that she would probably not.

"Please go through the diary with me and tell me which of her friends she kept company with, and something about each of them. I will call on them in due course, but your insight will be more acute than mine. You knew Mrs. Quixwood, and possibly her true feelings about these people rather than the socially polite face she showed. Also, I have learned to my cost that women can judge one another far more observantly than men can." He allowed himself a very slight smile.

He saw it echoed in a momentary easing in her expression also.

"Yes, my lord, of course," she agreed.

It took Narraway the next three days to meet with eight of the people mentioned in

Catherine's diaries. He found it difficult, which surprised him. They were all women very like those he had known and mixed with all his adult life, and yet when speaking of Catherine, the artificiality of polite conversation between strangers irritated him.

He began with a cousin of Catherine's, a dark, rather elegant woman with beautiful hair and a very ordinary face. Her name was Mary Abercrombie.

"Of course we are deeply grieved," she said earnestly, but without any signs of pain that Narraway could see. "I don't know what I can tell you; I was very fond of Catherine, of course. We grew up together." She fidgeted slightly with her skirts. "But as so often happens, when we both married we drifted apart. Our tastes were . . . different."

"But you still went to the British Museum together," he pointed out. "Or was the entry in her diary incorrect?"

Mrs. Abercrombie smiled and looked down at her hands. Narraway had a fleeting and irrelevant thought about how much uglier they were than those of Flaxley.

"It was incorrect?" he prompted.

"Yes . . . and no," she equivocated. "We did meet there, and visited a few of the exhibits. I ran into a friend and left to take tea with her. It was about that time in the afternoon. Catherine stayed on, I presumed by herself, but I don't know. When I spoke to Rawdon a few days later at a reception, he implied that Catherine had returned home very late. I'm afraid I rather let her down by saying to him that I had left the museum before four o'clock."

"And Catherine was not at the reception?" he asked.

"No." She shook her head, a shadow of disapproval crossing her face. "She found such light social exchanges rather tedious. So do many of us, but one must make the effort." It was a statement, as if it were a fact agreed to by all.

Narraway wondered if she had made the remark to Quixwood on purpose. Catherine had been beautiful. Even in violent death the remnants of it were there in her face. Mary Abercrombie was agreeable enough and without obvious blemish, but she was no beauty, at least not to Narraway.

"Was that the last time you saw her?" he asked.

"Yes. Except briefly at a concert about two weeks ago."

"Who was she with at the concert?"

"I'm not sure she was with anyone." She

raised her eyebrows slightly. "When we spoke she was alone."

"Did that surprise you?"

"Frankly, no. Catherine was inclined to go to events alone. If it was something she wished to do, she would prefer to be alone to indulge in it, rather than go with company, who might require conversation from her." Her disapproval of such behavior was clear, if still unspoken.

Narraway had a sudden vision of Catherine bent forward, listening to great, sweeping symphonies of music while the fashionable women around her were talking to one another, gossiping, flirting, or merely pretending to listen while they waited for the opportunity to recommence speaking. He imagined in her an inner loneliness he found disturbing, and frighteningly easy to understand.

Or was he simply projecting his own emotions onto her, because he had never known her alive and there was no one to refute his picture?

"Was there anyone to whom she was particularly close?" he asked.

"You mean someone who might know if she was . . . having an unsuitable friendship?" Mrs. Abercrombie asked, delicate eyebrows raised. "Possibly. But I cannot

125

imagine that they would be indiscreet enough to speak of it, even had she been that foolish and disloyal. Poor Rawdon is suffering enough, don't you think? And Catherine has certainly paid for any indiscretions."

Narraway smiled coldly, feeling the temper like an ice storm inside him. "Actually, Mrs. Abercrombie, I was thinking of someone who might know if she was being troubled by unwanted attentions," he corrected her. "Men sometimes look at a beautiful woman and imagine she has given them some encouragement, when in truth she was no more than civil — or at most, kind. Denials do not always persuade them of their error."

She opened her pale eyes very wide. "Really? I have never known anyone so . . . disturbed."

"No," he agreed without a flicker in his expression. "I imagine not."

The anger burned up her face. "But most perceptive of you to have realized Catherine may have," she retorted. "Remarkable, because apparently you did not know her. But then, perhaps you know women like her."

"Unfortunately not," he said, keeping his eyes on hers. "From all I hear, she seems to have been unique. Please accept my condolences on your loss, Mrs. Abercrombie." He rose to his feet and gave a very slight inclination of his head.

She remained seated, her eyes cold. "You are too kind," she said sarcastically.

Still annoyed and somewhat confused in trying to make sense of Catherine's seemingly innocent life, Narraway called on the police surgeon, Brinsley, to see if he had anything further to report.

Brinsley was busy with another autopsy, but he did not keep Narraway waiting more than fifteen minutes. He came into the sparse waiting room rolling down his shirtsleeves, his hair a little tousled.

"Afternoon, my lord," he said briskly. He did not hold out his hand. Perhaps he had experienced too many people's revulsion, their imagination picturing where it had just been.

"Good afternoon, Doctor," Narraway replied. "Am I too soon to learn if you have anything further to say about Mrs. Quixwood's death?"

"No, no. Preformed the autopsy this morning," Brinsley's face was pinched. "I've really nothing to add, unless you want the details of the rape? Can't think it'll help you. Very violent." His voice sank even lower, grating with anger. "Very ugly."

"Can you tell if she fought, or at least tried to?" Narraway asked.

Brinsley winced. "She tried. A few ugly bruises have come out. They do, after death, if they were inflicted just before. Wrists, arms, shoulders. He was unnecessarily brutal. Thighs, but you'd expect that. And the bite, of course, on her breast." His mouth was tight, as if his jaw was clenched. "Only thing that might make a difference to you is that I'm now quite certain she actually died of opium poisoning. Overdose of laudanum, dissolved in a glassful of Madeira wine. Pretty heavily laced, I must say. Far more than enough to kill her."

Narraway stood paralyzed, grief washing over him. He had hoped the doctor's initial reading had been an error. Now he couldn't help but picture the despair she must have felt, as if everything she was had been torn violently from her: her body, her dignity, the very core of herself damaged beyond hope.

"I'm sorry," Brinsley said hoarsely. "I keep thinking that one day I'll get used to it, but I never do. I can't say for certain that it was suicide, since we don't know if the man stayed long enough to force her to drink it, but that seems extremely unlikely. If he'd wanted her dead he could simply have broken her neck. I'm afraid everything suggests she crawled to the cabinet and poured herself enough to deaden the pain, and either accidentally or intentionally overdid the dose." His face was bleak. "I'm sorry."

Narraway struggled to picture it. "Could she have dragged herself that far? And why on earth would she keep laudanum in the cabinet in the hallway? Wouldn't she keep it upstairs? In the bedroom?"

"I've no idea," Brinsley said patiently. "But as far as we know, there was no one else in that part of the house, right? And from the bruising on her knees, I believe she crawled over to the cabinet. It isn't difficult to assume that from there she opened it and poured and drank the Madeira. The dregs were full of laudanum, both in the glass and in the bottle." He shook himself. "For God's sake! The poor woman can't have had the least idea of what she was doing. She just tipped the laudanum into the bottle and drank the whole damn thing. Can you blame her?"

"It doesn't make sense. Why would she pour opium into the bottle? Why not just straight into her glass, then?"

"I don't know," Brinsley said. "I've just

given you the facts, and I don't see what else you can make of them. But I hope to hell you find whoever did it, and if you can't hang him, literally, for murder, then find a way to get him for rape."

"I'll try," Narraway swore. "Believe me."

He visited and spoke with all the other people on Miss Flaxley's list. He gained a wider view of Catherine Quixwood, but it did not alter radically from that already given him by Mary Abercrombie. Catherine had been interested in all manner of science, in the artifacts of other times and places, in human thought and above all in the passions of the mind.

She seemed to have skirted more carefully around the edges regarding passions of the heart. He wondered if they had frightened her, perhaps come too close to breaching the walls of her own safety, or her loneliness.

Or was that his overfanciful imagination seeking in her a likeness to himself? He could understand being drawn to the music of Beethoven, and yet at the same time frightened of it. It challenged all the flimsy arguments of safety and dared beyond the known into something far bigger, both more beautiful and more dangerous. At times he wanted to stay with what his mind could conquer and hold. To be enchanted by the brilliance of the mind was exciting, but without the risk of injury.

Look at vases of flowers, not the wild paintings of Turner in which all the light was caught and imagined on canvas. Look at the artifacts of ancient Troy, but do not think of the passion and the loss of the time. Always keep the mind busy.

Was that what Catherine had been doing?

At the end of three days Narraway had a plethora of facts, statements, and stories, but no fixed frame in which to place them. If she had made secret assignations with anyone, she had been sufficiently clever in concealing them that he had found no trace. She was charming to everyone and intimate with none.

About the only thing she did not appear to have had any interest in was the last few years of extraordinary events in Africa. There was one brief note in her diary on the discovery of gold in Johannesburg, but no mention of the massacres carried out by Lobengula, or the extraordinary career of Cecil Rhodes, or even of the catastrophic Jameson Raid only months ago. For a woman interested in so many things it was a curious omission.

Finally Narraway was driven to going back again to speak to Quixwood himself, little as he wished to. He owed the man a report of his discoveries, fruitless as they were so far.

He found him in the library of the club, as before, but this time he was busy writing letters. He looked up as Narraway came in. He was clearly tired, the lines in his face more deeply scored.

"Have you found anything further?" he asked as Narraway sat down on the smooth, comfortable leather.

"I'm not certain," Narraway replied honestly. "I have been asking questions of her friends, mostly the people with whom she attended lectures and visited museums, that sort of thing."

Quixwood frowned. "Why? What might that have to do with her death?" His voice held a note of disappointment.

"She knew whoever killed her," Narraway said, gently but without hesitation. He could think of little more painful than the possibility Quixwood now faced. If he balked at it, or blamed the man who told him, it was a very human reaction. He needed someone to be angry with for his pain.

Quixwood blinked as if caught in a sudden, bright light. "And you think one of her friends might know who it is?"

"Possibly without being aware of the connection, but yes, I do," Narraway told him.

Quixwood stared at him for several long seconds, then he lowered his gaze. "Yes, you are quite right, of course. I suppose it is what I have been trying hard to deny to myself. Such things do not happen in isolation. And I can't willfully refuse to accept that she let him in. I appreciate your patience in allowing me come to it a trifle more slowly."

"I'm sorry," Narraway said with intense regret. "I cannot see any other answer that fits the facts we have."

"And . . . do you have any idea who it was?" Quixwood framed the words with difficulty, staring down at his half-written-on paper.

"No, not yet. But I have further questions I intend to ask Flaxley. She seems a sensible woman, and loyal. I believe she wishes to see this man punished, as far as is consistent with protecting Mrs. Quixwood's reputation."

Quixwood looked bleak but he forced a rather shaky smile. "I'm sure Flaxley will give you all the help she can. She was devoted to Catherine. I've no idea what she'll do now, because there is nothing for her to do in what is left of my household. I suppose I can offer her an excellent reference, but that feels like precious little to do for a woman who's given so many years of her life, and seen it end in such hideous crime." He took a deep breath. "And a pension, of course. Fortunately I'm in a position to do that."

"That would be good of you, and quite appropriate," Narraway agreed. "But I would be obliged if you kept her on until we have solved this case."

"Of course! I'll do all I can in every way. Good God, man, no one could care about it more than I do!" Quixwood reasserted control of himself with something of an effort. "Someone else who might be able to help is Alban Hythe, a young man with a good position in the Treasury. I know he shared many of Catherine's tastes." He made a slight gesture with his strong, slender hands. "He is a most intelligent and civil young man, who traveled widely earlier in his career. According to Catherine, he is a lover of music and art. If there is someone who became . . . who became obsessed with Catherine and imagined there was something between them, Mr. Hythe might have noticed it. Narraway, I would be extraordinarily grateful if you did not speak of the"

— he swallowed — "of the details of her death to him."

"Of course," Narraway agreed. "I will tell him nothing except that she was attacked in her own home by someone she had assumed to be a friend, and therefore she was not initially afraid of him. That will cover all the truth he needs to know."

"Thank you." Quixwood gave the ghost of a smile. "I'm sure he will help you if he can."

Narraway felt a chill. Was it possible this was the answer? He did not want to believe Catherine might've been having an affair. He could understand her loneliness. Everything he had learned about her indicated a woman unfulfilled in her life, desperately seeking something more. He had thought it was purpose she was looking for, to exercise her intelligence. But maybe it was simply a love more immediate to her nature than that offered by her husband.

He rose to his feet. "Thank you. I had better go and visit this man Hythe, and see what I can learn."

He arrived at Hythe's address in a very nice part of Holborn just before seven. It was not really a courteous hour to call — people would be preparing for dinner, or to go out for the evening — but he was not willing to wait another day. Added to which, if he was honest, he was concerned enough about the part Hythe might have played in Catherine's death that he had no concern whatsoever for the man's convenience.

Narraway was admitted by a parlormaid and had only moments to wait before Hythe himself appeared, looking startled but not worried. He was a handsome man, probably in his late thirties, tall and slender, his brownish hair streaked fair where already the summer sun had bleached it.

"Lord Narraway?" he said questioningly, closing the door of the parlor behind him. The house was charming but modest and had no separate morning room for visitors.

"I am sorry to disturb you so late," Narraway apologized blandly. "In fact for calling upon you unannounced at all. If the matter were not so serious I would have made an appointment in the usual way."

Hythe frowned, indicating Narraway should be seated. "Is it something at the Treasury?"

Narraway sat, and Hythe lowered himself into the chair opposite.

"No," Narraway replied. "As far as I am aware there is nothing amiss at the Treasury. This concerns the recent death of Mrs. Catherine Quixwood."

He saw the anxiety in Hythe's face change to deep grief, a look so genuine it was hard to disbelieve it. But he had known people before whose loyalties had been so violently torn apart that they could kill and weep for the victim at the same time.

"How can I possibly help?" Hythe seemed genuinely confused. "For heaven's sake, if I knew anything at all, I would already have contacted the police." He frowned. "Who are you? Clearly you are not a policeman."

"Until recently I was head of Special Branch," Narraway replied, caught slightly off guard by the question. He had not expected to have to explain himself except casually, and in his own way. "Mr. Quixwood asked me to help him as much as I am able, both to close the matter as quickly as possible and to keep it as discreet as circumstances allow."

"And the police?" Hythe said with some anxiety. "Is there need to be concerned as to their . . . clumsiness?"

Narraway smiled bleakly. He found Hythe agreeable. It was easy to see how Catherine Quixwood could have liked him also, even though he was perhaps a decade younger than she.

"Actually, I think Inspector Knox is both capable and discreet, but the situation is not easy to deal with," he answered.

"How can I help?" Hythe appeared still to have no idea how he was involved. "Both my wife and I were very fond of Mrs. Quixwood, but I have no idea what I could do to be of assistance."

"She was killed by someone she knew well enough to let into the house, quite late in the evening, and was comfortable enough with to not send for one of the servants to be present," Narraway answered. He saw the surprise in Hythe's face, and a degree of apprehension, perhaps even alarm. Was it because he was guilty, and had he not expected anyone to deduce so much?

"I see from Mrs. Quixwood's diary that she went to many interesting events," Narraway went on. "Lectures, displays at the British Museum, concerts, and the theater, many of which Mr. Quixwood was unable to attend. He tells me that these were events that also interested you, and that you might be able to tell me a little of others she would have become acquainted with." Narraway shrugged slightly. "It is unpleasant to have to question her friends in such a way, but we are trying to uncover the entire truth about what happened."

"I see." Hythe rose to his feet and went to the door. He excused himself and disappeared for several minutes, returning accompanied by a young woman who at first glance seemed quite ordinary-looking, apart from the steadiness of her gaze. Her hair was the color of honey and had a deep, natural wave.

Narraway rose to his feet immediately.

Hythe introduced her as his wife.

"How do you do, Lord Narraway?" Maris Hythe said with interest. Her voice was soft and surprisingly deep, giving her a gravity that her smooth, candid face belied.

"How do you do, Mrs. Hythe?" he replied. "I am sorry to intrude on your evening with such an unhappy subject."

She sat down gracefully and the men followed her lead.

"That is hardly of any importance, if we can assist you in any way." She dismissed it with a slight gesture of one hand. "I liked Catherine very much. She was funny and wise and brave. I have no idea who could have wanted to kill her, but if I can help you find him, then all my time is yours." She looked at him gravely, waiting for his answer.

He told her of his conversation with Flaxley, and then later with Quixwood, explaining why he needed to know Catherine's friends, but always skirting around the subject of rape. However, he was not subtle enough to deceive her.

"Was his intention robbery?" she said very quietly, almost under her breath. "Or did he attack her . . . personally?"

There was nothing to be gained by evasion, and he needed her help. "I am afraid it was the latter. The details of that would be better not spoken of."

"I see." She did not argue with him, nor respond to her husband's sudden look of surprise and distress.

"Perhaps if I give you a list of her most recent engagements," Narraway suggested, "then you can tell me who you remember as also being present, and who might have become close to her recently. I realize it is distasteful, but —"

"We understand," Hythe interrupted him. He glanced at Maris and then back at Narraway, holding out his hand for the list.

Narraway passed it to him, and watched as he and Maris read it together.

For half an hour they mentioned names back and forth, and Narraway learned something of each of the events Flaxley had described. Hythe appeared to have enjoyed those he had also attended, and there was pleasure in his voice as he told of each. If the grief Hythe exhibited as he remembered

Catherine was artificial, he was a superb actor.

But Narraway had known people every bit as convincing who would kill without hesitation if their own needs were thwarted or their safety in jeopardy. Quixwood was right: Hythe and Catherine had clearly been good friends, and Maris also, especially where music was concerned. If there had been an affair between Catherine and Hythe, then it was well concealed. But he had to grant that it was easily possible. Everything Hythe said seemed to be true, and yet looking at the tenseness in his shoulders, the awkward way he sat, without moving, Narraway grew increasingly certain that he was concealing something that mattered, something that frightened him.

Maris explained that she was close to one of her sisters, recently widowed, and she spent much of her time helping her, offering comfort, simply being there so her sister was not alone. Alban Hythe could not account for his time on most of these occasions, including the night of Catherine's murder.

The three conversed for nearly two hours. Afterward, Narraway thanked them both and left, walking out into the soft dusk of the summer evening, the last light fading pink in the west. He was saddened by the possibility that Alban Hythe had begun an affair with Catherine because of her loneliness and his temporary solitude, and perhaps a weakness in both of them, played on by the depth of intellectual understanding and mutual love of the interesting, beautiful and creative.

But what terrible change in their seeming friendship had led to such violence? Had he wanted more and she refused him? Or had she wanted more, possibly even a commitment, and he refused her? Had she threatened his safety in some way and he responded from a fearful darkness in his character she had not for a moment imagined?

Narraway walked along the pavement toward the lights of the main thoroughfare and felt sadness overwhelm him. His anger at Hythe also returned, for the life and passion that, he was beginning to suspect, Hythe might've destroyed.

CHAPTER 5

"Mama, I can't possibly wear that!" Jemima said indignantly. "I shall look terrible. People will think I am ill. They'll be offering me chairs to sit on, in case I fall over." Her face was flushed with temper and frustration. She appeared the picture of health, as if it would take a runaway carriage to knock her off balance, not a fainting fit.

Pitt looked up from the newspaper he was reading. They were all in the parlor, the summer evening air drifting in from the open French windows. Daniel was absorbed in a *Boy's Own Paper* and Charlotte had been looking at the *London Illustrated News*.

Pitt regarded the dress Jemima was holding up. "You wanted that last year," he pointed out. "It suited you excellently."

"Papa, that was last year!" she said with exasperation at his lack of understanding.

"You haven't changed all that much." He

looked her up and down quite carefully. "An inch taller, perhaps," he conceded.

"Two inches taller," she corrected him. "At the very least. And anyway, I'm completely different." It distressed her that he had not noticed.

"You don't look completely different to me," he answered.

"Yes, she does," Daniel argued. "She's a girl. She's getting all . . ." Suddenly he realized what he was saying and was lost for the appropriate words.

Jemima blushed. "You're trying to make me look like a child," she accused her father. "Genevieve's father does the same thing. He doesn't want her ever to become a woman."

"You're fourteen," Pitt said flatly. "You *are* a child."

"I'm not! That's a terrible thing to say!" Unaccountably Jemima was on the edge of tears.

Daniel bent his head back to his *Boy's Own Paper,* lifting it a little higher to hide his face.

Pitt looked at Charlotte. He had no idea how he had offended, or what to do about it. It was totally unreasonable.

Charlotte had grown up with two sisters and there was no mystery in it for her.

144

"You are not having a purple dress, and that's all there is to it," she told her daughter. "If you feel that that one is too young for you, then wear the blue one."

"Blue's ordinary," Jemima responded. "Everyone has blue. It's dull. It's safe!" That was the worst condemnation she could think of.

"You don't need anything special," Pitt told her gently. "You're very pretty whatever you wear."

"You just say that because you're my father!" Her voice choked as if she could not control her tears any longer. "You have to like the way I look."

"I don't!" He was surprised and a little defensive himself. "If you wore something I didn't like, I would say so."

"You'd have my hair in braids down my back as if I were ten!" she said furiously. She turned to Charlotte. "Mama, everyone wears blue, it's boring. And pink looks like you're a child!"

"Yellow?" Daniel suggested helpfully.

"Then I shall look as if I have jaundice!" she responded. "Why can't I wear purple?"

Daniel was not to be put off. "Green?"

"Then I'll look sickly! Just be quiet!"

"Aunt Emily wears green," he pointed out.

"She's got fair hair, stupid!" she shouted at him.

"Jemima!" Charlotte said sharply. "That was quite uncalled for. He was being perfectly sensible, and pale green would look very nice —"

"I don't want to be 'nice'!" Jemima said furiously. "I want to be interesting, different, grown up." The tears spilled from her eyes onto her cheeks. "I want to look lovely. Why can't you understand?" Without waiting for an answer she swung round and stormed out. They heard her feet banging on the treads up the stairs and then a door on the landing slam.

"What did I do?" Daniel asked incredulously.

"Nothing," Charlotte assured him.

"Then why is she like that?"

"Because she's fourteen," Charlotte replied. "She wants to look nice at the supper party she's going to."

"She always looks nice." Pitt was reasonable, and confused. "She's very pretty. In fact she looks more like you every day."

Charlotte smiled ruefully. "I'm not sure she'd appreciate your saying so, my dear."

"She did the other day," he argued.

"That was then, this is now," she answered. There was no use trying to explain it to him. He had grown up without sisters. Girls of Jemima's age were as incomprehensible to him as mermaids or unicorns.

Daniel shrugged and turned the next page of his *Boy's Own,* to the story of a pirate adventure off the coast of India. "Why couldn't she have been a boy?" he said resignedly. "That would have been better for all of us."

"It would have been easier," Charlotte corrected him. "Not better."

Pitt and Daniel exchanged glances, but both were wise enough not to take issue with her.

An hour later Charlotte went upstairs to Jemima's room and knocked on the door. When there was no answer she rapped sharply, then went in anyway. Jemima was sitting on the bed, her hair loose and tangled, her cheeks tearstained. She glared defiantly at her mother.

"I suppose you've come to tell me off," she said belligerently. "That I have to wear blue, and be glad of it. And that if I smile I'll look charming anyway . . . and about as interesting as a jug of milk!"

Charlotte did not ask whose interest Jemima was working to awaken; she already knew. His name was Robert Durbridge and he was eighteen. He was far too old for Jemima at the moment, but otherwise was a pleasant-seeming young man, the son of the local rector and bent on every kind of rebellion against the path in the Church that his parents had planned for him.

"Wear a green sash around your waist and you will be quite different from other girls," she suggested helpfully.

"What?" Jemima's eyes flew wide open. "Mama, you can't wear blue and green together! Nobody does that!"

Charlotte smiled at her. "Then you will be the first. I thought you wanted to be different. Have you changed your mind?"

"Blue and green?"

"Why not? Blue sky and green trees. You see it all the time."

"I don't want to look like a field," Jemima said in disgust.

"A willow tree against the sky," Charlotte corrected her. "Stop being so obstructive. There is nothing less attractive than bad temper, I promise you. Now wash your face and pull yourself together. It is not your father's fault, or your brother's, that you are full of emotion and indecision. It's part of growing up and we all experience it. You are behaving as if you are the center of the world, and you aren't."

"You don't understand!" Jemima wailed, her face crumpling.

"Of course not," Charlotte agreed with a smile. "I was never fourteen, I went straight from being twelve to being twenty. So did both of my sisters."

"Twenty!" Jemima was horrified. "You mean I'm going to feel like this for another six years?"

"Please heaven, I hope not!" Charlotte said with feeling.

In spite of herself, Jemima smiled, and then started to giggle. "Can I really wear a green sash on my dress?"

"Of course. So you had better walk with your head up, and smile to everyone, because they will all be looking at you, including young Robert Durbridge."

"Do you think so?" Jemima blushed. "But then maybe I should wear . . ."

"Jemima!" Charlotte interrupted.

"Yes, Mama."

"The subject is closed."

Charlotte and Pitt attended yet another reception that duty obliged them to, but Charlotte admitted to herself that there were elements of it she thoroughly enjoyed, not the least being that she was nobody's guest. She was here because Pitt was invited.

In the swirl of greetings, polite conversations, and the swapping of suitably trivial inquiries and answers, they began to move among the throng of people. Charlotte noticed Vespasia, strikingly elegant as usual. Pitt looked for those with whom he needed to speak.

Charlotte met various women she had encountered before, but found her attention wandering. They were discussing family matters: who was engaged to marry whom; love affairs and misfortunes she was thankful did not concern her. She realized that all too soon she would have to consider Jemima finding a suitable husband, but she had three or four years' grace yet before that needed to be a preoccupation. When she was young and single she had loathed being presented to various people in the hope that some young man might please her, and she him. Now she felt an embarrassing wave of sympathy for her own mother. She knew perfectly well that she had been extraordinarily difficult, and in the end decided to marry a policeman and virtually disappear from Society.

By that time her mother had been relieved to accept any settled life for her middle daughter and had put up barely any resistance.

She was still smiling at the memory when she saw Angeles Castelbranco with some other young women. They all appeared to be laughing with two young men, both of whom were quite openly admiring Angeles. Charlotte could not blame them or find it surprising. She was a beautiful young woman, and at the moment her face was flushed and her eyes brilliant.

Then Neville Forsbrook approached the group, smiling.

Seeing him, Angeles's face fell and she backed away sharply. It was an awkward movement, completely without grace.

One of the other young men laughed.

Angeles did not even look at him. Her eyes were fixed on Forsbrook. No one else in the room seemed to notice.

Forsbrook said something to Angeles and gave a slight bow. He was still smiling.

Angeles blushed hotly. She started to speak, but seemed unable to find the words she needed. She ended by apparently saying something angry in Portuguese, and the other young women moved away uncomfortably.

The young men looked at each other and laughed again, but weakly; it seemed more out of confusion than amusement.

Forsbrook took another step toward Angeles, this time with one hand forward as if he would touch her arm.

She snatched it away, and in stepping backward lost her footing a little. Forsbrook lunged forward and grasped her, preventing her from falling. She gasped, and then cried out.

Forsbrook held her more firmly. It could have been because he feared she might fall.

Angeles tried to wrench her arm away from Forsbrook but he held on to her. She swung her other arm and slapped him across the face as hard as she could. One of the young men let out a cry of surprise.

Forsbrook let go of her with a very slight push and she staggered backward, tripping on her skirt and collapsing into a couple of girls, who were giggling and oblivious of everyone else. The three of them clung together to avoid ending up on the floor, angry and embarrassed.

"For God's sake, what's the matter with you?" Forsbrook shouted at Angeles, as she struggled to find her balance. His voice was sufficiently loud that at least a dozen people heard him and swung around to stare.

Angeles's face was scarlet. She looked desperate, turning from left to right to find some way of escape.

Charlotte had been moving forward to

intervene. At the same moment she saw Vespasia several yards away, her face filled with deep anxiety. She also was trying to make her way toward the open space where Angeles and Forsbrook now stood facing each other.

"Stop it!" Forsbrook was still raising his voice and he took another step closer to her, again reaching for her arm.

She staggered backward again, her face twisted as if in terror.

"Stop it!" he repeated. "You're making yourself look ridiculous!" He lunged forward, reaching out as if to take her hand, just as a waiter with a tray of glasses passed within a yard of her.

She gasped and pulled away, and this time crashed straight into the waiter, sending the glasses flying in all directions, splintering on the floor. The poor man tripped in his effort to regain his feet and only made it worse. He ended up splayed across the floor, arms and legs wide, champagne and slivers of glass everywhere.

"Get a hold of yourself!" Forsbrook demanded furiously of Angeles. "You're hysterical! Are you drunk?"

Angeles picked up a dish of cakes from the table nearest her and hurled it at him. It struck him in the chest, covering his dinner suit with jam and cream.

He swore, in language he surely could not have intended anyone to hear in a public place, darting his arm out and grasping her shoulder firmly, as if to shake her. She screamed again and lashed out, kicking with all her strength, even turning her head and biting him on the hand. At that, he cried out and slapped her, and when she let go there was blood dripping scarlet from the flesh between his finger and thumb.

Now most of the room was staring, confused and alarmed. Everyone seemed paralyzed by the scene and unsure what to do.

Vespasia was helping the waiter to his feet, so Charlotte practically ran the remaining distance to Angeles, calling her name.

Angeles, however, seemed aware only of Forsbrook. She was swearing at him in Portuguese, her face still twisted in fear. So Charlotte turned to Forsbrook, at least to try to stop him from moving any closer to Angeles. But he was too angry to see anyone else.

"You stupid girl!" he said, waving his hand around as if the pain were unbearable. "You bite like a mad dog!" He continued moving toward her every time she backed away.

"Neville!" Charlotte caught his arm but all she managed to hold on to was the cloth of his coat. He tore it out of her hand, unintentionally bumping her, so she was forced to steady herself. She remained on her feet only with difficulty.

Angeles turned and ran, plunging through the knots of people, banging into tables and upsetting dishes. Twice she reached for plates of cakes or sweetmeats and threw them at Forsbrook. One sailed past him and struck one of the other young men, who was also shouting at her. A second one caught Forsbrook on the side of the face and left a gash along his cheekbone. At this, Forsbrook clearly lost the last remnants of his temper, letting out a bellow.

Angeles, terrified, ran straight toward the great window that overlooked the paved terrace two stories below.

Forsbrook was close behind her, his face contorted with emotion. Angeles screamed, her words unintelligible, her body twisting one way then the other until, arms flailing, she crashed into the high, multipaned window. It shattered, sending glass everywhere. One moment she was in front of it, all white silk and dark hair, the next there was only a jagged hole and wood splinters on the floor.

For a terrible second everyone was silent. Then there was a scream, a high, thin sound of utter despair. Isaura Castelbranco had appeared from nowhere with her husband, who was now staggering toward the remains of the window.

Forsbrook too was appalled. However, far from remaining still, he turned to those beside him, spinning round, as if to find someone to say it had not been his fault.

In the next room someone was shouting. Footsteps sounded, running.

Other people started to speak, to move aimlessly toward the window or away from it. There were shouts from outside on the terrace. Several women were gasping, and a few were weeping openly. The hostess went toward Isaura, and then stopped. Her face was deathly pale.

Castelbranco turned slowly from the window and faced the room. His grief was palpable in the air, washing outward to touch everyone.

Isaura took a step, then another, floundering as if she were wading through deep water. She called something to him in Portuguese.

Castelbranco replied abruptly, his voice hoarse. It was filled with anguish.

Charlotte remained rooted to the spot. The two were clearly racked with pain beyond bearing, and there was nothing any one of the horrified onlookers could do to help.

It was Vespasia who finally took action. She walked over to Isaura and took her arm.

"Come with me," she said firmly. "There is nothing for you to do here."

Isaura fought against her for only a moment; then, as if acknowledging some overwhelming defeat, she allowed herself to be led away.

No one went to Castelbranco. He stood stock-still, the cool wind blowing in through the remnants of the window ruffling his hair, chilling him until he shook with it. The sound of men's voices drifted up from the terrace below, very quiet, edged with shock. It must be the host deciding what to do, whom to call, giving directions to the servants.

Charlotte was undecided. Would it be intrusive, even socially inappropriate, for her to go over to Castelbranco? It seemed inhuman simply to stand here staring at him, but even worse to look away.

Where on earth was Pitt? Surely word of what had happened would have reached everyone in the house? The noise of the window smashing, the cries . . .

Then she looked at the tall clock against the wall and realized it had been only minutes. In another room with the doors closed, away from the back of the house and the window, no one would have heard anything.

She should find Pitt immediately. She turned away from the crowd now huddled into little groups trying to gain comfort from one another, and walked toward the main doors. She was just outside on the gallery at the top of the stairs when she saw Pitt coming up the steps two at a time. He looked pale, his eyes shadowed with horror. He crossed the few yards between them and stood in front of her. One look at her face was enough to make any questions unnecessary.

"How did it happen?" he asked quietly, so as not to be overheard.

"Ugly teasing," she answered. "A mixture of humor, at first, at least as far as the other boys were concerned. But then Neville was cruel. Even when it got out of hand, he didn't stop."

Her voice felt choked and thick in her throat. She was losing control. "It all happened so quickly." She took a deep breath. "I should have done something!" She was to blame. She had stood there watching. She was furious with herself for her stupidity.

He put his hand on her arm, holding on to her surprisingly hard. "Charlotte, stop it. You couldn't know she was going to go through the window. That was what happened, right?"

"Yes, but I didn't even try," she gasped. "And I knew something was wrong."

"And did you know what to do about it? In fact, do you know now?"

"No! But something . . ."

He slipped his arm around her and she relaxed a little against him. A wave of gratitude engulfed her that he was there, that in all the years his strength had never failed her.

"Thomas . . ." She did not know if she was going to sound foolish, or even if it mattered now that Angeles was dead.

"What?" he asked. "I can't just leave. I have to —"

"I know," she interrupted. "That wasn't what I was going to say." She pulled away so she could meet his eyes. He waited, frowning a little. Even as she said it she was uncertain. "She wasn't just angry, Thomas, she was terrified. We saw her over a week ago, Vespasia and I. She was frightened then too."

He frowned. "Are you certain? Frightened of what?"

"Yes, I am sure. Vespasia thinks — we both thought — that Angeles had been assaulted."

"Assaulted? Do you mean raped?" He was trying to keep the incredulity out of his voice but it was there in his eyes.

"Yes, I do." She pictured in her mind Angeles's face in the marquee when the young man had spoken to her. It was not distaste that had made her back away in such an extreme manner, it had been fear, a reaction to something else. "Yes, I do," she repeated.

"I'm sorry," he said very quietly. "I wish it were not so. But does it matter now? Would it not be better for everyone, especially her parents, if we did not raise that question?"

"If somebody did that to her, it's appalling!" she protested. "It's one of the worst crimes you can commit against a woman. It's the reason she was so terrified."

"Do you know that for certain?"

"No, of course I don't! But what does anyone know about a crime for certain, before you investigate?" Even as she said it she knew her words were hollow. It was a nightmare dancing at the edge of her mind. She did not know the shape or even the reality of it. "I . . ." she started, and then stopped again.

"I know." He touched her cheek. "You feel as if there ought to have been something you could've done. We all feel that after a tragedy."

"Can we at least do anything to help now?" Charlotte asked.

"I doubt it, but I'll try. Perhaps you should find Aunt Vespasia. I won't be any longer than I have to. No doubt the police will come quickly."

"I suppose so. Should I say anything, if they ask me?"

"Tell them exactly what you saw. And be careful — only what you saw, *not what you think it meant.*" It was a warning, softly spoken but grave.

"I know!" She calmed herself deliberately. "I know."

All around her people were huddled together, many in silence. The police had arrived and were speaking to them, making notes of what everyone said. Footmen moved among them almost silently, offering whatever refreshment might help, including quite a few stiff shots of brandy.

As Charlotte had expected, the police spoke with her. She was very deliberate in her answers, adding nothing to the facts.

"Is that all you saw?" a gaunt-faced older policeman asked her doubtfully. "You seem much more . . ." he searched for the word, ". . . composed than the other ladies I've spoken to. Do you know something more about what happened?"

She met his eyes. "No." Was that a lie? "My husband is head of Special Branch," she explained. "Perhaps I am just a little more careful of what I say. I want to tell you what I saw, not what I felt or might have imagined."

"Special Branch?" His eyes opened wider. "Is this — ?"

"We came socially," she answered him. "The entire incident happened without any warning. One moment it was nothing, and then within seconds it became ugly."

He frowned. "Ugly? What do you mean, Mrs. Pitt? Were there threats? An assault of some kind? Or something that Miss Castelbranco might have interpreted as an assault?" He looked puzzled now.

"No, just hectoring, though it seemed mean-spirited. Miss Castelbranco was clearly upset, and Mr. Forsbrook didn't let it go. Everyone else could see that it was no longer funny, but he seemed to . . ." She stopped, aware that finishing her train of thought was more than she wished to say.

"Yes?" he prompted her.

"I don't know. He just wouldn't leave her alone."

"Were you acquainted with Miss Castelbranco, Mrs. Pitt?"

"Only slightly. If you are asking if she confided anything to me, she did not. I can tell you only what I saw."

She met Vespasia later, just before they were permitted to leave. Vespasia was as immaculate as always, but she looked tired and pale, and she was clearly distressed.

"What are you going to say?" Charlotte asked her when they had a few moments alone in a small anteroom off the main hallway.

"I have been turning over all possibilities in my mind," Vespasia answered slowly. "But we do not know the reason for what happened; we can only guess. I think the bare truth, without interpretation, is all either of us can afford to say."

Charlotte stared at her. "That is what Pitt said. But we know she was terrified. If we say nothing then aren't we lying, by omission?"

"Terrified of what, or of whom?" Vespasia said very quietly.

"Of . . . of Neville Forsbrook," Charlotte replied.

"Or of something she believed about Neville Forsbrook," Vespasia went on. "That may or may not have been true."

Charlotte felt helpless. If they voiced their own fears about what had happened to Angeles, speculation would run wild. Neville Forsbrook was alive to defend himself, and so were his friends. He could say that Angeles was hysterical, that she had misunderstood a remark; perhaps her English was not so fluent as to grasp a joke or a colloquialism. Or even that she had had rather too much champagne. Any of those explanations could even be true, though Charlotte did not believe any of them.

"So there is nothing we can do?" she asked aloud.

Vespasia's eyes were full of pain. "Nothing that I know of," she replied. "If it were your child, what would you want strangers to do, apart from grieve with you, and make no speculation or gossip?"

"Nothing," Charlotte agreed.

She rode home silently with Pitt. When they alighted and went inside, Charlotte went directly up the stairs. As gently as she could, she opened Jemima's bedroom door and stared at her daughter, sleeping in the faint light that came through the imperfectly drawn curtains. Her face was completely untroubled. Her hair, so like Charlotte's own, was spread across the pillow, unraveled out of its braids. She could have been a child still, not on the verge of womanhood at all.

Charlotte found herself smiling, even as tears ran down her cheeks.

CHAPTER 6

Vespasia was deeply troubled by the terrible death of Angeles Castelbranco. She went over and over it in her mind, waking in the night and turning up the light in her elegant bedroom. She felt the urge to see her familiar belongings, to become rooted again in her own life with the beauty and the pleasures she was accustomed to. But with that came also the deep, almost suppressed loneliness that underlay it all.

At least she was physically safe from everything except illness and age. As the events at Dorchester Terrace a short while ago had reminded her so painfully, no one was free from those. Death need not be gentle, even in one's own home. The only thing one could do was have courage, and keep faith in an ultimate goodness beyond the limited sight of the flesh.

Of course faith was of little use now to Isaura Castelbranco; and Angeles, poor child, was beyond the reach of any of them.

But whoever had brought about her death, even indirectly — and Vespasia was certain that someone had — he need not be beyond the reach of justice, and maybe even more important, of being prevented from ever doing such a thing again.

Vespasia had heard of the death of Catherine Quixwood, and the speculation as to the nature of her attack. She knew that Victor Narraway had involved himself in the case and wondered if he really had any perception of the horror behind such a terrible act. In thinking this, she realized she had been avoiding approaching him about the matter because it would hurt her if he could not — or would not — grasp the true breadth of suffering such pain.

That made the decision for her. If she feared talking to Victor, then she must face that fear. She sent him a note in the morning arranging to meet him for luncheon in one of her favorite restaurants.

She found him already waiting for her when she arrived. There were some tables in the open air, placed well apart under the dappled shade of trees. They were set with white linen, and the ever-moving light caught the edges of cut-crystal glasses. The air smelled of earth and flowers, and the murmur of the river nearby made private conversation easy.

He greeted her with evident pleasure. For the first few minutes they laughed and considered the menu and made choices, as if nothing ugly or sordid ever thrust itself into the beauty of their world.

When they were served and the waiter had excused himself, Vespasia finally approached the subject that had caused her to arrange the meeting.

"How is the case going regarding the death of Catherine Quixwood?" She tried to make it sound as if her interest were casual concern.

He did not answer immediately but studied her face, searching for the depth behind her words.

She felt foolish. She should have known that even with her years of experience in Society at saying one thing and meaning another, she could not delude him. He was not so very much younger than she, and he had been in Special Branch much of his life.

"I have a reason for asking," she said, then realized she was offering an explanation that had not been asked for. She smiled. "Am I transparent?"

His answering smile was quick. "Yes, my dear, today you are. But have we ever

168

spoken idly to each other, looking for something to say?"

She felt a faint warmth creep up her cheeks, but it was from pleasure, not discomfort. "Perhaps I had better be frank and start at the beginning. It just seemed a little clumsy to bring it up at the luncheon table."

With his back to the light, his eyes were so dark as to be black. Now they widened slightly in surprise. "Disturbing, perhaps, forthright always, but never clumsy. Is it my involvement you fear may be inappropriate? Or is it something to do with Catherine Quixwood herself? Did you know her?"

"No. So far as I am aware, I never met her," she said with a strange touch of regret. "And it had not occurred to me that you would behave other than as always. It is the subject of . . ." She found herself reluctant to use the word, and yet to circle around it was somehow an insult to the victims. "The subject of rape," she said distinctly. They were not close enough to anyone else to be overheard. "I am afraid that there may have been another incident, ending equally tragically, and I am uncertain what to do for the best."

The concern in his face became profound. "Tell me," he said simply.

Quietly and without elaboration she recounted what had happened at the party during which Angeles Castelbranco had met her death. She was startled and even a little embarrassed that her throat ached with the effort to keep her tears in check. She had not intended him to be aware of the depth of her feelings.

"There was nothing you could have done," he said gently when she had finished.

The pity in his eyes, almost tenderness, caught her with a raw edge, awakening other, more complex emotions.

"But I didn't try to do anything," she said sharply.

"What could you have done?" he asked. "From what you say it was all over in a few terrible moments."

She took a deep breath and stared down at the tablecloth, the silver and crystal still winking in the light as a breath of wind stirred the leaves above them. "I knew there was something wrong over a week ago," she answered. "I should have done something then."

"You knew, or you suspected?" he said.

"That's splitting hairs, Victor. It doesn't help."

"What is it you want me to say?" he asked reasonably.

She felt a completely uncharacteristic flare

of temper. She wanted to lash out at him for being patronizing and completely missing the point, but she knew that was unfair. She sipped her wine for a moment before answering.

"I suspect Angeles might have been assaulted, possibly raped, and that is why she reacted to young Forsbrook so violently. She was terrified, of that I am quite certain. What I do not know is what to do about it now."

"Is Pitt aware of this?" he inquired.

"I imagine so; most certainly Charlotte is. But it is not a police matter, let alone one for Special Branch. I very much doubt the Castelbrancos will report it to anyone. They are foreigners here, in many senses alone in a strange country."

"Vespasia —" he began.

"I know," she said quickly. "It is not my right to interfere, and if I do so I will assuredly make it worse. But regardless of what the law may think, it is a monstrous wrong. I didn't think so at first, but I realize now that if there is something I can do, then I must do it. I am not involved with the police, or law, or government. There are avenues I can explore that they cannot. And I have no other demands on my time."

"It could be dangerous," he began urgently, his face creased with anxiety. "Pelham Forsbrook is a very powerful man, and you have no proof that Angeles's death was anything other than a simple tragedy. You —"

She fixed him with a withering look.

He stopped speaking and smiled, but did not lower his gaze.

She realized with surprise that the look that froze almost anyone else was having no effect upon him, but she did not avert her gaze either.

"What is it you wish of me?" he asked. "Other than my discretion, which you have."

"I want to know what the law does about rape, when they are tragically certain of it. For example, what the police are doing to find out who raped Catherine Quixwood," she replied. It was a guess — she had only suspected as much from the bits of gossip she had heard — but the shadow that fell over his face immediately confirmed it.

"How did you . . ." he began, his face troubled.

"I thought it was a possibility, given the circumstances," she said gently.

Narraway sighed. "It seems that whoever attacked her was someone she knew — she let him in without fear," he said simply. "The rape was violent and brutal, but in itself it didn't kill her. It seems, according to the doctor, that she managed to drag herself to the cabinet and pour herself a glass of Madeira, which she heavily laced with the laudanum. I thought the hall cabinet was an odd place to have laudanum, but apparently that's where it was. Perhaps she liked it with the wine because the wine masked the taste. I don't know."

Vespasia was stunned. The ugliness of the act and its aftermath crowded in on her and she felt crushed by its inevitability. So Catherine herself would be blamed for her circumstances; drinking the laudanum would be interpreted as an act of shame, an admission of some kind of guilt, and the fact that she had opened the door to her attacker would be read as an invitation to intimacy, not her innocent trust in the man.

Narraway was watching her. She saw the pain and confusion in his eyes and wondered how much he understood of what people would say, and what the additional burden would be for Quixwood: all the searing confusion and anger, his own life violated also.

"I see," she said in little more than a whisper.

"I don't," he answered. "Not really. I can't shake it from my mind. To realize that another human being has experienced such horror stays with me, as if a part of myself has been touched unforgettably."

She looked at him with surprise and then felt unexpected warmth for this sensitivity in him she had never perceived before. She wanted to reach out and touch his hand, but it was too intimate a gesture and she did not do it.

"Tell me about her," she asked instead. "Have you learned anything that might be of use in discovering who her assailant was?"

The waiter came and removed their dishes, replacing them with the next course.

At the table closest to them a couple was talking, heads bent close together. He laughed and moved his hand across the white cloth to touch hers. It was a possessive gesture. She pulled away from him, her face coloring.

Vespasia looked away. She could remember being so young, so uncertain. But it felt very long ago.

Narraway began slowly, feeling his way. "Knox seems to be a competent man and I think he understands the crime better than many. He moves very carefully. To begin with I wished he had been quicker. Now I'm starting to appreciate how very complicated the situation is."

"And Quixwood?" she said gently. "He must be torn apart."

"Yes. And I fear that if we find who did it, it will be even harder for him when it comes to trial. It will be as if it is all happening again, but this time in public. Strangers will be discussing the intimacy and the dreadfulness of it, pulling apart the details and speculating as to what happened. Even if it is done with compassion, it hardly makes things any easier."

"No, it won't," she agreed. "Perhaps that is why the people who do such things are not afraid. They know most of us will do nothing about it. We would rather suffer in silence and even lie to protect them, before living the horror all over again in front of everyone else. Except Catherine is dead, and can do nothing for herself now." She saw him flinch.

"You are right." He shook his head fractionally. "I have looked at least to a deeper side of her life. She seems to have been intelligent, sensitive, full of imagination and interested in every kind of beauty, discovery or invention that one can explore. And lonely. She had nothing to do that mattered —" He stopped abruptly, a shadow of self-knowledge in his face. Then he went on quickly. "There's a young man called Alban

175

Hythe whom Mrs. Quixwood seems to have met much more frequently than would be accidental."

"An affair?" she asked.

"I don't know. It seems a strong possibility."

"How very sad." For several moments Vespasia said nothing, picturing in her mind the arrival of a lover, the expected excitement, the emotion, the vulnerability, and then the sudden shock of violence. Had there even been a quarrel? What could possibly have happened that made emotions change from love to uncontrollable fury in such a way?

Narraway waited, watching her. She could not read his expression.

"Do you think it was this man?" she asked him.

"Reason says it is likely," he replied. "Instinct says not. But that may be only what I want to think. I also want to think she didn't mean to take her own life, that she just . . . misjudged the dose. But the police surgeon said it was many times the appropriate amount."

"She might have meant to, Victor," Vespasia said gently. "I have no idea how I would feel were such a thing to happen to me. I don't think it is something I have power to imagine. People can do desperate things when they are frightened.

"It isn't so very difficult to understand," she continued, quickly, urgently, leaning forward over the elegant table. "If somehow rape is the victim's own fault — she said or did something, wore indiscreet clothes, behaved in a certain way — then if we do not do whatever it is they did, it will never happen to us. It's not compassionate, it's not realistic, but it is understandable."

Anger burned in Narraway's eyes. "I don't disagree with you. But that sounds monstrous to me, callous and brutal. It is almost like consenting that rape is okay, by omission of defense. I find it is contemptible, the final betrayal."

"Admitting it can happen to a decent and completely innocent woman is to accept it could happen to anyone," she pointed out. "That is the unbearable truth. It tears away the last defense. And, of course, some even hate the woman, the victim, for creating what seems like an uncontrollable passion in someone. They don't understand that it is a crime of hatred, or of power, not of passion." She had a sudden afterthought. "Or perhaps they do, and it is wakening that animal inside the man which they hate her for. Because they want to pretend such an animal does not exist anymore."

"Are we so fragile?" he said unhappily.

"Some of us, yes." She thought for a moment. "And, of course, they might also be afraid for the men who love them — the rage in them, the need for revenge, even if only to prove themselves in control," she added. "It might lead them not to comfort the victim, hold her in their arms and assure her that she is still the same, still loved, but instead to go out and beat, or even kill, the man who has taken from her so much. And in their blindness of pain they might not even choose the right man."

"I begin to see why Angeles Castelbranco did not denounce Forsbrook, if you are right and she was raped," he said very quietly. "And why Catherine Quixwood, in the despair of that moment, chose to take her own life rather than go through the ordeal of what would inevitably follow."

"What are the chances of a successful prosecution anyway?" Vespasia searched his face now, looking for an answer. "Even if Knox finds the right man, will the verdict be worth the price it will cost?"

"I don't know," Narraway admitted. "But what happens to the law itself if we don't try?"

"What does Quixwood want?" she asked

instead of answering.

Narraway spoke slowly. "At the moment he wants to know the truth, but he may well find that he would rather not, if it turns out that Catherine was having an affair with Alban Hythe, or some other man. I don't know. I think he wants to do whatever is possible to clear Catherine's name and show she was innocent. Perhaps all he really wants is to be doing something rather than nothing. To feel he is fighting the reality and not simply submitting to it. I can understand that . . . I think."

"You are being very honest," she observed.

"Are we not past pretending?" he asked. "I can return to it, if you wish, but I would rather not. I have lived with secrets for as long as I can remember. Some were worth keeping, probably most were not. Being too careful has become a habit."

"Not a bad one," she responded, smiling again. "Most of us tell others far too much, and then are embarrassed by it, always trying to remember exactly how much we said and then replaying it over and over to convince ourselves it was less indiscreet, less revealing than it seemed."

"I cannot imagine you being indiscreet," he remarked.

"Don't be polite," she said a little tartly.

"You don't know me as well as you might think. Certainly, at times, I have been at the very least duplicitous."

"I'm greatly relieved," he said fervently. "A few imperfections and the occasional vulnerability are very attractive in a woman. It allows a man to imagine he is, now and again, just a fraction superior. In your case, of course, he is not, but it is a necessary illusion, if we are to be comfortable."

"I should like you to be comfortable," she said, hiding a smile and turning to the waiter, who was inquiring as to their choice for the final course. She was not certain if she saw a faint color in Narraway's cheeks or not.

Thanks to their conversation, Vespasia had made up her mind what she would do regarding Angeles Castelbranco. To begin with she must acquire as much information as possible. If Angeles had indeed been raped, then it must have been very recently. It should not be difficult to find out which functions she had attended in the last month. There were a considerable number of them, but they involved largely the same people. Diplomatic circles were fairly small, and occasions suitable for a girl of sixteen were limited.

A little invention, a great deal of tact, and half a dozen inquiries of friends produced a list of such parties over the previous four or five weeks.

It required all of the following day, and more evasion than was comfortable, before Vespasia had a rough draft of the guest lists. It would have been simpler to ask Isaura Castelbranco which parties Angeles had attended. However, for that she would have had to give a reason, and there was none that would not cause pain, or for which she could in any way account as her concern. She could not even imagine how the woman felt. Vespasia's own family had caused her many emotions over the years. To love was to be vulnerable, especially regarding children. One feared for their safety, their happiness, their good health. One felt guilty for their unhappiness or their failures. One was bothered by their dependence, and terrified by their courage. One forgot one's own mistakes, risks, high and absurd dreams and wanted only to protect them from hurt.

Then they grew up, married, and too often became almost strangers. They could not imagine that you were also afraid, fallible, could still dream and fall in love.

Perhaps that was just as well.

So she wrote and rewrote guest lists, and

asked questions in roundabout ways. Two days after lunching with Victor Narraway, she had found what she believed was the event at which Angeles had been raped. Obtaining details was more difficult. She pondered for some time whom she could ask to give her an account of the evening, who was willing and observant enough. More than that, what reason could she offer for making such a request?

And who would be discreet enough afterward to keep their own counsel and not mention it to anyone at all? How could she even suggest to whoever it was that the matter must remain confidential? To most people, the very secrecy of it would be a spur to gossip. Each retelling would grow and mutate in the exercise.

She studied more closely the list of those who had been present at that event. There seemed to have been a considerable number of young people. It was in observing how many that the answer came to her.

It was far easier making such inquiries face-to-face than on a telephone. Accordingly she arranged to have luncheon with Lady Tattersall; the following day they sat pleasantly chatting over a dessert apple flan, and far more cream than was good for either of them. Vespasia introduced the name of a fictitious sociable friend.

"She heard the party was a great success, and knew she would have to make hers equally delightful," Vespasia said, broaching the subject at last. "She does not know anyone who was there whom she might approach, so I promised her I would ask you."

"Of course," Lady Tattersall said agreeably. "What would she like to know?"

Vespasia smiled. "I think a simple account of how it went would be excellent, perhaps with a little detail, particularly as to how the younger guests responded to the evening. That would serve very well, and be most kind of you."

Lady Tattersall was delighted to recount everything she could remember. Vespasia had been careful enough to make her fictitious friend live quite out of the way, in Northumberland, so the absence of word of such a party ever taking place would not be noticed. She learned a great deal: a vivid firsthand account of a large but outwardly successful event. The only person less than happy had been Angeles Castelbranco, but her distress had been put down to her youth, and her foreign blood.

Vespasia left, certain in her own mind that Neville Forsbrook had raped Angeles at Mrs. Westerly's party, exactly as she and

Charlotte had feared. Now the question was what to do with that knowledge, besides informing Thomas Pitt.

In the late morning of the day after her luncheon with Lady Tattersall, Vespasia was taken very much by surprise when her maid announced that Mr. Rawdon Quixwood had called and asked if he might take a few moments of her time. He had a matter of some importance he wished to discuss with her.

She gave the maid permission to ask him in. A moment later he was standing in her quiet sitting room with its view onto the garden. It was in full summer bloom, hot colors of roses and, in the background, the cool blue spires of delphinium.

Quixwood was a stark contrast to the gaudy profusion beyond the windows. He was smartly dressed, but in black, relieved only by the white of his shirt. His thick hair was combed and his shave immaculate, yet his face was that of a man haunted by grief. His skin was pale and the lines around his mouth furrowed deep.

Vespasia struggled to think of anything to say that would not be banal.

"Good morning, Mr. Quixwood," she began. "May I offer you tea, or — if you would prefer it — something more?"

"That is kind of you, Lady Vespasia, but I shall return to my club for luncheon. I am presently living there. I . . . I cannot yet face returning to my home."

"I can imagine not," she agreed quickly. "I would not find it hard to understand if you never did. I am sure there are other properties that would be equally agreeable, and convenient for you."

He smiled very slightly. "You are quite right. Forgive me for intruding on you without warning. If the matter were not of some urgency and moral importance, I would not do so."

She indicated the chair opposite her and, as he sat down, she resumed her own seat. "What can I do for you, Mr. Quixwood?" she invited.

He looked down, smiling very slightly in a wry expression of amusement and pain.

"I have heard from a friend of mine that you have been making certain inquiries about Pelham Forsbrook's son, Neville, after the tragic night where young Angeles Castelbranco met her death." He winced. "It is . . . it is a painful reminder of my own wife's death." His voice was husky and he clearly found mastery of his emotions almost impossible.

Vespasia tried to think of something to

ease his awkwardness, but she had no idea what he meant to say, so nothing appropriate came to mind.

He looked up at her. "I don't know how to say this graciously." He bit his lip. "I know that young Neville behaved in a manner that can be described only as crass when he teased the poor girl. If he were my son, I hope I would have raised him to be more sensitive, more aware of the feelings of others, no matter how much wine he might have taken. His behavior was disgusting. There can be no argument on that. I imagine he will regret his cruelty for the rest of his life."

His eyes searched her face. "But I know that he did not assault her, seriously or even trivially, at Mrs. Westerley's party. I was there myself, when young Angeles appeared looking a trifle disheveled, and her face tearstained. I assumed at the time that she had had some youthful quarrel, perhaps even an unexpected rejection. I'm afraid I thought no more of it than that, and possibly I was horribly wrong." Now his face was filled with distress. "Since I . . . since . . ." He faltered to a stop.

Vespasia was overwhelmed with pity for him. He must feel doubly guilty, for not being able to protect his wife, and now for having failed to see Angeles's terrible distress, masked by her own need to hide it, and his assumption that youthful tears came and went easily.

She leaned forward a fraction. "Mr. Quixwood," she said very gently, "no sane person would have assumed otherwise in the circumstances. Of course girls her age both laugh and cry over things they barely remember the day after. There was nothing you could, or should, have done." She hesitated, and then continued, "It is natural when there has been a tragedy that we relive the time before, wondering how we could have averted it. In most cases there was nothing at all to be done, but we torture ourselves anyway. We want to have helped. Above all we want to do over the past with greater wisdom, more kindness; but as the pain settles, we know we cannot. Only the future can be changed." She wanted to comfort him regarding Catherine as well, but there was no comfort to give.

His smile was now rueful. "I am beginning to realize that, Lady Vespasia, but slowly, and I am some distance from acceptance. What I came to say, which matters, and why I took the liberty of disturbing you, was that whatever happened to Angeles Castelbranco, I know it was not

Neville Forsbrook who caused it. I was with him when she left the company and went to look at the paintings in the gallery. It was not Neville she went with, although I admit I don't know who it was."

Vespasia drew in her breath to ask him if he was certain, then realized it would be pointless and a trifle insulting. Of course he was certain. He had come out of his grief and his cocoon of protection to say so.

"Thank you, Mr. Quixwood," she said gravely. "It would be monstrous to blame the wrong person, even for a day. Whispers are not easily silenced. You have told me this before I had the chance to speak to anyone, and perhaps have saved me from a profound error. I am grateful to you."

He rose to his feet, moving with stiffness, as if he hurt inwardly.

"Thank you for seeing me, Lady Vespasia. Thank you for your wisdom. In time it will be of comfort." He bowed, just a gesture of the head, and went to the door.

She sat for several minutes afterward without moving, thinking, in the silent, sunlit room, how desperately fragile the illusion of safety could be.

CHAPTER 7

Pitt found it extremely difficult to forget the tragedy of Angeles Castelbranco's death. Every time he heard the clink of glass or the sound of someone's laughter, it took him back to that terrible party. In his mind he saw the ambassador's face as he stood by the window, all expression wiped from it as if he were dead.

Worse was the raging grief of the ambassador's wife. She reminded him of Charlotte somehow, although she looked nothing at all like her. Yet both were fiercely devoted mothers, and that gave them a similarity greater than all differences of appearance could be.

He sat in his office in Lisson Grove, which used to be Narraway's. He was trying to concentrate on the papers in front of him to the exclusion of every other thought, but not very successfully. He was relieved when there was a knock on the door. The moment after, Stoker looked in.

"Yes?" Pitt said hopefully.

There was no pleasure in Stoker's bony face. "The Portuguese ambassador is here and would like to see you, sir. I told him you were busy, but he said he'd wait, however long it took. Sorry, sir."

Pitt pushed his papers into a rough pile, turning the top one facedown. "Putting it off won't make it any better. Ask him to come in," he requested.

"Do you want me to interrupt in fifteen or twenty minutes?" Stoker asked.

Pitt gave him a bleak smile. "Not unless it's genuine."

Stoker nodded and withdrew. Two minutes later the door opened again and Rafael Castelbranco came in. He looked ill, and ten years older than he had a few days ago. His cheeks were sunken; there was no color in his skin. His clothes were neat, even elegant, but now they seemed a mockery of other, happier times.

Pitt rose to his feet and came around the desk to offer his hand.

Castelbranco gripped it as if that in itself were some promise of help.

At Pitt's invitation they sat in the two armchairs between the fireplace and the window. With a small gesture of his hand,

Castelbranco declined any refreshment. He had fine hands, brown-skinned and slender.

"What can I do for you, sir?" Pitt asked. There was no point in inquiring after his health, or that of his wife. The man was shattered by grief, and she could only be the same.

Castelbranco cleared his throat. "I know you have children," he began. "Mrs. Pitt has been most kind to my wife, both before my daughter's death, and since. You may perhaps imagine how we feel, but no one could know . . . could even think of . . ." He stopped himself, took several deep breaths, and continued in a more controlled tone. "I wish you to help me find out as much as I can about what happened to my daughter, and why." He saw Pitt's expression. "I am not looking for justice, Mr. Pitt. I realize that may be beyond anyone's reach." He closed his eyes a moment; whether to regain control of his voice or to hide his thoughts it was impossible to tell.

Instead of interjecting, Pitt waited for Castelbranco to continue.

The ambassador opened his eyes again. "I wish to silence the rumors, not only for my own sake, and my daughter's, but for my wife's. Until we know what happened we cannot refute even the ugliest whispers. We

191

are helpless. It is a . . ." Again he stopped. Clearly none of his diplomatic skills or experience came to his aid in trying to describe what he was feeling.

This matter was not specifically within the area of Special Branch's duties. But Castelbranco was the ambassador of a foreign country with whom Britain had a long and valued relationship, and the death had taken place in Britain.

Apart from that, simply as a human being with a daughter of a similar age, Pitt felt a sharp, very personal understanding of Castelbranco's grief.

"I'll do what I can," he promised, wondering as he said the words if he was being rash and would regret it. "But I must be discreet, or I may risk making the rumors worse, rather than better." Did that sound like an excuse? It was not. Pitt simply knew from experience that inquiring into a rumor, or even denying it too vehemently, could result in it spreading much further.

"I understand the risks," Castelbranco said grimly, "but this is intolerable. What have I left to lose?" His voice trembled in spite of himself. "Angeles was betrothed to marry Tiago de Freitas, a young man of excellent family, with a bright future ahead of him and an unspotted reputation. It was in all ways an excellent match." His hands tightened, even though they were resting in his lap. "She told me that their decision to end the engagement was mutual. But now people are suggesting that he discovered something about Angeles that was so shameful he could not live with it, and that is why the engagement was broken."

Pitt felt a wave of fury flow through him, then one of terrible pity. The ambassador's body was visibly so tense, Pitt knew every muscle in him must ache, and yet how could the man possibly rest? Did he sleep at all? Or perhaps in nightmares he saw his daughter crash through the glass into the night, again and again as he watched, helpless to save her?

Or was it even worse than that? Did he see her laughing, young, and excited at all that lay ahead of her? Did he feel her hand in his, small and soft, and then waken and remember that she was dead, broken on the outside by glass and stone, inside by terror and humiliation?

"Exactly what has this young man said?" Pitt asked.

"That it was Angeles who really ended the betrothal," Castelbranco replied. "But he has not denied the rumor. He smiles sadly, and says nothing." His voice shook with anger and the color washed up his face. "Sometimes a silence can speak more than words."

Pitt searched for something to say that would draw away the poison of what was being whispered, and failed. In Castelbranco's place, Pitt would want to strike out at de Freitas — verbally, physically, anything to let loose some of the agony inside himself.

"I'll speak to him," he promised. "See if he's willing to tell me anything, and if he does I'll follow up. If not, I'll warn him of the dangers of careless speculation at the expense of someone else's reputation. I don't know what result that will have, but I'll try. Is his business in Britain?"

For a moment Castelbranco's eyes softened. "At least some of it. Your words may have an effect on him. Thank you. There is no one else to defend my daughter. It makes me wonder if de Freitas was as good a choice to marry Angeles as we thought. How do you know the measure of a person, when often the event that betrays them comes too late?"

"Half my job would be unnecessary if I knew the answer to that," Pitt replied.

Castelbranco rose to his feet. "Perhaps it was a foolish question. I thought I knew Tiago. I concentrate on the lesser pain of disillusion, to take my mind off the greater one of loss, imagining it will ease my grief."

"I would do the same," Pitt acknowledged, rising also and holding out his hand. "I will inform you as soon as I have anything to say."

Tiago de Freitas received Pitt reluctantly. Pitt was sure he did it only because he could not refuse, considering Pitt's station and the power it gave him. They met in a side office in de Freitas's father's highly prosperous wine import and export offices, just off Regent Street. The rooms were somber, but luxurious in their own way. There was a lot of exquisite wood, much of it carved. The furniture was embossed leather, and beneath the feet rich carpets silenced all movement.

De Freitas was a handsome enough young man, with fine dark eyes and a magnificent head of black hair. He would have been more striking still had he been a few inches taller. He regarded Pitt somewhat cautiously.

"What can I do for you, sir?"

He did not invite Pitt to be seated, which pleased Pitt. There was a certain informality to sitting, and he wanted the interview to be courteous, but not easy.

"First of all, Mr. de Freitas, I regret having to disturb you during what must surely be a difficult time. I will try to be as brief as I can," he replied.

De Freitas stiffened almost imperceptibly, with just a movement of the muscles in his neck.

"Thank you," he acknowledged. "But I am sure you did not come here just to express your condolences about my fiancée. Your card says that you are commander of Special Branch, which I am aware is a part of the Intelligence Service of this country. I will do all I can to assist you as a guest here, but I am Portuguese and I'm sure you understand the interests of my own country must come first."

Pitt was about to deny that his business was anything to do with national interest, then he realized that would rob him of the power he needed.

"I would not ask it of you, sir," he replied smoothly. "You just now referred to Miss Castelbranco as if she were still betrothed to you. I was informed that the engagement had been broken. Was that incorrect?"

De Freitas's black eyebrows rose. His voice was not openly defensive, but it was guarded. "How can that concern you, Mr. Pitt?"

196

Pitt answered with a slight smile. "It has to do with another matter, one I cannot discuss. If you won't tell me, I am obliged to suppose that the rumors I've heard regarding the entire situation may be correct. I am hoping they are not, and that for the sake of the pleasant relations that have existed between Britain and Portugal for half a millennium, I can lay them to rest." He let the invitation hang in the air for de Freitas to pick up.

The younger man hesitated, caught in uncertainty. A very slight flush of annoyance colored his cheeks.

"I had preferred not to speak of it for the sake of her family, but you force my hand." He gave a very slight shrug, not perhaps as discreetly as he had intended. "The engagement was ended."

"How long before her death did that happen, Mr. de Freitas?"

Tiago looked startled. "I really don't see how this can be of concern to the British Secret Service." There was a touch of anger in his voice now. "It is a very personal matter."

"The announcement of a betrothal to marry is a very public event," Pitt pointed out. "It is not possible to end it entirely

197

privately, however personal the cause may be."

De Freitas seemed to hover between irritation and capitulation. Seconds passed as he fought with a decision.

"I am trying to quell rumors that can only hurt the Portuguese ambassador to Britain, Mr. de Freitas," Pitt pressed. "It is a small courtesy we can accord him at the time of a very dreadful loss. Miss Castelbranco was his only child, as I am sure you are aware."

De Freitas nodded. "Yes, yes, of course." He let out a very slight sigh. "We broke our engagement less than a week before she died. I'm sorry about it, of course I am."

Pitt noticed how gracefully de Freitas had evaded the issue of who made the initial move to end the relationship. The way he said it, the decision sounded like an inevitable mutual agreement.

"Was Miss Castelbranco extremely upset?" Pitt asked, determined to force the young man into an answer.

De Freitas looked up sharply, his face reflecting a sudden anger. "If you are suggesting that her death was . . . was a result of my breaking off an engagement, then you are completely mistaken." He lifted his chin a little. "It was she who ended it."

"Indeed? What reason did she give? One

does not do such a thing lightly. Her parents would have been most distressed. As I imagine yours were also."

De Freitas did not answer for several moments, then he gave a brief, tight smile. "You have me at something of a disadvantage, Mr. Pitt. I had hoped to give you a vague answer, and that you would be gentleman enough to accept it. I'm afraid I cannot say anything further without dishonoring a young woman I had thought to make my wife. Of course I understand you wish to protect her reputation, and give her family whatever comfort is possible, and I respect you for it. Indeed, I admire it. However, to assist you in that I must decline to say anything more. I'm sorry."

"So it wasn't she, but you who broke the engagement," Pitt concluded.

De Freitas shrugged. "I've told you, sir. I can say nothing more. Let her rest in peace . . . for everyone's sake."

Pitt knew he would get no more from Tiago de Freitas. He thanked him for his time and walked back through the hushed, wood-lined corridors.

"You mean he implied that it was he who broke it off, and that he was lying to protect her?" Charlotte said incredulously that evening when Pitt was home and dinner was finished and cleared away. They were in the parlor, with the windows ajar. The slight breeze carried in the rustle of leaves and the smell of earth and cut grass. The door to the passageway was closed. Daniel and Jemima were in their respective bedrooms reading.

"More or less," Pitt conceded. He was not sitting. He felt too restless to settle down; perhaps because Charlotte was so angry she also could not sit.

She looked stricken. "So whatever it is they are saying, he either believes it or he doesn't care because he wanted to be rid of her anyway," she accused.

"The engagement was broken off before she died," Pitt pointed out, shaking his head.

"Exactly!" she retorted. "He listened to some rumor and abandoned her!" Her face was flushed and her eyes brilliant. She was so quick to defend the vulnerable. He loved her for it and he would not change her, even in situations when it would be far wiser to weigh the matter first. She had been wrong before, dangerously so, but that did not stop her.

"I know what you're thinking," she accused him. "Of course I might be wrong. Would you be weighing it this carefully if it had happened to someone we were close to?"

"But it isn't," he said reasonably.

"It isn't this time! What about when it is?" she demanded.

He took a deep breath and turned to face her. "If something like this were to happen to someone we love, God forbid, I would be just as furious as you are, just as hurt, and just as impetuous," he admitted. "And it would also probably do no good at all. Loving someone makes you care passionately. It makes you a decent person, warm, vulnerable, generous, and brave. But it doesn't make you right, and it certainly doesn't make you effective in finding the truth."

"I think the truth is she was raped," she said quietly, tears suddenly bright in her eyes.

"And I still can't believe that anyone would truly blame her for that," he responded.

"Oh, Thomas! Don't be so . . . blind!" she said desperately. "Of course they can blame her. They have to! If they don't, they have to accept that it can happen to anyone, to them or their daughters."

She shook her head. "Or else you're the kind of person who has to stand and stare at it, probe to see where it hurts the most, and make yourself important by knowing something other people don't." Her voice was brittle with contempt. "Then you can be the center of attention while you tell everyone else, making up any details you might not happen to know."

He took a step toward her, touching her lightly. Her arms were rigid under his fingers. The wind outside rattled harder in the trees and blew in through the door with the first patter of rain and the sweet, rich smell of damp earth.

"Aren't you being a little hard on everyone, generally?" he asked.

Her eyes widened. "You mean I'm being a bit hysterical, perhaps? Because I'm afraid that one day it could be our daughter?"

"No," he said firmly. "Rape is very rare, thank God, and Jemima will not be allowed to keep the company of any young man we don't know, or whose family we don't know."

"For the love of heaven, Thomas!" Charlotte said between her teeth. "How on earth would you know how many rapes there are? Who is going to talk about it? Who's going to report it to the police? And do you really think that it's never young men we *know* who could do such things?"

Pitt felt a sudden icy twinge of fear, and

then helplessness. His imagination raced.

She saw it in his eyes, and bent her head forward to rest her brow against his neck. The wind ruffled her skirt and then pushed the door wider, so it banged against the wall.

"It's a hidden crime. All we can do is bite the heads off anyone who speaks lightly or viciously about Angeles Castelbranco. And don't tell me I shouldn't do that. I don't care if it's appropriate or suitable. I care about protecting her mother."

He slid his arms around her and held her very tightly.

Pitt could not devote his own time to making discreet inquiries into the character and reputation of Angeles Castelbranco, and to send anyone else might raise more speculation than it would answer. Why would any man unrelated to the girl be asking such questions unless there was cause to suspect something; for example, her virtue?

He was still weighing the various possibilities open to him, and discarding them one by one, when two days later Castelbranco came to his office again, his face even more haggard than before. He seemed barely able to stand and he gripped his hands together when he sat in the chair Pitt offered him, as though to keep them from trembling. Twice he began to speak and then stopped.

"I visited de Freitas," Pitt told him quietly. "He equivocated. First he said it was Angeles who broke off the engagement, then he admitted it was he. I have been considering how to prove it either way without raising even further malicious speculation."

"It is too late," Castelbranco said, shaking his head. "I don't know what happened or who is behind it. I cannot think who would say such things, or why they would. I fear it is some enemy I have made who is taking the cruelest possible revenge on me."

"If that is so, there may be something Special Branch can do," Pitt began, then realized he might be offering a false hope. "What makes you think this?"

"Someone has said that her death was not a terrible accident but a deliberate act of suicide." Castelbranco had difficulty keeping his voice from choking. "And suicide is a mortal sin," he whispered. "The Church will not bury her with Christian rites — my . . . my child is . . ." The tears slid down his cheeks and he lowered his head.

Pitt leaned forward and put his hand on Castelbranco's wrist, gripping him hard. "Don't give up," he said firmly. "That decision is hasty and may be born of serious misinformation." He tried to keep the contempt for men who would make such a cruel decision — childless men without pity or understanding — out of his voice and knew he failed. He didn't want to add that grief to Castelbranco's all but unbearable burden. Now, above all else, the man needed his faith.

"Perhaps this should be the subject of a proper inquiry after all," he said. "If such a thing is being alleged, then the discretion I have tried to exercise may be pointless."

"It is," Castelbranco said hoarsely. The tears were now running down his cheeks. He was too harrowed to be self-conscious. "It has been suggested that she was with child, and the disgrace of it drove her to take both their lives. That is a double crime, self-murder and murder of her innocent babe. I don't know how my wife can live with it. She is already dying inside. I fear that would . . ."

His eyes searched Pitt's face as if to find some hope he could not even imagine there. He was teetering on the edge of an abyss of despair. "I need the truth," he whispered. "Whatever it is, it cannot be worse than this. I loved my daughter, Mr. Pitt. She was my only child. I would have done anything to make her safe and happy . . . and I could not even keep her alive. Now I cannot save her reputation from the mouths of the filthy, and I cannot save her soul to heaven. She was a child! I remember . . ." He lost command of his voice and faltered to a stop.

Pitt tightened his grip. "I know. My own daughter is willful, erratic, hot-tempered one moment, tender the next." He could see Jemima in his mind. He remembered holding her as a baby, her tiny, perfect hands clinging to his thumb. He remembered her discovering the world, its wonders and its pain, her innocence, her trust that he could make everything better, and her laughter.

"She can seem so wise I marvel at her," he went on. "Then the instant after she's a child again, with no knowledge of the world. She's a baby and a woman at the same time. She looks so like my wife, and yet when I look into her eyes, it is my own I see looking back at me. I can imagine what you are suffering well enough to know that I know nothing of it at all."

Castelbranco bent his head and covered his face with his hands.

Pitt let go of his wrist and sat back in his chair, silent for several seconds.

"I have a certain degree of discretion as to what I can investigate," he said at last. "As you are the ambassador of a country with whom we have a powerful and long-standing treaty, it could be in the national interest that we do not allow you to be victimized in this way while you and your family are in London. That I can do, as a courtesy to you as the representative of your country."

Castelbranco rose to his feet awkwardly, swaying a little until he regained his balance.

"Thank you, sir. You could not have offered more. I appreciate your understanding." He bowed and turned round slowly before walking upright to the door. Once outside he closed it softly behind him.

Pitt shifted only slightly, to look out his window, to bring order to his thoughts. He had meant what he said: he could not grasp the enormity of the man's pain, his helplessness that his child had been destroyed both on earth and, in his belief, in heaven as well; and he had been unable to do anything to prevent it.

Pitt was not sure what he believed of heaven. He had never given it much consideration. Now he was certain he did not worship a God who would condemn a child — and Angeles was little more than that — for any sin, let alone an unproven one, and for which she had already paid such a hideous price.

Castelbranco must be wrong about God's nature. Such judgment was a law of men, who flexed their muscles to dominate, to keep the disobedient under control, to frighten the willful into submission. God must be better than that, or what exactly is His mercy for?

But that was an argument for another time. Nothing would bring Angeles back. The truth might restore at least her good name, and perhaps help to find some way around the bitter damnation of the Church, the judgment of men who, by their very calling, had no children of their own, no understanding of the endless tenderness a parent feels, no matter how tired, frustrated or temporarily angry.

Did any parent ever put his or her child beyond forgiveness, truly? He could not imagine Charlotte doing so, for all her impetuosity, her high hopes and at times instant judgments, hot tempers, impatience, ungoverned tongue; no, she would defend those she loved to her last breath.

He smiled as he thought of her. She was exasperating, sometimes even a professional liability with her crusading ideas, and, in the past, her incessant meddling in his cases. But she was never, ever a coward. She might have been a lot less trouble if she had been, and a lot safer. And, he admitted, a lot less help. But without question, he would never have loved her as he did.

Heaven help him, was Jemima going to be the same? At three years younger, Daniel was already more levelheaded; Jemima, however, would instinctively, without thought or planning, leap to his defense, right or wrong.

One day she would be a mother like Charlotte: protect first, and chastise afterward. Punish, but forgive. And having forgiven, she would never mention the offense again. Charlotte had once sent Daniel to his room without supper for carrying a grudge after a matter had been resolved.

Pitt knew now at least where he would begin. He rose to his feet and called for Stoker. When he arrived, Pitt gave him his task. Then he went alone to see Isaura Castelbranco.

He caught a hansom with ease, and all too rapidly made his way through the busy, jostling streets to the ambassador's residence. Perhaps Castelbranco had prepared her, because Isaura received Pitt without any excuses or prevarication. He was asked to wait in the private study, where mirrors were turned to the wall, pictures draped with black and the curtains on the windows pulled all but closed.

Isaura came in quietly. The only sound he heard was the click of the latch as the door closed. She stood straight, but she seemed smaller than he remembered, and her face was bleached of all color except the faint olive of her complexion.

"It is kind of you to come, Mr. Pitt," she said with a slight huskiness, as if she had not used her voice for quite some time, after so much weeping.

"The ambassador asked me to look into the events leading up to Miss Castelbranco's death and find out whatever facts I can," he explained. In the face of her dignity it would be faintly insulting to be anything but direct. "I expect you can tell me at least some things that I do not know."

A slight movement touched her mouth, almost a smile.

"My husband is deeply grieved. He loved his daughter very much, as did I. But I think perhaps I am a little more realistic as to what may be done." She looked down for a moment, then up again, meeting his eyes. "Of course part of me wishes for revenge. It is natural. But it is also futile. Anger is a quite understandable reaction to loss. And he has lost his only child. You did not know her, Mr. Pitt, but she was lovely, full of life and dreams, warmhearted . . ." She stopped, unable for a moment to keep up her brave demeanor. She turned half away from him, concealing her face.

"As you may know, I have a daughter myself, Senhora Castelbranco," he said. "She is fourteen and already half a woman. I suppose that is why the case matters so much to me. I could easily be in your place."

"Please God, you will not be." She turned back to him slowly. Something in his words had allowed her to reclaim at least a semblance of self-mastery. "If you were, you might feel the fury my husband does, the desperate desire to clear our daughter's name from the slander that is being spread. But your wife would tell you, as I tell the ambassador; we are helpless to bring any charges. It will only prolong the speculation and the gossip. It will cure nothing."

Pitt was taken aback. She was as much ravaged by grief as her husband, and yet she seemed quite calm in her refusal to take the issue further. It was not defeat. Meeting her eyes he knew she was not emotionally frozen by shock. She spoke from determination, not emptiness.

"Don't you want to know what happened?" he asked. "If only for your peace of mind . . . for the future, perhaps?"

Her lips tightened a moment, not a smile so much as a grimace. "I do know, Mr. Pitt. Perhaps I should have told my husband, but I did not. I knew it would . . ." she drew in a deep breath, ". . . it would hurt him, with no purpose. There is nothing we can do."

Pitt was surprised and confused. He knew what Charlotte and Vespasia suspected had happened, where and when, and almost certainly by whom. But would Isaura respond this way if their suspicions were indeed correct?

"I can't act without your permission, Senhora, but for the sake of the valued relationship between England and Portugal, I must discover what happened," he said gently.

She blinked her dark eyes. "What happened? A young man who has a twisted soul raped my daughter, and then made light of it. He sought out opportunities to mock her in public with pretended courtesies, and when she retreated from him, he taunted her all the more, until in hysteria she backed away as far as she could, and beyond, crashing through a window to her death. I saw it, and was helpless to do anything to save her. That is what happened." She stared at him, almost challengingly.

"Forsbrook?" He breathed the name rather than speaking it. He had known from

Vespasia and Charlotte, who had witnessed Angeles's final moments, and yet there was still a monstrousness about it.

"Yes," Isaura said simply.

"Neville Forsbrook?" he repeated, to be certain. "You knew? When did it happen, and where?"

"Yes, Neville Forsbrook, the son of your famous banker who is responsible for so much investment for your countrymen," she answered. "I knew because my daughter told me. It happened at a party she attended. Forsbrook was there, among many other young people. He found Angeles alone in one of the apartments looking at the art there. He raped her and left her terrified and bleeding. Here at home one of our maids found her weeping in her room and sent for me."

"She said she had been raped, and who it was?" He hated pressing her. It seemed pointlessly cruel, and yet if he did not he would only have to come back later to ask.

"She was bleeding," Isaura replied. "Her clothes were torn and she was bruised. I am a married woman, Mr. Pitt. I am perfectly aware of what happens between a man and a woman. If it is anything like love, or even a heat-of-the-moment weakness, a hunger, it does not leave bruises such as Angeles had." She lifted her chin. "Do I know it was Neville Forsbrook? Yes, but I cannot prove it. Even if I could, what good would it do?"

She gave a tiny, hopeless shrug. "Angeles is dead. He would only say she was willing, a whore at heart. And his father would turn the goodwill of the people he knows against us. They would close ranks, and we would find ourselves outcast for making a fuss and exposing to the public what should have remained a private sin."

Pitt did not argue. His mind raced to find a rebuttal, but there was none. Politically, socially, and diplomatically it would be a disaster. The most that would happen to Neville Forsbrook would be that he might marry less fortunately than otherwise. Even that was not certain. He might continue to make people believe that it was all the imagination of a hysterical young foreign girl who had stepped willingly into disgrace, like Eve, possibly even gotten pregnant, then blamed him for it. And there would be no way to prove him a liar.

Even the testimony of the maid who had found Angeles crying and bleeding would hardly be viewed as impartial. The girl's humiliation would be painted in detail for everyone, and branded in their memories even more deeply than it was now. Isaura was right: they were helpless.

Forsbrook would never allow his son to be blamed, and he had the power to protect him. He would use it. Perhaps it was Pitt's job to see that it did not come to such a thing.

What would he tell Castelbranco? That England was powerless to protect his daughter's reputation, or bring to any kind of justice the young man who had raped her and driven her to her death? Not only that, but they felt it better not to try to seek any kind of justice, because it would be uncomfortable, raise fears and questions they preferred to avoid?

And if Castelbranco then thought them barbarous, would he be wrong?

"What about his mother?" Pitt said aloud, casting around for any other avenue at all. "Do you think . . . ?"

She shook her head. "Eleanor Forsbrook died a few years ago, I'm told. There was a terrible carriage accident in Bryanston Mews, just off the square where they live. People speak very well of her. She was generous and beautiful. Perhaps if she were still alive this would not have happened."

"Probably not," he conceded. "But the loss of a mother does not excuse this. Most of us lose people we love at some time or

215

other." He thought of his own father, taken from him when he was a child, unjustly accused of theft and deported to Australia. It was a long time ago now. Nobody was deported anymore. His father had been one of the last. Pitt had no idea if he had even survived the voyage, or what had happened to him if he had. He might still be alive, but he would be old, close to eighty. Pitt wasn't sure if he even wanted to know his father still lived. He had never returned, or made any contact. It was an old loss better left alone.

"Most of us have wounds of some sort," he said quietly.

"Of course," Isaura agreed. "But you see, there is nothing you can do. I am grateful for your kindness in coming to me in person rather than sending a letter."

He did not want to accept her dismissal.

"I would still like to speak to your maid, Senhora," he said grimly. "I will be discreet, I give you my word, but I want to know for myself all that I can. Special Branch has a long memory."

Her eyes flickered for a moment. With hope?

"Of course," she agreed. "I shall ask her to come." She turned and left, going out of the door with her head high, her shoulders awkwardly stiff.

Pitt wondered how rash his promise was, and when Isaura Castelbranco would tell her husband the truth. Probably when she was sure he would not take his own revenge. She had faced more than enough grief already.

CHAPTER 8

Narraway went to Lisson Grove reluctantly. It had been his office, his domain, for so many years that going back as a visitor heightened his sense of being superfluous. He did not belong anymore. He looked much the same as he always had, not even noticeably any grayer, certainly not heavier or stiffer. His mind felt just as sharp — in fact, in some ways more so. It was emotionally that he felt different. Surely gentleness, an awareness of others, a greater humanity, was part of wisdom?

He had time in which to do anything he wanted, to travel anywhere, if he wished. It wasn't possible that he had forgotten how to enjoy himself. He could go to the beautiful cities of Europe he had only visited in haste before. He could admire the architecture, steep himself in the history of the cultures, the music, the great art created through the centuries. He could stop and talk to people purely for the pleasure of it. He could ignore or forget anything that bored him. There were no boundaries, no responsibilities.

Was that what troubled him? He needed boundaries? What for — an excuse? Responsibilities, or he felt unimportant? Did that mean there was little to him except the job? He had started in the army at eighteen, straight from Eton, where he had excelled academically. The military had been his father's idea, much against his own intention.

He had arrived in India almost coincidentally with the beginning of the Mutiny, and seen firsthand the horrors of war. It had been brutal and desperate — innocent men, women, and children slaughtered as well as soldiers. It was there that he had first become aware of the unnecessary human errors — "stupidity" would not be too strong a word in some cases — that caused such tragedy. It had sparked his appreciation for military intelligence and, even above that, the understanding of people and events, of political will, the perception of social movement that had eventually matched him with his true gifts, Special Branch. He had given the rest of his life to it.

Was it the loss of purpose that hurt now, or the loss of power? Who was he without those things? It was the question he had avoided asking himself, but now that it was in his mind in so many words, he could not sidestep it anymore. He had never been a coward before. He could not be one now. There was still something left to play for.

He had brought Pitt into Special Branch, originally as a favor to Cornwallis when Pitt got himself thrown out of the Metropolitan Police because he knew too much about a particular area of corruption. Now Pitt was head of Special Branch and Narraway was retired to kick his heels in the House of Lords, very much against his will. After the miserable Irish business he had had no chance of remaining in office.

He walked up the steps and in the door self-consciously, aware of the surprise and then discomfort of the men who used to snap to attention and call him "sir." Now they were uncertain how to greet him. He could see in their faces the indecision as to what to say. He should have the grace to relieve them of that.

"Good morning," he said, giving a very slight smile, which was not familiarity, just good manners. "Would you please inform Commander Pitt that I am here, and would like to speak with him regarding a matter in which my advice has been requested. He is already aware of it."

"Yes, sir . . . my lord," the man replied, relief filling his face that Narraway seemingly knew his place. "If . . . if you'll take a seat, sir, I'll deliver that message."

"Thank you." Narraway moved back from the desk and obeyed, feeling ridiculous, slightly humbled in what had been his own territory, asking favors of men he used to command. Would Pitt feel obliged to see him, however inconvenient it was? Might he even feel a slight pity for him, a man with no purpose? He was too tense to sit down. Perhaps he should not have come to the office, but rather, met Pitt at some other location.

He was not old; he was still more than capable of doing the job. He had been dismissed because of a scandal deliberately and artificially created in one of the most dangerous plots of the decade, perhaps of the century. But he had made enemies. The very nature of Special Branch made it impossible for Narraway to justify himself without also telling the truth as to what had happened. And that he could never do. He acknowledged with a bitter irony that the very act of talking to the public would have made him unfit for the position.

And Pitt was a worthy successor. He would grow into the job. He had both the intelligence and the courage. With luck he would last long enough to gain the experience. The only quality in doubt was the steel in his soul to make the decisions where there was no morally clear answer, where other men's lives were at stake and there was no time to weigh or measure possibilities. That required a particular type of strength, not only to act, but afterward to live with the consequences. Narraway could not count the number of times he had lain awake half the night, second-guessing himself, regretting. There was no other loneliness quite like it.

The man returned. Narraway remained where he stood, waiting for the response.

"If you'll come with me, my lord, Commander Pitt has a little free time and would be happy to see you," the man said.

Narraway thanked him, wondering whether the "little free time" was Pitt's wording or the messenger's. It was very faintly patronizing and did not sound like Pitt.

"Morning." Pitt rose to his feet as if Narraway were still the superior. "The Quixwood case?" he asked as Narraway closed the door.

"Yes," Narraway replied, accepting the seat offered him. He felt a touch of surprise at Pitt's serious tone, and the fact that he had brought up the subject so quickly. "You're not interested in the Quixwood case, are you? I mean officially?"

"Not quite. As far as I know, thus far it's an ordinary tragedy, no political implications. But I'm just beginning to realize what a complicated, misunderstood, and horrible crime rape is. I was actually thinking of Angeles Castelbranco, before you came."

Narraway blinked. "The Portuguese ambassador's daughter who died in that appalling accident?"

"I think it was probably an accident, to some degree," Pitt answered. "At least on her part. On his, I don't know."

"His?" Narraway raised his eyebrows. "What are we talking about?"

Pitt's face creased with distaste. "It was a public taunting — baiting, if you like — that led to her fall, largely orchestrated by Neville Forsbrook. I don't think she had any intention of going out the window, as is now being suggested."

Narraway frowned. "What are you saying, that she was raped too? By Forsbrook?"

"I think so. But I have no way of proving

it. But this isn't why you came. What can I do to help you with Catherine Quixwood?"

There was a horrible irony in Pitt's sudden switch from Angeles to Catherine. Narraway tried to marshal his thoughts.

"Knox is a good man," he began. "But he doesn't seem to have gotten anywhere beyond the fact — which now seems inescapable — that she let the rapist in herself." He watched Pitt's face closely, trying to see if his thoughts were critical, or open. He saw no change in Pitt's eyes at all. "I can see that he hates it, that he believes she had a lover," he went on.

"What do you think?" Pitt asked.

Narraway hesitated. "I've done a lot of digging into her actions over the last six months or so." He measured his words carefully. When he had been in Pitt's job he had not allowed emotions to touch his judgment. Well, not often. Now he was thinking of Catherine Quixwood as a woman: charming, interested in all kinds of things, creative, probably with a quick sense of humor, someone he would have liked. Was it because the whole tragedy had nothing to do with danger to the country, no issues of treason or violence to the state, that he allowed himself to really visualize the people involved? People with dreams, vulnerabilities like his own? He could not have afforded to before.

"Was her marriage reasonably happy?" Pitt asked.

"Happy?" Narraway thought about it and was puzzled. "What makes a person happy, Pitt? Are you happy?"

Pitt did not hesitate. "Yes."

For an instant Narraway was overtaken by a sense of loss, of something inexpressible that he had missed. Then he banished it. "No, I don't think it was," he answered. "She was making as much happiness for herself as she could, but through aesthetic or intellectual appreciation."

"Has Knox given up looking for suspects?" Pitt asked.

"There's a young man named Alban Hythe who seems likely," Narraway replied. "He is smart, likes the same arts and explorations that she did, and attended many of the same functions. He admits to being acquainted with her, although since they were seen together a number of times he could hardly deny it."

Pitt frowned. "Then what troubles you? Her reputation, if she was known to have a lover? Or are you concerned for Quixwood's embarrassment? There's nothing you can do about that." His face was filled with regret. He gave a very slight shrug. "I'm finding it hard to face that fact myself."

Narraway heard Pitt's dilemma and for the moment ignored it.

"My problem is, I'm not certain I believe it was Alban Hythe," he argued. "I met him and he seemed a decent chap. The rape was violent. Whoever did it hated her. It doesn't seem like the crime of a lover unexpectedly denied — not a sane one."

Pitt shook his head. "If rapists didn't appear perfectly natural we'd find them a lot easier to catch."

"I can believe it of an arrogant young pup like Neville Forsbrook a lot more easily," Narraway retaliated, startled by his own anger.

Pitt looked at him in silence for several moments before replying. "If Hythe is innocent, then someone else is guilty," he said at last. "Whether he was her lover or not, whoever it was raped her violently and killed her. That can never be excused."

Narraway took a deep breath. "That's another part of the problem," he admitted. "The medical evidence suggests it's possible he didn't kill her directly. She actually died of an overdose of laudanum — it very easily could have been suicide. It will be difficult to convince a jury otherwise. It's easy to believe, given the violence of the rape, that she was traumatized to the extent that she wanted to end her life."

Pitt continued to stare at him, his gray eyes steady and full of pain. "We know far too little about it, this rape or any other," he said levelly. "Perhaps we know too little about ourselves as well. But if Alban Hythe isn't the man, and the circumstantial evidence is piling up against him, then you need to prove he's innocent, or he may eventually be imprisoned, or worse, for something he didn't do. Not to mention the fact that whoever did do it will escape entirely, and probably do it again. And there may be something to be salvaged of Catherine's reputation, at the very least." His mouth turned down in a bitter twist. "People are now suggesting that Angeles Castelbranco was with child, and that was why she killed herself."

"Like you said, it's doubtful she wanted to go out that window," Narraway said with some heat. "Judging by what you know, I don't believe she thought of anything except getting away from Forsbrook and his taunts."

"I agree," Pitt said. "But if I say so, then Pelham Forsbrook will defend his son." The misery and the anger were cut deep in his face. "How does anyone prove Neville is truly to blame for anything beyond cruel words and insensitive behavior?"

Narraway clenched his fists, hardly aware of it until his nails dug into the flesh of his palms. "I refuse to be so bloody helpless!"

"Good." Pitt smiled bleakly. "When you discover how to accomplish that, please share it with me."

Narraway rose to his feet. "Can't you at least prove Angeles wasn't with child? There would have been signs, surely?"

"That isn't the point," Pitt answered wearily. "If she thought she was, or could have been, then her reputation is equally ruined."

Narraway no longer had the energy for this. He felt a coldness close around him, in spite of the warmth of the day and the sunlight streaming through the window. The brightness seemed curiously far away. He should recall what he had come for and ask Pitt, before the opportunity slipped away.

"I haven't dealt with rape before," he said. "What kind of proof do the police look for if the victim is dead and can't say anything herself?"

Pitt thought for several moments. "I'm not sure that they would try to prove rape," he said at last. "If she was badly beaten that might be enough to convict the guilty party. That is a crime, and the jury would read more into it, under the circumstances. The sentence could be just as heavy; obviously she could not have done that to herself. If you can prove the accused was there, and no one else could have been, it should be sufficient."

"I see. Then that is the approach I shall take." Narraway rose to his feet. "Thank you."

Pitt relaxed a fraction. "It was good to see you," he replied.

Narraway was still turning the matter over in his mind early that evening. He sat with the windows open onto the deepening colors as the sun lowered toward the horizon. He was startled when his manservant knocked discreetly and stood in the doorway to say that Mrs. Hythe was in the entryway and wished to speak with him.

"Shall I bring tea, my lord?" he added with elaborate innocence. "Or a glass of sherry, perhaps? I don't know the lady sufficiently well to guess."

"But you know her sufficiently well to assume that I will see her?" Narraway said a trifle waspishly. He was tired, more by frustration than action, and would have been happy to forget the whole issue of the Quixwood case for a few hours.

"No, sir," the manservant replied, his eyes momentarily downcast. "But I know you, my lord, well enough to be certain you would not refuse someone in considerable distress, and who is counting on you to be of help."

Narraway stared at him and did not see even a flicker of irony in the man's face. "You should have been a diplomat," he said drily. "You are far better at it than most of those I know."

"Thank you, my lord." A light glinted for a moment in the man's eyes. "Shall I bring tea or sherry?"

"Sherry," Narraway answered. "I would like it, whether she would or not."

"Yes, my lord." He withdrew silently and a moment later Maris Hythe came in. Her face was as charming as before, with the same blunt gentleness, but she could not hide the fact that she was both tired and frightened. Instantly Narraway regretted his self-absorption.

He rose to his feet and invited her to sit down in the chair facing the window and the deepening sunset.

"I apologize for coming uninvited, my lord," she said a little awkwardly. "Normally

I would have had better manners, but I am frightened, and I don't know of anyone else who might help."

Narraway sat down opposite her, leaning forward a little as if he too were tense. "I assume the situation has worsened with regard to Mr. Knox's investigation? I haven't spoken to him for a day or two. What has happened?"

Her answer was forestalled by the return of the manservant with a silver tray bearing sherry and two long-stemmed crystal glasses.

Maris hesitated.

The manservant poured a little of the rich dark golden liquid into one of the glasses and placed it on the table beside her. He poured a second and gave it to Narraway.

After he had gone Narraway picked his up, so she might do the same, and waited attentively for her to speak.

"Nothing Mr. Knox finds could prove my husband's guilt, because he is not guilty," she said, forcing herself to meet his eyes. "But every new fact does make it look worse for him."

"He has never denied that he and Mrs. Quixwood were friends," Narraway pointed out. "What new information has been added to that?"

She kept her composure with difficulty, taking a sip of sherry, probably more to hide her eyes for a moment than because she wished for its taste.

He waited.

"Small gifts he gave her," Maris replied very quietly. "I didn't know about them. I think he felt sorry for her. She . . . she was very lonely. Mr. Quixwood has been both honest and contrite about it, as if he blames himself for putting so much effort into his work that he did not accompany her to the places she wished to go."

"It is natural to feel guilty when it is too late to go back and make a better task of it," he said with a twinge of guilt for his own sins of omission.

She smiled very slightly. "I think he is a kind man who did not see how she really felt. And perhaps she did not tell him. One doesn't. It sounds so like complaining, and when you have comfort, position, no need to worry . . . and respect as well, from a man who is honorable, to ask for more is . . . greedy, don't you think?" She looked at him as if she genuinely wished for an answer.

"I have no idea," he admitted. He tried to think of the women he knew. Charlotte would certainly want more. She would sacrifice financial security or social position for love, she had already proved that. Perhaps within the definition of "love" she would include a sharing of purpose, and a commonality of interest. Above all she might require to be needed, not an ornament but a part of the fabric of life.

Her sister Emily loved her husband and had considerable wealth and social standing, and yet she envied Charlotte her purpose, her excitement, the danger and variety. Narraway had seen it in her eyes, heard it in the sharp edge of her voice in a rare unguarded moment.

And what of Vespasia? That was a question perhaps he preferred not to consider. Because of her title and extraordinary beauty she had lived in the public eye all her adult life, but she was still acutely private with her emotions. He had never thought of her as vulnerable, capable of such frailties as doubt or loneliness.

"My lord . . ." Maris interrupted a little anxiously.

He returned his attention to her, slightly embarrassed to have been discourteous. "I'm sorry. I was considering what you had said about Catherine Quixwood." That was true, in a way. "It is perceptive of you to have seen the possibility of her loneliness."

A look that he could not read flickered

across her face. The only thing he recognized in it for certain was fear.

He leaned forward a little more to assure her that she had his attention, in spite of his earlier lapse. "What is it you would like me to do, Mrs. Hythe?"

"Mr. Knox is still working on the case," she replied. "I really don't think he will give up until his superiors tell him he must. He seems to me to be a good man, gentle, in spite of the terrible things he has to deal with every day." The ghost of a smile was in her eyes for an instant. "He speaks of his family once in a while, when he is in my house. He admired a teapot I have, and said his wife would like it. It seems she collects teapots. I wondered why. Surely two or three are sufficient? But he said she likes to arrange flowers in them, so I tried it myself — daisies. It worked extraordinarily well. Now every time I look at the thing it makes me think of him, and then of Catherine."

Narraway did not know how to respond to that. How had Pitt dealt with the reality of people, the details of their lives that stayed in the mind? He thought of Catherine lying on the floor, and the ornaments in the room. Had she chosen them, put them there because they pleased her, or reminded her of someone she cared for?

"You have not told me what it is you wish of me, Mrs. Hythe," he said, bringing the conversation back to the practical.

"Every detail he finds makes it clearer that Catherine was fond of my husband," she answered. "And that they liked and trusted each other, and met . . . often." She swallowed with a tightening of her throat that looked painful. "He believes that she let her attacker in herself, and that could only be because she knew him —"

"Yes," he cut in. "There was no break-in."

She lowered her eyes. "I know that too. But I also know that my husband is a good man — not perfect, of course, but decent and kind. He felt sorry for her and he liked her, no more than that." She looked up at Narraway earnestly. "If they were having an affair, perhaps I would have hated her for it and — if I were crazy enough — wished her harm. But I could not have raped her. And my husband didn't either."

She gave a little shiver. "On the other hand, her husband could have, but that doesn't work either, does it, as he was at a party while she was being attacked. Don't mistake me; I care very much that you catch whoever did this. I think any woman would. It was a terrible way to die." She took a deep breath and continued. "But in spite of his kindness to her, the small gifts he gave her, the times they met at one exhibition or another, my husband was *not* her lover. And, as I've said, even if he had been, he could not have committed such an atrocious crime against her."

Narraway was brutal, to get it over with: "And if he found her fascinating, flattering to his vanity, a beautiful older woman with sophistication and intelligence, and she suddenly rebuffed him?" he asked. "How would he react to that? Are you certain that it would not be with anger?"

Color burned up her face, but she did not look away from his gaze. "You don't know Alban, or you wouldn't ask that. I'm aware you think I am being idealistic and naïve. I'm not. He has his faults, as do I, but losing his temper is not one of them. Sometimes I wish he would. For some time, I am ashamed to say, I thought him something of a coward because he was so gentle." She winced. "Now I risk seeing him hanged for a crime he could never even imagine committing. I think perhaps he even helped her with something that troubled her, although I don't know what. He never mentioned it to me. Don't let him be destroyed for that."

Narraway stared at her, trying to assess if she truly believed what she said, or if, even more than to convince him, she was trying to convince herself.

"Are you positive you have no idea what it was?" he urged. This was a new thought and perhaps worth pursuing.

She looked down at her hands for a moment, weighing her answer before she spoke.

"Alban is a banker. I know he is young yet, but he knows a great deal about business, especially investment. I . . . well, I think it may have something to do with that, investments, in Africa, the Boers, and Leander Jameson. I know Alban read a lot about the raid, and the difference it might make to people if Dr. Jameson is found guilty. He listened to Mr. Churchill, and his talk of the possibility of war."

Narraway drew in his breath to interrupt her. Surely she was being fanciful, desperate to say or do anything to defend her husband, and was tossing out any idea she could think of, even if it was ridiculous? But then, maybe it wasn't ridiculous. Quixwood was a man involved in major finances. He might have made an investment that his wife feared was risky, even potentially ruinous. Was it conceivable that she had sought advice behind his back, from an independent source?

And she might have feared Quixwood

would see that as a betrayal, a complete failure of loyalty to him, a lack of belief in his judgment.

It sounded desperately unlikely that a woman such as Catherine — beautiful, dependent, without any knowledge of international affairs, let alone of finances — would have undertaken to learn such things, and from a young man like Alban Hythe, no less, not her learned husband.

Narraway wanted Alban to be innocent, as did Maris Hythe, albeit for different reasons. Were they not both reaching too far, grasping for impossible answers and refusing to see what was right in front of them?

She looked at him, breathing in as if to say something else. Then she changed her mind and some of the light faded from her eyes.

Knowing he would regret the words even as he said them, Narraway spoke. "I'll do all I can to follow this lead, Mrs. Hythe. I shall see Knox straightaway."

She blinked hard and smiled. "Thank you, Lord Narraway. You are very kind."

He did not feel kind as he waited for Knox in the police station the following day; in fact, he felt particularly foolish. When Knox finally came in, hot and tired, his boots covered in dust, his face tightened when he saw Narraway.

"I don't know anything more, my lord." There were smudges of weariness under his eyes, and when he took his hat off his hair stuck up in spikes. "I can tell you half a dozen places where she met with this Alban Hythe, but I can't tell you for certain whether it was by accident or arranged." He put his hat on the hat rack. "They turned up at an awful lot of the same events. Hard to see it as always accidental like. They were things she was interested in, but far as I can tell, he hadn't been, until he met her." He sat down heavily in the chair opposite Narraway.

"Do you really think they were having an affair passionate enough to cause him to rape her and beat her like that if suddenly she ended it?" Narraway asked, allowing his doubt to reflect in his expression.

"No," Knox said frankly. "But somebody raped her. It looks like it's Alban Hythe, and there's nothing to show it wasn't him, except my own feeling that he's a decent young man. But haven't you ever been wrong about a gut feeling?"

"Yes," Narraway admitted. "Sometimes seriously. I suppose you've looked into his background? And, also, how on earth did he have time to wander around art galleries and National Geographic luncheons and exhibitions of crafts from God knows where? I certainly don't!"

"Nor I," Knox said ruefully. "But I'm not a venture banker with fancy clients to please. And apparently he's very good at his job indeed."

Narraway was startled. "Is that what he says he was doing? Taking clients out?"

Knox gave a bitter smile. "Yes. He quite willingly offered me the names of some of the clients concerned, and I contacted them. Of course they didn't discuss their business, but they affirmed that they had dealings with him, and that they were quite often made in social surroundings — usually over a damn good lunch or dinner. It seems that introductions are made in such places. He mentioned an exhibition of French art, in particular, where certain British investors met with French wine growers, all very casually. Pleasantries were exchanged, and then agreements about very large sums of money were made."

"That would hardly involve Catherine Quixwood," Narraway pointed out. "It could be an explanation for one or two meetings, not more."

"Three or four maybe," Knox corrected. "Quixwood himself is one of the investors."

Narraway was puzzled. He could not see how this explained what appeared to be a very personal friendship with Catherine. Unless, of course, Maris Hythe's extraordinary idea had some truth in it?

He pursued it with Knox because he very much wanted an answer that exonerated Catherine from any type of wrongdoing, and Alban Hythe as well. He acknowledged to himself that he also was angry enough, wounded enough, that he wanted someone to be provably in the wrong. He needed someone to be punished for the pain and the humiliation she had suffered.

"What does Quixwood say of him?" he asked aloud.

"Nice young man, and good at his job — in fact, gifted at it," Knox replied unhappily. "He seemed very distressed at the thought that Hythe could be guilty." He sighed. "It would be a very personal kind of betrayal, both for Quixwood, and for Mrs. Hythe. But then rape is, when the people know each other. I sometimes wonder which is worse, to be attacked so intimately by a complete stranger, or by someone you had trusted."

"But you still don't think Hythe is guilty?"

Narraway pressed again.

Knox looked up again, meeting Narraway's eyes. "Have you ever been really surprised by who was a traitor, or an anarchist, Lord Narraway? Did you have that kind of sense for judging people, regardless of evidence, or what anyone else said?"

Narraway thought for a moment. "Occasionally," he replied. "Certainly not most of the time. But rape is . . ."

"Bestial?" Knox said for him. There was a bleak humor in his eyes that could have meant anything.

Narraway was going to answer, then as he looked at Knox longer he saw the intelligence in the man, the perception and experience of things Narraway had passed by without seeing, never considering them.

"Depends on who you believe, doesn't it, sir?" Knox answered his own question. "I daresay if I were to ask a few ladies you'd loved and left, if they bore some kind of resentment they would tell a tale you wouldn't recognize as the truth — my lord." He sat motionless, as if half waiting for Narraway to be angry at his impertinence. But there was no shame in his face.

Narraway did not answer immediately. Memories raced through his mind: women who had attracted him intensely and on occasions women he had used because they were attracted to him. Certainly he was not proud of it and he would have found it difficult to explain to someone else had any one of them accused him of rape. Nothing like that had ever been suggested — although in Ireland he had earned the undying hatred of one man by seducing his wife. Recollection of that burned with hot shame up his face, even now. It had been years ago, and the man and woman in question were both dead. Still, it did not lessen what he had done.

Were it recent, and someone had charged him, how could he account for it with any honor? What words would he find to tell a courtroom why he had acted as he did, all the little details, the lies, the carefully fabricated deceptions, why he had felt it was the only thing to do . . . at that time? The thought of Vespasia's ever hearing about it scalded him. Would it be the end forever of their friendship, her trust, her respect? No wonder people lied!

And of course there had been other women over his long life. Some he had loved, briefly, knowing it would end. He had never seduced an unmarried woman, or made a promise he had not kept. He would like to think he had never intentionally lied unless it was for a greater good.

What a piece of spurious self-excusing! Would anyone else see it like that? Even the simplest act could be viewed in so many ways. The mind could create a dozen different interpretations of a word, a gesture, a meeting, a gift. People believed what they wanted to, saw what they expected to see.

"Could you defend yourself, if you had to, my lord?" Knox said softly. "I've had times when I couldn't have."

No one had accused Narraway of anything, and yet he felt the fear as closely as if it had touched his skin. Of course he had incidents in his life he would prefer other people knew nothing about. He cared surprisingly much what his friends thought of him — Charlotte, Pitt, other people he had known and worked with; above all, Vespasia.

He faced Knox again. "There was no misunderstanding in what happened to Catherine Quixwood," he said grimly. "Whether it was a lover or not, whether she lied to him, betrayed him, seduced him, or whatever else, he beat and raped her and now she is dead, not of natural causes. He did that to her. He is responsible."

"I know," Knox said, the pain back again in his eyes, all the lightness gone. "If I can, believe me, I will see that he pays."

Narraway said nothing, but felt his face relax into a kind of smile. It was not pleasure so much as an ease in Knox's company, a respect for this man he had not felt for anyone else except Thomas Pitt.

In keeping with his promise to Maris Hythe, Narraway sought out Rawdon Quixwood, who was still spending much of the time at his club. He waited impatiently for him in the lounge, well into the late afternoon. Most of the time he tried to concentrate on the newspapers and their comments on the forthcoming trial of Leander Starr Jameson for the armed raid he had led in Africa, patriotically inspired but disastrously misguided.

Occasionally Narraway was too restless to remain seated, so he paced up and down the largely deserted room. Then an elderly man, almost hidden by the wings of the huge armchair he was sitting in, coughed repeatedly and glared at him over the top of his spectacles. Narraway realized that he was being inconsiderate and returned to his seat.

He picked up the newspaper again and found his place in the varied accounts and letters to the editor.

He was still reading when the steward

informed him that Mr. Quixwood had returned, and inquired if he would like tea, or perhaps whisky.

"Ask Mr. Quixwood if he will join me," Narraway answered. "And then serve whatever he chooses."

The steward inclined his head in acknowledgment and withdrew.

Fifteen minutes later Narraway was sitting opposite Quixwood in the quietest part of the lounge. He studied the man for several moments while they both sipped their whiskies in silence. Narraway would rather have had tea, but he was not here for his pleasure.

Quixwood looked exhausted. His skin was pale except for the dark circles under his eyes, but the hand holding his glass was perfectly steady. Narraway admired his self-discipline. He must be feeling both the ordinary grief of losing a wife suddenly and violently, and the loneliness, but he had the additional torture of imagining her last moments, and then there was the speculation in the press, which was no doubt read by almost everyone he met. It was not only a question of who had raped her, but whether the man had been her lover. It was written about in daily newspapers for everyone in the street to think about, talk about, even make jokes over.

Until it was solved, there would be no end to it.

"Do you know something new?" Quixwood asked. His voice was so low that Narraway had to concentrate to hear him.

"I imagine Knox has told you that he suspects Alban Hythe?" Narraway answered. "Or at least that the evidence suggests that he and Mrs. Quixwood knew each other unusually well."

Quixwood shook his head fractionally. "Yes, but I find it very difficult to believe." He smiled faintly, and with obvious effort. "But then, I imagine a man always finds it difficult to believe that his wife was having an affair."

A day ago Narraway would have agreed with him. After his experience with Knox he responded differently. "It is very disturbing to realize how easily we go through life assuming," he said, watching Quixwood's face. "People change slowly, so infinitesimally that day by day we don't see it. Like glaciers — so many feet in a year, or maybe it's inches."

Quixwood looked down at his glass and the light reflecting in its amber depths. "I thought I knew her. I'm slowly facing the fact that perhaps I didn't." He glanced up abruptly. "You know the worst thing? I'm not even as certain as I was that I really want to know exactly what happened. I . . . I don't want all my illusions shattered. I trusted my wife and believed she loved me, and even at our most cool or difficult moments, she would never have betrayed me."

A smile flickered across his lips for a moment and vanished. "I thought Hythe was someone I could trust, and now that I know his wife a little better, I know that she also trusted him. She still cannot accept even the possibility that he could be guilty of this. I suppose it is part of my own grief that I want to comfort her."

Quixwood sipped his whisky again. "Am I a coward to want not to know?"

Narraway considered it for a moment before replying, wanting to be honest.

"I think you may be unwise," he said at last. "I can imagine how you would prefer to leave your wife's last days, and especially her last moments, unknown. In your best times you will not think of it at all. In your worst you will visualize it brutally."

Quixwood was watching him, waiting for him to finish.

"But it isn't only you," Narraway continued. "Maris Hythe may find she cannot live with the uncertainty. If Hythe is innocent, he surely deserves to have that proved. How could he live with it otherwise, hinted at but unproven, for the rest of his days?"

"And if he's guilty?" Quixwood asked.

"Then he deserves punishment," Narraway said without hesitation. "And even more than justice toward him, what about the rest of society?"

Quixwood blinked.

"Do you want to live in a country where such appalling crimes go unpunished?" Narraway asked. "Where we are sufficiently indifferent to the horror of it that we prefer not to inquire too closely in case the answer is one we don't like? What about other men's wives, or daughters? What about the next woman raped?"

Quixwood closed his eyes. His hands clenched around his glass so tightly that had it not been heavy cut crystal, it would have broken. Narraway did not press him to answer.

They spoke of other things, briefly, and after a little while Narraway left, wishing there were more he could do and knowing there was not.

CHAPTER 9

It was early evening but the sun was still high. Charlotte was at the stove, her back to the kitchen table, but she could hear Pitt's fingers drumming irritably on the wood. She could have asked him to stop, but she knew it was pointless. He was not even aware of doing it. His sense of helplessness was eating away at him. The death of Angeles Castelbranco was unexplained; in his mind it was still a bleeding wound.

She knew that it was not just a matter of solving a crime. It was not even the taking of some small step to absolve England's reputation as a gentle and civilized country where women, children, the vulnerable were treated with respect; they must show that brutality was punished swiftly, and that no one pleaded for justice in vain.

Beyond that, it was the deep, visceral nature of the crime that ate at him, the knowledge that those he loved could as easily have been the victims, could yet be, and he had found nothing he could do to prevent it.

She never doubted that he loved his family fiercely. Sometimes he was too strict, true, expected too much of the children; other times she thought he was too lax, but either way, whatever the disappointments, the love was as certain as the ground beneath her feet or the warmth of the sun.

All over the country there were other men the same, in every town and village — people who loved, who worried, who protected their loved ones the best they could, who lay awake at night thinking about the unthinkable, praying that they would never have to face it.

But Pitt had had to face it, to see it in Rafael Castelbranco and be unable to do anything, unable even to try, because there was nothing to grasp, no evidence. Witnesses abounded, and yet they had seen nothing that did not lose substance, like mist, when it was examined.

Isaura Castelbranco had said her daughter's violator was Neville Forsbrook. Charlotte herself had seen him taunt Angeles and felt her terror as if it were palpable in the room. But then you had Rawdon Quixwood, stricken and bereaved by the rape of his wife, who had sworn to Vespasia that he had been at the event where the rape of Angeles must have taken place, and he knew young Forsbrook could not be guilty. It was not a reference to his character but to his whereabouts.

Who was lying? Who was mistaken? Who was so prejudiced as to be unable to see or tell the truth?

To Pitt it was more than that. He felt uniquely responsible because he had been present when Angeles had died; he was a guardian of the law, supposed to protect people, or at the very least to find justice for those who were wronged. Charlotte knew that fact was in his mind far more than the angry words, the long silences, the overprotectiveness that was infuriating Jemima or the lectures begun and broken off that confused Daniel.

She wanted to say something to help, at least to let Pitt know that she understood and did not expect him, or any man, to slay all the dragons or keep safe all the dark corners of life, whether they were far away or in the familiar rooms of one's own house.

Pitt was still drumming his fingers on the tabletop.

Charlotte lifted the lid of the pan with potatoes and pushed a skewer into one, then another, to see if it was time to put on the cabbage. She hated it overcooked. The potatoes could do with a few more minutes. The table was already set and the cold meat carved. There were three separate dishes of chutney out: apple and onion, orange and onion, spiced apricot. She was rather pleased with herself for that.

"Only three places," Pitt said suddenly. "Who's not here?"

"Jemima," she replied. "She's spending the evening with a friend."

Pitt's voice sharpened. "Who is it? Do you know the family? What is she like, this friend? How old is she?"

Charlotte put the lid down on the potato pan and turned around to face him. She saw again how tired he was. His hair was as untidy as usual, even though it had been cut recently. The light caught on the gray at his temples. His skin was pale and there were fine lines around his eyes she had not noticed before, although they must have come slowly.

"A very pleasant girl named Julia," she replied as lightly as she could, as if she had not seen the tension in him. "She is rather studious and she likes Jemima because Jemima makes her laugh and forget to be self-conscious. I know her mother — not well, but enough to be certain Jemima is quite safe there. And before you ask, yes, Julia is fourteen as well, and she has no older brothers."

Pitt lowered his head wearily. "Am I being ridiculous?" he asked.

Charlotte sat down on the chair opposite him. "Yes, my dear, completely. But I might think less of you if you weren't." She reached out her hand and put it lightly over his on the table, stopping his fingers in their nervous movement. "How could we look at people living our worst nightmare and feel nothing? If that happened, I would think Special Branch had changed you from the man I love to an efficient person I could only respect."

He was quite still for several moments, and she had no idea what he was thinking. She wanted to ask, but knew it would be intrusive.

"I don't know what to do," he said suddenly, avoiding her eyes. "I looked at Isaura Castelbranco a couple of days ago. She has courage, and immense dignity; in a way, more composure than her husband. But she's broken inside. Whoever did this has destroyed far more than just one person. The pain he's inflicted is beyond measure, and it will go on all their lives. Even if we catch the rapist, it seems a poor sort of justice, doesn't it?"

"I don't know," she said honestly. "Maybe, at times. But don't we all need there to be justice, however cold the comfort of it is? What safety is there for anyone if people can do what this man did and then walk away free? If there's no price, why shouldn't he do it again, whenever he wishes to and has the chance? And surely if there's no public justice, won't there be people who'll look for it privately? What are the chances they'll take it from the wrong person? Or the right person, but who was guilty only of being intimate with the wrong person, not of rape?"

Pitt pushed his hair back hard as he straightened and leaned again against the hard frame of the chair. "Isaura knows it is Neville, and she's right, prosecution would only make it worse."

Charlotte was stunned. "But you told me Vespasia had said it couldn't be him! Quixwood was there! You must make absolutely certain that the ambassador doesn't take —"

"Isaura didn't tell him anything," he cut across her. "She won't. She knows as well as you do that the temptation to take revenge would one day be more than he could resist. She didn't even confirm to him that Angeles was raped, although I imagine he suspects."

She frowned, tense now.

"You are sure?"

"Yes." There was no uncertainty, no equivocation in his voice. "By the way, I questioned the maid." He winced as he spoke. "Angeles was bleeding and badly bruised. Whoever it was, he must have used considerable force."

Charlotte thought about it for several moments, her mind racing. The pain inside her was not only for Isaura Castelbranco, but for every other woman who lived with fear or grief, or who would do so in the future; everyone else who felt humiliated and helpless.

"But she did say it was Forsbrook?" she said aloud.

"Apparently that is what Angeles told her mother. But if Quixwood is telling the truth, she must have been mistaken. Perhaps someone even pretended to be Forsbrook. That's not impossible. I've asked a few questions . . ." He smiled bleakly. "Don't look like that. I was discreet. I asked people about functions over the last month or two, who attended and any incidents concerning the Portuguese. This damned Jameson Raid is an excellent cover for all kinds of inquiries."

Charlotte had forgotten about the Jameson trial. It was on everybody's lips, and yet it had held no meaning for her, because of the other things she had heard being discussed. There was pity for Isaura Castelbranco, certainly; however, in too many instances it was tempered by cruel remarks about foreigners and their different standards, as if the girl were to blame for her own death. Since the gossip had begun about the Church's decision that she could not be buried with Catholic rites, the conclusion was that she must have committed suicide. The kindest speculation was that she was in love with someone who did not return her feelings. The cruelest that she was with child, that her fiancé had very understandably called off the betrothal, and in despair she had killed herself and her unborn baby.

Charlotte had seethed with anger, but all she could do was accuse the speaker of malice. And that would gain nothing, except enemies she knew she could ill afford, for Pitt's sake as well as her own. If she was helpless, how much more so was Isaura Castelbranco?

"Did you learn anything?" she asked Pitt.

"Not that could be proof," he replied.

257

"What else did Mr. Quixwood say about the party?"

"Only that Forsbrook was charming, flattered Angeles in the way most young women enjoy, but that she seemed to be upset by it. He implied that either she thought herself too good for Neville or her English was not sufficiently fluent for her to have understood him properly. The prevailing opinion was that she was too young, and too unsophisticated to be in Society yet, even when her mother was present at the same function, as she usually was. They suggested that perhaps Portuguese girls were more sheltered and less prepared to conduct themselves with appropriate grace." He stopped, looking at Charlotte with a frown.

"That doesn't mean anything. Everyone is saying whatever makes them feel most comfortable. It's disgusting! How desperately alone she was . . . and her family is now." She wanted to encourage him, but what was there to say? "There must be something you can do," she tried. "Even indirectly, perhaps?"

Pitt raised his head.

"I haven't given up." His voice had an edge to it he failed to hide.

"I'm sorry," she said quickly. "I'm asking for miracles, aren't I?"

"Yes. And your potatoes are boiling over."

She leaped to her feet. "Oh blitheration! I forgot them. Now it's too late to put the cabbage on." She pulled the pan off the stove and lifted the lid cautiously. She jabbed the skewer into one. They were very definitely cooked, a little too much so. She would have to mash them.

Pitt was smiling. "We'll just have more pickle," he said with amusement. She was always teasing him that he used too much.

The following morning Pitt sat in his office studying the papers, mostly looking for information he could use professionally. Often Stoker selected articles for Pitt, to save him time.

"Lot about the upcoming Jameson trial," Stoker observed drily, putting more papers on Pitt's desk.

"Anything I need to know right now?" Pitt asked, hoping he could avoid reading them.

"Not much." Stoker's face creased in distaste. "Still haven't solved the murder of Rawdon Quixwood's wife. Sometimes I think I'd understand it if somebody murdered a few of these journalists, or the damn people who write letters expressing their arrogant opinions."

Pitt looked at Stoker curiously. It was an

unusual expression of emotion for him. More often he showed only disinterest, or occasionally a dry humor, especially at political contortions to evade the truth, or blame for anything.

Rather than ask him, Pitt turned over the pages of the first newspaper until he came to the letters to the editor. He saw with anger what Stoker meant. A good deal of space was devoted to the subject of rape.

One writer expressed the heated opinion that morality in general, and sexual morality in particular, was in serious decline. Women of a certain type behaved in a way that excited the baser appetites in men, leading to the destruction of both and to the general degradation of humanity. But the author conceded that rapists, if caught and the matter proved beyond any doubt, should be hanged, for the good of all. No names were mentioned, but Pitt noted that the writer lived in a neighborhood not two streets away from Catherine Quixwood.

"Why the devil does the editor print this sort of thing?" he demanded angrily. "It's vicious, ignorant, and will only stir up ill feeling."

"And produce more letters in answer," Stoker replied. "Dozens of them, of all opinions. And loads of people will buy the paper, to see if their answer has been printed, or just for the fun of watching a scrap. Same thing as the idle who gather to watch a street fight, and then demand we clean up the mess afterward, all the time shaking their heads and saying how terrible it is. But heaven help you if you get between them and the view."

Pitt looked up at Stoker with surprise. There had been more heat in his voice than Pitt had heard in a while. It flickered through his mind to wonder if Stoker had known and cared for someone who had been violated: a sister, even a lover at some time. He knew little of Stoker's personal life — or that of most people in Special Branch, for that matter. And he wasn't likely to learn more about them through this subject, as it was the sort of thing a man did not talk about even to those he knew best, let alone relative strangers.

"Of course." Pitt looked down at the newspaper again. "It was a stupid question. People attack what they're afraid of. Like poking a hornets' nest with a stick. Makes you feel brave, as if you're doing something. Don't care who the damn things sting afterward. Poor Quixwood must feel like hell."

"Yes, sir," Stoker agreed. "But I've met

Knox before; I know he is a good man. If anyone can find the truth, it's him."

Pitt looked up at him again. "I notice you didn't say 'catch who did it.' Do you think it wasn't murder, then? Suicide, because she allowed herself to be raped?" He heard the anger in his own voice and could not control it.

Stoker looked slightly embarrassed. "Whoever it was, sir, she let him in herself, with no servants around. That doesn't make attacking her right, but it does make it a lot more complicated."

"Sometimes, Stoker, I look back to my time in Bow Street, when murders seemed simpler. Greed, revenge, fear of blackmail I can understand. I quite often felt a degree of pity for even the worst people, but I knew that I still had no acceptable choice but to arrest them. If the jury decided they were innocent, then I could live with that and it was a comfort to know they might catch my mistakes, if that's what they were. But who catches ours?"

Stoker chewed his lip. "Sometimes we do," he said with a raised eyebrow. "Otherwise, probably no one. You'd like me to say different?" He was polite, just, but there was a challenge in his voice, one he would not have dared use with Narraway.

"No, not if you can't do it believably," Pitt retorted. "At least we're not in the diplomatic service, or the Foreign Office. Thank God Leander Starr Jameson and his damn raid aren't on our desks."

"No, sir. And neither is poor Angeles Castelbranco."

"Yes she is," Pitt replied grimly. "Someone raped her here in London, and brought about her death."

"Not a diplomatic incident, sir," Stoker said firmly.

"Are you sure?" Pitt stared at him, holding his gaze.

Stoker blinked. For the first time uncertainty showed on his face as he considered other possibilities. "Rape, as a tool of fear, civil disruption? I don't think so, sir. It's just a regular crime of selfishness, violence, and uncontrolled appetite. She was a very pretty girl, and some vicious bastard saw his chance and took it. I don't see it makes any difference that she was Portuguese, except maybe it made her easier to get at." He swallowed. "And maybe he reckoned her parents would be in less of a position to insist on his arrest, punishment — although honestly, I don't believe he'd even have thought of that. Rape's a kind of hot-blooded crime, isn't it?"

"Not necessarily. But does that make any difference?" Pitt asked, still holding Stoker's gaze. "If an anarchist throws a bomb on impulse, or shoots a political figure, is it less dangerous than if he'd planned it ahead of time?"

This time Stoker's answer was immediate. "No, sir. D'you think it'll become an international incident? That might put it on our plate. Castelbranco didn't seem the sort of man to use his daughter's death like that. Although I suppose his temperament and philosophy might change if no one is charged."

"And if he doesn't, others might, in his — Angeles's — name," Pitt pointed out. "I'm pretty sure most fathers would want to see someone pay for this."

Stoker looked bleak. "Except the father of whoever did it, sir. He sure as hell wouldn't. Maybe some of that is what's behind it?"

"We've opened up some ugly possibilities, Stoker," Pitt admitted. "We need to look further into the thought of people taking advantage of the event for political manipulation, repulsive as that is. Bring me what we know about Pelham Forsbrook and any interests he might have that connect in any way to Portugal, or Castelbranco personally." He rose to his feet. "I think I need to

264

know a lot more about this. With the Quixwood case we will — it's on everyone's
minds — but not this one, poor girl."

"We'd better try our best to figure it out,
sir. We don't want to be caught looking as if
we didn't care. Someone could dig a real
deep hole for us with that."

"Yes," Pitt agreed with a shiver. "You'd
better see if you can find out who else was
at that party I told you Lady Vespasia
mentioned. See if you can find a servant
who noticed people, things. Some of them
do. Claim robbery as a cover. Be careful
what you say."

"Right, sir. Thank heaven the Quixwood
case is nothing to do with us," Stoker said
with feeling. "Count it up how you want, it
looks as if it had to be a lover. I'm sorry for
Quixwood. Not only lost his wife pretty horribly, but the whole world knows she was
betraying him. There's another man you
couldn't blame if he lost his control and
killed the bastard . . . if they find him."

"If they find him they'll hang him," Pitt
replied, taking his hat and jacket from the
coat stand.

"Even if she took her own life, which is
what some people are saying?" Stoker questioned.

"She was a respectable married woman,"

Pitt answered, jamming the hat on his head. "Important husband with influence. And she was British."

Stoker pulled a sour face, but he did not reply.

Pitt went to Lincoln's Inn Fields to find the man he had been advised was the best and most experienced prosecuting lawyer in cases of rape. He had telephoned in advance to make an appointment, using his position as leverage to force himself into the man's already busy schedule.

Aubrey Delacourt was tall and lean, with a shock of dark brown hair. He had a long face with heavy-lidded eyes, which were surprisingly blue.

"I can spare you about twenty minutes, Commander," he said, shaking Pitt's hand briefly, then indicating a chair opposite his desk. His manner was impatient, making it clear he resented being obliged to disrupt his day. "You might be best served by omitting any preamble. I already assume this is important to you, or you would not waste your own time, never mind mine."

"You are quite right," Pitt agreed, sitting down and crossing his legs comfortably, as if he refused to be hurried. "I wouldn't. However, I must start by saying that what

I'm about to tell you is in absolute confidence. If you require me to retain your services for that, give me a bill for your time."

"Not necessary," Delacourt replied. "You have told me you are the head of Special Branch, and I took the precaution of confirming that for myself. What is the advice you wish?"

Very briefly Pitt summarized his account of the rape and death of Angeles Castelbranco. Before he had finished, Delacourt interrupted him.

"You have no case to bring," he said bluntly. "I would have expected you to know that." There was brisk condescension in his tone. "Even if you find the man who raped her, from what you have said you cannot prove it. All you will do is damage the poor girl's name even more."

"I know that." Pitt did not hide his own irritation. "I have advised her father to that effect, but quite naturally he cannot bring himself to accept it. I myself have a daughter only two years younger, and when I look at her I know perfectly well I would not accept it either. I would want to beat him senseless, even tear the man apart with my own hands. Knowing I would end up in jail for assault, and it would leave my wife and children in an even worse position perhaps might stop me, but I can't swear to it."

Delacourt's eyebrows rose slightly. "You want me to advise you how to stop Castelbranco? Say to him exactly what you have said to me."

"I want to know more about rape cases," Pitt answered sharply. "It can't always be as hopeless as this. If it is, then we need to do something about the law. Does everyone just . . . give in? One of the misfortunes of life, like a cold in the head, or measles?"

Delacourt smiled and the anger seeped out of him, his body easing in his chair into a different kind of tension.

"I won't wrap it up for you, Commander. Rape is a crime that is desperately difficult to prosecute. That is partly why I chose to specialize in such cases. I like to delude myself that I can achieve the impossible."

He steepled his fingers. "People react to it in different ways. Most often, I believe, it is not even reported. Women are so ashamed and so hopeless of any justice that they tell no one. Strangers tend to think they must have deserved it in some way. That is the most comfortable thing to think, especially for other women. Then it cannot happen to them, because they do not deserve it."

He moved slightly again. "Some people

believe that if a woman defends herself thoroughly, she will not be raped." He smiled bitterly. "Only beaten to a pulp, or murdered, which would, of course, show she was a virtuous woman, albeit a dead one.

"Men whose daughters are raped feel the rage you just described," Delacourt went on, his face puckered with his own anger and sense of futility. "The younger the girl, the deeper the pain and the fury, and usually the sense of personal failure, that they did not prevent the atrocity from happening. What use are you as a father if your child is violated in this terrible way, and you were not there to stop it?"

Pitt could imagine it only too easily.

Delacourt was watching him. "We don't want our children to grow up, except in the sense of happiness," he said. "We want them to find someone who will love them, when they are ready for the idea, not before. We want them to have children of their own, and if they are sons then to have successful careers — all without the pain and the failures that we have had."

Pitt shook his head, not able to find words.

"We know it's not possible," Delacourt agreed. "But we are still not ready for reality. If it is our wives who are raped, then we are confused, outraged not only for her but for ourselves. She has been violated, and something we considered ours has been taken away — not only from her but from us. Life will not ever be the same again. Somebody must be punished. Our civilized minds say it should be long imprisonment. Our more primitive core demands death. In our dreams that we would not admit to, we would accept mutilation as well."

Pitt opened his mouth to protest, then merely sighed, and again said nothing.

Delacourt had not yet finished. "And thoughts we don't want to have enter our minds." Delacourt had not yet finished. *"Was it really rape? Did she in some way invite it? Surely she must have. Why did it happen to her, and not to someone else? She's different now. She doesn't want anyone to touch her, even me! And I'm not certain that I want to touch her anyway. This man has ruined my life. I want to ruin his, slowly and with exquisite pain, as he has done to me.*

Delacourt leaned forward a little. "And if it is brought to trial she will have to tell the whole court, detail by detail, everything he did to her, and how hard she fought, or not. He will be there, in the dock, watching, listening and reliving it himself. Possibly as you look at him you will see the light in his eyes, his tongue flickering over his lips. His lawyer will say everything he can either to suggest she has the wrong man, is mistaken, hysterical, deliberately lying — or else that she was perfectly willing at the time, but is now crying otherwise to try to protect her reputation. Perhaps she is afraid that she is with child, and her husband knows perfectly well it is not his, but a lover's?"

"I am back to the beginning, then," Pitt replied, now paralyzed by futility. "We can do nothing. We rule an empire that stretches around the world, and we cannot protect women from the depraved among us?"

Delacourt gave a very slight shrug, rueful, but there was a gentleness in his face. "It's not impossible, Commander, just extremely difficult. And even when we succeed, the cost is high — not to us, but to the women. You have to be certain that you think it's worth it. Are you sure you are willing not only to live with the result yourself, but to watch this girl's family live with it?"

Pitt managed a bleak smile. "Do you tell this to all your clients?"

"Perhaps not quite as brutally," Delacourt admitted. "What is it you want to achieve, Mr. Pitt? Angeles Castelbranco is dead. Her reputation is ruined. If you could prove she was raped, and that would be extremely difficult without her alive to speak, then you might achieve something. But the young man would no doubt defend himself vigorously, and whatever he says, there is no one to say otherwise."

"Yes. But if we do nothing, then the Portuguese ambassador will believe we don't care," Pitt argued. "It might damage the relationship between our two countries for some time — not vastly perhaps, but how can you trust a nation that allows such a thing to occur and then lets it go unpunished?"

Delacourt grimaced. "I can see the ugliness of that. I don't know what help I could suggest, Commander, but I will give it some thought."

"And the other part of it is that if the young man gets away with it completely, as seems the case, will he do it again?" Pitt asked. "Put simply, why shouldn't he?"

"There you have the worst of it. Almost assuredly he will. From the little you've told me, it was hardly a crime of passion." Delacourt clenched his teeth and shook his head very slightly. "A crime of hate, the desire to dominate and to shame. Have you ever been in the slightest tempted to take a woman for whom you had some regard, at any cost?"

The thought was repulsive. "Of course not!" Pitt said with more feeling than he had intended. "But I am not —" He had been going to say "a rapist," but stopped, realizing the thought answered itself.

"A man subject to desire?" Delacourt asked with quite open amusement.

Pitt felt himself coloring with embarrassment, not that he had felt desire, almost overwhelmingly at times, but that he should have sounded so naïve.

"I'm sorry," Delacourt apologized. "I led you into that, partly to show you how easy it is to twist someone's words and feelings on the subject. Even a man as experienced as you are in police work and evidence in sensitive matters can be led to awkwardness. Imagine being on the witness stand, vulnerable, trying desperately to be both honest and to give evidence that will trap a dangerous man and still preserve some dignity and reputation for the woman concerned."

"But you're pretty certain he'll do it again?" Pitt said.

"Yes," Delacourt agreed. "Don't most thieves do it again? Most arsonists? Most embezzlers, vandals, liars, anyone whose crime benefits them in some way in their appetite for money, power, revenge, or excitement?"

Pitt rose to his feet.

"There is one thing," Delacourt added, looking up at Pitt. "All that I have said is true; I know it by bitter experience in the courtroom. But if this young man is as violent as you say, then it is possible he has shown it in other ways. Look for loss of temper when he is crossed, when he is beaten in some sport or other, or even loses badly at cards. If he is a risk-taker, look for gambling losses that are heavy or unexpected."

Pitt was not certain he grasped the importance of things so trivial. "How will that help the Castelbrancos? Proving Forsbrook is ill-tempered is a far cry from rape."

"Not so very far, if he is a bully who can't take losing," Delacourt replied. "But that isn't my point. I've tried to convince you of the difficulty of proving rape at all, never mind the danger to the victim of trying. Sometimes one can settle for what is admittedly far less, pathetically so: a prosecution for assault can damage a man's reputation; people don't want to do business with him, invite him to the better social events, have him marry into the family. Several such convictions, or even prosecutions without a serious sentence, can mar his life."

Pitt said nothing, thinking slowly.

Delacourt was watching his face. "A small victory," he admitted, "when you want to beat the man to pulp, and then tear him apart for what he has done to a woman you care about. But it is better than nothing — and it can be a foundation on which to build if you ever do get him to court on a heavier charge."

"Thank you, Mr. Delacourt," Pitt said. "You have spared me more time than you can probably afford. And although only moderately encouraged, I am at least wiser. I understand why people take the law into their own hands. They have looked hard at those of us who are supposed to protect them, or at the very least avenge them, and see that we are powerless. I shall try to prevent the Portuguese ambassador from taking action . . . even though I still can't say that I am entirely averse to it. In his place I would do so, and then leave immediately for Portugal and never return."

Delacourt shrugged. "Frankly, Mr. Pitt, so would I."

Pitt hesitated, wanting to say more, but not knowing what, precisely. "Thank you," he said finally. "Good day."

Outside in the street he walked slowly, oblivious of passersby, of the traffic, even of the open brougham with a beautifully dressed woman riding in it, parasol up to protect her face from the sun, colored silks fluttering in the slight breeze.

What Delacourt had said to him filled his mind. He believed that it was true, but he was unable to accept that there was no possible way to fight. There had to be. They must make it so, whatever that demanded of them. To be helpless was unendurable.

He came to the curb and waited a moment or two for a brewer's dray to pass, then crossed the road.

Instead of thinking of Jemima, he was now thinking about Daniel. How many men feared for their sons? What would Pitt do if Daniel, grown to adulthood, should be wrongly accused of such a violent and repulsive crime?

The answer was immediate and shaming. His instinctive reaction would be to assume that the woman was lying, to protect herself from blame for some relationship she dared not acknowledge. His own assumption would be that Daniel could not be at fault, not seriously.

In six or seven years, Daniel would be a young man, with all the hungers and the curiosity that were there for every young man. His father was probably the last person with whom he would discuss such things. How would Pitt know what Daniel thought of women who perhaps teased him, provoked him, with little or no idea what tigers they were awakening?

He crossed Drury Lane into Long Acre, only peripherally mindful of the traffic.

How would he prevent Daniel from becoming a young man who treated women as something he had the right to use, to hurt, even to destroy? Where did such beliefs begin? How would he ever make certain his son could lose any competition with the same grace as when he won? That he would govern himself in temper, loss, even humiliation? The answer was obvious — he must learn at home. Would it be Pitt's fault if Daniel grew up arrogant, brutal? Of course it would.

If Neville Forsbrook was guilty of raping Angeles Castelbranco and thereby causing her death, was it Pelham Forsbrook's fault as well as Neville's? Probably. Would that same father defend him now if he was accused? Almost certainly. Any man would, not only to save his child, and out of a refusal to believe he was guilty, but also to defend himself. Pelham Forsbrook would be socially ruined, and perhaps professionally damaged irreparably, if his son was convicted of such a crime.

The defense would be savage, a fight for survival. Was Pitt prepared to involve himself in that? Winning would not bring Angeles back, and the risks were great.

But if he did not try? What would that cost?

Without being aware of it he increased his pace along the footpath. How would he feel if it was his daughter, his wife who was violated in such an intimate and terrible way? What if it was not so immediate, so visceral? What if it was Charlotte's sister Emily? He had known her as long as he had known Charlotte.

What if it was Vespasia? Age was no protection. No woman was too young, or too old. Vespasia had such courage, such dignity. Even to imagine her violation was a kind of blasphemy. It jerked him to a stop on the footpath with a pain that was almost physical. He must not allow Neville Forsbrook, or anyone else, to break his world in pieces like that. Whatever the cost, to stand by and do nothing, paralyzed with fear and hopelessness, was even worse. He must think how to attack. It was they who should feel frightened and cornered, not he, not the women he cared for, or any others.

He started along the pavement again, moving as if he had purpose.

CHAPTER 10

While studying Catherine Quixwood's diaries more closely, Narraway found something he hadn't taken notice of before. Notations like reminders: small marks, sometimes initials, quite often figures, as if for a time of day. Others were larger numbers, and he copied them down to see if they might be telephone numbers, even though there were no names of exchanges in front of them. Perhaps she knew the areas in which people lived sufficiently well that a reminder was not necessary.

He questioned the staff at Quixwood's house about the numbers.

"No," Flaxley said unhappily when he showed her the pages. "I don't know what she meant by that."

"Telephone numbers?" he asked.

She looked at them again. Most of them were four digits. "Perhaps — I don't know."

They were sitting in the housekeeper's

room again, a sudden squall of rain batter-
ing against the windows. Flaxley was pale
and tired, even though she had little to do
except consider what position she would be
able to obtain after it became known she
had worked for a victim of rape and murder.
People were terrified of scandal and there
were plenty of good lady's maids. Narraway
was acutely conscious of that as he sat opposite her.

Having achieved nothing with his questions so far, he changed direction and
became blunter.

"Did she ever speak to you about Mr.
Hythe?"

"Not often," she replied. "Just that he was
a very pleasant gentleman. It was only really
in connection with what dress to wear." She
smiled for a moment. "She did not care to
dress in the same gowns if she was aware
she had done so on a previous meeting with
the same person." There was affection in
her voice, in her eyes, and for a moment it
seemed her mind was back in the happier
past.

"She knew he would notice?" Narraway
said quickly. He hated to break the spell of
memory, and yet he had to learn all he
could.

For an instant there was a flicker of

281

contempt in her eyes, but she carefully concealed it. "No, my lord, most gentlemen don't know more than if they like a thing or if they don't. Another lady, of course, would know exactly, and might even be unkind enough to remark on it, but mostly ladies dress to make the best of their appearance and have the confidence then to forget about themselves and behave with wit and charm."

Narraway had never considered the subject before, but it made perfect sense. He could see it true, above all, of Vespasia. He could not imagine her dressing to impress anyone else.

But that did not answer the question of whether Catherine had been in love with Alban Hythe or not. Or, for that matter, anyone else.

Was there any point in asking Flaxley? He looked at her rather bony face, still smudged with grief and now anxiety. Her skin was scrubbed clean, her eyelids a little puffed. Her hair was pinned up neatly, but without softness, without care. He suddenly felt profoundly sorry for her. A year ago he would have brushed by the idea of being no longer needed as merely a part of life that had to be accepted. But now it was a pain he felt in his own flesh and understood.

"Miss Flaxley," he said, leaning forward slightly and meeting her eyes with more urgency, "it was clearly important to Mrs. Quixwood that she meet with Mr. Hythe. She seems to have made arrangements to do so increasingly as often as every week or even twice a week, in the month before her death. Other plans were set aside to fit with his convenience, and as far as I can find out, she mentioned these meetings to no one else. In fact she barely referred to the acquaintance at all. It was not exactly secret, but it was certainly discreet."

Flaxley did not reply, but her gaze never left his.

"It was important to her that they meet," he went on. "She dressed carefully, but not so as to draw undue attention to herself, not as if she were meeting a lover with whom she dared to be seen." He stopped as he saw the flare of anger in Flaxley's eyes.

"Please describe her manner before she went out on these occasions, and when she returned," he pressed. "I know I am asking you to speak of things that normally you would regard as a trust that you could not ever betray, but someone abused her terribly, Miss Flaxley. Someone beat her and caused her death as surely as if they had put their hands around her throat and choked the life out of her." He saw the tears spill over and run down her cheeks and he ignored them. "If that was Alban Hythe, then I want to see him hang for it. And if it was not, then I want to save him. Don't you?"

She nodded so minutely it was hardly a movement at all.

"How was she, Miss Flaxley? Excited? Frightened? Anxious? Sad? Tell me. It is too late to protect her now. And if it is loyalty to Mr. Quixwood you are considering, either for his sake, or for your own — and I am aware that you will need his goodwill in securing another position — I will tell him nothing that you say unless I have to, and even then I will attribute it to another source."

She was surprised, confused, sad to the point of rocking herself back and forth very slightly, as if the movement offered some relief.

"She was anxious," she said in little more than a whisper. "But not as if she were going to meet a lover, more as if she was going to hear something that was good news, or . . . or bad news. She liked Mr. Hythe, but more than that I think she trusted him."

She looked down, avoiding Narraway's eyes. "I have known her, in the past, when she was a little in love with a gentleman — though, of course, she never did anything . . . wrong. She wasn't excited like that over Mr. Hythe. But she would never miss an appointment, no matter what else had to be rescheduled. And it seemed to grow more important to her as time went by. I swear, my lord, I don't know why. I'd tell you if I knew, whatever it was. I'd tie a rope myself to hang whoever did that to her."

Narraway believed her. He said so, thanked her and took his leave. There was nothing more to be gained. He made a note in his mind to speak to Vespasia and see if a position could be found for Flaxley among her friends. Then he smiled as he walked out of the front door, down the steps, and turned toward the square. He was becoming soft. What was the fate of one maid in a city of millions? A year ago he had held the fates of whole nations in his hands!

How the mighty have fallen! Or was it just a realignment of his focus? Perhaps one a trifle overdue.

When he spoke to Quixwood a couple of days later, again in the library of the club, they seemed to have achieved nothing new. Quixwood was tired. It was easy to imagine he had found sleep elusive. He looked thinner than before and the lines in his face deeper. There was a certain hectic light in his eyes.

Narraway felt a gnawing pity for him, and a guilt that he had no real progress to report.

"She saw him often?" Quixwood said, his voice curiously flat, as if he was deliberately trying to keep it unemotional.

"Yes, at least once a week, or more, in the last month of her life," Narraway agreed. "But judging from her diary, and what Flaxley says of her dress and her manner, it was not a love affair."

Quixwood gave a tiny, painful laugh. "Dear Flaxley. Loyal to the end, even when it has become absurd. She's a good servant. It's a shame I have no possible position for her now. If Catherine was not meeting Hythe for an affair, what could it have been? He is a handsome man, at least ten years younger than she was, maybe more."

He smiled, blinking hard. "Catherine was beautiful, you know? And perhaps she was bored. After all, I could not spend all day with her. But I loved her." He stared at some point in the distance, perhaps at a vision or a memory only he could see. "I assumed she knew it. Maybe I should have told her so more . . . more believably."

"She seemed to have many interests," Narraway said after a few moments of silence that dragged heavily. The footsteps of servants could be heard on the wooden floor in the passageway outside.

Quixwood looked up. "You mean other than going to museums and galleries?"

"She seemed to find Africa as fascinating as many others do, especially with the present unrest."

"Unrest?" Quixwood said quickly.

"The Jameson Raid in particular," Narraway elaborated.

"Oh." A brief smile crossed Quixwood's face and vanished again. "Yes, of course. That trial should start soon. The man can't have had the wits he was born with." He sighed. "Although I admit that in the beginning I can see how many would have thought it was a grand adventure, with money to be made." He drew in a deep breath and let it out slowly, his voice thick with unshed tears. "I . . . I went home the other day. I can't stay away forever."

Narraway waited.

Quixwood kept his eyes lowered. "I collected some of my clothes, a few personal things. I thought I might be ready to move back again, but I . . . I can't. Not yet." He looked up at Narraway. "I was looking at

Catherine's jewelry. I thought I should put it in the bank. I don't really know why. I don't know what to do with it, except keep it safe. I suppose there will be something to do with it . . . one day. I . . ." Again he stopped and took a long, jerky breath. "I found this." He held out a small, delicate brooch, not expensive but very pretty — three tiny flowers in various stages of opening, like buttercups. It could have been gold, possibly pinchbeck. "It's new," he said softly. "I didn't give it to her. I asked Flaxley where it came from. She didn't know, but she could tell me when she last saw it. It was after Catherine had met with Hythe at an exhibition of some sort."

Narraway looked more carefully at the piece, without touching it. "I see," he said with sharp regret. "Is there any proof that Hythe gave it to her?"

Quixwood shook his head. "No. Only Flaxley's word that that was the day she first had it."

"And Flaxley would know?" Narraway pressed.

"Oh, yes. She is very good at her job, and completely honest." Quixwood smiled. "She hated admitting it, but she would not lie . . . to me or to anyone. Of course it proves nothing, I know that. But I have no idea

288

what would!" He looked very steadily at Narraway. "Perhaps it will help?"

Narraway took the brooch. "I'll see if I can find out anything about it. It's very attractive — individual. If I can trace it, it would at least be indicative."

Quixwood stared at the floor. "Whatever happens, I'm grateful to you for your time and your patience, and . . . and for your great compassion."

Narraway said nothing. He was embarrassed because he felt he had done so little.

He took the brooch to a jeweler he had consulted with in the past when wanting to know the origin or value of a piece.

"What can you tell me about it?" Narraway asked, offering the old man the delicate little golden flowers.

The jeweler took it in his gnarled fingers, turned it over, and squinted at the back, then looked at the front again.

"Well?" Narraway prompted him.

"Old piece, perhaps fifty or sixty years. Pretty, but not worth a great deal. Perhaps two or three pounds. Individual, though, and women tend to like that. Come to it, I like that." He looked at Narraway curiously. "Stolen? Who'd bother? Couldn't sell it. Come from a crime?" He shook his head.

"Shame. Somebody took care and I'd say a lot of pleasure in making that. Innocent little flowers. Tainted with blood and treason now?"

Narraway evaded the question. "Where would you buy or sell something like this?"

The old man pursed his lips. "Sell it to a pawnshop, not get more than a few shillings for it at most. Buy it there again for a bit more."

"And if I wanted to be discreet?" Narraway pressed.

"Barrow in Petticoat Lane. You don't need me to tell you that."

"Gold or pinchbeck?"

"Pinchbeck, Mr. Narraway. You don't need me for that neither. Pretty thing, nice workmanship. Sentimental, not worth money." He handed it back. "You got as much chance of tracing it as you have of winning the Derby."

"Somebody has to win," Narraway pointed out.

"You've got to ride in it first," the old man said with a dry laugh. "You thought I meant putting money on it? Any fool can do that."

Narraway thanked him and went outside into the sun, the little brooch in his pocket again.

Reluctantly he visited Maris Hythe in her

home that evening to show her the brooch and ask if she had ever seen it before. He loathed doing it, but he would be derelict not to find out.

She took it and turned it over in her hand. She looked puzzled.

"Have you seen anything like it before?" he asked.

"No." She looked up at him. "Whose is it? Why do you bring it to me?" There was fear in her eyes.

"It was Catherine Quixwood's," he replied. "Her husband says he didn't give it to her."

"And you think Alban did?" It was a challenge. "He would hardly have told me."

"Is it the sort of thing he would like?"

She looked down, avoiding his eyes. "Yes. It's individual. It's old. I expect it has history. Several people might have owned it, worn it." She held it delicately, as if she too would have been pleased with it as a gift. "She might have bought it for herself," she said at last, passing it back to him.

He took it. Had he achieved anything more than to raise doubts in her mind, more questions as to her husband's involvement with the woman who had owned it? He felt slightly soiled by the act.

"I suppose it will make no difference if

my husband tells you that he has not seen it before?"

"It means nothing one way or the other without proof," Narraway replied. "Mr. Quixwood mentioned it to me as something among her jewelry he had not seen before."

"Or not noticed," she corrected wryly. "Men frequently do not notice an entire garment that is new, let alone one small item. Ask any woman, she will tell you the same."

"But a man knows which jewels he has bought for his wife," he pointed out. "That's rather different." There was also the matter of Miss Flaxley's not seeing the brooch before.

Maris looked up at him, meeting his eyes, her face very pale. "I have told you what I know, Lord Narraway, which is only that my husband was doing Mrs. Quixwood a favor in a matter that was of great importance to her." Her voice wavered a little, but her eyes did not.

He admired her, but he was aware with deep sorrow and a chill inside that she might one day have to face an ugly truth. Still, let her keep hope as long as possible. He was not yet certain beyond doubt that she was mistaken. If a woman loved him as Maris Hythe loved her husband, Narraway would wish her to keep faith in him, whatever the evidence appeared to be, no matter what a jury might decide. That only irrefutable proof, or his own confession, would be enough to break it.

They were discussing other avenues to explore when Knox came unexpectedly through the door behind the maid.

"What can I do for you?" Maris asked, startled, her voice trembling and slightly defensive. "My husband is in his study. He still has work to complete. Do you require to see him at this hour?" There was reproof in her voice, as if Knox were uncivil.

He looked tired and deeply unhappy. There was a light summer rain outside and his coat was wet. He seemed bedraggled, like a bird whose plumage was molting.

"I'm afraid I do, Mrs. Hythe. I'm glad Lord Narraway is here to be with you."

She looked startled, but said nothing, still sitting on the sofa as if afraid her legs would not support her.

Although it seemed incredible, Narraway suddenly realized what Knox was here for. He stood up.

"Why?" he demanded. "Aren't you being precipitate?"

Knox looked at him sadly, biting his lip. "No, my lord. I regret not. Unfortunately in our search of Mr. Hythe's possessions we found what can only be described as a love letter from Mrs. Quixwood."

"When?" Narraway demanded, his mind racing to think of some innocent explanation for such a thing. "When did you search Mr. Hythe's belongings? Just now?"

"No, my lord, earlier today, with Mrs. Hythe's permission."

"But you didn't arrest him then?" There was challenge in Narraway's voice, one based on emotion rather than reason.

"No, my lord. Mr. Hythe denied knowing about it. I wanted to give him every opportunity, even on the assumption that the letter was not genuinely in Mrs. Quixwood's hand. I have, however, verified that it is unquestionably hers, and the contents of the letter could not be interpreted as anything but words between lovers. I'm sorry."

Maris rose to her feet at last, swaying a little, her chin high.

"That . . ." Narraway swallowed hard. "That does not prove that he raped her . . . or killed her!" He sounded ridiculous, and he knew it, and yet he seemed unable to help himself.

"If it were innocent, my lord, Mr. Hythe would explain it, not deny it," Knox said with a shake of his head, barely a movement at all. "Don't make it harder than it needs to be, sir."

Narraway had no answer. His throat was tight, his mouth dry. He looked across at Maris's ashen face and turned his attention to her, going across to stand beside her, even put his arm around her as she struggled to keep her balance, giddy with horror and grief.

They heard footsteps on the stairs, and then the opening and closing of the front door.

Without speaking, his shoulders bowed, Knox left, disappearing into the night and the rain.

CHAPTER 11

Stoker came into Pitt's office and closed the door behind him.

"Sir, something's happened I think you should know about." His expression was bleak, his eyes sharp and troubled.

"What is it?" Pitt asked immediately.

Stoker took a deep breath. "There's been another very nasty rape of a young woman, sir, and I'm afraid she is dead. Seventeen, her father says. Respectable, good family. Walking out regular with a young man in the Grenadiers."

Pitt felt horror ripple through him, then an overwhelming pity for the father, but also a sense of relief he was ashamed of. This was not Special Branch business. He could leave the pain and the bitter discoveries to someone else.

"I'm very sorry to hear that," he said quietly. "But it's for the police to handle, Stoker, it's nothing to do with us."

"I'm not sure about that, sir," Stoker said, shaking his head. "Very violent, it was. Quite a lot of blood, and her neck was broken with the force of the blow." Stoker stood rigid, almost to attention, like a soldier.

"It's still not ours," Pitt said hoarsely. "It's for the regular police. Unless . . . you're not going to tell me she's a foreign diplomat's daughter, are you?"

Stoker raised his chin a little.

"No, sir, her father is an importer and exporter of some sort. But her young man's a friend of Neville Forsbrook and his crowd, even met Miss Castelbranco once or twice, so her father says." He waited, staring at Pitt.

"You think Neville might be to blame?" Pitt framed the words slowly.

"Don't know, sir." Stoker attempted to smooth his face of anger and frustration, but failed. "I doubt the newspapers will make that connection. Nobody else knows for sure that Miss Castelbranco was raped, and she was certainly alive until she fell through that window. And, by the way, they've arrested someone for raping Mrs. Quixwood, but it's a close thing as to whether he was in custody at the time of this most recent attack."

Pitt was startled. "Have they? Who was it?"

"Alban Hythe," Stoker said flatly, his voice expressionless. "Young man. A banker, so they say. Married. Not what you'd expect. Seems they were lovers — at least that's what I hear from a friend I have in the police."

Pitt said nothing. He wondered what Narraway would think of Hythe's arrest. He had not wanted to think Catherine Quixwood was in any way to blame, even remotely.

"What's her name?" he asked, meeting Stoker's eyes again. "The new victim, I mean."

"Pamela O'Keefe, sir. It'll make a big splash in the newspapers, I should imagine. When it does, the Portuguese ambassador's going to be very upset. I would be." He stood still in front of the desk, his bony hands moving restlessly.

Normally Pitt would have resented the pressure, even the suggestion of insolence; however, he knew it sprang from Stoker's own sense of helplessness in the face of what he felt was an outrage. He expected Pitt, as head of Special Branch, to do something about it.

"Be careful, Stoker," Pitt warned. "The

Home Secretary personally sent me a note warning me that there's nothing we can do about Angeles Castelbranco."

Then suddenly Pitt's anger overwhelmed him, the obscene injustice of it. His temper snapped — not with Stoker, but Stoker got the brunt of it simply because he was there.

"Damn it, man! I was in the building when the poor girl went through the window. Forsbrook says she was hysterical, and so she was. The only question is, what made her so. Was she terrified of him, and for good reason? Was she blaming him for something that someone else did to her? Or was it all in her own fevered imagination?"

Stoker's eyes blazed but he knew to keep silent.

"Do you think I wouldn't arrest the bastard if I could?" Pitt shouted. "No charge would stick to him and we'd end up looking ridiculous. Far more to the point, the poor girl is —" He stopped, appalled. "God! I was going to say decently buried — but she isn't. She's just shoved into some hole in the ground, because the sanctimonious bloody Church has decided she might have taken her own life!"

He very seldom swore, and he heard the echo of his own voice with disgust. He was shaking with fury. Every instinct in him was to attack, to punish Forsbrook until there was nothing left of him. And all he could do was stand by and watch.

And now Stoker too was expecting something of him he could not give. He wondered for a brief instant if Narraway would have done better.

Stoker did not flinch. "So are we going to let it go . . . sir?" he asked. His voice was so tight in his throat it was a pitch higher than normal.

"When was Alban Hythe arrested?" Pitt asked coldly.

"Last night, sir, or more accurately, late yesterday evening," Stoker replied. "Shortly after Pamela O'Keefe was raped and killed, if that's what you're asking. Too close to call."

"Of course that's what I'm asking!" Pitt snapped. "So could he be guilty of killing Pamela O'Keefe, regardless of the crimes against Mrs. Quixwood or Angeles Castelbranco?"

"It doesn't seem likely, sir," Stoker said grimly. He took a breath. "I'd say we've got two violent men raping respectable women. Maybe three. Unless you're thinking Angeles Castelbranco wasn't actually raped."

"No, I'm not thinking that!" Pitt all but snarled. He knew he was being unfair, but

300

the sense of outrage and futility suffocated him. "Coincidences happen, but I don't believe in them until there's nothing else left." He stared at Stoker's blank face. "Find out if there's any further connection between Forsbrook and this poor girl. Maybe he is the leader of a whole bunch of cowards that go after women."

"A gang of them?" Stoker said with disgust, his hands curled into fists. "Isn't that some special sort of crime?" There was a lift of hope in his voice.

"If he or any of them killed the O'Keefe girl, we can hang them just as high for that as for Angeles's death," Pitt replied. "Go and find out. But, Stoker . . ."

The younger man halted at the door and turned. "Yes, sir," he said.

"Be careful," he warned again. "I would very much rather the Foreign Secretary had no occasion to think of us at the moment, let alone know anything. I've been told to leave it alone. It was an order. I need to be damn careful not to be seen disobeying. Your inquiries are for the purpose of making certain Mr. Forsbrook is not mistakenly blamed for any of this. Do you understand?"

Stoker snapped to attention, his eyes brilliant as sunlight on ice. "Absolutely, sir. We must protect our national honor. An upstanding young gentleman like Mr. Forsbrook musn't be slandered by some foreign ambassador, no matter how upset the poor man might be about his daughter's most unfortunate death in our capital city." He took a breath and went on. "And we must make certain there is no connection in anyone's mind between that and this other poor girl's rape and murder, sir. Mrs. Quixwood is quite another matter . . . no connection whatever. Regrettably London appears to be full of rapists, and I suppose young ladies are not careful enough who they keep company with —"

"Stoker!" Pitt barked.

"Yes, sir?" Stoker opened his eyes wide.

"You've made your point."

Stoker lowered his voice. "Yes, sir." There was something close to a smile on his lips. "I'll report to you as soon as I have anything, sir." And without waiting to be dismissed, he turned on his heel and went out.

Pitt picked up the telephone to call Narraway.

Two hours later Pitt and Narraway walked along the Embankment with the magnificent Palace of Westminster towering above them in the sun. On the telephone Pitt had very briefly told Narraway of the new rape case, keeping the details until they met. Narraway in turn had given him nothing beyond the bare fact of Alban Hythe's arrest. His own ambivalent emotions about it were clear in his voice.

On the river to their left a pleasure boat passed with people crowding the decks, laughing and pointing, straw hats waving, bright with ribbons. Somewhere out of sight a barrel organ was playing a popular song. The sound of laughter drifted on the breeze.

"Stoker told me this morning," Pitt said quietly. "Apparently it happened yesterday evening. They can't be sure as to the exact time. Quite early, though."

"Alban Hythe was arrested by nine," Narraway replied. "I know that beyond doubt."

Pitt looked across at Narraway's face, trying to read his emotions. As always, it was difficult. But he was getting to know Narraway far better now than he had when the man had been his superior. In the short time Pitt had been in charge of Special Branch he had carried the burden that Narraway had borne for years, and with that came a different kind of understanding between them.

In Narraway's features he saw uncertainty

and unhappiness. In a way, they had changed positions: Narraway was tasting the personal shock and pain, the dismay in the face of crime; Pitt was feeling the terrible loneliness and weight of responsibility he could not pass on to anyone else, could not even share.

"You don't think he's guilty of raping Catherine Quixwood, do you?" Pitt observed.

Narraway looked at him sharply. His eyes were nearly black in the sunlight, the pale streaks at his temples silver.

"I don't know," he admitted, expression half-concealed. "I'm not used to this . . . this sort of crime. It's nothing like anarchy or treason. I don't know how the devil you dealt with it, with the people and their . . . lives."

"One at a time," Pitt replied drily. "It's not worse than being the one who decides who gets charged, who doesn't, who's let go quietly, and who gets killed. It's just different. In the police you find the facts, then pass it all over to someone else to make the judgment."

"Touché," Narraway said quietly, glancing at Pitt and then away again. "And no, I don't think I believe Alban Hythe raped Catherine Quixwood. But that may well be because I don't want to. I liked him. And I like his wife. I don't want to watch while all her hopes and dreams are laid bare and broken for the public to watch."

"Liking people has very little to do with it," Pitt pointed out. "Even sympathizing with them sometimes. More than once I've thought I could have done the same thing — had I been in the same situation."

Narraway stared at him, incredulity in his eyes. As Pitt did not flinch, slowly the disbelief became the beginning of an understanding. "You mean kill someone?"

"Well, I certainly don't mean rape them!" Pitt retorted a little waspishly. "But yes, I've felt like killing those who beat and terrify women, children, the weak, the old; those who blackmail and extort and yet manage to ensure the law doesn't touch them."

"And rapists?" Narraway asked.

"Yes, them also."

"Pitt . . ." Narraway started.

Pitt smiled with a twisted humor. "Perhaps only if it happened to my wife, or daughter. But I can understand someone who would feel that way, who would want to take justice into his own hands."

Narraway bit his lip. "So can I, and I have no wife or daughter. Do we need to watch Quixwood, once he knows that it's Hythe?

305

Or if Hythe gets off?"

"If he gets off, yes, very possibly," Pitt admitted.

"And the Portuguese ambassador?" Narraway added quietly.

Pitt shivered. "I am watching. Castelbranco taking matters into his own hands is one of several things I am concerned about."

Narraway looked at him closely. "And the others?"

"That whoever is doing this will not stop," Pitt replied.

"All the same man? It can't be, unless Hythe is innocent." Narraway said it with something that could have been hope.

"Or we have two, or even three, men of such violent and brutal disposition loose in London right now," Pitt finished the thought.

Narraway had no answer to that.

Pitt had not seen Rafael Castelbranco for nearly a week. There had been no news to report that would ease any of the man's distress. However, Pitt felt compelled to inform him of the arrest of Alban Hythe, and that as far as he was aware, Catherine Quixwood's death had nothing to do with Angeles's attack.

He made the appointment formally and

306

presented himself at the Portuguese Embassy at four o'clock, as requested.

He was received in a large study with elegant furniture, a wooden floor with beautifully woven rugs and on the walls portraits of past kings and queens of Portugal.

Castelbranco came forward to greet him. He was at least outwardly composed, but was still wearing black relieved only by a white shirt, with no jewelry, not even a pocket watch. His face was calm but his eyes looked hollow, and his skin brittle and drained of color. He did not even pretend to smile, nor did he offer refreshment.

"Good afternoon, Commander Pitt," he said in little more than a whisper, as if his throat was painful. "Have you come to tell me again that you can do nothing to prosecute the man who drove my daughter to her death?" There was no bitterness in his voice, no accusation, just pain.

Pitt hesitated. He had been prepared to be less blunt and this took him by surprise, but to be evasive now would be insulting.

"I suppose, for the present time, that is the truth," he replied. "But the reason I came today is to tell you that a man has been arrested for the rape, and thus causing the suicide, of another woman. It is not public news yet, but it will be by tomorrow morning."

Castelbranco was startled. His body stiffened. His dark eyes met Pitt's with bewilderment. "Another woman? And you can arrest him for raping her?"

Pitt was embarrassed and he knew it showed in his face. "He appears to have had a relationship with her that can be proved," he explained, feeling as if he was making excuses. "They were seen together. There are letters, gifts between them."

Castelbranco said nothing, his eyes unmoving, his mouth closed tightly.

"She let him into her house, after dark," Pitt went on. "When her husband was at a function in the course of his business, and she had dismissed the servants. The man raped her and beat her extremely badly. She was very seriously injured indeed, but it was actually an overdose of laudanum that directly caused her death."

Castelbranco was stunned. He stepped back and sank into one of the chairs. He breathed in and out heavily, his fingers gripping the leather of the arms. For several moments he did not speak. When he did, it was with difficulty.

"Are you saying that this same . . . creature . . . raped my daughter, Mr. Pitt?"

Pitt felt again as if he was making excuses, totally ineffectually.

"No, Ambassador, I'm not. Nor am I suggesting that your daughter had any relationship with the man who did. I'm telling you of this only because the case bears a superficial resemblance, and I don't want you to hear of it without some warning. Also, the man is only accused. He has not stood trial yet, and he has denied his guilt completely. Indeed, it is possible he is innocent."

"You said there was a relationship between this man and the woman he raped? Letters, gifts, meetings?" Castelbranco accused.

"Yes, it seems so. And he cannot account for his time on the evening the poor woman was attacked."

"She let him in? What kind of a woman was she?" Castelbranco glared at him, bewildered and hurt, desperately seeking escape from the thoughts that crowded in on him.

"According to what I have heard, a beautiful woman in her early forties, trapped in a lonely and sterile marriage," Pitt replied.

"And so she took a lover who was depraved?" Castelbranco closed his eyes as if by not seeing Pitt he could deny the reality of what he had said. "Her poor husband. He must be insane with grief. I hear my daughter spoken of as if she was a loose woman, without virtue, but at least I know it was not true." The tears seeped between his eyelids and it took him some moments to master himself. "What must he feel, poor man?"

"I can't imagine," Pitt confessed. "I've tried to. I think about my own wife and daughter. And son," he added.

Castelbranco stared at him. "Your son?" Clearly he saw no sense in the remark.

"I look at my son." Pitt did not avert his eyes. "He's nearly twelve. What will I do to make certain he never misuses any woman, no matter who she is, or how she uses him?"

"Do you imagine this man's father is thinking such a thing?" Castelbranco asked bitterly. "What guilt could be greater than that?" He gave a slight shrug, painfully, as if his shoulders ached. "Or perhaps he refuses to believe it? It takes great courage to accept the very worst you can imagine."

"It would be better to have the courage to accept the possibility beforehand, and do what you can to prevent it, I suppose," Pitt answered him. "But it is too late for that now."

Castelbranco did not answer, just inclined his head in acknowledgment.

Pitt weighed his words carefully. He still

had not delivered the message that was his reason for coming. He must do so.

"If this man proves to be guilty of raping Mrs. Quixwood — and that is by no means certain yet — but if he is, I would not blame Rawdon Quixwood if he were to find the opportunity to kill the man himself," he admitted. "But much as I daresay Inspector Knox, the policeman concerned, would regret it, he would still have to arrest him and charge him with murder. He would then be tried, and if found guilty . . . perhaps not hanged, but he'd certainly spend many years in prison. It would magnify the tragedy immeasurably for his family. He has no children, but no doubt there are those who love him. Parents, maybe a brother or sister."

"And if the law excuses this man who raped Mrs. Quixwood or you cannot find sufficient proof of his guilt?" Castelbranco asked. His voice was hoarse, barely audible, his eyes fixed on Pitt's. "What if he murders him then? Or what if this man was found dead, how hard would Knox, or any of you, search to discover and prove who killed him?"

"You are hoping I'll say we would make only a token effort, and be delighted to fail," Pitt said with considerable compassion. "I would be tempted to, believe me. I daresay Knox would also. But then, this man has a young wife who not only loves him but believes in his innocence. Perhaps he has a father, or brothers who would look diligently for whoever killed him? How long does it go on?"

Castelbranco lowered his head, his eyes closed. "I understand your message, Mr. Pitt. I shall not murder my daughter's rapist, even if I believe I have found him. Who would then look after my wife? She needs, and deserves, more of me than that. She too has lost her only child."

"I'm sorry" was all Pitt could think of to say.

Castelbranco did not respond.

Pitt arrived home a little early. He had received a brief report from Stoker. So far there was nothing to suggest that Alban Hythe had ever met, or even heard of, Angeles Castelbranco. He had not attended any of the same social events, or moved in the same circles. Added to which, any theaters, dinners, or balls he enjoyed, he had gone to with his wife. The galleries and museums where he had met Catherine Quixwood were not places to which Angeles Castelbranco had ever been.

Charlotte must have heard his footsteps because she greeted him in the hall, kissing him quickly and then pulling away.

"Is it true?" she said urgently. "Have they arrested a man for the rape and murder of Catherine Quixwood? Is he the same man who raped Angeles? They won't have to charge him with both, will they? Or would it be better if they did, then at least people would know she was a victim. I heard that he and Catherine were lovers. Is that true? Then why would he rape Angeles?"

"Where would you like me to begin?" Pitt said with a half smile. The warmth of his own home, the smells of clean laundry, of lavender, of furniture wax on polished wood all closed around him, and he wanted to forget the violence and loss of other people's lives. He needed to build a barrier around himself and, for a time, push all the questions and worry outside, beyond his awareness. But he looked at Charlotte's troubled face, the anxiety in her eyes, and knew he could not.

"Don't equivocate, Thomas!" she said. "Tell me!"

"I know what you would like me to say," he replied, his lips stiff, his tongue fumbling with the words. "That yes, we have someone. That he's locked away and we'll prove him guilty. That one day everyone will know Angeles was an innocent victim and her good name will be restored."

"You think I want a comfortable lie?" she said incredulously. "We've been married for fifteen years, Thomas, and that's what you think? It makes me wonder how many times you have told me what you imagined I wanted to hear rather than the truth. Sometimes? Often? Always?"

"Why are you so invested in this?" he demanded furiously. "You think someone's going to attack you? No one is."

"No one is?" She looked at him with real anger and fear. "Who's to say? Or are you implying these brutes attack only foreigners? Catherine Quixwood was as English as I am!" She drew in a deep breath and went on. "You said he was her lover! So it was someone she knew and trusted. That could happen to any of us, especially someone young, who doesn't know the difference between real love and —"

"Charlotte!" He cut across her words sharply. "I didn't actually say anything at all; I just asked which question you wanted answered first."

She was hurt, all the more so because he was right. "I want all of them answered. Have you told the Castelbrancos?"

"Yes, I have. They would hear of it soon enough, but I wanted to take this as an opportunity to warn Rafael not to do anything foolish."

She paled, the anger in her eyes instantly replaced by horror.

He put his arm around her and gently led her toward the parlor. When they were inside he closed the door.

"They have arrested a very respectable young married man named Alban Hythe," he told her, his voice calmer now. "His wife is young and charming, and so far still believes in him totally."

Charlotte's eyes widened, all fury turned to pity. "Poor woman," she whispered. "I imagine she loves him — loves what she thought he was. She won't be able to bear thinking anything else . . . until she has to." She shook her head, and all the tiny muscles in her face tightened as she imagined the other woman's pain. "I didn't think there would be anything worse than losing a child, but perhaps this would be. It has robbed her not only of the present and the future, but of all that she believed of the past."

"We don't know that he's guilty," Pitt said gently. He wanted to comfort her, but he would not dare say anything less than the truth.

"Narraway isn't at all sure that Hythe is guilty," he said, watching her face.

She was startled. "Victor isn't?"

Pitt didn't mind that Charlotte had used his given name, that there was a degree of familiarity between his wife and his friend. He was perfectly aware that Narraway had been in love with Charlotte during the Irish adventure, and for some time before that, and that Charlotte knew it. She was quite certain that the feelings would pass, if they hadn't already. Pitt wasn't sure he agreed, but he trusted Narraway entirely.

"No," Pitt agreed. "And he has been doing some investigating of his own."

"So this Hythe man, he was Catherine's lover?" she asked.

"He says not. She was lonely, intelligent, starved for someone with whom to share ideas, discovery, beauty."

"And her husband is . . ." she chose her words delicately, ". . . a bore?"

"Perhaps insensitive," he amended. "Yes, from her point of view, very possibly a bore. Maybe he was too involved in his business affairs."

"And she was lonely enough to take a lover?" she pressed.

"Enough to seek a friend," he corrected. "At least that is what Narraway thinks. He says Mrs. Hythe is also warm and interesting, and quite individual."

Charlotte smiled. "For him to have noticed, she must be! So do they have the wrong man?"

"I don't know, but it seems quite possible."

"And what about Neville Forsbrook?" she challenged. "There is no doubt he is the one Angeles Castelbranco was terrified of."

"Isn't there?" Pitt thought back to his conversation with Stoker. "I wanted to ask you about that. You don't think it could have been one of the other young men he was with? Think carefully, remember exactly what you saw."

"Would that be his defense, if you charged him?" she said quickly.

"I imagine so."

"Well, it was him. The others were only following his lead. She was looking at him all the time she backed away." There was absolute conviction in her voice and in the bright anger in her eyes. "I'll swear to it if I have to," she added.

"You won't." Suddenly he was weary. "There's nothing with which to charge him."

"So Hythe may be innocent, and yet he'll go to trial, whereas Forsbrook is guilty, and he'll walk away without anyone even mentioning his name? What's the matter with the world?" Now there was fear in her face again: fear of the unreason, the lack of justice.

Pitt wanted desperately to give her an answer that would offer comfort, or at least hope. She was looking at him, wanting it not only for herself but for everyone, for her children, and there was nothing he could say.

"Hythe hasn't been tried yet," he said quietly. "He may be found not guilty, clear his name."

"Will it clear his name?" she asked. "Or will people go on thinking it was him, but that he just got away with it? Do you suppose people in general will really listen to the evidence?"

"We may get someone else for it," he said, trying to force hope into his voice and his eyes.

"And Forsbrook?" she went on. "Will justice ever catch up with him? Or will people go on, happy with the easy answer that Angeles was a foreigner who lacked propriety?" Then she saw his face, and blushed miserably. "I'm sorry, Thomas. I know there's nothing you can do. I wish I hadn't said that."

He smiled and kissed her gently. "I'm still looking for proof."

"Be careful," she warned. "It won't help anybody if the government throws you out."

"I won't give them the excuse. I promise." But even as he said it, he wondered if that was possible.

They ate dinner at the kitchen table with the late sun streaming in through the back windows. The smell of clean cotton emanated from the sheets on the airing rail, and there was fresh bread on the rack above the oven.

Daniel ate with relish, as usual, but Jemima pushed her food around her plate. Her face was miserable, eyes down.

"If you don't want that potato, can I have it?" Daniel asked hopefully, looking at her plate.

" 'May I,' " Charlotte corrected him automatically.

Daniel was disappointed. "You want it?" he said with surprise.

"No, thank you." She stifled a smile. "The word 'like' is better than 'want,' in that way. 'I would like it, please.' But 'can' refers to ability. If you are asking permission for something you say, 'may I please.' "

Wordlessly Jemima passed the potato over

to her brother.

"Papa, what happened to Mrs. Quixwood? Why did she kill herself?" she asked suddenly.

Charlotte drew in her breath, held it a second, staring at Pitt, who looked quite taken aback. Then she let it out in a sigh.

"Was she in love with someone she shouldn't have been in love with?" Tears brimmed in Jemima's eyes and her cheeks were pink.

"You don't kill yourself over that!" Daniel said with disgust. "Well, I suppose girls might . . ."

"It's usually men who run out of control in that area, not women," Charlotte said sharply. "And we don't know what happened yet. Maybe we never will."

"She was attacked in a very personal way," Pitt replied, looking at Daniel. "Parts of the body that are private. And then she was badly beaten. She drank some wine with medicine in it, possibly to dull the pain, and she took too much, perhaps by accident, and that is what she died of."

Daniel looked startled by all of this information, and suddenly very sober.

Pitt plowed on. "When you are older you will develop certain appetites and desires toward women. It's a natural part of becoming a man. You will learn how to control them and, most important, that you do not make love to a woman unless she is as willing as you are."

"You do not make love to her unless you are married to her!" Charlotte corrected him firmly, with a quick glance at Jemima, then back to Pitt.

In spite of himself, Pitt smiled. "We will have a long talk about that, a little later," he told his son. "And not at the dinner table."

"If he really hurt her, and it was his fault, why does everybody seem angry with her?" Jemima asked.

"Because they're frightened," Charlotte said before Pitt could frame an answer he thought suitable for his daughter, not really knowing how much she knew of the whole subject.

Jemima blinked and a tear slid down her cheek. "Why are they frightened?"

"Because rape can happen to any woman," Charlotte said. "Just like being struck by lightning."

"Hardly anyone gets struck by lightning," Daniel pointed out. "And if you don't go out and stand in the middle of a field in a thunderstorm, there's nothing to be afraid of."

"Thank you." Charlotte smiled at him.

"That was the point I was trying to make. But when it does happen to someone, then people become afraid and they blame the person it happened to, because if it was their own fault, rather than the lightning's fault, then everyone else is safe."

"Was it her own fault?" Jemima did not seem comforted.

Charlotte looked at her steadily. "We have no idea, and it would be cruel of us to assume it was until we know. But perhaps you and I should have a longer talk about it this evening, at a more suitable time. Now please eat the rest of your dinner, and let us discuss something more pleasant."

The conversation could not be avoided. Charlotte knew from Jemima's unhappy face that something was troubling her profoundly, something more than the usual day-to-day dreams and nightmares of being fourteen.

"Would it be my fault if — if I . . . really liked someone?" Jemima asked, her eyes lowered, too afraid to look up at her mother.

"What you feel is not your fault," Charlotte picked her way through the minefield. "But what you do about it is your responsibility. Perhaps in view of what everyone is talking about, it is a good time to discuss what is wise behavior, what is becoming, and what is very likely to be misunderstood and taken as permission you really do not mean to give."

"We've already talked about it, Mama."

"Then why are you still unhappy and apparently confused?"

Jemima looked up and blinked, tears in her eyes again. "What is rape? I mean exactly? Could it happen to me? Would I die? I mean, would I have to commit suicide? That's a terrible sin, isn't it?"

"If someone is so desperately unhappy that she is driven to suicide, then I think I would forgive her," Charlotte answered. "And I am certain God is better than I am, so I think He would forgive her too. There might be a price to pay, I don't know. There normally is for anything done less well than we could have done it, for acts of omission as well as commission. But it is not my place, thank heaven, to judge anyone else. And as far as Mrs. Quixwood is concerned, we don't know if she meant to die."

"So she'll be all right? In heaven, I mean?" Jemima said earnestly.

"Certainly. It is the man who raped her who will not."

"Everybody says 'rape,' but they don't say what he actually did to her."

Charlotte knew that she must face the issue now, or make it even worse.

"We have talked about love and marriage before, and having children," she said frankly. "If you love someone, and he is gentle and funny and wise, as your father is, then the acts of intimacy are wonderful. You will treasure them always. But if you imagine that kind of act with someone you do not know or like, and he tears your clothes off you and forces you and hurts you —"

Jemima let out a gasp of horror.

"That is what is called rape," Charlotte finished. "It is terrible at the time — it must be — but that is not all. You may find that you are with child, which will have consequences for the rest of your life, because the child is a person, and one you have brought into the world. You will love him, or her, but the child will also remind you of what happened."

Jemima stared at her, blinking slowly, tears on her cheeks.

"And as you have already heard, people will tend to blame you," Charlotte continued. "They will say that somehow it was your own fault. You were dressed in such a way that he thought you were willing, or that you invited him and only said 'no' at the last moment. Or he may even say you were perfectly happy at the time, but that you are now claiming it is his fault now so that you are not to blame for losing your virginity, and therefore your reputation."

"I think I might kill myself too," Jemima said slowly.

"There will be no need," Charlotte told her steadily. "It will not happen to you. You will not see young men alone until you are a very great deal older, by which time you will also be wiser and more able to make your own wishes known, unmistakably. No one ever treated me that way, nor will they treat you less than as the woman you choose to be."

Jemima nodded. "And Papa will catch the man who did that to Mrs. Quixwood, won't he?"

"Mrs. Quixwood is not his case, but he will help how he can. I fear, though, that it will not be easy, and it may take some time."

Jemima smiled. "We're lucky, aren't we, to have Papa to look after us?"

"Yes, we are. But you will still not see young men alone, no matter who they are."

"But . . ." Jemima began.

Charlotte raised her eyebrows slightly.

"But with others? If Fanny Welsh is there too, it's all right?" Jemima insisted.

"I will take it under advisement, and let you know," Charlotte replied.

CHAPTER 12

Narraway hated prisons, but it had quite often been necessary in the past for him to visit people awaiting trial, and sometimes even afterward when they were convicted. However, seeing Alban Hythe was more personal, and therefore painful in a quite different way.

Hythe looked ill. He was clearly exhausted and he seemed undecided as to whether he should even try to appear calm. He greeted Narraway courteously, but with fear jumping in his eyes.

Narraway tried to dismiss the overwhelming pity from his mind. He needed clarity of thought if he was to be of any help. They sat opposite each other across a scarred wooden table. Narraway had to use considerable influence to gain access and be left alone with Hythe, while the barrel-chested jailer remaining outside the door.

"I haven't seen that brooch, and I never

received love letters from Catherine!" Hythe said urgently. His voice shook a little. "We were friends. That's all! Never more than that. Maris is the only woman I've loved."

"Did they show you the letter?" Narraway asked him.

"Yes, but I swear it's the first time I ever saw it!" Hythe was barely in control. His hands twitched and there was a wild desperation in his eyes.

"Do you believe she wrote it?" Narraway pressed. "They say it is undoubtedly her handwriting, but is it also the kind of language she would've used?"

"I've no idea! The letter is all about love, and we didn't speak of love. We only —" He stopped abruptly.

"What?" Narraway asked. "What did you talk about? This is not the time to be modest or circumspect. You're fighting for your life."

"I know!" Hythe shivered uncontrollably.

Narraway leaned forward. "Then tell me, what did you talk about? If it wasn't you who did this, then who else could it have been?"

"Don't you think I've racked my brain to remember anything she said that could help me?" Hythe was close to panic.

Narraway realized he had made a tactical

error in frightening Hythe by bringing up the stakes so soon. He moderated his voice. "Have you any idea how often you met? Once a week? Twice a week? Her diaries suggest at least that."

Hythe looked down at the scarred table-top. His voice when he spoke was quiet. "The first time we met by chance, at a dinner party. I forget where. It was a business matter, and rather tedious. Then a little while later I was at an art gallery, filling time before meeting a client for luncheon. I saw Catherine and recognized her. It seemed quite natural that we should speak."

"What did you discuss?" Narraway asked.

Hythe smiled for the first time, as if a pleasant memory had given him a few moments' respite from reality. "Pre-Raphaelite paintings," he answered. "She wondered what the models were thinking about, sitting still for so long while the artist drew them in such fanciful surroundings. We thought about where they had actually been — some studio or just an ordinary room — and if they even knew the legends and dreams into which they were painted.

"Catherine was very funny. She could make one laugh so easily. Her imagination was . . . quite unlike that of anyone else I have ever known. She always had the right words to make one see the absurdity of things, but she was never mocking. She liked eccentricity and wasn't afraid of anything." His expression became sad. "Except loneliness."

"And Quixwood never noticed that, clearly," Narraway observed.

"A clever man, but with a pedestrian soul," Hythe answered without hesitation. "Her soul had wings, and she hated being made to spend her time with her feet in the dust." He bent his head suddenly. "I'm sorry; my judgment is unwarranted and cruel. She was just so alive; I hate whoever did this to her. They have spoiled something that was lovely and destroyed a friend I cared about. She was . . . she was good." He seemed to want to add more. It was in that moment that Narraway knew Hythe was lying, in essence if not in word.

"Just a friend?" he asked skeptically.

"Yes!" Hythe jerked his head up. "Just a friend. We talked; we looked at pictures painted from great imaginations, at pages from books written on papyrus from the very first poets and dreamers in the world. We saw carvings of grace made by artists who died before Christ was born. She escaped from her loneliness, and I from my world of facts and figures, interest on loans, duty on imported treasures, and prices of land."

His voice trembled.

"Haven't you ever had friends, Lord Narraway? People you like enormously, who enrich your world, and without whom you would be poorer in a dozen ways — but you are not in love with them?"

Narraway instantly thought of Vespasia.

"Yes, I have," he said honestly, feeling the warmth himself, for a moment.

"Then you can understand." Hythe looked relieved. The ghost of a smile returned to his pale face.

Narraway felt a sudden stab of surprise, a question in his mind. What exactly did he feel for Vespasia? She was older than he by several years. He had been elevated to the House of Lords because of his skills, and possibly as a sop to his pride for being dismissed from his position as head of Special Branch. She had been born into the aristocracy. They had become friends by circumstance. He had begun a little in awe of her, and he was quite aware that she had never been in awe of him — nor perhaps of anyone else either.

But she could be hurt. He had realized that only recently. Her feelings were far deeper than he had imagined, and she was not invulnerable. Was she also, occasionally, as lonely as Catherine Quixwood had been?

He forced it out of his thoughts. He was concerned with Alban Hythe, and whether the younger man was guilty or not, and what it was he still lied about, even though the shadow of the noose hung over him.

"Did you ever write to her?" Narraway asked a little abruptly.

"No," Hythe said urgently. "We met by chance, or . . ."

"Or what?" Narraway demanded. "For God's sake, man, they've charged you with rape, and the victim died. If they find you guilty they'll hang you!"

He thought Hythe was going to pass out. The last vestige of color drained out of his face and for a moment his eyes lost focus.

Narraway jerked forward and grasped hold of his wrists and forced him upright.

"Fight!" he said between his teeth. "Fight them! Damn it, give me something to use! If you weren't lovers, then what the hell were you doing meeting a married woman in half the galleries around London? You have no room and no time to protect anyone else!"

Hythe sat up against the hard back of the chair, breathing in and out slowly, trying to steady himself. Finally he lifted his eyes.

"We met by arrangement," he said huskily.

Narraway bit back the angry answer that was on the edge of his tongue.

"So why were you meeting with such elaborate care as to make it appear by chance?"

"I promised her . . ." Hythe began, then tears of grief filled his eyes.

"She's dead!" Narraway said brutally. "And precisely three weeks after they find you guilty, you will be too!"

The silence in the room was thick, as if the air had turned solid, too heavy to breathe.

Had Narraway gone too far? Had he frightened Hythe into a mental collapse? His mind raced for something to do, anything to rescue the situation. He had been irretrievably stupid, lost his touch completely. No wonder they had retired him!

"Hythe . . ." he started, his voice choking.

The other man opened his eyes. "She wanted something from me," he began, then released a heavy sigh. "Advice."

Narraway felt the sweat break out on his body and relief flood through him.

"What kind of advice? Financial?"

"Yes. She . . . she was concerned for her future," Hythe said miserably. He was breaking his own professional code of honor by speaking of it, and it was obvious how profoundly difficult that was for him.

Still, Narraway sensed an evasion. There was something incomplete. Hythe might feel guilty about breaking a confidence, but there was nothing immoral in a woman being afraid her husband was rash with money, even a husband usually skilled in such affairs.

"Go on," he prompted.

"Her husband was involved in investments," Hythe said quietly. "She was afraid that something he was doing would end up being disastrous, but he wouldn't listen to her. She wanted to have her own information and not depend on what he told her. It was . . . detailed. It took me a long time to find it and I gave it to her piece by piece, as I could. Each time it fell into place she would ask for something further. She believed that some investments currently worth a fortune might become useless, and others gain enormously."

He was still lying, at least in part. Narraway knew it, and he could not understand why. Did Hythe still not understand his own danger?

"Was she trying to save her husband's finances?" Narraway asked. "Did she have money of her own, or expectations?"

Hythe stared at him. "I don't know. She didn't tell me why she needed the information, but I think it was more than that. I had the increasingly powerful feeling that she was afraid of something calamitous happening. I asked her, and she refused to say."

"Why?"

"I don't know. I didn't press her."

"How many times altogether did you meet?"

"A dozen maybe." He lifted his shoulders in a gesture of helplessness. "I liked her, but I never touched her in a familiar way, and I certainly didn't rape her! Why on earth would I? We were friends, and both her husband and my wife were perfectly aware of it!"

"You are sure that Quixwood was aware of it?" Narraway pressed.

"Of course! He and I even talked about an exhibition at the National Geographical Society, photographs of Patagonia. He told me how beautiful Catherine found it: great sweeping wilderness country; all pale, wind-bleached colors, light and shadow. Superb."

"Did she speak to anyone else about the financial issues?"

Hythe thought for several moments, then met Narraway's eyes.

"I don't think so. From what she said to

me, I gathered I was the only person she trusted."

"She came to you for financial information, but you said she was warm, amusing, a lovely woman."

"She was!"

"And Quixwood was cold, without a true understanding of her?" Narraway insisted.

"Yes."

"So she was lonely, maybe desperately lonely?"

Hythe swallowed painfully. "Yes." His voice was husky with emotion, guilt, and perhaps pity. "But I did not take advantage of that. I had no wish to. I liked her, liked . . . cared . . . but I did not love her." He added no oaths, no pleas, and his words were the more powerful for it.

"It's not enough. You have to think harder!" Narraway leaned forward again, a note of desperation in his voice. He heard it and forced himself to speak more levelly. "Whoever it was that raped her, she let him in." He swallowed hard. "She wasn't afraid to be alone with him. What do you conclude from that?"

"That she knew him," Hythe said miserably. He shook his head a little. "It doesn't sound like Catherine at all, not as I knew her."

"Then as you knew her, how do you explain it?" Narraway demanded. "What do you believe happened?"

"Do you think I haven't tried to work it out?" Hythe said desperately. "If she let the servants go then she *wasn't* expecting anyone. Letting them all retire for the night like that makes it obvious; Catherine was never careless in that way. It would be . . . unnecessarily dangerous. What if a footman had come down to check a door, or the butler came to ensure she didn't need anything? Isn't that what actually happened?"

"More or less," Narraway agreed.

"So the person at the door had to be someone unexpected," Hythe argued.

"But then why did she let him in?" Narraway persisted. "Why would the woman you knew have done that?"

"It must have been someone she knew and had no fear of," Hythe answered. "Maybe he claimed to be hurt, or in some kind of trouble. She wouldn't hesitate to try and help." He stopped abruptly. He made no display of grief, but it was so deeply marked on his face that it was unmistakable.

Narraway suddenly was completely certain that Hythe had not raped Catherine or beaten her. Someone else had, but Hythe was going to face trial. The letter and the gift would damn him. And there was no one else to suspect. He felt a jolt of fear.

Who was going to defend Hythe in court, at the very least raise a reasonable doubt? That would not clear his name, but guilt would hang him, and finding the right person after that would matter little. Hythe would be dead, and Maris a widow and alone.

"Do you have a lawyer, a really first-class advocate?" Narraway asked.

Hythe looked as if he had been struck. "Not yet. I — I don't know of anyone . . ." He trailed off, lost.

"I will find you someone," Narraway promised rashly.

"I can't pay . . . very much," Hythe began.

"I will persuade him to represent you for free," Narraway replied, intending if necessary to pay for the barrister himself. Already he had the man in mind, and he would speak to him this afternoon.

He remained only a little longer, going over details of facts again so they were clear in his mind. Then he excused himself and went straight from the prison to the chambers of Peter Symington in Lincoln's Inn Fields, a short distance away. If any man would take on the case of defending Alban

Hythe with a chance of winning, it was he.

Narraway insisted on seeing Symington immediately, using the suggestion of more influence than he possessed to override the clerk's protests.

He found Symington standing in the middle of the well-carpeted floor, a leather-bound book in his hand. He had clearly been interrupted against his instructions. He was a handsome man in his early forties. Most remarkable about him were his thick, fair hair, curling beyond the barber's control, and the dazzling charm of his smile.

"My lord?" he said quietly, reproof in his voice.

Narraway did not apologize. "A matter of urgency, it can't wait," he explained as the clerk closed the door behind him.

"You've been charged with something?" Symington said curiously.

Narraway was in no mood for levity. "Inspector Knox has charged a man with the rape of Catherine Quixwood, and therefore morally, in the minds of the jury, with her murder. I would like you to defend him. I believe he's innocent."

Symington blinked. "You'd like me to defend him? Does he mean something to you, to the government, to Special Branch? Or is it just because you think he's innocent?" There was amusement in his voice, and curiosity. "I presume he told you he is?" He put the book down on his desk, closed, as if it no longer interested him. "Why me? Or am I the only one you think fool enough to take it?"

In spite of himself Narraway smiled. "Actually, the last," he admitted. "But you are also the only one who would stick to it long enough to have a chance of winning. I really believe he's innocent, and that there is something large and very ugly behind the whole case — maybe more than one thing. Certainly someone raped and beat the woman so badly she died as a result. She was a funny, brave, and beautiful woman. She deserves justice — but even more important, whoever did it needs to be taken off the streets and put where he can never hurt anyone else."

Symington raised his eyebrows. "Like a grave?"

"That would do nicely," Narraway agreed. "Will you take the case? I would like Hythe to believe it is without charge, because he doesn't have the means to meet it. I'll pay you myself, but he must never know."

Symington's utterly charming smile beamed again. "I'm not a fool, my lord. The case sounds like a challenge. I think I can clear my desk sufficiently to give it my very best attention. And I'll weigh the matter of my bill, and send you what I feel appropriate. I give you my word that Hythe will believe I do it for the love of justice."

"Thank you," Narraway said sincerely. "Thank you very much."

He hesitated, wondering if he were risking the frail thread of trust he had just established with Symington — and yet it was the only hint he had that there might be someone else besides Hythe to blame. But he also believed that at least in some sense Hythe was lying, or at the very best willfully concealing something.

Symington was waiting for him to speak.

"Hythe admitted meeting Catherine Quixwood as often as her diaries suggested, but he said she arranged it. He said she wanted him to give her financial advice."

"And you believed that?" Symington said with a twisted smile. "Quixwood's a financier himself, and an extremely good one."

"I know," Narraway admitted. "Hythe said she was afraid Quixwood was into something dubious, and over his head. She wanted to know more about it. If she was afraid for her future, if he had been reckless, then that would be believable."

"Ah. But do you? Believe it?" Symington

asked. "If he has any proof of it, why didn't he tell Knox?"

"I don't know," Narraway admitted. "He's lying about something. I just don't know what."

"But you're sure he didn't rape her?" Symington looked puzzled and not angry.

"Yes," Narraway answered, unable to explain himself.

"Then I'll take the case, try to win the trial," Symington promised.

"Thank you," Narraway said.

That evening Narraway went out rather later than was customary to call on a woman alone, particularly one with whom he had only the slightest acquaintance. He stood in the small parlor of Alban Hythe's house and told Maris what he had achieved.

Maris was so pale that her dark dress, more suitable for autumn than summer, drained the last trace of the vitality from her face. However, she kept her composure and stood straight-backed, head high, in front of him. What effort it must be costing her he could only guess.

"And this Mr. Symington will defend my husband, in spite of the evidence?" she asked. "Why? He can't know that Alban is innocent. He's never even met him. And we

342

can't pay the sort of money such a man as you describe would ask." She struggled to keep control of her voice and very nearly failed.

"Then I did not describe him very well," Narraway apologized. "Symington cares far more about the case than the money."

She studied Narraway's face for several moments, searching his eyes to judge whether he was lying to her, or at the least prevaricating. Finally she must have come to the conclusion that he was not. But her words were interrupted by a maid at the door telling her that Mr. Rawdon Quixwood had called and wished to speak with her.

Narraway was startled but, turning to look at the maid, saw that her face was completely expressionless. Clearly she was not surprised.

Maris looked pleased.

"Thank you. Please ask him to come in," she instructed.

The maid withdrew obediently and Maris turned to Narraway.

"He has been so kind. Even with all his own grief, he has found time to call on me and assure me of his help." She lowered her eyes. "I fear sometimes he believes Alban guilty, but his gentleness toward me has been without exception." She gave a small, very rueful smile. "Perhaps he feels we are companions in misfortune, and I have not the heart to tell him it is not so, because it does seem that Catherine was more familiar with someone than she should have been. I would so much rather think that was not true, of course, but I have no argument that stands up to reason."

She had not time to add any more before Rawdon Quixwood came in. The hollowness of his face had eased a little, perhaps because at last someone had been arrested for the crime, even though the loss must still feel just as bitter.

"Maris, my dear —" he began, stopping abruptly when he realized Narraway was also in the room. He checked himself quickly. "Lord Narraway! How agreeable to see you. I wonder if we are here on the same errand. I'm afraid I can offer little comfort. Perhaps you have better news?"

Narraway met Quixwood's eyes and found he could read nothing of what the man was thinking. The idea occurred to him that the effort of hiding his own pain might be the only way Quixwood could turn his mind from his grief.

Still, Narraway found himself reluctant to trust him, or to risk wounding him still more deeply with the possibility that they

344

had not actually caught his wife's attacker.

"I am still searching," he replied quietly. "Without much profit so far, for all the information I can find. I hear contradicting stories of Mrs. Quixwood."

Quixwood gave a very slight shrug, a graceful gesture. "I daresay they are exercising the customary charity toward the dead who cannot defend themselves. I appreciate it. Women who are . . . assaulted . . . are often blamed almost as much as the men who assault them. The euphemisms and occasional silences are a kindness."

"But not helpful," Narraway pointed out. "We need the truth if we are to obtain justice, for any of the people concerned."

Maris gestured for both men to be seated. As soon as they were, Quixwood spoke.

"Justice." He seemed to be turning the word over in his mind. "I began wanting justice for Catherine as a starving man wants food. Now I am less certain that it is really what I wish. Silence might be more compassionate. After all, she can no longer speak for herself."

Maris looked down at her hands folded in her lap, white-knuckled.

"Rawdon, you have been the essence of kindness to me," she said gently. "In spite of the fact that it is my husband the police have arrested for the terrible wrong done to your wife. But Alban is not guilty, and he needs justice also. Apart from that, do you not wish the real monster to be caught, before he goes on and does something similar to another woman?"

Quixwood's face reflected an inner conflict so profound, so intense, he could barely keep still. His hands in his lap were more tightly twisted than Maris's. In that moment Narraway knew beyond any doubt that Quixwood was certain that Alban Hythe was guilty, and he was here to do what he could to help the man's wife face that fact. It was a startling generosity. But . . . well, what did he know that Narraway and Maris did not?

Quixwood was still searching for words, his eyes on Maris's face, troubled and almost tender. "I don't think it is likely," he said at last. "It is far better that you do not know the details, but I assure you, it was not a random maniac who did this deed. It was very personal. Please, think no more of it. You must concern yourself with your own well-being. If there is anything I can do to help, I will." He gave a very slight smile, wry and self-deprecating. "It would be a favor to me. It would give me someone to think of other than myself."

A warmth of gratitude filled her face, and also a very genuine admiration. Narraway was sure that Quixwood had seen it, and it must indeed have given him some small comfort.

The following day Narraway called early at the club where Quixwood was still living. He had to wait until the man rose and came into the dining room for breakfast, then joined him without asking permission, because he had no intention of accepting a refusal.

Quixwood looked startled, but he made no objection. He regarded the older man with some curiosity.

Narraway smiled as he finished requesting poached kippers and brown toast from the steward. As soon as the servant left, he answered Quixwood's unspoken question.

"I hear several different accounts of Catherine," he said, watching Quixwood's eyes. "I assume that you loved her, and also that you knew her better than anyone else. Nothing need come out in court that puts that in doubt, and still less in the newspapers, but I think it is time we discussed her without the glittering veil of compassion that usually shrouds the dead."

Quixwood sighed, but there was no resistance in him. He leaned back a little and his dark eyes met Narraway's. "Do you not think it was Alban Hythe who killed her?" he said anxiously. "It will bring terrible grief to poor Maris if it is, of course. She still believes in him."

Narraway did not answer the question directly.

"If they were lovers, Catherine and Hythe, why on earth would he suddenly turn on her like that?" he said instead. It was a reasonable question.

"Does it matter now?" Quixwood wrinkled his brow.

"If we are going to convict the man and hang him, it has to make sense," Narraway said bluntly.

Quixwood winced. "Yes, of course, you are right," he conceded. He began to speak in a very low voice. His eyes were downcast, as if he was ashamed of being forced into making such admissions.

"Catherine was a very emotional woman, and she was beautiful. You never saw her alive, or you'd understand. She hated going to the sort of functions where you and I might meet. And to tell you the truth, I didn't press her. It wasn't only out of kindness to her, but also because she was so charming, so very alive, that she attracted attention she was not able to understand for what it was, or deal with."

Narraway was puzzled, but he did not interrupt.

"She loved attention," Quixwood continued, a warmth lighting his face, probably for the first time since the night of Catherine's death. "She responded to it like a flower to the sun. But she also was easily bored. When someone did not live up to her expectations, or have the imaginative enthusiasm she did, she would drop their acquaintance. It could cause, at the very least, a degree of embarrassment."

At last he looked up and met Narraway's eyes. "I loved her, but I also learned not to take her sudden passions too seriously. She lived a good deal of her life in a world of her own creation: mercurial, entertaining, but quite unreal." He shrugged his shoulders. "I fear young Alban Hythe would have had no idea how changeable she was, how . . . fickle."

He made a slight gesture of dismissal. "She would mean no cruelty, but she had no concept of how deeply an idealistic, rather naïve young man might fall in love with her, and — when she rejected him — feel utterly betrayed."

He blinked and looked away. "If they were

lovers, or he thought she had implied they would be, and then without warning she felt he had not lived up to what she expected of him, he surely would have felt utterly cheated. He might have damaged irreparably his relationship with a wife who was devoted to him in favor of a woman who seemed incapable of loyalty to anyone — who had built a castle in the air out of his dreams and then destroyed it in front of him. Do you see?"

Narraway did. It was a persuasive image. And yet he did not quite believe it.

"But what about taking the laudanum to end her life?" Narraway asked, his voice sounding harsher than he had meant it to.

"Perhaps she realized what she had done," Quixwood said with a small, helpless gesture of his hands, barely a movement at all. "She was passionate, but she was not strong. If she had been, she would have lived in the real world . . ." He left the rest and all its implications unsaid.

"Thank you," Narraway responded quickly, as the steward arrived with his poached kippers, and bacon, eggs, sausage, and deviled kidneys for Quixwood. They both turned, with little joy, to their food and harmless, matter-of-fact subjects of conversation as the dining room filled up.

■ ■ ■ ■

After leaving the club, Narraway decided that he still did not know enough about Catherine Quixwood. The woman her husband had described was very different from the one Alban Hythe had seen and believed he knew and had liked so deeply. Moreover, both were different again from the one Narraway had seen in death.

Who would have known all of her, fitted the disparate pieces into a whole, however complex? No one wished to speak ill of the dead, and most particularly of someone who had died so horribly.

Would there be any point in asking Knox for his help? Probably not. He had arrested Alban Hythe, which meant that he had formed a picture of Catherine he could now not afford to alter.

Narraway circled back to the idea that perhaps the person who knows a woman best is her lady's maid. But he had already spoken to Flaxley, more than once. Did she have anything left to tell him? He decided it was worth one more try.

Narraway stepped into the street and hailed a cab, giving Quixwood's address.

Then the obvious way around Flaxley's

reluctance came to him like sudden daylight. If anyone could persuade a loyal servant to discuss the details of her mistress's character, it would be Vespasia.

He leaned forward and knocked on the front of the cab, asking the driver to take him instead to Vespasia's house.

"Really, Victor," she said with slight surprise when he told her what he wished her to do. "And what shall I give the poor woman as a reason why I consider her mistress's character to be any of my concern?"

They were sitting in her morning room, all cool colors and stark white frames to the windows. There was a bowl of early blooming white roses on the low table, and the sunlight through the glass was hot and bright. In spite of his reason for calling, Narraway found himself relaxing. It was extraordinarily comfortable here.

"I'm sorry," he said. He found himself telling her not only what Alban Hythe had said of Catherine, and what Quixwood himself had said, but also his own impressions and the depth of feeling it aroused in him.

She watched him gravely the whole time, without interrupting.

"I see," she said when she was certain he

352

had no more to add. "It is not possible for both opinions to be entirely true, and perhaps neither of them? It would be a curious thing to see yourself as others do. I imagine it would seldom be comfortable." She smiled very slightly. "I am very glad that I shall not be present at my own funeral, even to hear the eulogies that, I'm sure, will make me sound quite unreal."

He was caught with a sudden icy coldness. He had never imagined Vespasia dying. The thought was so painful, it shocked him.

"My dear, don't look so tragic," she said with a slight shake of her head. "I quite see the necessity of someone speaking to Flaxley, and your argument that it should be I who does so is perfectly sensible. I shall make the arrangements."

"Thank you," he said a little awkwardly, afraid she might suddenly understand what it was that had really shaken him so much.

Narraway dined with Vespasia the following evening. He chose to make it a formal affair — a dinner at the finest restaurant he knew. For his own pleasure, he wished to behave as if it were a celebration of something, rather than the pursuit of the last act of a tragedy.

She flattered him by dressing with all the glamour he had associated with her when they had first met. She wore heavy ivory silk with guipure lace at the neck and over the bodice, and as she did so often, she ornamented it with ropes of pearls. He saw other diners, especially several gentlemen and senior members of Parliament, look at him with distinct envy.

Vespasia conducted herself with the nonchalance he would have expected, although a slight flush of pleasure did rise in her cheeks as they entered the dining room.

He wanted to find out if she had succeeded in learning anything, but it would be unbecoming to ask too soon. Additionally, it might give her the totally mistaken idea that that had been his sole motive in inviting her.

They had reached the dessert (a most exquisite French apple tart) before the subject was raised, by Vespasia.

"I spoke at some length to Catherine's maid," she said, setting her fork down on her plate. "At first she was naturally reluctant to say anything but the sort of respectful praise that loyalty would dictate. I'm afraid I took the liberty of mentioning that if we did not prosecute the right man, the real murderer would escape detection and very probably commit a similar crime against someone else. I am not certain if that is true, of course, but I am quite sure that Catherine herself would not wish the wrong man convicted."

"I'm afraid it probably is true," he replied gravely. "What did she tell you? Is Quixwood right about Catherine?"

"No," she said without hesitation. "But, of course, I can't say whether he *believes* he is. It is quite clear that she did not find in him either the love or the friendship she wished for. His defense against that may have been to see her as the cause of the problem rather than he himself, or the simple fact that perhaps they were mismatched."

"And you are sure the maid was not merely being loyal?" he pressed.

She smiled. "Yes, Victor, I am quite sure. I have had a lady's maid all my life. I can read between the lines of what they say, or decline to say." Her eyes were bright with amusement, but there was no impatience in them, no condescension. He had the distinct feeling that she was pleased to have been asked for her help.

"Would you like Armagnac, perhaps?" he said impulsively.

"Champagne is sufficient for me," she

answered, smiling.

He hesitated.

She looked at the light, sparkling wine in her glass and raised her delicate eyebrows. "Is this not champagne, then?" she asked.

For a moment he was not certain of the compliment. Then, meeting her eyes, he understood and found himself coloring with pleasure, and even a little self-consciousness. He raised his glass to hers without answering.

In the morning Narraway went to find Knox again. He began at the police station and was told that there had been an unpleasant brawl down on the waterfront and Knox had been called to the scene.

Narraway obtained the precise location, thanked the constable, and left to find a hansom to take him there. It was not a long journey but it took time weaving in and out of the traffic, dense at that time of day, the roads crowded with drays, wagons, and men and women on foot busy with their early errands. He passed lightermen, stevedores, crane drivers, wagon masters, and ferrymen, already busy. Gulls wheeled and dived, screaming as they fought over fish. Up and down the highway of the river Narraway saw strings of barges ride the tide, and on the land behind them men shouted at one another and the rumble of wheels jolted over the uneven cobbles.

He found Knox standing on the stone slipway where the fight had taken place, his jacket collar high round his ears, wind whipping his hair.

Fortunately, in this crime no one was dead, although there was still blood on the stones from a knife wound.

"I know you didn't want Hythe to be guilty," Knox remarked after he had greeted him. "Neither did I. Sometimes I don't understand people at all. I'd have sworn he hadn't it in him, but you can't argue with that letter." He pushed his hands into his coat pockets. "And don't tell me it isn't in her hand, because it is. First thing I did was have it checked by the experts who can spot a forgery. Although I don't know why anybody'd bother with that; it's not as if we had any other suspects."

Narraway felt crushed by the logic of it. "Then there's something about this case that we've missed," he said stubbornly, although he could think of nothing.

Knox looked at him with a frown, puzzled. "Haven't you ever found that an anarchist, who wanted to bring the whole social order down around our ears, was actually quite a

357

nice fellow if you met him down at the pub, my lord?"

"Yes, of course I have," Narraway said irritably. "But Hythe liked Catherine Quixwood, and he understood her a lot better than her husband did."

Knox hunched his shoulders and pulled his coat more tightly around him, as if he were cold, although the wind off the river was mild.

Water slopped noisily on the stones as the wash from a string of barges reached them.

"My lord, we both know what was done to Mrs. Quixwood. Think what you like about Hythe, but if he's the guilty party — and he is the one charged — there was no like nor understanding between him and Catherine Quixwood at the end."

Narraway said nothing. He stood in the sun by the water. The rising tide would wash away the bloodstains at his feet, but, remembering the injuries Dr. Brinsley had described, he thought nothing would ever rid his mind of the images they conjured, or the sick misery that filled him.

CHAPTER 13

Several days later, Charlotte was attending a luncheon at the very beautiful town house of her sister Emily, which she had inherited from her first marriage to Lord Ashworth. His early death had left her with a considerable fortune, and several very fine properties, held in trust for her son, who was heir to his father's title as well as the benefits that went with it.

Her very happy second marriage was to Jack Radley. Early in his career he had been a gentleman of fashion, and little else. Now he was a member of Parliament, and had grown into a position of considerable responsibility.

Half a dozen ladies were sitting in the large garden room, which was open onto the paved terrace and the sloping lawn with flowers beyond. It was as beautiful a place in which to dine as any in London, and they were taking full advantage of the very pleasant weather. Pastel silks and muslins fluttered in the fitful breeze. Parasols carefully placed kept the sun's harsher light from fairer skins.

"Everything seems to be in such turmoil," Marie Grosvenor said with a slight frown. "People are talking about all kinds of wealth, and loss. I have friends who are saying they'll end up with unimaginable money, and others who are terrified they'll be ruined. Some say Dr. Jameson's a true patriot, and others that he's an irresponsible madman. I really don't know what to believe."

Charlotte glanced at Emily and saw her attention quicken. The presumably harmless conversation had suddenly taken a darker turn with talk of financial ruin. Was she going to struggle against the tide, or go with it? It was her duty as hostess to govern the mood of the party, but it would require a very strong will to alter its course. Not that Emily was without such a will; it was more about her desire to use it when not doing so might prove far more entertaining.

"Will you attend the trial?" Arabella Scott asked, her fair eyebrows raised, interest sharp in her pale blue eyes. "I'm thinking of it myself. Poor Dr. Jameson. But heroes are often vilified, do you not think?" She looked from one to the other of them, her gaze finally resting on Charlotte.

Everyone else turned to look at her also, clearly thinking she had some special knowledge. They had heard, at the very least, that Pitt had been in the police. Of course it was not an occupation for a gentleman, but there was a certain gruesome fascination in it, all the same.

Charlotte was annoyed. She had to guard her tongue in so many things, she was compensating for it by being less conciliatory in others. Right now she was ready for battle. She looked at Arabella with a smile.

"Oh, yes, I agree with you," she replied, ignoring Emily's look of surprise. "We are very hard on heroes, exactly as you say. And often we praise the wrong people, not even realizing who has done what. We can accept the most superficial of explanations and attribute courage to people who are merely foolhardy, or even stupid and self-serving. Then we totally ignore those who set the good of others before their own profit. How wise you are to see it, and brave to point it out, if I may say so."

Arabella looked completely nonplussed. The last thing she had intended to be was brave, as Charlotte well knew.

Flora Jefferson blinked. "Maybe I am not

paying due attention, but I am not certain if you mean that Dr. Jameson is a hero, or that he is not," she said pointedly.

Emily drew in her breath, watching Charlotte.

"Neither am I," Charlotte said charmingly. "I hear one story, then I hear another. According to some people, Dr. Jameson led an army of patriots to save Mr. Rhodes's railway in the Pitsani Strip, which I believe borders on the Transvaal, which belongs to the Boers and, of course, is said to be riddled with gold and diamonds."

"He did it to protect the Uitlanders," Arabella explained with slightly condescending patience. "They are being thoroughly exploited by the Boers."

Flora and Sabine Munro nodded agreement.

Charlotte's smile became a little more fixed. She was not about to back down. "And then I hear that this army of about five hundred well-armed men actually crossed over into the Transvaal and marched on Johannesburg," she went on. "And were met by the Boers, whose city it is, and thoroughly thrashed." The moment she had said it, she wished she had used less emotive words, but it was too late.

"Heroes do not have to win in order to be

heroes," Arabella said with a flash of anger reddening her face.

"Of course not," Charlotte said quickly, before anyone else could attack or defend her. "It is hardly heroic to fight if you cannot lose. Any jackanapes can do that. It was unquestionably brave. The question I hear raised is as to whether it was wise or not. In fact, I suppose, as to whether it was right."

"Right?" Arabella said indignantly.

"Morally right," Charlotte elaborated patiently. "We invaded Boer land."

"For heaven's sake, do you want the Boers to rule South Africa?" Arabella asked, aghast at the idea.

"Not at all," Charlotte answered levelly. There was no backing out now. "But the fact that I want a thing does not automatically make it right — or wrong."

Marie Grosvenor now returned to the fray. "It is a matter of loyalty," she said stiffly. "Loyalty is always right." It was a statement and she expected no dissent.

"Is it?" Charlotte looked from one to the other of them, all sitting in gorgeous silks and delicate embroidered muslins in the dappled shade. "So if we are loyal to opposing sides, we can all be equally right?"

"Charlotte," Emily said quietly.

"We are all equally right, then," Charlotte

continued, ignoring her. "It is just that the Boers, being loyal to their own homes and fighting for their own lands, were better at it than we were, so they beat us?"

"We were fighting for the Queen and Empire," Arabella said stiffly. "Are you not British, that you don't understand that?"

"I am British." Charlotte kept her voice level. "But that doesn't mean I am always right."

"Indeed you are not!" Sabine agreed heatedly.

"If always being right is a quality intrinsic to being British, then none of us are British," Charlotte added. "Even Dr. Jameson. We can all make mistakes, especially when we are frightened . . . or when there is a great deal of money involved."

"It has nothing to do with money!" Sabine was openly angry now. "That is a dreadful thing to say."

"Of course it has to do with money," Flora put in. "Those who invested in this raid stand to lose a fortune, if the verdict goes against Dr. Jameson."

"So you think he's guilty?" Marie accused.

"I think he could be found guilty," Flora corrected. "That is not always the same thing. Has he ever denied he led the raid?"

"Of course not!" Arabella snapped. "He's

no coward!"

"I wonder how much of it is his money?" Emily said, and the instant afterward clearly regretted it. She scrambled to make amends. "I suppose he risked everything?"

There was a moment's silence while each one of them weighed what they thought, and what they judged wise to say.

"I don't know what will happen," Charlotte said thoughtfully. "Trials sometimes disclose evidence no one had foreseen, and make the verdict quite unexpected. I have heard that Mr. Churchill said the trial may lead to war. Is that not so?" She looked at Emily.

Emily shot her a look like daggers. "So I am told," she conceded grudgingly. "And Mr. Chamberlain of the Colonial Office is caught in a most embarrassing situation because he can neither deny knowledge of the raid nor admit to it."

"I daresay the British South Africa Company will have to pay a great deal of compensation to the Transvaal," Charlotte added, hoping she had her facts correct. "It will depend, of course, on who has staked fortunes in that." She had overheard this and did not really know for certain, but it seemed a reasonable thought.

Flora and Sabine looked at each other,

both now clearly anxious.

"A great deal?" Arabella said with an edge to her voice. "What do you mean by that?"

It occurred to Charlotte that the "great deal" to be made or lost in such ventures might include the fortunes of those in this quiet London garden. She had meant to discomfort their unthinking arrogance, not seriously frighten them.

"There is gold in the Transvaal, and diamonds," she replied. "Where there are fortunes to be made, there are fortunes to be lost as well. The raid failed. It was a big gamble, and we have no idea yet what the end may be. Perhaps you are right and, to take the chance with such high stakes, Dr. Jameson is a hero."

There were several moments of silence. No one was comfortable. The peace and satisfaction of the party had been shattered by a sudden and very chilling reality.

"There won't be war," Sabine said dismissively, waving her hand with its heavy emerald ring. "Mr. Churchill is talking nonsense, as usual. He will say anything to draw attention to himself. All kinds of people have invested in Africa. They won't allow a war to break out. If you knew a little more about real money, finance, and investment, you wouldn't even say such a thing."

Charlotte decided to let it go. "Perhaps not," she agreed. "And undeniably, Mr. Rhodes is usually very successful. No one needs to win every skirmish to win a war."

"It's not a war," Arabella said waspishly. "It was an attempt to —" She realized she was not sure what she meant and stopped abruptly. "Mr. Churchill is a buffoon," she finished, glaring at Charlotte.

At last Emily was stung to defend her own position. "I cannot allow you to say that unchallenged." She spoke quietly and with a smile, but there was a degree of steel in her voice. "He is not always right — I know of no one who is — but at times he is remarkably perceptive, and a voice of warning that should be heeded. The Jameson Raid was a fiasco, and Mr. Chamberlain has had to order Sir Hercules Robinson, the Governor-General of the Cape Colony, to repudiate it."

"He wouldn't have if it had succeeded," Marie pointed out.

"Of course not." Emily made a slight gesture of conciliation.

"If." Charlotte smiled also. "If wishes were horses, then beggars would ride. Unfortunately, they aren't. Perhaps that is what heroes are about, which is why one nation's heroes are another nation's enemies."

"Well, I am British, and I shall honor our heroes." Arabella fixed Charlotte with a glare. "You must choose whatever you will."

Charlotte kept her smile, although she felt it false. "I shall wait until I know more about it. At the moment I confess my ignorance."

"That is an excellent decision, all things considered," Arabella snapped.

In spite of herself, Charlotte laughed, which was the last thing Arabella expected. Her argument was derailed.

Emily stepped in quickly. "Perhaps we should attend the trial and at least become somewhat informed about the affair?" she suggested.

"Half of London will be there," Marie said, nodding her head.

"I daresay the other half will be at the other miserable trial," Flora remarked with a shudder. "I think I prefer not to know anything about that one. I should have nightmares."

"I'm sure you have no need," Marie said comfortingly. "You are in no danger whatever."

For a moment Charlotte was not certain what they were referring to.

"Another news item about which you know nothing?" Arabella inquired with a slight smirk, seeing Charlotte's blank expression. "Why, Catherine Quixwood was having an affair with a younger man, and he assaulted and then murdered her. All dreadfully sordid. No doubt they will hang him."

Charlotte felt her fury return like a tidal wave, all but taking her breath away. Any consideration of Emily's party was swept aside.

"No, I had no idea," she said with cloying sweetness. "But then, I do not interest myself very much in other people's more . . . intimate lives. As you so correctly say, it is all dreadfully sordid." She enunciated each word with distaste. "I merely know of Catherine Quixwood as a woman who had great charm. That was all I wished to know."

Flora stifled a giggle. Charlotte realized with sudden perception that she also disliked Arabella, but could not afford to let it be known. Now she remembered the sense of freedom she had felt at being no longer involved in Society, the loss of its glamour far outweighed by the opposing gain of autonomy.

Emily rushed into the thick silence to rescue what she could of her party.

"I feel so sorry for poor Rawdon Quixwood," she said, looking from one to the other of them, except Charlotte. "He must be suffering appallingly. I can't even imagine it."

"What a terrible thing," Marie agreed. "Is there anything more painful than total, devastating disillusion? Poor man. He must be distracted with grief."

"Disillusion?" Charlotte heard her voice become hard-edged with incredulity. "His wife was raped and beaten half to death, then in her unbearable pain she dosed herself too heavily with laudanum, and died of that. I should imagine *that* is the cause of his devastating grief. Not any disillusion."

"My dear Mrs. . . . Pitt?" Arabella hesitated as if she were not certain as to exactly who Charlotte might be. "Decent women do not get raped. Perhaps you did not read in the newspapers that she let the man in herself? I ask you, what respectable woman dismisses the servants for the night, then lets a younger man into the house and entertains him alone, while her husband is out?"

Charlotte raised her eyebrows. "Oh, was he younger? You clearly read different articles of the newspapers than I do. Or perhaps different newspapers altogether."

Arabella's face flared red. It was an insult she could not ignore. Ladies with the slightest pretension to gentility did not read

370

sensational papers. "It is common knowledge!" she snapped.

"Very common," Charlotte said under her breath. Only Flora, sitting closest to her, heard it. She affected a fit of sneezing to stifle her laughter. Sabine handed her a glass of water.

"Standards are slipping all over the place," Marie remarked, perhaps to fill the silence. "That poor Portuguese girl committed suicide as well. Heaven only knows why."

Sabine looked at her in surprise. "Well, everyone says she fell in love with Neville Forsbrook, and when he didn't want her, she completely lost her senses and threw herself out of the window. Far too highly strung, these younger girls. And to blame young Forsbrook is awful. His poor father; first he lost his wife, now this wretched scandal. Not that it's in the remotest way his fault, of course."

"Yes, his wife," Flora said. "She died —"

"She died in an accident," Emily interrupted.

"Nobody imagined she was having an affair," Arabella added. "It was a tragic accident in a coach."

"An ordinary hansom, I believe," Sabine corrected her. "Late at night. The road was wet and something made the horse bolt.

Poor cabby was killed as well. Dreadful."

"Such a terrible thing to happen," Charlotte said with as much sincerity as she could manage through her anger. She remembered Vespasia telling her of the tragedy. She hadn't known Eleanor Forsbrook, but she would not have wished her any harm. Her son's brutality would surely have caused her as much grief as it would any other woman. "Perhaps we should treasure our own safety with a little more gratitude."

"I don't know what you mean," Arabella said coldly.

Flora looked at her with a bright smile. "I do. You are perfectly right, Mrs. Pitt. We take our happiness and our safety far too much for granted. I am alive and well. It is a beautiful day and I am in a lovely garden, among friends. I shall enjoy it to its fullest." She looked at Charlotte, meeting her eyes directly. "Thank you for a most timely reminder. I'm so glad you came this afternoon."

There was another moment of startled silence, then Emily picked up a dish of tiny cakes and passed them round. She bit her lip to stop herself from smiling, and carefully looked away from Charlotte's eyes.

Pitt stood in his office facing Rafael Castelbranco. He had dreaded this moment since he had heard the date set for Alban Hythe's trial. The Portuguese ambassador was white-faced, except for the bruised shadows around his eyes and the hectic spots of color high on his cheeks. If Pitt had not known his story, he would have thought he was drunk.

"This man raped a married woman with whom he was having an affair. You arrested him and you are now bringing him to trial," Castelbranco said, his voice wavering, catching in his throat as if he could barely force the words out. "If he is found guilty, you will hang him, and her family will have at least a sense of justice. Yet you *know* who raped my child, and you can do nothing? Is this how your justice works?"

He made it sound absurd, outrageous, as if it were a deliberate action against him. He was trembling with the savagery of his emotions.

"Rafael," Pitt said gently, "I do not know who raped Angeles. I had believed it was Neville Forsbrook, but the husband of Catherine Quixwood, the married woman who was raped, says that he was in the company of young Forsbrook at the time we believe Angeles was attacked. Also, although I do not doubt that it did happen, we have no proof. In Mrs. Quixwood's case her beaten body was found on the floor of her own house. There was no place for doubt as to what happened, only as to who the man was."

Castelbranco gulped. "It was Forsbrook. Angeles told her mother so."

Pitt knew better than to argue. Castelbranco believed his daughter. He had to: every loyalty in him demanded it.

"If I could prove it, I would charge Forsbrook and bring him to trial," Pitt said with absolute honesty. "But if I charge him and can't bring it to trial, then public sympathy will be with him. If I can rake up enough evidence to try him, and fail to convict — which needs evidence beyond a reasonable doubt — then I will have made all the details public and given him the opportunity to say whatever he pleases about Angeles, blacken her reputation with whatever he wants to invent. No one can claim innocence or purity for every minute of his or her life — you and I both know that. And an accused man has the right to defend himself."

Castelbranco stared at him in horror, swaying a little on his feet.

"Rafael," Pitt continued, his voice even lower, "the jury will be composed entirely of men, as it is everywhere. Some of them may be fathers, some may not. Most of them will have seen women who were not their wives, whom they lusted after, particularly when they were young and unmarried. They will all, at times, have been tempted to behave badly, and I daresay most of them will have done so, to one degree or another. And most of them will have been accused of things they considered unfair, whether related to love affairs or not. Forsbrook would be there, sober and sad-faced, swearing to his innocence, very English, very gentlemanly. He will say that she was beautiful and he complimented her. She misunderstood, her English not being fluent."

Castelbranco blinked back tears.

Pitt forced the pictures of Angeles out of his mind, and then — with even more difficulty — made himself forget Jemima: her passionate face so like Charlotte's; the trust in her eyes when she looked at him, the father who had protected her all her life.

"Angeles will not be there to tell them what truly happened," he said. "All I can offer you is the promise that I will not forget it, and if I can ever prove Forsbrook's guilt without crucifying Angeles in the process, I will do it. But if I rush forward and try, and fail, then even if I had all the proof in the world afterward, I could not try him a second time. The law does not allow anyone to be tried twice for the same offense. And he will know that as well as I do. Let the threat, at least, remain over his head."

Castelbranco nodded very slightly. Too broken to speak, he turned and walked out of the door, leaving it open behind him, and Pitt alone in the room.

CHAPTER 14

It was a hot summer day at the Old Bailey, the central criminal court in London, when the trial of Alban Hythe, charged with the rape of Catherine Quixwood, began.

The gallery was crowded. Narraway was thankful for his influence — without it, he would not have been able to find a seat, except possibly at the very back. He had wanted to ask Vespasia if she would come. He would have valued her opinion, possibly even her advice. If he was honest with himself, most of all he would have liked her company. He knew this was going to be painful.

He had considered calling her; his hand had hovered over the telephone, and then he'd realized how often he had asked for her time recently, and never for any social or pleasurable reason, such as attending the opera or the theater. She had always been willing, even gracious about accepting, but

377

surely one day she would politely and gently refuse. She must have put up a warning hand to hundreds of men during her life, to tell them that they were asking too much, presuming on friendship a trifle too often.

Was he doing that?

He was not used to rejection, not when it actually mattered, and he realized with a shock like a stab of physical pain that it mattered. If she were to turn away from him it would hurt him in a way and with a depth that he had not experienced for years.

He had been attracted to women who had chosen someone else before. It happened to almost everyone. It had stung his vanity more than his heart. He had felt embarrassment, even self-doubt and despondency at times. But to be rebuffed by Vespasia, however softly or reluctantly, would wound him in a place he had considered invulnerable. He must not allow it to happen. The friendship was important enough to him that the loss of it was frightening.

So he sat alone near the front of the gallery as the proceedings began. The jury was called and sworn in, and the charge was read. Symington was willing to defend Hythe free of charge, simply for the interest and fame of the case. But clever, inventive, and individual as he was, Narraway was concerned. Not only the evidence but the mood of the court was overwhelmingly against Hythe.

Hythe stood in the dock, high above the well of the room. He looked so pale as to seem almost gray. He made no movements, no sounds, except to state his innocence in a voice so quiet that the judge had to ask him to repeat it.

Maris Hythe would be waiting outside, perhaps alone. She would not be permitted to hear the evidence, in case she might be called to testify. Could there be a more exquisite torture of the mind?

The charge did not include murder, only the brutal rape and beating. In his opening statement, Algernon Bower, Queen's Counsel for the prosecution, faced the jury and spoke with a soft but curiously penetrating voice. He was not a large man, barely of average height, but he had a presense that could not be ignored. His face was powerful, with a dominant nose and keen eyes. He had a high forehead where, Narraway knew, his dark, straight hair was beginning to thin; although today, of course, Bower wore the lawyer's costume of a white wig.

"We will prove to you, gentlemen," he said levelly, removing almost all emotion from his tone, "that the accused man was having a love affair with the dead woman, Catherine Quixwood, and that he visited her late on the evening of her death. She herself was the one who let him into her home. No servants saw him, but that is because she wanted it so. She herself had dismissed them."

The jurors stared at him, somber and unhappy. There was a distinct rustle of movement in the gallery.

Next to Narraway, a large man pursed his lips in disapproval. His thoughts were almost as clear on his face as if he had spoken them aloud.

"We may never know exactly what happened," Bower continued. He looked at the jurors as an actor regards his audience, weighing them. "But we will prove beyond any doubt at all that there was a terrible quarrel, which became physically violent. You may surmise the cause of it to be that Mrs. Quixwood had grown tired of Mr. Hythe's attentions, or even that her conscience had at last asserted itself and she had decided to think again of her loyalty to her husband." He held up a hand, although Symington, in his seat on the other side of the aisle, had made no move to interrupt him.

"We will prove to you, through medical

and other evidence," Bower went on, "that this quarrel ended in the most brutal rape and beating of Mrs. Quixwood, leaving her broken and bleeding on the floor. Later she crept on her hands and knees over to the sideboard, where she poured an overdose of laudanum into her glass of Madeira wine and thus took her own life."

There were head-shakes in the jury box. A woman in the gallery let out a cry of horror.

Narraway winced. Despite the heat in the room, he was cold, as if despair were settling inside him and filling his body. It was as well he had not asked Vespasia to be here, even had she been willing to come. This was, in a sense, the beginning of a public execution. She could be spared that.

Bower finished and Symington stood up. His face looked as it had in his office when Narraway had engaged him on the case: smooth, handsome, younger than he actually was. The light caught his pale wig, which concealed almost all his hair, but there was no sign whatever of his quick, wide smile or the totally irresponsible sense of humor that was ordinarily characteristic of him. Watching him now, Narraway had no idea if Symington had a plan, much less a believable idea how to defend Alban

Hythe. Narraway himself certainly had none.

Symington stood in front of the jury. He smiled at them charmingly, but the warmth was without lightness. One of them frowned at him, looking as if he disapproved that anyone should attempt to excuse Hythe. Two smiled back, maybe sorry for him because in their eyes he was already beaten.

"A dreadful crime." Symington's smile vanished and it was as if the sun had gone down, changing him entirely. "I'm sorry that you will have to listen while the police surgeon tells you, probably in detail, how poor Mrs. Quixwood was raped and beaten, almost to death." He shook his head fractionally. "It will be a terrible experience for you. I have had to go through the details as part of my duty, and I admit it turned my stomach and all but made me weep in pity for her."

Bower fidgeted. He neither liked nor trusted Symington, and as much was clear in his face.

Symington was still facing the jurors. "And just as powerful as grief, it frightened me, because it could happen to any woman, to those I love." He lowered his gaze and met theirs individually. "And to those you love — your wives, your daughters. Cather-

382

ine Quixwood was a respectable, married woman, behind locked doors in her own house on the evening of the crime. Who could be safer?"

He hesitated.

The jurors were clearly uncomfortable. Many of them looked away.

Symington spread his hands. "It would be much more comfortable if it were in some way her fault. If she brought this upon herself, then we are all right, because we won't do the things she did, will we?"

Suddenly his voice became stronger, darker in tone and yet also more intimate. "But we are not here to think of ourselves, or even to thank God for our own comfort and safety. We are here to learn the truth about the tragedy and horror of other people's lives — to look at them honestly, to rise above our own fears and prejudices, should we have them. We all feel terror, not just of violence, but of loss, of disgrace, of public humiliation, of the impulse to lie rather than be stripped in front of the world."

He shrugged very slightly, and the smile lit his face again. "But we are chosen by our fellows, by fate, if you like, to be fair, to be honorable above our everyday selves and to set our natural proclivity toward self-protection aside. I ask you to be merciful to the quirks and the weaknesses that we all have, and to be relentlessly just to the facts."

The jurors looked puzzled. One middle-aged man blushed hotly.

"I will show you how else this terrible thing could have happened," Symington said finally. "And why Alban Hythe had no part in it at all. I will convince you of this until in good conscience you cannot return a verdict of guilty. You cannot see him hang." He smiled again, warmly, as if he liked them, and turned away, walking quite casually back to his place.

Narraway wondered how much of that was bluff. Watching him, listening, he could see no doubt in Symington at all.

Bower called his first witness: a very nervous man in a plain, dark suit that did not fit him comfortably. Narraway recognized him only when he told the court that his occupation was as butler to Rawdon Quixwood.

"I'm sorry, Mr. Luckett," Bower started, as he walked over toward the high witness box, which was something like the prow of a ship, or a tower several feet above the floor of the courtroom, "but I must ask you to turn your mind back to the evening of May the 23rd. Mr. Quixwood was in the city at a function, I believe, at the Spanish Embassy, and Mrs. Quixwood had allowed all the servants to retire early, leaving her alone in the withdrawing room. Is that correct?"

Luckett was clearly distressed and having some difficulty composing himself. The judge looked at Symington to see if he objected to Bower putting so many words into the witness's mouth, but Symington remained seated in his place, smiling and silent.

"Mr. Luckett . . ." the judge prompted.

"Yes . . ." Luckett said jerkily. "Yes, she often allowed us to retire if she knew she would need nothing." He gulped. "She was very considerate."

"She did not even retain a footman to answer the door?" Bower said with surprise.

"No, sir," Luckett replied, shifting his weight from one foot to the other.

"Did you yourself go to bed, Mr. Luckett?"

"No, sir. I went for a walk. I know some of the younger servants, girls, went to the servants' quarters before I left, and the housekeeper was sitting up with a pot of tea. The cook was doing something in the kitchen, I believe." He was twisting his hands. He knew, as did the rest of the court, what was coming next.

In the gallery no one moved.

"Did Mrs. Quixwood send for you?" Bower asked.

"No . . . no, sir."

"But you did return to the front of the house? What time would that have been?"

"I . . . can't say, sir. I didn't look at the clock. It was late."

"Why did you go back after Mrs. Quixwood had expressly dismissed you?"

"I returned from my walk and saw the lights still on, sir. It was a lot later than Mrs. Quixwood usually retired. I thought she must have forgotten to turn them down. And . . . and I wished to check the front door a last time."

"Would you tell us what you found, Mr. Luckett?" Bower looked grave. He was an excellent prosecutor. It flickered through Narraway's mind that he would also have been a good undertaker. He had an expression made for disaster.

Luckett gulped. "I — I went into the vestibule and I saw . . . I saw Mrs. Quixwood lying on the floor. For an instant I thought she had slipped and fallen, perhaps fainted." He was not looking at Bower but at some terrible memory within himself. "She was sort of . . . sprawled out, on her side. There . . . her . . . her clothes were torn and there was blood on the floor. I bent to touch her and I could see that she was . . . dead."

"What did you do then, Mr. Luckett?" Bower said gently.

"I — I sent the footman for the police. Then I went back into the housekeeper's room and informed her of what I had found."

"Thank you, Mr. Luckett," Bower said gravely. "Did you let anyone into the house that evening, before Mrs. Quixwood's death? Did you hear the doorbell ring, or were you made aware in any way of anyone entering the premises?"

Luckett stared at him with the same expression of revulsion he might have worn had he discovered a caterpillar in his dinner.

"No, sir, I did not."

Bower raised his eyebrows. "Then how did any visitor gain entrance?"

"I don't know, sir."

"But you locked the door before leaving for your walk?" Bower would not allow him to evade the issue.

"Yes, sir."

"So who unlocked the door and let in whoever attacked Mrs. Quixwood?"

Luckett said nothing.

"You did place the bolts in their sockets, did you not?" Bower insisted.

"Yes, sir. Mr. Quixwood expected to be very late from his function. When that happens he stays at his club." Luckett looked as if he were having teeth drawn.

"Just so," Bower agreed. "So who let in the man who raped Mrs. Quixwood and beat her?"

"I don't know, sir."

"Must she not have let him in herself?" Bower demanded.

"It would seem so," Luckett said very quietly.

"Thank you." Bower turned to Symington.

Symington rose to his feet. He smiled up at Luckett.

"It does seem rather as if she let him in herself, doesn't it?" he said ruefully. "But my learned friend has run the whole question into one. Let me rephrase it. Did Mrs. Quixwood ring for anyone to open the door? Or was there anyone else in the house who could have answered the door and let someone in, for whatever purpose?"

"No, sir." Luckett regarded him warily.

"So Mrs. Quixwood opened the door. Is there any way to know whom she expected to be on the other side? A friend? Someone in trouble needing her counsel or help, perhaps? Even Mr. Quixwood, returning from his function earlier than he had expected? Or someone with an urgent message?"

"Yes, sir. It could have been any of those," Luckett agreed with relief.

"Had Mr. Quixwood ever mislaid his key?"

"He did not carry a key, sir. It was his house. He would expect one of us to answer the door. But, like I said, he had intended to spend the night at his club."

"Quite my point." Symington smiled dazzlingly. "You have been butler to the household for several years, and a footman before that, I believe? You must have known Mrs. Quixwood since her marriage?"

"Yes, sir." There was warmth in Luckett's face, swiftly followed by grief.

"My learned friend said she must have let in the man who attacked her so terribly. Do you suppose she imagined he was there for that purpose?"

"Of course not!" Luckett was astonished.

"My thought exactly," Symington agreed. "She let him in believing him to be harmless, even a friend. Thank you, Mr. Luckett."

The judge looked at Bower, who declined

to pursue the subject and instead called Inspector Knox.

Narraway realized he was sitting with his shoulders so tense his neck ached. At least Symington was putting up a fight. But he had been given no ammunition. Every avenue Narraway had followed regarding Catherine's inquiries for financial advice had proved useless. She had inherited no money of her own, and Quixwood himself kept his affairs from her. They were complicated and extremely successful, as was to be expected with his profession.

Knox was sworn in and Bower began immediately asking him about the message he had received, and his arrival at the Quixwood house. Knox described what he had seen, being as brief as he could about the details. Apart from the fact that his voice trembled, he might have been speaking of a burglary, not what at that point had seemed to be a particularly dreadful murder.

"After you had sent for the police surgeon, what did you do then, Inspector Knox?" Bower asked.

"I sent my men to see if they could find how the attacker had gained entry, sir," Knox replied. "We found nothing out of order at that time, and in the daylight the following morning we ascertained that that was indeed the case. He must have been let in through the front door."

"And did you ever find evidence to contradict that?"

"No, sir."

"But you looked?" Bower insisted.

"Yes, sir."

"I shall call the police surgeon to give his own evidence," Bower warned him. "But from the information he gave you, what did you conclude had happened to cause Mrs. Quixwood's death?"

Symington rose to his feet. "My lord, Mr. Bower has asked the witness a question, and at the same time directed him not to answer it. How can the poor man know what to say?" He looked apologetic, and slightly amused.

"Perhaps you should rephrase your question, Mr. Bower," the judge suggested. "Or else have the police surgeon testify now, and recall Inspector Knox after you have established how Mrs. Quixwood met her death."

There was a rustle of interest in the gallery. Two of the jurors nodded. But it was light without substance, and Narraway knew it. It would make no difference in the end.

Without any outward loss of composure Bower said he would release Knox, and he sent for Dr. Brinsley.

Narraway half listened as Brinsley described the appalling injuries sustained by Catherine Quixwood. He used no emotive adjectives, and somehow his calm voice and bleak, sad face made the brutality of it even more horrific. The packed court could not but be reminded of the intimate and intense vulnerability of all of them.

Narraway had heard it before, but it still appalled him. He had seen her body lying on the floor, but he had not then imagined the fearful damage done to her. Only when Knox and Brinsley had described it to him had it become real.

The court listened in silence. There was no sound in the gallery, no whisper or rustle of movement, only the occasional gasp. A little farther along the row Narraway saw a woman reach out and take hold of her husband's hand, and his fingers close over hers tightly.

What could have possessed any man to do such things? Surely only gut-wrenching fear or insane hatred drove this kind of depravity?

Why had he gone there, whoever he was — Hythe or anyone else? If she had intended to break off an affair, why had she let him into the house without a servant within call? Had the man in question never lost his temper before, never shown any inclination toward violence? Was that possible? Had she never had any other bruises, cuts, abrasions, from him before — nothing to show his nature?

Narraway fished in his pocket and found a pencil and paper. Hastily he wrote a note to Symington, then gave it to the usher to pass it to him.

"And what was the ultimate cause of Mrs. Quixwood's death, Dr. Brinsley?" Bower asked after the doctor had finished.

"Her wounds were severe," Brinsley replied. "But she actually died of an overdose of laudanum, taken in Madeira wine."

"Self-administered?" Bower asked.

"No idea," Brinsley said tartly.

"Could it have been just a little more than the usual medicinal dose?" Bower persisted.

"It was several times the usual medicinal dose," Brinsley answered him. "No one could take that much by accident."

"You are saying it was suicide," Bower stated.

Brinsley leaned forward over the railing of the witness stand, his face flushed. "I am saying it was approximately four times the usual medicinal dose, Mr. Bower. She appears to have drunk it voluntarily, but whether she put the laudanum in the wine herself, or it was added by someone else, I have no idea, and — so far as I know — neither do you."

Bower's eyes flashed with temper but he did not retreat. "Is it possible that, out of shame at her betrayal of her husband, and the pain and humiliation of being raped by her lover — which inevitably her husband would come to know of — she deliberately took her own life?"

Brinsley glared at him. "I am not going to speculate, sir. I am a doctor, not a clairvoyant."

"Have you known of women who have been raped who have taken their own lives?" Bower said between his teeth.

"Of course. People take their own lives for all sorts of reasons, and frequently we do not ever fully understand them," Brinsley answered.

"Thank you, Doctor," Bower responded with exaggerated patience. "Your witness, Mr. Symington."

Symington rose and strolled over to the witness stand. He looked up at Brinsley and smiled.

"You must see many tragic and distressing cases, Dr. Brinsley."

"I do," Brinsley agreed.

"You have described poor Mrs. Quixwood's wounds in some detail for Mr. Bower. I won't ask you to go over them again. I think all of us are distressed enough. Just tell me one thing about them, if you please. Were they all sustained during that one awful attack?"

Bower stood up slowly. "Is my learned friend suggesting some other attack took place that same evening, my lord? That is preposterous! There are no grounds whatsoever for such a suggestion. And even if there had been such a . . . a mythical attack, how would Dr. Brinsley differentiate one wound from another?"

Symington looked at Bower as if he had taken leave of his wits.

"Good gracious," he said incredulously. "Such a thing never occurred to me. She would hardly have let a second attacker into the house after sustaining one attack. What on earth are you saying?"

"It was your suggestion, sir!" Bower all but spat the words.

"Not at all," Symington shook his head. "I was thinking that if her lover was prone to violence, then there might have been old bruises, half-healed scars, abrasions, from earlier quarrels. A deep bruise can take some time to disappear altogether."

"I saw no older injuries at all," Brinsley

replied, but now his face was keen with a spark of interest.

"Then would it be reasonable to assume, from the evidence, of course, that the attack was sudden, and would have been completely unexpected?" Symington pushed his hands into his pockets and leaned back a little to look up at the doctor on the stand.

"It would indeed," Brinsley agreed. "In fact, if the same man had ever shown any violence toward her, I imagine she would've been very careful not to let him in without male servants well within earshot. We can't say for certain, but I think it is safe to assume that it was unexpected."

"Then one may also assume that she was not afraid of him?" Symington waved his hands in denial. "Oh, I'm sorry. That was simply my own thought. Foolish of me. Of course she was not afraid of him, or she would not have let him in. Thank you, Dr. Brinsley."

Bower half stood, then changed his mind and sat again, his face hard-edged and angry.

The court adjourned for luncheon. Narraway glanced up at the dock and saw Alban Hythe rise to his feet, looking back at the court only once before the jailers led him away. His face was white, terrified, and despairing, searching for even one person who believed in him.

Was Narraway such a person? He thought he was, but even still, he was glad Hythe had not met his eyes, or recognized him, because he was not certain what his own eyes would've revealed. The only thing he was sure of beyond any doubt at all was that he had no idea how to help him.

In the evening Narraway sat alone in his study and weighed in his mind everything he knew or believed about Catherine Quixwood and Alban Hythe. He had read Catherine's social diary. Was it really credible, as Hythe claimed, that she had been seeing him in order to learn more about major investments her husband might have made.

Did she actually know or understand enough of Quixwood's finances to fear that he would lose badly? There was no hint of economic study or skill in what Narraway had learned of her. Her education was what would be expected of a young woman of her social class. She was well read in literature, spoke a little French, knew English history, and had the usual familiarity with the classics. She had added greatly to the last of these in her own private reading and attendance at various lectures. As far as he could see, none of them had concerned economics or investment strategy.

Her own private spending involved supervision of the kitchen expenses, and a dress allowance, which she had never exceeded. Quixwood himself saw to all other bills, and he was more than comfortably situated.

Was Hythe telling the truth, or building an elaborate, and frankly rather ridiculous, excuse for having met Catherine so frequently, where they could speak without being watched or overheard? If he offered that to Symington, without highly credible evidence, no jury would believe it.

What would such evidence be? Was it all paper investment, or real? Was it conceivable that the figures in Catherine's diary were not telephone numbers but amounts of money? Thousands of pounds? Had Quixwood sunk a lot of his fortune in something Catherine had feared was morally or ethically questionable? Or in something she feared to be against British interests? In the Transvaal? Or in diamonds or gold specifically? In some venture with Cecil Rhodes? In the Pitsani Strip, in railways, in building? If Catherine was worried, why on earth look for vague information from Alban Hythe? Why not simply tell Quixwood that she was afraid, and ask him for assurance that he was not taking risks with their safety?

Was there any point in learning as much as he could about some dubious investment Quixwood might have considered, this late in the game? And what could any of it have to do with the rape?

The answer was almost certainly, nothing at all.

He went to bed tired and discouraged, and slept badly.

CHAPTER 15

On the morning of the second day of Alban Hythe's trial, Knox sent a message to Pitt to meet him at the home of a Mr. Frederick Townley, on Hunter Street, just off Brunswick Square. The footman had instructions to admit him as soon as he arrived.

It was a damp, hazy day, already warm at half-past nine, with a very fine drizzle falling. As Knox had been promised, a grim-faced footman opened the door so immediately after Pitt's pulling of the bell that he had to have been waiting for him. He was shown into the morning room, where Knox and a very clearly distressed Frederick Townley were waiting.

Knox introduced Pitt with his full title.

Townley was gaunt, middle-aged, with dark hair receding at the brow. At the moment he was restless, fidgeting, and unable to control his nerves.

"I've told you, Mr. Knox, I was in error,"

he said urgently, looking at Knox, then at Pitt, then back again. "I do not wish to make any such complaint. You may say anything you please. I withdraw the complaint. I have no idea in the world why you should think to involve Special Branch. It is completely absurd." He turned to Pitt. "I apologize to you, sir. This is just a domestic matter. In fact, it is no more than a misunderstanding."

Pitt looked at the man's face and saw fear and grief, which at this moment were overridden by acute embarrassment.

"I'm sorry." Townley regarded Pitt with discomfort. "You have been disturbed unnecessarily. Now I must return to my family. I would like to hope you understand, but at this point it really makes no difference to me. Good day to you, gentlemen."

"Mr. Townley!" Knox said with asperity. "I may not have the authority to require a statement from you, if you choose to let this matter go unreported, but Commander Pitt cannot ignore it if the safety of the realm is in question."

Townley's jaw dropped in disbelief. "Don't be absurd, man! How can my daughter's . . . misfortune possibly concern the safety of the realm? I don't know what it is you want, but I am laying no complaint whatever. You have wasted this gentleman's time." He gestured toward Pitt. "Please excuse me." Again he moved toward the door, lurching a little and regaining his balance with a hand on the jamb. "My footman will be happy to see you out," he added, as if he thought his meaning might have been unclear.

"If you do not speak the truth, Mr. Townley, whether in the form of a complaint or not, then an innocent man may hang," Knox said peremptorily.

Townley swung around and glared at him. "Not because of anything I have said, sir!"

"Because of what you know, and have not said," Knox retorted. "Silence can lead to damnation as much as speech, and still cost a man his life."

"Or a woman her reputation!" Townley snapped back. "I look after my own, sir, as does any decent man."

"Have you a son also, Mr. Townley?" Pitt said suddenly.

Townley stared at him with disbelief. "And what is that to you, sir? None of this . . . this supposed affair has anything to do with him."

"I have a son and a daughter also," Pitt told him. "They are children still, but my daughter is fast turning into a woman. It seems to me that she grows more and more like her mother with every few months that pass."

Townley tried to interrupt him, but Pitt overrode him.

"Because of an incident involving someone she knew, my daughter has asked me, and her mother, very urgent and awkward questions about rape. She wishes to know what it is, and why people are so terribly upset about it. We have tried to answer her both delicately and honestly, bearing in mind that she is only fourteen."

"I wish you well, sir," Townley said, succeeding in interrupting this time. His face was gray-white and he seemed to have trouble forming his words coherently. "But that is of no concern to me."

"And I look at my son," Pitt went on, disregarding the interruption. "He is nearly twelve, and has no idea what we are talking about. How do I explain it all to him, so that his behavior toward women is never coarse or, worse still, violent? But perhaps more terrible than that, how do I protect him from being accused of something he did not do? What father, what mother, would see their son at the end of the hangman's rope, jeered at by the crowd, insulted, and abused, for a hideous crime of which he was innocent, but could not prove himself so?"

Townley was trembling where he stood, his fists clenching and unclenching. "Then you will understand, sir, why I make no complaint. You have answered your own question." He took a shaky step closer to the hallway and his escape.

"Mr. Townley!" Pitt said as if it were a command.

"You have my answer," Townley said between his teeth.

"I am not asking that you lay a complaint," Pitt said, quietly now. "Only that, man to man, you tell me the truth. You can deny it afterward. I will not ask you to sign anything, or to swear anything. I need to know, because the daughter of a foreign ambassador was also a victim recently. That is why Special Branch has become involved."

Townley hesitated. "I will not testify!" he said, his voice a little shrill.

"I'm not sure that I would if it were my daughter," Pitt admitted. "I'd do what I thought was best for her."

"I will not allow you to speak to her," Townley warned. "Even if I was so inclined, her mother would not. Seeing the doctor . . . was bad enough."

Pitt drew in his breath to say he understood, but realized he had no idea. Instead he simply asked what she'd told them had happened.

Townley closed his eyes and said in a flat hesitant voice, "Alice is nearly seventeen. She was at a ball in the house of a friend. I will not tell you her family's name. There were naturally young gentlemen present also. She enjoys dancing and is particularly skilled. She was flattered when a young man in his early twenties asked her to dance, imagining he thought her older, more sophisticated, which she has a great desire to be. To . . . to get to the point . . ." He gulped. "He spoke pleasantly to her, inviting her to see one of the galleries in the house where there were some remarkable paintings. Alice likes . . . art. She suspected nothing and went with him."

Pitt felt himself clenching inside.

"He took her first to one gallery with some art as lovely as he had said it would be," Townley continued. "Then promised more works, even better, but said they were in another part of the house . . . a private part where they should not trespass, but he said they would touch nothing, merely look at the paintings."

Pitt almost said it for him, to break the unbearable tension, and to save the man from having to say it himself. Then Knox moved a fraction, no more than shifting his weight from one foot to the other, but reminding Pitt of his presence. Pitt let out his breath without speaking.

"He . . . violated her," Townley said hoarsely. "She had not the power to fight him off. He left her bleeding and bruised on the floor. She had hit her head, and was knocked senseless for a while. When she came to she climbed to her feet, and was staggering to the door when a different young man met her. He assumed that she had taken too much wine, and rather than tell him the truth, that she . . . had lost her virginity, she said it was true, she was inebriated, and she accounted for her bruises and the blood by saying she had fallen down some steps. That was the story she gave her hostess too, and no one pressed her further." Townley's chin lifted and he glared at Pitt, then at Knox. "And that is the story I shall tell if I am pressed. I will swear to it under oath."

"Did she say who the young man was who assaulted her?" Pitt asked.

"It will do you no good," Townley said bluntly.

"Possibly not, but I wish to know," Pitt insisted. "It would be very much better if she tells me than if I have to investigate all the balls in London last night to find out who attended which. People will inevitably ask why I need to know."

"You are a brutal man," Townley said icily, but his eyes filled with tears.

Pitt was silent for a moment. Would it really help to know? Yes, it would. Not just for Rafael Castelbranco, but for all other young women. He needed to get Neville Forsbrook off the streets — if he could just be certain it was he.

"Please?" he said.

Wordlessly, Townley led them upstairs and across a wide landing, to a door with a porcelain floral handle. Townley knocked, and when his wife answered, he told her that this was unavoidable. At his insistence, she allowed Pitt inside, but not Knox.

The girl propped up in the bed was white-faced, except for the tearstains on her cheeks, and the pink on the rims of her eyes. Her long honey-brown hair was loose around her shoulders. Her features were soft, but in a year or two would also reflect a considerable strength.

Pitt's step faltered as he walked across the carpet and stood near the bed, but not too close.

"My name is Thomas Pitt," he said quietly.

"I have a daughter who will be your age soon. She looks quite a lot like you. I hope she will be as lovely. I understand you like paintings?"

She nodded.

"Yesterday evening you were shown some particularly beautiful ones, is that correct?"

Again she nodded.

"Were they portraits or landscapes?"

"They were mostly portraits, and some animals, very out of proportion." She almost smiled. "Horses whose legs looked so thin I don't know how they could stand on them."

Pitt shook his head. "I've seen some like that. I don't like them very much. I like to see horses with movement in the lines rather than standing still. Who showed you these pictures?"

"He wasn't going to steal them," she said quickly. "At least I don't think. He has lots of money anyway . . . or his father does. He could just buy them."

"Maybe he was thinking of offering to buy them," Pitt said kindly, then, just as soft, "Who was he?"

"Do . . . do I have to tell you?"

"No, not if you really don't want to." The minute the words were out, he regretted them. Narraway wouldn't have been so weak.

"It was Neville Forsbrook," she whispered.

He let his breath out in a sigh. "Thank you, Alice. I appreciate knowing. And thank you for letting me visit with you."

"It's all right." She gave him a tiny, uncertain smile.

He thanked Mrs. Townley as well and walked onto the landing, Townley at his heels. The door closed behind them with a faint click.

Townley stood on the landing by the window, surrounded by vases of carefully arranged flowers. His face was ravaged with fear and grief.

"Thank you," he echoed. "Now that is the end of it."

Pitt nodded and followed Knox down the stairs.

Alice Townley's face haunted Pitt as he walked away from the house. It was as if he had met a ghost of Angeles Castelbranco, and what troubled him like an open wound was the fact that in his own mind he was certain that there would be other girls in the future, perhaps not lucky enough to escape with their lives. Perhaps Pamela O'Keefe had been one of them? They would probably never know.

He could not blame Townley for wanting

to protect his daughter. Had it been Jemima, Pitt doubted he would try to prosecute. In fact, if he were honest, he knew he would not. Whatever Forsbrook went on to do, one protected one's own child first.

Alice Townley had been violated, but not seriously injured, certainly not beaten as Catherine had been. Pamela O'Keefe had been murdered, her neck broken. Why the difference? What injuries had Angeles Castelbranco sustained?

Were there two different men, then? One Neville Forsbrook, the other — Alban Hythe? Perhaps — perhaps not.

Had Pamela O'Keefe's death been an accident? Had Forsbrook forced himself on her, and in the violence of her struggle snapped her neck? Was he terrified, then? Or exhilarated?

Was the difference in his perception of the woman, or in the way they reacted to him? Did he need their fear to excite him?

Pitt knew he must check on the degree of violence, the bruises of self-defense, and note all the differences and the similarities.

It was not difficult to find Brinsley; he was in the police morgue performing a post-mortem on another body, a man stabbed in a bar-room fight. Pitt waited half an hour until he was finished. He came out of the autopsy room cold, his hands still wet. He carried a faint odor of carbolic with him.

"Commander Pitt, Special Branch," Pitt introduced himself.

"What can I do for you, Commander?" Brinsley asked. "Tea? I'm tired and I'm cold and I've still a long evening ahead of me."

"Thank you," Pitt accepted. "I'm looking into several rapes, to see if I can compare them to one that concerns me particularly. I need to know if they're related."

Brinsley reached his office and put a kettle onto a small burner. It was only moments before it boiled and he made tea for them both in a round-bellied china pot.

"Look for similarities," Brinsley said with a shrug. "I assume you have no testimony, no description?"

"I have some, but if it is accurate, the man seems to be far more violent with some women than with the others."

"Interesting," Brinsley said thoughtfully. "Usually they escalate with time. Are you certain it's all one man?"

"No, I'm not. Can you describe the injuries to Catherine Quixwood?"

"They were very grave, but not fatal," Brinsley replied. "She was deeply bruised on her body, upper arms, more so still upon her thighs, and there was tearing of her genital organs by forceful penetration." His mouth twisted in a grimace. "There was also a fairly deep bite on her left breast. The man's teeth had torn the skin and left distinct bruise marks, which became more pronounced after her death."

"Thank you," Pitt said quietly. "Was there anything about these injuries that would be distinct to the man who inflicted them?"

"If it was the same man, I'd say he was more deeply sunk in his state of . . . depravity . . . with Catherine. I can't imagine any victim beaten more terribly than she was."

"But that crime happened first," Pitt said unhappily.

"Then it seems you have at least two rapists." Brinsley shook his head. "I'm sorry."

"Thank you anyway." Pitt turned to leave, his tea only half-drunk. His throat felt too tight to swallow.

Brinsley took a breath.

Pitt turned back. "Yes?"

"Was there anything particularly different about the victims? Or about the places of attack, or the circumstances?"

"Would that account for it being two men?"

"I don't know. It's possible." There was no lift in Brinsley's voice, no brightness in his face. "But you should look."

"Thank you," Pitt said again.

He did not tell Charlotte what Brinsley had said when they sat alone in the parlor late into the evening. There was no need for her to hear the details Brinsley had told him. He could spare her that much. She sat in one of the big armchairs. Pitt was too restless to sit, and too angry. The sense of helplessness burned inside him like acid, eating away at his belief in himself.

"He'll go on," he said bitterly, staring out at the familiar garden. This was where his children had grown up. They had played here with hoops, a skipping rope, had built castles with piles of colored bricks, ridden imaginary horses, used as make-believe swords the garden canes that now held up the delphiniums in bloom.

What good was he if he could not protect Jemima from such hideous violation of all her future promise? Or Daniel from turning into a monster? Would they ask of him one day, "Papa, why did you let it happen?" Charlotte wouldn't accuse him, but it would be in her mind, it would have to be. Try as she wished, she would never again see him as the man she trusted always, the man he wanted to be.

And what was he doing? Advising Townley and Castelbranco to do nothing, admitting that the law, his law, was helpless to
protect them or to find any justice. The legal
system too would look the other way and
pretend nothing had happened: timid,
circumspect, afraid of making a fuss.

Neville Forsbrook, and anyone else like
him, would go on without someone standing in their way or calling them to account.
He reached to pull the curtain closed and it
stuck. He yanked it harder and it tore.

"Thomas . . ." Charlotte began.

"Don't tell me to sit down!" he shouted,
yanking harder at the curtain and pulling
the whole thing down off the wall to lie in a
heap.

"I wasn't going to," she replied, standing
up herself and walking over to join him at
the glass, completely ignoring the pile of
velvet on the floor. "You are sure Forsbrook
will go on and rape other people?"

"Yes. I'd stop him if I could, Charlotte!"
He felt his hands clench. He was behaving
like a fool and he knew it. It was not her
fault, but every word seemed like criticism,
because he blamed himself. It was his
responsibility to do better than this.

She took a deep breath and held it a moment or two. She was controlling her own

temper, and he was sharply aware of it. There was no point in apologizing because he knew he would do it again, probably within moments.

"I was going to say . . ." She was choosing her words carefully, still ignoring the curtain. "I was going to say that if this pattern of violence stretches into the future, how do we know that it does not also stretch into the past?"

"I imagine it does," he said slowly.

"Then might there not be something there that you could find, and prosecute, without mentioning Angeles, or this new poor girl?" she asked. "Perhaps it was something less serious, but still enough to bring a charge?"

He let the idea take form slowly, testing every step of it. "Anyone who did not accuse him then would be unlikely to do so now," he pointed out. "The disgrace would be the same, and the proof even harder to find."

"But if you know the pattern of the past, then you can predict the future more accurately, maybe even prevent him next time he tries?" She would not give up. "One woman alone can't do anything to him, but several might be able to. Or at least the fathers of several, if they know they are not alone."

He turned to look at her. In the evening light the tiny lines of her face were invisible. To him she was more beautiful at forty than she had been in her twenties, though the softness of youth was gone. She still looked at life bravely and honestly with her steady eyes, but was better able to deal with it in a measured way.

"And do what?" he asked quietly, but he was not dismissing it. "It still may not be possible; Pelham Forsbrook will defend Neville to the very last ditch. It is not only his son's reputation on the line, but his own."

"The victims won't accuse him because to do so would ruin them socially for the rest of their lives," she began.

He almost interrupted her, but bit back the words.

"Surely the accusation from many people, all prepared to stand together, whether it was proven in a court of law or not, would also ruin him?" she asked. "Reputation doesn't require legal proof. If it did there'd be thousands of people still in Society who are not here now, because ill is believed of them, although never more than whispers. They do not fight because there is nothing said plainly enough for slander."

He blinked. "You mean we should spread

416

a rumor?"

"No!" Now she was angry too. "You don't need to do it! Just prove you could, so Pelham Forsbrook knows it is true, and that you mean to stop his son because he has to be stopped."

He turned it over in his mind, carefully, uncertain.

"Thomas?" She put her hand on his arm. He felt the strength of her fingers as well as the warmth.

He waited.

"How would you feel if it were not Alice Townley, but Jemima?"

"The same as Townley, exactly," he answered. "I would see Neville in hell, if I could, but more than anything else I would want to protect my daughter."

"And if it were me, instead of Catherine Quixwood?"

He felt cold to the bone. "I would want to kill him," he said honestly. "I might even do it."

"So isn't this worth at least trying?" She smiled very slightly, pleased at his anger, as if it were a shield for her, at least in her mind.

"Perhaps," he said. "A little unorthodox, but then the orthodox isn't working. But don't do anything yourself, Charlotte. Do

417

you understand me?"

"Yes, of course," she said obediently. "If I were clumsy, it would warn him. Give me credit for a little sense, Thomas."

He had several answers for that, but he forbore from giving them. Fifteen years of marriage had taught him something at least.

"I want to know anything that might be interesting," he told Stoker the next morning. The door was closed and he had given orders that he was not to be interrupted. "The man's a rapist. He may have started years ago." He explained Charlotte's reasoning, without mentioning her name.

Stoker looked a little puzzled. "What am I looking for, sir?"

"I don't know," Pitt admitted. "Why does a young man have this kind of rage inside him? He barely knows the young women concerned. Who does he really hate? Could he help himself if he wanted to? Who else did he hurt in the past, who also dared not accuse him? Does his father know? Does he care? Has he ever disciplined him himself, or paid off anyone to keep their silence?"

"Pelham Forsbrook?" Stoker said in surprise. "Why would he need to? He's one of the most influential bankers in London. If he grants you a loan for business venture capital, you're made. If he puts word out against you, then no one else'll back you either. Although whisper has it that he'll lose pretty badly if the British South Africa Company has to pay damages to the Boers after the Jameson Raid."

Pitt was suddenly interested. "Really? Has he partners in the venture, or is he all on his own?"

"No idea. Do you want me to find out?"

"Not unless it has anything to do with his son."

Stoker shrugged. "If I had a son like that I'd keep an eye on him, and definitely want him where I had enough influence to protect him."

"Would you? Would you protect him?" Pitt thought for several moments. "I'm not sure what I'd do if it were Daniel. Maybe I'd ship him off to Australia, and let him take what's coming to him if he didn't straighten himself out. I've no idea. I need to make damned sure it doesn't happen, so I won't ever have to find out. I like to think I'd have the strength to deal with it, but maybe in the end I'd see the child in him that I'd loved, and I wouldn't be able to. God knows."

"I'll bring you all I get, sir. It'll take a day or two."

"Good. And do be discreet, Stoker!"

"Yes, sir. Believe me, I don't want to get caught at it."

"Neither do I," Pitt said with feeling. "We can't afford to. Oh, and Stoker?"

"Yes, sir?"

"Find out where young Forsbrook was the night before last. And if a girl called Alice Townley was at the same place. And for God's sake, be doubly discreet about that!"

"Yes, sir."

Pitt followed a different path himself. If there was something in the past with which they could trap Neville Forsbrook, then the home in Bryanston Mews, where he had grown up, would be the place to find it.

He knew from experience in his police days that servants were almost always loyal, so instead of going to the Forsbrook house, where failure was certain, he went to the servants of neighbors, beginning with inquiries that were completely fictitious.

He was very careful to start with, perhaps too much so. He had concocted an imaginary story, of which the Forsbrooks, father and son, could have been the heroes. He thought it necessary, in case any whisper of it should leak back to them, and thus to the Home Secretary. He was quite open about who he was, though. To be caught in an evasion could be damning, and make him seem ridiculous.

He had been to a dozen houses without learning anything more than a general impression that the Forsbrooks were feared but not liked. He was growing a bit desperate when he found in Bryanston Mews an elderly groom, busy brushing down horses.

The smells of leather polish, dung, hay, and horse sweat brought back a sudden and very sharp memory of childhood on the big estate where he had grown up. His father had been the gamekeeper and his mother had worked in the house, before tragedy struck them and his father was deported.

Reminder of that childhood bewilderment and pain made the present injustice burn the more intensely. He had tried everything he could then to help his father, and been helpless. He had been a country boy, educated alongside the son of the manor house, as companionship and competition for him, but still a nobody, dependent upon Sir Arthur Desmond's patronage even to survive. Now he was a man in his late forties, and head of Britain's Special Branch. He would not allow himself to be helpless this time.

He smiled at the groom. "Good animal you have there," he remarked, looking at the horse.

"Aye, sir, she is that," the man agreed. "Can I 'elp yer?"

"Unlikely," Pitt said with a slight shrug. "I grew up in the country. I miss the friendship of horses, the strength . . . the patience." Memory flashed back again. "I used to clean the harness for the groom sometimes. There's a satisfaction in working the leather, in making the brass shine."

"There is that, sir," the man agreed. He was thin and strong, a little bow-legged. His hair stuck out in wisps from under the cap he was wearing. "But if I can say so, you don't look like a country boy, sir." He regarded Pitt's well-cut city suit. For once there was very little stuffed in his pockets and his cravat was almost straight. The only detail familiar from the past was the fact that his hair was too long and curled in no particular shape.

"Ambition," Pitt admitted. He found himself wanting to be completely honest with this man. He was tired of evasions that achieved nothing. "My father was a gamekeeper, accused of poaching, a serious crime back then. I always believed him innocent, still do, but it didn't save him. Injustice cuts deep."

The man stopped working for a moment

and stared at Pitt with sudden interest deeper than mere politeness. "Ye're right about that, sir," he said with feeling. "Yer got summink as yer workin' on right now, then?"

"Yes." Pitt knew well enough to stop far short of the truth this time. "Looking for a bit of understanding of the past, to get the present right, if you know what I mean. See that blame doesn't fall where it shouldn't."

The man nodded. "So wot d'yer want to know?" The horse swung its head round and nudged him. He patted it and began to brush again. "All right, girl," he said with a smile. "I ain't forgot yer." He smiled at Pitt. "Like women, 'orses are. Don't like yer to put yer mind to someone else when it's their turn."

"I know," Pitt agreed. "But horses don't ask much."

"Ye're right," the man said happily. "Give yer their 'ole 'earts, they do. Don't yer, girl?" He patted the horse's smooth neck without altering the pace of the brush. "What d'yer want ter know, sir?"

Pitt gestured behind him, toward the back of the Forsbrook house. "Do you know Sir Pelham Forsbrook and his family?"

The man's face tightened so very slightly that had Pitt not been watching closely he would have missed it. "Yeah, some," he said. "Knew Lady Forsbrook — Miss Eleanor, as she used to be." His face softened with memory. "Wild, she was, but so alive. Couldn't 'elp but like 'er in the end. Wot they call ironic, in't it?"

"Is it?" Pitt said curiously. "I heard she died in an accident. How was it ironic?" He sensed something further, something unsaid that the man half seemed to expect him to know.

The groom concentrated on brushing the horse's gleaming flanks for several seconds before he replied. "Accident, right enough," he said at last. " 'Ad her cases with 'er, an' all. Knew that from Appley, 'e were the groom there then. Runnin' away, she were. Some said it were to go with the feller she was 'avin' an affair with. Others said it were just that she couldn't take the beatin' no more. Dunno the truth of it, but beat black and blue that night she were. Face all swole up."

Pitt held his breath, afraid even to acknowledge that he had heard.

"Accident, all right," the man was almost talking to himself as memory filled his mind. "In an 'ansom, an' the 'orse got spooked by summink. Some said it were a dog went fer it. Dunno. Terrible thing. Poor driver got killed too."

"How long ago was that?" Pitt asked, trying to keep his voice level, the razor-sharp interest at least half-concealed.

"Four years, maybe?" The man turned back to the horse. "There y'are, girl. That's yer lot for now. Got other things ter do but talk ter you all day. Spoiled rotten, you are, an' all." He picked up his brushes and patted her gently with his free hand.

"Going to clean the harness?" Pitt asked.

"Gotter," the man replied. "Not as I mind, like. It's a good job." He led the way to the tack room and Pitt followed.

"May I help?" Pitt asked, mostly to keep the man in conversation, but also because it would be a physical job with good memories attached, something with assured purpose. He found he wanted very much to do it.

The man looked Pitt up and down. "Get yourself dirty, 'ands and cuffs all messed."

Pitt answered by taking off his jacket and rolling up his sleeves.

A few minutes later they were both working hard. It took one or two fumbles before Pitt had the art back, but the rhythm of it returned quickly, to his intense satisfaction.

"That must have been very hard for Sir Pelham," Pitt said, returning their conversation to the main subject

"Took it bad," the man agreed, nodding as he watched Pitt work. "Strange one, that. Never know wot 'e's thinkin'. Mind, that's true of a lot o' the gentry. Never knew whether 'e loved 'er, or was just angry 'cos she were leavin'. Not as I s'pose she'd 'a got away very far, poor soul."

"Unless there was somebody else?" Pitt made it half a question.

"If there were, they were so bleedin' careful no one ever knew of it." The man looked sad, as if he had wished there had been. Pitt could see it through his eyes; Eleanor Forsbrook had belonged to another world: one he served, and caught glimpses of in unguarded moments, one whose inner life he could only imagine — still, he had liked her. In a sense she was a prisoner of her circumstances also, but with less freedom than he, a neighbor's groom.

Pitt worked on the leather silently for a few more minutes before pursuing the thought.

"I suppose young Neville found it hard too. Was he close to his mother?" he asked casually. Pitt had been close to his own mother. They were survivors together after his father was sent away. His education, equal with that of Sir Arthur Desmond's son, had separated them in mind, and in language, but the affection, although hardly ever put into words, had never been doubted. When she had died it had been the end of a part of his life.

Perhaps that had been at least in part why he had found it easy to love Charlotte. He had trusted women all his life. He had seen too closely their loyalty, sacrifice, and stoicism for it not to be part of his belief system.

"Did it change him?" he asked aloud, referring again to Neville Forsbrook.

"No," the man said, shaking his head. "More's the pity. Always was a cruel little bastard. Sorry, sir. Shouldn't 'a said that." But there was not a shred of regret in his weathered face.

"Said what?" Pitt asked with a smile.

"That's right, sir. Thank you," the man agreed, his eyes bright.

"Fancy a glass of cider when this is done?" Pitt invited him.

The man surveyed the harnesses a little doubtfully.

"It'll take less time with two of us," Pitt pointed out.

"In't yer got nothin' else ter do, important gent like yerself?"

"Probably, but it'll wait. Everybody has to have an hour or two off sometime. And a glass of cider and a sandwich. Cheese and pickle?"

"Done," the man agreed instantly. "You're a rum one, an' no mistake. Maybe we'll be all right after all!"

Pitt bent to the harness again to hide the pleasure he felt at the compliment, and the hope that he would live up to the trust.

CHAPTER 16

It was a quiet summer evening as Vespasia walked along the gravel path beside Victor Narraway, moving from dappled sunlight into the shade. They had met by design at the end of a busy and, for him, unsatisfactory day. He was troubled, and as had happened so often lately, he sought her company. He couldn't help it.

"Do you believe it?" she asked him directly.

He sighed. "I would like to, but frankly it is highly unlikely, and I know of nothing whatever to substantiate it. It makes no sense."

She measured her words with care. "What did he actually claim? That Catherine had asked for further information about various financial investments because she was concerned her husband might lose money? Or that the money might be invested in ventures of dubious morality?"

"Briefly, yes, the latter," he agreed. "But if Quixwood had money invested dubiously, why not simply ask him? She was his wife. Surely he would tell her? He would have to, if indeed he lost heavily. They would need to reduce their circumstances, possibly even sell the house and move to somewhere less expensive." He matched his step more evenly with hers. "It doesn't seem reasonable that she would need to know the details to the depth a banker such as Hythe could explain them to her."

Vespasia could think of no counter for that. He was correct.

"But if he is telling the truth, then she did want exactly such details," she argued.

"He is not telling the truth," Narraway said patiently. "If something is unbelievable, then do not believe it." His smile was twisted, unhappy. With anyone else he might have been impatient.

"Alternately," she continued, "suppose that he is telling the truth. Then there must be some facts of which we are not aware. It does not make sense, therefore it is incomplete. Why would an otherwise sensible woman seek financial facts about her husband's affairs by secretly cultivating the company of another man in financial business?"

"Because he is younger, handsomer, and a great deal more affectionate and interesting," he answered sadly. "The explanation is not difficult."

"Or else she does not trust her husband to tell her the truth," she offered. "That also is a very old story."

"It would be a stronger argument if it were her money and he invested it foolishly and dared not tell her," he said. "But she had no money of her own, as far as I can tell."

"I know," she replied. "I took the precaution of finding out about that myself. It is his money. He is a man of remarkable financial acuity. He has multiplied his original inheritance from his grandfather at least ten times."

"Then she should've trusted him," he pointed out.

"To be wise, certainly, even to be fortunate," she responded. "But not necessarily to be ethical."

He was startled. He stopped and turned to face her. "Hence the detailed information. What is she afraid he might be doing?"

"Ah." She stopped also, and met his eyes. "That I don't know," she admitted. "I'm going to attend the Jameson trial tomorrow, and see what more I can learn of the whole affair of the British South Africa investment, including Dr. Jameson's part in it, and his connections to Mr. Cecil Rhodes, who apparently has financed this fiasco."

"You won't get in," Narraway warned. "Three-quarters of London Society have been trying to obtain seats. They are harder to find than tickets for the opening night of a play."

"The trial is probably more dramatic," Vespasia said drily. "Don't concern yourself. I have done favors for certain people in the past. I have called upon one or two in particular, and I believe I shall be fortunate."

"I see." Different emotions conflicted in his face. "I hope you will tell me if you learn anything at all that would be of use. The situation for Alban Hythe has become desperate."

She stared at him, and he colored very slightly. She was about to make a fairly sharp retort when she realized he was in some way uncomfortable, but she did not know why.

"Of course I shall tell you," she said more gently. "That is my purpose in going. If it were merely for the result of the trial, I should be perfectly content with reading it in the newspapers. I don't see how they can do anything other than find him guilty.

Whether you approve of it or not, he is unquestionably guilty of a serious misjudgment."

His smile was wry, and quite gentle. "Of course he is guilty, my dear," he replied. "He failed. It wasn't even a glorious failure; it was an idiotic one."

"Oh, Victor, how wise we have become. It isn't always very pleasant, is it," she asked with a smile.

"I think politics, and military escapades in particular, already have fools enough," he answered. After a moment or two, he offered her his arm so they might continue their stroll under the trees.

Vespasia needed to draw on more than one favor in order to obtain a seat at the High Court of Judicature for the second day of the trial of Leander Starr Jameson. It was June 21, the longest day of the year. She was also obliged to rise early and be at the court over an hour before the proceedings commenced, such was the interest in the issue, and the almost hectic support for Dr. Jameson himself.

She accompanied the Hon. Hector Manning, a longtime friend who had held a position of some weight in the Foreign Office, and thus was able to obtain a place in the gallery himself. No one had the temerity to question the fact that he brought a lady with him. There were many among the crowd who recognized her. She smiled and nodded to a few of them.

She had dressed in muted colors: silvers and grays, and a charcoal silk so dark as to seem almost black in the shadow, as befitted the occasion. A man was fighting not only for his freedom, but also for what was probably of more value to him: his honor.

After they had taken their seats, Hector, still a very distinguished-looking man, leaned toward her and spoke quietly. "Unless you've changed beyond recognition, you have some better reason for being here than mere curiosity. Were that all, you would never have forced yourself to ask a favor of me. As I recall our last meeting, some twenty years ago, you did not view me with particular pleasure."

She did not wish to be reminded of it, but his question was fair and he deserved an answer.

"You are quite right," she conceded, looking not at him but straight ahead of her at the rapidly filling seats. The slight buzz of conversation made their voices inconspicuous among the rest. On impulse she decided to be moderately frank. "A friend of mine is concerned about some of the financial repercussions of this whole affair. I wish to learn far more of it than I know at the moment . . ."

He swiveled in his seat to stare at her with concern, even anxiety. "I hope you do mean a friend, and not yourself? And even if it is merely a friend, please do not involve your own finances in any way at all; not yet."

She saw the gentleness in his eyes and was a little abashed to recognize an affection she had once dismissed.

"I have no money whatever in Africa, nor shall I, I promise you," she said with a slight smile. "But I appreciate your warning."

"I have no right to tell you not to rescue anyone . . ." he began, then drew in his breath and let it out in a sigh, "but don't, please."

Should she tell him the truth? It was unpleasantly deceitful to cause him completely unnecessary anxiety, and yet the rape of Catherine Quixwood seemed to be so far from the escapades of Leander Jameson that she could hardly expect Hector Manning to believe her. She did not have any explanation to make sense of it.

"It is a matter of proving someone innocent of a terrible act," she said, choosing her words carefully. "So far as I know, no one I am acquainted with needs financial assistance, I promise you."

He relaxed fractionally. "This whole venture was an appalling mess, you know. Is this friend of yours involved in it?"

"I don't know yet," she said frankly. "I am not being deliberately evasive, Hector. I really don't know. If I can understand the raid better, it may answer a few very delicate questions."

"You're not going to tell me any other details, are you?" he concluded.

She smiled at him. "Not unless I have to. It would be indiscreet."

Before they could discuss it any further the court was called to order and the trial commenced.

Vespasia listened with total attention. She already had a certain amount of information with which to catch up. She had never personally met Dr. Jameson, and now studied him with interest while the totally predictable formalities were conducted.

He entered the courtroom and walked toward his chair, taking his seat with care to arrange his dark frock coat so as not to crease it.

Every single person in the room was watching him, a fact of which he could not have been unaware. There was a dull flush visible over his complexion, even darkened by sun as it was. If he recognized anyone, he gave no sign of it.

Vespasia watched him with a growing interest. He was a physician by training, not a soldier, and looking at him now she wondered what course of events had led him to this situation. She could very easily imagine him listening with attention to the symptoms of an injury or illness, then gravely prescribing a treatment. He sat with his large head a little to one side, as if weighing some deep consideration. He had fine, dark eyes — half concealed by drooping lids — a prominent nose and a full-lipped mouth. His hair was receding a trifle, his mustache neatly trimmed. It seemed the face of a city man, a doctor, a professor, or even a clergyman, not a soldier leading adventurers across an African border, armed with Maxim guns and Lee Metford rifles.

As the witnesses testified one by one, Jameson seemed unconcerned, even uninterested.

"Does he not care?" Vespasia whispered to Hector Manning. "Is he expecting a dramatic rescue of some sort?"

"Looking at him, one would think so," Hector murmured back to her.

"By whom?" she asked. "What am I not

understanding? Mr. Chamberlain? Lord Salisbury?"

"I doubt it," he said so quietly she had to strain to hear him. "Poor old Joe Chamberlain is in a hell of a mess himself with this, and it'll get worse before it's over. He'll be lucky if Salisbury doesn't ask for his resignation."

As the evidence and arguments continued, she remembered what she'd heard earlier of the entire matter.

In November of the previous year, 1895, a piece of territory known as the Pitsani Strip, a part of Bechuanaland bordering on the Transvaal, had been ceded by the Colonial Office to the British South Africa Company. The reason given at the time had been for the safeguarding of a proposed railway to run through it. The Prime Minister of the Cape Colony, Cecil Rhodes, had been very keen indeed to bring the whole of South Africa into British dominion. To that end he was willing to encourage the disenfranchised outsiders of the Boer republics into the fold, and thus out of the dominion of the Boer Afrikaners.

This was the spark that lit the fiasco of what came to be known as the Jameson Raid. It was in effect a British South African Company private army of about five hundred men, armed to the teeth. Their purpose was to rouse the workers on the Pitsani Strip, and with them to march across the border into the Transvaal, and overthrow the Boer government there, and then annex the territory, with its fortune in diamonds and gold.

They got within twenty miles of Johannesburg before the Boer forces captured them, forcing them to surrender.

Sir Hercules Robinson, the Governor-General of the Cape Colony, had been ordered by Chamberlain to repudiate the actions of Jameson. The Company's charter was in jeopardy if he did not.

Jameson was shipped home to England for trial. There could be no other action taken if the Company was to survive. Even so, there would be massive reparations to pay to the Boers of the Transvaal. Fortunes would be lost.

Was Jameson a hero betrayed? Or an adventurer who had jeopardized British interests for his own foolhardy ends?

At the end of the day Vespasia was still uncertain. As she walked away from the courtroom with Hector Manning she felt an urgent need to ask him for much more information. She already knew that there was too little time left to wait for a verdict on Jameson. Alban Hythe was also on trial, and his jury might return far sooner. There was hardly any evidence for Peter Symington to use in a defense. She needed more knowledge of the financial side of the venture before she could form any judgment at all as to whether Catherine Quixwood had really asked Hythe for advice.

Vespasia was walking beside Hector Manning, holding his arm, when she glanced to her left and caught sight of Pelham Forsbrook. He looked very pale, and his long face was clenched in an expression of extreme tension. She was afraid he would see her and realize that she was staring at him, until the fixedness of his eyes and the way he moved through the crowd, bumping people without care, made her realize he was oblivious of anyone else.

"Pelham Forsbrook looks distressed," she observed to Hector, as soon as they were on the steps and clear of being jostled. "Could he be financially involved in this, do you suppose?"

"Almost certainly, poor devil," Manning replied. "He's pretty thick with Cecil Rhodes, and everybody knows Rhodes was behind this bloody silly adventure. Pardon my —"

"For heaven's sake, Hector, I've heard the

word before," Vespasia said impatiently. "Jameson was administrator general for Matabeleland, so of course he was tied up with Rhodes too. This idiotic escapade must have pulled troops out of Matabeleland and left it vulnerable."

"Naturally," he agreed, going down the steps, matching his pace to hers. "That is almost certainly why the Matabele revolted in March. Don't know the casualties yet, but it'll be into the hundreds."

"I can't imagine it will stop there," she said quietly. "What a tragedy. But I need to know if many people will have taken serious financial loss. Do you know?"

"There can be no question about it at all," he answered. "Only I don't know who, or how much."

"To judge from his face, Pelham Forsbrook will be one of them."

They reached the bottom of the steps and turned left along the footpath, now clear of the crowd. "Do you think he believed the raid would succeed? If it had, would there have been a profit? I mean, one worth the risk?"

He smiled. "Not as it turns out, but could there have been? Yes, of course. If they'd taken the Transvaal, with its diamonds and gold? Unimaginable wealth."

"Do you know Rawdon Quixwood?" There was no time to be wasted in approaching the subject obliquely. She must have something to tell Narraway before it was too late.

"Slightly," Hector replied. "Poor devil's rather out of things at the moment. What a nightmare." His face was creased with pity. "Can't even imagine it. I hear the wretched man who did it is being tried right now. I hope they hang him." He said it with a sudden surge of feeling.

"Providing, of course, that he is guilty." Vespasia could not help putting that in, even though it was irrelevant. It surprised her. She was usually able to hold back her emotions more effectively.

He was startled. "Do you doubt it?" he said, his eyes wide.

"I don't know." She kept on walking, but slowly. She did not want to discuss the subject. She did not want Hector Manning to know the real purpose of her attendance at Jameson's trial. "Probably they are perfectly right. Poor Quixwood — I don't really know what would be the most painful."

"I don't know what you mean." Hector sounded confused. "Surely he must want the man convicted?"

"If he's guilty, of course," she agreed. "But

442

if it was he, then it also seems as if he was having an affair with Catherine Quixwood. That can hardly be what anyone would want to have happen at all, let alone be made public news."

"Yes, I see. Of course." He too was walking very slowly now. "He loses, whatever the verdict. God help him."

"Did he lose money in this miserable Jameson business as well, do you suppose?" she asked as artlessly as she could.

He stopped completely now, looking at her with a mixture of puzzlement and concern. "What makes you think so?" he asked, frowning.

"There is a suggestion that Catherine was very afraid that he had," she answered truthfully, or at least without telling any direct untruth.

"Really? And you mean she was already looking for someone else, in case he did? What a —" He stopped himself in time before using language he would afterward be ashamed of.

"No, I don't think so." She tried not to sound too firm, or as if she might actually know anything. "It seemed to be rather more a concern that she might be able to give him advice to prevent it."

"Bit too late for that!" he dismissed it out

of hand. "Any good advice should have been before this trial and whatever judgment they reach!"

"But do you suppose Quixwood invested in Africa?" she pursued.

"Thought about it, then didn't, I heard. Could be nonsense, but Quixwood is pretty astute."

"Are you sure?"

"Yes, actually, I am," he said reluctantly. "But that's confidential. He took a better look at it, and could see the pitfalls."

"But he didn't tell Pelham Forsbrook," she added.

"I think that's clear from the look on Forsbrook's face, no. But, of course, he could have told him, and Forsbrook might've just thought he knew better and ignored the advice. Well, he'll pay for it now, poor devil."

"Indeed," Vespasia said quietly. She stopped as they reached her carriage. "Thank you so much, Hector. I have found it one of the most interesting afternoons I have spent in a long time. It is most kind of you, and a great pleasure to see you again."

"Always," he said graciously. He seemed about to add something more, then looked at her again, and knew it would be unwise. He smiled and bowed, then handed her up into her carriage.

■ ■ ■ ■

There was no time to waste. Vespasia went to Victor Narraway's flat, prepared to wait for him if it should prove necessary. His manservant showed her to the sitting room and brought her tea, which was all she wished. She had no more than half an hour to occupy herself before he arrived.

When he did, he was disconcerted to find that she had been obliged to wait for him, but there was no time to indulge such emotions.

"I have learned a great deal that may perhaps be relevant," she said as soon as greetings were exchanged and the manservant had brought fresh hot water and a second cup so Narraway could join her.

"The Jameson trial? Did Quixwood invest unwisely? Or could Catherine reasonably have feared he did? How could we find proof?"

She smiled very slightly at his eagerness. He so badly wanted to believe Catherine innocent, and somehow show it to the court.

"Several people will have invested unwisely," she replied, measuring her words. Perhaps she had not learned as much as she had assumed, or led him to hope. "The prospects looked good enough to tempt many people. Had the raid succeeded, Jameson would have been instrumental in causing an uprising that could have led to us annexing the Transvaal, with its incalculable wealth. The Uitlanders would have given us the excuse. As it is, those who invested in the raid will not only have lost everything, but also cost the British South Africa Company and its investors a fortune in reparation to the Boers."

"And that was what Catherine was afraid of?" he said, carefully controlling his excitement, but it flared up in his eyes. "Perhaps the figures in her diary were not telephone numbers, but really were money! Did Quixwood invest? Do you know?"

"Apparently he considered it, then withdrew in time," she answered. "But Pelham Forsbrook did not. He has lost a great deal. Whether it will ruin him or not, I don't know. He certainly looked very grim at the trial today."

Narraway considered this for several moments before replying.

"But Quixwood withdrew?" he said at last. "I think we need to know a lot more about the relationship between those two men. Is it the mere acquaintance we assumed it to be? Even in his bereavement, Quixwood has

446

gone out of his way to show that Forsbrook's son could not have been guilty of raping Angeles Castelbranco. Under the circumstances, that is the act of an extraordinary friend."

"Thomas does not believe it is true," she pointed out. "Which leads one to wonder if he is mistaken, or deliberately lying. And if it is a lie, why would Quixwood do such a thing? Does he believe Neville Forsbrook innocent anyway, or has he some other reason?"

Narraway frowned. "I don't see how that could be connected to the Jameson Raid, or the trial. There seems to be something very important that we have missed. And now we have little time indeed in which to find it."

"How much longer do you think the trial of Alban Hythe will continue?" she asked quietly. The sitting room was calm, elegant, a little masculine for her taste, but very comfortable. The summer evening was still light. She could see the trees against the sky beyond the windows, clouds of starlings sweeping around in circles, all moving with some infinitely subtle communication, as though they had one mind.

There was no sound inside, not even the ticking of a clock.

"I don't know," he admitted. "Perhaps two more days, three at the very outside, but by then Symington could be stretching the judge's patience, and the public's credulity."

She said nothing. There was no need to struggle for hopeful words. Neither their understanding nor their companionship required it.

CHAPTER 17

Stoker came into Pitt's office and closed the door.

"Morning, sir," he said as he walked over and sat down on the other side of the desk. Pitt would not have presumed to sit without permission when this had been Narraway's office, he thought wryly. Stoker was becoming comfortable. Possibly that was a good thing; on the other hand, it might be a mark of the changing times.

"What do you have on Neville Forsbrook?" Pitt asked him.

Stoker pursed his lips. "Not sure it's a lot of use," he said a little awkwardly. "He's never crossed the law, or if he has then his father paid people off for him and they kept quiet. Couple of whispers . . ." He hesitated.

"What, exactly?" Pitt pressed. "If it's nothing out of the usual I don't care: bad gambling debts, or fights . . . unless someone was very badly hurt. Did he seriously damage anyone? Use a knife? Maim or disfigure anyone?"

"No. Most of his trouble was with prostitutes," Stoker replied with evident distaste. "One or two brothels had to be paid off, and accepted the money only on the condition he didn't return."

"Go on," Pitt said sharply.

"Well, I don't know if it's true," Stoker said tentatively. "But there's word going round, very quietly, that Neville beat a prostitute pretty badly, and her pimp returned the favor, but with a knife. Left a few marks Forsbrook'll carry for the rest of his life. At least that's how the story goes."

"How much credit do you give it?" Pitt was interested, but he was well aware that people boasted for many reasons, perhaps to build up their reputations as bad men to cross. It was a part of their image, and their vanity.

"Difficult to check," Stoker replied. "Couldn't get a precise date, but I have a guess. Forsbrook took a sudden holiday, and no one saw him at any functions for a couple of months. Told everyone he took a trip to Europe, but I haven't been able to confirm that yet."

"Where in Europe did he supposedly go?"

"Somewhere unusual," Stoker answered

with a twisted smile. "Nowhere on the Grand Tour, where he'd expect to be seen. Sofia, or Kiev, or someplace like that. Not going to run into any of your neighbors there."

"You believe the story?"

Stoker chewed on his lip. "Put it this way: if he raped those two girls — Angeles Castelbranco, and then Alice Townley — it would fit the pattern that he tried it on a prostitute first, and got himself beaten for it. So badly he had to get away from London until he was healed."

He shifted his weight. "On the other hand, if he didn't rape either of them, then he could quite genuinely have taken a holiday in Sofia, or anywhere else. We might be able to prove he went to those places, if we dig, but there's no real way we can prove he didn't — unless we can show with certainty where he actually was. But I'd give a week's pay if it turns out his father didn't cover the tracks so no one'll find them."

"Interesting," Pitt said thoughtfully.

"But of no use," Stoker pointed out.

"Unless we can find the pimp who allegedly cut him and learn exactly where the scars are."

Stoker grinned. "Yeah? I can see young Mr. Forsbrook letting us take a good look

451

at the more private parts of his body to verify a pimp's story!"

Pitt pulled a sour face. "But if it's true, then it's undoubtable that Forsbrook fits the pattern of rage and savagery extremely well. Tell me, do you believe it, Stoker?"

Stoker was suddenly grim and very steady. "Yes, sir, actually I do. I talked to quite a lot of people. No one is willing to say much against him. His father's got a great deal of power in financial circles."

He chewed his lip uncertainly. "There is a bit of a whisper that Pelham took a pretty hard fall over this Jameson Raid affair. Put more money into it than he can afford to lose. Bit of bad advice, I should think. Reckoned on us annexing the Transvaal."

"Bad advice?" Pitt questioned. "From whom?"

"Well, you'd have to think you knew something before you risked your shirt on a raid like that, wouldn't you?" Stoker said reasonably. "Inside information somewhere."

"Yes," Pitt agreed. "But that doesn't excuse Neville Forsbrook of anything, even if it's true."

"And it would be difficult to trace Pelham Forsbrook's dealings," Stoker said. "A lot of it's confidential, and there's no way to judge why he backed one person and not another."

"You're right," Pitt agreed. "It's a waste of time, and could make us a lot of enemies where we need friends. Just look for anything recent in young Forsbrook's life that seems odd."

"There's nothing Portuguese," Stoker said straightaway. "Him or his father, I looked at that already."

"And what about Neville Forsbrook's income? Is all of it directly from his father? Any inheritance from his mother?"

"Not much, and he doesn't come into it until he marries," Stoker said with a shrug. "He's tried one or two things, a couple of years in the army, but he didn't take kindly to the discipline. Gave it up. Good leader, not such a good follower."

"Thank you, Stoker. See what else you can find that'll tie into rape."

"Yes, sir."

"Let me know as soon as you can. Now I have to go and see the Home Secretary."

"About this?" Stoker was concerned.

Pitt smiled bleakly. "I don't know. He didn't inform me."

Pitt stood on the carpet in front of the Home Secretary's desk, too angry, and too aware of his own guilt, to do anything but remain at attention.

"The situation in Africa is very delicate, Pitt," the Home Secretary said irritably. "You can hardly be unaware of the Jameson fiasco, and the massive reparations we are going to have to pay to Kruger and the Boers." He said it with considerable bitterness, and Pitt could not help wondering if he too had suffered some personal reversal in the disaster.

"Yes, sir, I am aware of that," Pitt said grimly. "And of Mr. Churchill's warning that sooner or later, if we are not very careful, we will find ourselves at war with the Boers in Africa, which will include the Cape as well. In my own judgment he is probably correct. I am also aware that feeling is very divided here in England, and many regard Jameson as a hero. We are doing what we can to forestall any violent demonstrations — either for him or against him — but it is largely a police matter of public order."

"I know it is not Special Branch's responsibility!" the Home Secretary snapped. "That's not why you are here. I want to know why the devil are you inquiring into the personal affairs of Pelham Forsbrook. I thought I made it clear in my note to you that the very nasty scandal surrounding the Portuguese Ambassador and his family was to be left alone. What was it about my orders that you failed to understand?"

Explanations raced through Pitt's mind, but he knew none of them were what the Home Secretary wanted to hear.

"For God's sake, Pitt!" the Home Secretary went on furiously. "Even Castelbranco himself understands that there is no proof of anything, and irresponsible accusations will serve no one. The poor girl is dead and nothing can bring her back. Let what is left of her reputation be preserved from further speculation, for her parents' sake, if nothing else."

He prodded a finger in Pitt's direction. "You are not a policeman to hound the case to its bitter end, you are head of Her Majesty's Special Branch! Your concerns are the safety of this nation within its own borders, the catching of anarchists, traitors, enemies of the state and its people. Didn't Narraway make that clear to you, for heaven's sake?"

Pitt clenched his hands behind his back, where the Home Secretary could not see them, and let his breath out slowly.

"Yes, sir. Lord Narraway explained my responsibilities in some detail, and the width of my remit, in pursuit of those ends. I believe that an attack on the family of a friendly nation's ambassador falls very clearly within that realm. We cannot afford the reputation of being a country where foreign women are not safe from rapists. Still less can we appear to be indifferent to such atrocities, as if they were commonplace in London, and we thought nothing of it."

"Don't be absurd!" the Home Secretary snapped, his face scarlet. "And offensive. Nobody is dismissing the tragedy, but to say that it is rape is irresponsible. There is only a hysterical girl's account, totally without proof, that anything at all took place. You cannot and must not slander a man's reputation with such a suggestion. Not to mention the wretched girl's. What on earth do you imagine people are saying about her? Have you thought of that?"

Pitt made an intense, almost painful effort to keep his self-control. His body ached. His mouth was dry. "I have made no remarks at all to suggest that Miss Castelbranco was raped, or even assaulted, sir," he said between his teeth. "Her own church has declined to give her proper rites of burial, on the assumption that she lost her virginity, became with child in an illicit affair, and then intentionally took her own life." He was unable to stop his voice from shaking. He was angry enough to face down the Queen, never mind a mere Cabinet Minister.

The blood drained from the Home Secretary's face, leaving him gray. "The matter is tragic indeed," he said quietly. "But it is not our fault —"

"It is our fault if we do nothing about it," Pitt cut across him, quite aware of what he was doing. He was past caring for the niceties.

"Slandering Neville Forsbrook's name will not help." The Home Secretary was growing angrier as the exchange slipped out of his control. "One injustice does not help another. And if you imagine it will, you are the wrong man to have replaced Narraway. I didn't like the man, but by God, he had better judgment than this!"

"Actually, sir, my inquiries about Neville Forsbrook's past behavior had nothing whatever to do with the death of Angeles Castelbranco," Pitt said very carefully, measuring every word. "The Portuguese ambassador will become aware of it only in the future, if it should prove relevant. Which is why I considered it prudent, as well as morally right, to inquire now."

The Home Secretary glared at him. "What the devil do you mean? Explain yourself," he demanded.

"Another young woman was raped, and survived the assault, although she was injured," Pitt replied, fixing his gaze on the Home Secretary's eyes. "The family does not wish to make a complaint, for the girl's sake. She is only seventeen. It would ruin her socially, prevent her from making a fortunate marriage, and ensure that for the rest of her life this repulsive violation follows her everywhere."

The Home Secretary stared at him, aghast. "And what has this to do with Forsbrook?" It was clear in his face that he knew what Pitt was going to say. He had tensed, as if anticipating a physical blow.

"She named Neville Forsbrook as her rapist," Pitt said. "She described the circumstances, the time, and the place. Naturally I had it looked into. She refused to tell me the house in which it happened, but it was very easy to find out. There were not so many balls held in London that night. Her attendance was not secret, nor was that of Forsbrook. The rooms, the paintings, the other details were simple to ascertain."

The Home Secretary let out his breath slowly.

"I see. And what is it you imagine this will accomplish? Let alone what it has to do with Special Branch?" he asked.

Pitt raised his eyebrows. "I would like to find out if Neville Forsbrook raped Angeles Castelbranco and thus brought about her death. I think that is the concern of Special Branch, but if you think the Foreign Office better equipped to handle the investigation, I shall be delighted to turn over all the facts that I have so far obtained."

"Don't be so damned impertinent, sir!" the Home Secretary snapped. Then he leaned back in his chair and stared at Pitt, still standing on the carpet in front of the desk, towering over him. "Be careful! Pelham Forsbrook is a very powerful man indeed. If you malign his son and you cannot prove it, he'll have your job, and I can't save you. Not that I shall try."

Pitt felt the cold seep through him as if he were sinking into icy water. "I shall be very careful, sir," he said in little more than a whisper. "But the man has to be stopped. The next victim could be your daughter."

"Granddaughter," the Home Secretary corrected him bitterly. "Again, be careful!"

"Yes, sir."

Late in the afternoon Pitt went again to the Portuguese Embassy. He must see Castelbranco and tell him the latest news, as he had promised he would.

When he reached the embassy, Rafael received him immediately in the quiet study. Pitt had considered what he was going to say, and knew perfectly well what it might cost him, but he had no doubt as to what it would cost him if he did not.

"You have news," Castelbranco said softly. "I can see it in your face. What has happened?" There was anxiety in his voice and his eyes looked Pitt up and down.

His gentle tone stiffened Pitt's resolve. He had gained a profound regard for the Portuguese ambassador over the last weeks, even a kind of affection. In many people grief shows more vividly their weaknesses; it shakes the fault lines in their character. In Castelbranco, though, it had marked more profoundly his strengths. There was a fortitude in him that was rare.

"It is good of you to come," the ambassador said quietly. "May I offer you some refreshment? I have whisky, if you wish it, but in view of the pleasantness of the weather, you might prefer something lighter? I have been drinking a concoction my wife enjoys, a mixture of fruit juices." He stood still, waiting for Pitt's answer.

"That sounds excellent," Pitt agreed honestly. "We'll keep the whisky for the autumn."

Castelbranco took a glass from the cupboard and filled it from a jug on the sideboard, then they both sat down. Under different circumstances, Pitt reflected sadly, they would have truly enjoyed each other's company.

On the way to the embassy, he had been trying to reach a decision. Now in this calm room he no longer wavered. It was disobedience to the spirit of the Home Secretary's orders, but to obey would be a betrayal of this man Pitt had come to think of as almost a friend.

Castelbranco was waiting for Pitt to speak. The silence would stretch comfortably only so long.

"They are almost certainly going to find Alban Hythe guilty in the next few days," Pitt said at last. "I'm not certain it is the correct verdict, but there is little to refute it. However, the man who was head of Special Branch before me, and for whom I have an immense regard, believes Hythe is innocent."

Castelbranco's face creased with an even deeper sense of tragedy.

"More injustice," he said softly. "The whole matter of violence toward our women stirs a hysteria in us we don't seem to manage very well. Terror and unreason rage through it all. Can you do anything to help?"

"I doubt it," Pitt admitted. "But I know Lord Narraway won't give up. As you will recall the charge is that they were lovers who quarreled, not that he attacked her at random."

Castelbranco smiled bleakly. "I am aware of your point, Mr. Pitt. I do not imagine that this young man assaulted my daughter. She told her mother it was Neville Forsbrook. I do not doubt her." There was a question in his eyes. It was not a challenge, but his gaze was direct and unwavering. "I don't know why this man Quixwood would say that it could not be. Perhaps in his own grief his memory is disturbed. His loss is terrible, and the whole of London knows that his wife betrayed him."

"It is an awful situation," Pitt agreed. "But not what I came to discuss. I have made it my business to learn much more about Neville Forsbrook, and that is the reason I came this evening in particular. The Home Secretary has commanded me to cease my investigations in the matter. If I don't he has threatened to remove me from my command — in fact, I imagine from the Service altogether."

"Then you cannot continue!" Castelbranco said in alarm, leaning forward in his chair, his eyes wide. "You have done all you can to find justice for my daughter, and been a good friend to me. What ill return I would offer you to ask more!"

"I can at least tell you what I know," Pitt answered. "I have, in fact, discovered quite a lot about Forsbrook." He repeated what Stoker had told him regarding the incident with the prostitute and the resulting violence from the pimp, as well as Neville Forsbrook's prolonged absence from England. He also mentioned the rumors of Pelham Forsbrook's violent nature, and that his wife, Neville's mother, had supposedly fled — whether to an imaginary lover or a real one, no one knew — and had been tragically killed in a carriage accident.

"It explains much," Castelbranco said quietly, staring into his empty glass. "But it does not excuse it. Neville is dangerous. Do you not think he will continue to hurt others?"

"Yes, I do," Pitt answered. "I would very much like him to be stopped, but so far I have no idea how I can do that." He fished in his pockets and brought out a folded piece of paper. On it was a name and address. He held it out to Castelbranco. "This is a man I knew on and off when I was in the regular police. It would be necessary to

463

pay him, but he is not greedy and he is extremely discreet. He can make inquiries for you, if you wish."

Castelbranco took the paper and read it. "Elmo Crask? Is that how you pronounce it?"

"Yes. He is unimpressive to look at. He appears harmless, untidy, as if easily fooled, but he cultivates that intentionally. He is very clever indeed and has a memory like an elephant. But consider before you approach him." Even as he said it Pitt still wondered if he was doing the right thing. It was what he himself would want, but that did not make it wise. He had not told Charlotte what he intended because he thought she might well disapprove.

Castelbranco was waiting, watching him.

"No matter how careful he is, it is possible that one way or another Pelham Forsbrook will come to hear of it. There may be no proof that you are behind the inquiry, but it would be the obvious conclusion."

"What can he do that is worse than what his son has done?" Castelbranco asked with a quiver in his voice.

"He can certainly strike where it hurts," Pitt said miserably. "He can start more rumors about your daughter, ask even crueller questions. Please don't take it for granted that he wouldn't. If he believes he is protecting his son's reputation, he will be as determined as you are, and far less scrupulous."

"Such behavior would surely prove his son's guilt," Castelbranco pointed out. "But I hear what you say, and I shall weigh it before I approach this . . ." he looked again at the piece of paper, ". . . Elmo Crask. I know it is not only a matter of the past — there is the future to consider as well, all the other young women Neville could destroy, the other families who will be wounded forever by loss."

Pitt stood up and held out his hand. "I'm sorry to offer so little."

"It is much." Castelbranco stood as well, his voice suddenly husky. "You have already gone far beyond the bounds of your office. I hope you do not suffer for it." He firmly held on to Pitt's hand for several seconds before releasing it.

Pitt left, and went out into the warm summer night hoping desperately that he had made the right decision, that he had acted with wisdom, not merely out of emotion.

He took a hansom cab and rode through the heavy traffic barely noticing it, his mind in turmoil. He wanted to be at home, surrounded by the comforts he was familiar with, and put other people's grief out of his mind, at least for a few hours.

But he knew home would not afford him that. He would look at all he had, the things that were precious to him beyond measure, the center of all value and happiness in his life, his wife and children, and he would not be able to forget. By the time he reached the quiet of Keppel Street, and his own house, he had no answers, only a greater clarity as to the questions.

Charlotte was happy to see him, as always. If she had concerns, she was wise enough to keep them until after supper when he would undoubtedly be more willing to listen — or, at the very least, not hungry.

Jemima was excited and full of energy, her eyes shining, her face flushed. He half listened as she told him in hectic detail about something to do with a musical performance. He had learned to feign an appearance of understanding, nodding at the right times. She did not expect him to understand. Charlotte understood, and that was sufficient.

Daniel rolled his eyes now and again, then when it was his turn to receive the attention he asked numerous questions about the geography of the Empire, and answered them himself. His knowledge was impressive and Pitt told him so, to his son's immense pleasure.

Later, Pitt was standing in front of the French windows, which were wide open, the perfume of damp soil drifting into the room, when Charlotte approached him. The last of the light was on the tops of the neighbors' trees. Starlings circled in the air. Apart from a very slight breeze moving the leaves, and a dog barking on and off in the distance, there was hardly any sound.

"What is it?" she asked quietly, coming to stand beside him.

"What is what?" His mind had been wandering and he could not remember the last thing he had said to her.

"Thomas! I know you are worrying about something. I imagine it is to do with Angeles Castelbranco." There was a degree of exasperation in her voice, but it was gentle.

"Questions, to which I don't know the answers," he replied.

She linked her arm through his and stood close enough so he could feel the warmth of her body. "About Angeles?" she asked. "You are not sure it was Neville Forsbrook, are you? It was. I saw him taunting her. He knew exactly what he was doing, and why it would hurt her."

"In spite of the fact that Rawdon Quix-wood swears Neville was somewhere else and couldn't have been involved?" He smiled very slightly, disengaging his arm from hers and then putting it around her and holding her even closer.

"Is that the question you're asking your-self?" she said. "Why on earth Rawdon Quixwood would lie to protect Neville Fors-brook?"

"Yes," he agreed. "Assuming he is lying."

Charlotte weighed it in silence for several moments before she spoke.

"People lie for several reasons," she said thoughtfully. "To protect themselves, or someone they love; or, of course, someone they are being pressured to protect. Or they lie to achieve something, or to avoid some-thing. Do people lie to protect an ideal? Or because the truth is something they can't afford to believe, for some reason? Some-thing they just don't want to believe? Refuse to?" She watched him, waiting for the answer. "Or are afraid to?" she added.

"Or maybe because of blackmail?" he answered. "Or debt? And if that's the case, then the question arises, what could Raw-don Quixwood possibly owe either Neville or his father?"

"Maybe they knew something about Catherine that he wants to keep secret?" she suggested. "After all, the poor woman can't protect herself now."

"But she was already dead when Quixwood stepped forward to swear Forsbrook was innocent regarding Angeles," he said grimly.

"Then it would have to be something that mattered very much. Considering how Catherine died, Rawdon Quixwood would be the very last man in London to protect a rapist."

"And yet I think he's lying," Pitt responded. "I just can't work out what the truth could be. Nothing I imagine makes any sense."

"Let's go through the scenarios one by one, then," she suggested. "What might Forsbrook have, either father or son, that Quixwood would want? Not money, I don't think. Vespasia said Quixwood got out of an African investment before the Jameson Raid, and she is all but certain that Forsbrook didn't. She said he looked like a ghost at the Jameson trial."

"All right," Pitt agreed. "Not money. To protect someone? That's obvious — to protect Neville, but why? Pelham Forsbrook certainly had nothing to do with Angeles's rape. And she and the other young girl, Alice Townley, specifically said they were raped by Neville. Neither of them mentioned his father."

"You're right," she said, biting her lip. "It's difficult. Fear? Who is afraid of what? Or . . . Quixwood and the Forsbrooks are not related, are they?"

"No," he said, turning it over in his mind. "Not by blood, or any business alliance that we can see."

"Then something else," Charlotte suggested. "If we start off assuming that Angeles and Alice Townley are telling the truth, then Quixwood is lying."

"Indeed," Pitt said, putting his other arm around her and tightening his hold. "But how do we find out why?"

She laid her head on his shoulder. "If it isn't the men, try the women," she suggested. "Neville Forsbrook's mother must have had some influence on him."

"She's dead," he reminded her, but as he said it the beginning of an idea stirred in his mind. "But I'll try that tomorrow."

CHAPTER 18

Narraway had hardly started his breakfast when his manservant interrupted him to say that Commander Pitt had called to see him, and the matter was urgent.

Narraway glanced at the clock, which read just before half-past seven.

"It must be," he replied a trifle waspishly, perhaps because he was touched with a moment of fear. Only an emergency could bring Pitt at this time of the morning. "Ask him if he would like breakfast, and show him in," he instructed.

A moment later Pitt came into the dining room dressed formally, and rather more neatly than usual. He looked excited more than alarmed.

Narraway waved at the opposite chair and Pitt sat down.

"Well?" Narraway asked.

"Let's assume that Angeles Castelbranco and Alice Townley were telling the truth,"

Pitt began without preamble. "We are left with the conclusion, then, that Rawdon Quixwood must be lying about being with Neville Forsbrook at the time of Angeles's rape." He leaned forward a little. "Which raises the question as to why he would do such a thing. One would presume he would be the last man in England to defend a rapist."

"So why should we presume it?" Narraway asked. With anyone else he would have been sarcastic, but he knew Pitt better than to assume he spoke without an answer in mind. "What have we missed?"

Pitt gave a very slight, rueful gesture. "I'm not certain. Some connection between Forsbrook, either father or son, and Quixwood. Or if not that, then possibly between the women."

"What women? There's no connection between Angeles and Quixwood. And no connection between Catherine and Angeles, or Catherine and either of the Forsbrooks," Narraway pointed out. "And as far as the men are concerned, Vespasia says there appears to be a connection between Pelham Forsbrook and Quixwood, but it's tenuous. They both considered investing in the British South Africa Company. Forsbrook did. Quixwood changed his mind in time and lost nothing. Quixwood does a lot of financial advising, so possibly he told Forsbrook to leave it alone."

"But what if he didn't give him the advice?" Pitt suggested.

Narraway sipped his tea. "Why wouldn't he?"

"We need to find that out," Pitt answered. "It might make sense of why Catherine Quixwood was so intent on learning about investment, and the British South Africa Company. Perhaps she discovered Quixwood was misleading people in that manner — or perhaps only Forsbrook — and she needed more knowledge from Hythe in order to be certain?"

Narraway thought about it for a moment or two. The manservant came in bringing Pitt a full breakfast, including fresh tea.

"It could make sense," Narraway finally answered when the manservant had gone. Pitt was eating hungrily. "Except then we are left with a complete stranger raping Catherine, rather than Hythe, which doesn't fit."

"That's true," Pitt admitted. "But we don't have any other solution that makes sense either."

"Unless it is exactly what it appears to be." Narraway did not like the answer, but he could not deny it. "Catherine was desperately lonely and she gave in to temptation to have an affair with a charming and intelligent man, who shared her interests."

"But why did Hythe start the affair?" Pitt pressed. "He had nothing of value to gain, and everything to lose."

"She was lovely and smart," Narraway said simply. "Perhaps his wife had become boring compared with her?"

"Then why did he rape and beat her?" Pitt said. "Forcing a woman is a crude and vicious thing to do, but to beat her half to death is the act of a man driven by demons within himself, a man completely out of control. Is there anything else in Hythe's life to draw a picture of him like that?"

"No," Narraway said thoughtfully. "Nothing at all. But do we always see it? If we do, why does sudden, terrible violence ever happen?"

Pitt smiled reluctantly and swallowed his mouthful of bacon and eggs. "You can't arrest a man for what you think he could be capable of. And we know a lot more about Hythe because of all this than we do about most people. We also know a lot about Neville Forsbrook. Compare the two of them. Who seems more likely to commit such crimes?"

"But like I said before, there's no connection between Catherine and either of the Forsbrooks. I would go so far as to say Neville had likely never even met Catherine Quixwood," Narraway argued.

"No. But if he called on her, would she have let him in? Would she have any reason to fear him?"

"No," Narraway conceded. "But would she have let the servants retire and sit up alone waiting for him? Unless you are suggesting she was having an affair with Neville? There's absolutely no evidence at all of that! He's a generation younger than she is. What on earth could they have in common?"

"I don't think she was having an affair with him," Pitt replied, pouring himself more tea. "Or anyone else, for that matter."

Narraway raised his eyebrows. "What, then? He simply called by because he wanted to rape someone, and he chose her?"

"Of course not," Pitt answered impatiently. "There's something important that we don't know. There must be a connection between the Quixwoods and the Forsbrooks. And somehow these other girls — Angeles, Alice — have gotten caught up in it."

Narraway felt the panic well up inside

him. They were losing the case, and the trial of Hythe might not last beyond today — tomorrow, if they were lucky. He had spoken with Symington. The barrister was going to face the final battle with no more than charm and imagination, which was too little against all the supposed facts.

"It's too late to look for evidence now," he said quietly. The taste of failure was bitter in his mouth. "Whatever we find, we couldn't hope to prove it in a day."

Pitt's face was set hard with determination. "Then Symington will have to find a way to suppose, to raise possibilities and doubts."

Narraway tried to calm his thoughts and compose some line of reasoning. "Is this how you work, Pitt?" he asked. "No, please don't answer that. I don't want to know."

"Do you have a better solution? Aside from giving in, I mean?" Pitt reached for the toast. He was smiling, but there was tension in the lines of his body, and his eyes were perfectly serious.

Narraway swallowed. "What sort of a possibilities do you have in mind?" he asked.

"The women," Pitt repeated. "Actually, it was Charlotte who suggested it. Apart from the business connection between Forsbrook and Quixwood, what about Eleanor Forsbrook? We haven't thought about her very much."

"She's been dead for several years," Narraway said patiently. "She can hardly have anything to do with this."

"About four years, actually," Pitt agreed.

"Then how can she be involved? None of it goes back that long, unless you think she's responsible for Neville being . . . violent? Lots of young men lose their mothers. It doesn't turn them into rapists."

"I'm not suggesting that. I've no idea why Neville became a rapist. But it's possible Eleanor was beaten by Pelham Forsbrook, and that she was running away with a lover when she was killed in a carriage accident."

Narraway was confused. "So what if she was?"

"Well — who was her lover? What happened to him?"

"What are you thinking? That it might've been Quixwood?" Narraway said incredulously.

"Why not?" Pitt asked. "Then there could be a hatred between the two men; what if Quixwood deliberately advised Forsbrook to invest in the British South Africa Company, knowing he'd lose badly, and that is what Catherine suspected and was trying to guard against?"

"To save Forsbrook? Why?"

"Does it matter why? It could be she simply thought it was wrong. Or maybe that it would rebound on Quixwood and perhaps on her also."

"But then why would Quixwood protect Neville? And how can we prove any of this?" Narraway's mind was racing now, grasping for possibilities, for hope.

"I'll look into the possibility that Quixwood could have been Eleanor Forsbrook's lover, and for some evidence that Forsbrook beat her over it. Someone must have seen her body after the accident. If I can find the doctor and he's someone I know, or at least can impress, he might be able to swear some of her injuries happened before her death. Just make sure Symington knows what we are doing, so that he can use whatever information we find."

"I'll go and see him again before court starts today. But one thing, Pitt: if Hythe's connection with Catherine was strictly professional, why hasn't he admitted the entire truth about the information he found for her? Why would he hang in order to protect Quixwood?"

"He wouldn't," Pitt admitted, biting his lip. "There has to be a reason for that too."

"You're supposing an awful lot of other

reasons," Narraway said unhappily.

"Yes," Pitt said, taking the last mouthful of his breakfast. "I am."

"And, truly, what has this to do with Angeles Castelbranco and her family?"

"I don't know, except that I believe Neville Forsbrook raped her. And if he raped her, and he raped Alice, it isn't ludicrious to suppose he could be connected to Catherine's attack in some way. I want him off the street."

"Would you like the moon as well?" Narraway asked, sounding more sarcastic than he meant to, only because he desperately wanted Pitt to be right.

Narraway arrived at court early and was waiting for Symington when he came in, also early, in hope of preparing some kind of defense. When he arrived he was neat, immaculate as always, but his face showed lines of weariness, making him look older.

"I have no good news," Symington said when he saw Narraway in the hallway, but led him into his chamber and closed the door behind them.

"Neither have I," Narraway responded. "But I have some ideas."

"A little late," Symington replied wryly. "I'll hear them anyway, though. Bower was good yesterday, with his questioning of Knox, and I have nothing to come back with. He's calling Quixwood today, and I don't know whether to attack him or not. Sympathy is with him entirely and I don't know a damn thing to shake him."

"I might," Narraway replied. Quickly, he summarized what he and Pitt had discussed over breakfast.

Symington listened patiently, but there was no spark of hope in his eyes.

"Conjecture," he said when Narraway finished. "It could be true, but there are big holes in your theories. The biggest one to start with: if Hythe was only getting financial information for Catherine, why hasn't he disclosed the details of their exchanges? He knows any concrete information he can offer us might help save his life, after all." He shook his head. "Secondly, you found no evidence in Catherine's belongings that she was collecting financial evidence. If she made notes, what did she do with them? The diary is so brief and so careful it proves nothing. And thirdly, this still doesn't offer the possibility of another suspect. If it wasn't Hythe who raped her, who was it? If what you say is true, Quixwood himself is the most obvious choice as attacker — he found out his wife was investigating him and

480

decided to put a stop to it — but we know that can't be because he was with you at the time! Bower could call you to testify to that if he had to."

"Yes, we know Quixwood didn't rape her," Narraway agreed. He tried to make his voice hopeful. "But we don't know who put the laudanum into the wine. Just because the laudanum bottle was found with the wine and the glass in the cabinet, we assumed Catherine must've. But really, anyone could've done that, including Quixwood."

"To say she did it herself seems a reasonable supposition, though, and that is what Bower will insist happened," Symington responded. However, he stood a little straighter, shoulders more square, chin a little higher. "If someone else put the laudanum into the Madeira, it was either the rapist — which means he knew where the wine was, left her and went to get it, put the laudnam in, and then roused her and dosed her with it. Or else Quixwood put it there himself, which suggests very strongly that he had some ulterior motive, and that Catherine drank the wine without realizing it was laced. Frankly, neither of those sounds anywhere near as likely as her taking it herself in despair."

Narraway nodded slowly.

"And Bower will say that even if Catherine didn't do it herself, Hythe must've known where the laudanum was kept and fed it to her so she would die, and thus could not testify against him."

"He beat her nearly to death, and then stayed in the house, risking the servants finding him, so he could fetch and mix laudanum and dose her with it?" Narraway edged his voice with disbelief. "Bower has painted Hythe as a raving madman who completely lost his mind and savagely raped a woman he had been in love with, because she suddenly rejected him. So why not just break her neck at that point?"

"True," Symington agreed again. "But the bottom line is, if Hythe wasn't her lover and their whole friendship, and the secrecy of it, was to do with finding financial information about Quixwood's investment, or not, and his advice about it to Forsbrook, then why doesn't Hythe just say so?"

"Perhaps either Forsbrook or Quixwood has some power over him?"

"Such as what?" Symington frowned as if he was searching his mind desperately for any thread to weave into a defense.

Pitt had said Charlotte told him to think of the women. She had meant Eleanor and Catherine. But what about Maris Hythe?

"If he's found guilty and hanged, what will happen to Maris?" Narraway said aloud, a new urgency in him impelling him forward.

Slowly the light came into Symington's vivid blue eyes. "Disgrace and probably destitution," he said, letting his breath out slowly. "Hythe's keeping silent to protect Maris. Quixwood must have promised to look after her." He leaned forward, desperately urgent. "Find out if that's true, Narraway! Get somebody onto it! Get Pitt — now! Today! Then maybe we have a chance."

Narraway rose to his feet. "Can you send a message to Lady Vespasia Cumming-Gould that I am pursuing evidence and will not be in court today? It is important."

Symington smiled. "The beautiful Lady Vespasia. I should be delighted to have an excuse to speak to her. Of course I shall tell her. Do you wish me to say where you have gone, and what you are pursuing?"

"By all means. Thank you."

Vespasia was in a seat reserved for Narraway himself and had received the message from Symington that Narraway had gone on an urgent errand. Symington had expressed no emotion in words, but there was a visible excitement in him that had no explanation other than hope.

As she sat watching the proceedings begin she could see no reason for hope at all, unless there really was some powerful new evidence that had totally eluded them before. However, she clung to that belief with difficulty when Rawdon Quixwood appeared. There was a buzz of heightened emotion when he took the stand. Vespasia felt her breath catch. The man looked ten years older: paler and withdrawn into himself. He climbed the steps up to the stand as if it cost him an effort. When he finally faced Bower he leaned very slightly against the railing to support himself. His dark hair was thick and tidy but his eyes were hollow and there was no color to his skin. He seemed thinner as well. His clothes hung on him. He wore black, as was appropriate for a man still in mourning for his wife. Looking at him as he faced Bower, no one could forget that he was the living victim of this terrible crime.

In the dock, Alban Hythe appeared like a man already sentenced to death.

When Quixwood was sworn in, Bower approached him with both respect and grave compassion.

"Mr. Quixwood, I regret having to call you to this ordeal at all, and I will make it as quick as I can so that you soon may be excused from this experience, which can only be a terrible suffering for you." He said it quietly, but his voice carried in the utter stillness of the courtroom. No one stirred in the gallery. There was not even a whisper of movement. "Were there some other way, I would take it," Bower continued. "But I promise you we will obtain justice for your wife, and it will not be much longer now."

"I know that, sir," Quixwood answered somberly. "You do only what is necessary, as justice demands. Please ask whatever you wish."

There was a murmur of approval from the gallery, and several of the jurors nodded.

Bower inclined his head gravely, milking every moment for sympathy.

Vespasia had expected it, but she was still impatient. "Proceed with it, man," she sighed under her breath.

As if he had heard her, Bower looked up at Quixwood.

"I have kept your testimony until last, Mr. Quixwood, because I want to give you the opportunity to sum up for the jury exactly what happened, as you are aware of it, and the desperate, even emotionally fatal blow that this terrible crime has dealt you. Let me begin at the beginning, so far as you are aware of it."

He glanced up toward the dock, briefly. The eyes of all the jurors followed him to where Alban Hythe sat motionless, then back again at the silent, wounded figure of Quixwood.

As theater it was superb. Vespasia found herself clenching her teeth and wondering where on earth Narraway had got to and what he hoped to achieve now. Time was slipping away from them.

"Are you acquainted with the accused, Mr. Alban Hythe, sir?" Bower asked.

"Yes, I am. We have done business with each other on various occasions," Quixwood answered.

"And do you know him socially also?"

"Much less so, but yes, we have attended the same functions from time to time."

"Mr. Quixwood, were you aware of the friendship your wife had found with the accused, Mr. Alban Hythe? That they had met on a number of events over a matter of months, at lectures, museums, galleries, and so on, when neither you nor Mrs. Hythe were present?"

"I was aware they met on occasion," Quixwood replied. "She mentioned something about his being very pleasant. I can't remember any more than that."

"Did you know that Mrs. Quixwood attended such events quite often?"

"Yes, of course I did. She had many interests, and friends. These were natural and very pleasant places to meet." He sounded a little annoyed, as if Bower were tainting Catherine's reputation gratuitously.

"But you had no idea that she was seeing him increasingly often, up to as much as two times in a week, toward the end of her life?" Bower went on.

Quixwood gripped the railing in front of him. "No."

"Would you have acted differently had you known?" Bower asked.

"Naturally. I would have required an explanation from her, and then forbidden her to continue. It was foolish . . . and . . ." he swallowed convulsively, ". . . ill-considered, at best. As it turned out, it seems to have been tragic. I had no idea she was so . . . so emotionally fragile. I had not seen it in her character."

Bower nodded sagely. "She had always been of good judgment until this . . . friendship?"

"Yes. Excellent. Catherine was a beautiful and gracious woman."

"You were happy in your marriage?"

"Very. No one who knew Catherine would be surprised at it. Many men envied me my good fortune. And I held myself to be fortunate." Quixwood stood quite still. Never once did his eyes stray up toward Hythe in the dock, or toward the jury.

"Did she ever give you cause to be concerned that she was forming a romantic attachment to another man? Please think carefully. I regret asking such an ugly question, but circumstances force me to." Bower looked genuinely distressed.

"I understand," Quixwood said softly. "If you please, let us get it over with. Allow me to answer the question you are leading toward too delicately." He straightened his shoulders with an effort. "Yes, looking back with hindsight, it is perfectly possible that my wife was having an affair with Alban Hythe. He is a charming man and has many interests Catherine shared — interests I myself had not time to indulge in. She may have hungered for someone with whom to discuss them. It never occurred to me at the time. I trusted her absolutely. She had the freedom to come and go as she wished. We — we did not have children, and I asked no social duties of her except the occasional dinner party."

Vespasia could feel a wave of sympathy for him emanating in the courtroom. The jury was all but overcome by emotion.

Quixwood took a deep breath and let it out with a sigh. "Perhaps I should have asked more of her; then she would not have . . ." He was unable to complete the thought aloud.

Bower did not press him.

"We have heard that you were attending a function at the Spanish Embassy when the police informed you of Mrs. Quixwood's death," Bower continued.

"Yes," Quixwood agreed. "At the Spanish Embassy. I was in conversation with Lord Narraway when I was told . . . told that Catherine had been . . . attacked."

There was a shudder of horror in the gallery, a sigh. Two or three women let out little moans of pity and grief.

"Quite so." Bower nodded. "I regret raising the question, had you noticed any change in Mrs. Quixwood's behavior over the last few months before the incident? Was she absentminded? Did she wear any very attractive new clothes? Did she seem to take more than the usual care over her appearance? Was she evasive about where she had been or whom she had met?"

Quixwood smiled bleakly and the pain in his face was evident.

"You are asking me if she was having a love affair. The answer is that I noticed nothing at the time. Perhaps I should have, but I deal in major finance, enormous sums of money, all of which belong to other people. It is a great responsibility. I paid her too little attention." He blinked several times and took a moment to regain control of his grief.

Quixwood had said nothing against Hythe whatever, and yet at this moment Vespasia knew the jury would have convicted him without even retiring to debate the issue. The anger and the pain in their faces testified to it more vividly than words. Symington would have to be more than a genius, he would need to be a magician to turn this tide.

"Mr. Quixwood, I will not harrow you by asking you to describe for us your feelings as you traveled back home, or when you saw your wife's body broken and bleeding on the floor, hideously violated," Bower said gravely.

"Please tell the jury, Mr. Quixwood — briefly, if it is easier for you — what you yourself did after that terrible night, in order to assist the investigation. As much as you can recall. I am sure the Court appreciates that it has been a nightmare for you, one in which your memory may be imperfect."

Vespasia was aware of the skill of the question, the careful making of room for error. It would be almost impossible now for Symington, who was furiously scribbling notes to himself, to trip him up. Was that on purpose because Bower feared Quixwood would make errors? Or was it a usual precaution he would have taken with anyone?

Quixwood hesitated, as if arranging his thoughts, then began. His voice was low and very clear, his eyes downcast. He looked like a man controlling terrible pain.

"That night, as I recall, I asked Lord Narraway to give me any help he could personally. He was very gracious, and seemed to me to care deeply, both for justice in general, and in this case in particular. I knew of him, of course, when he was head of Special Branch, but I found him in this instance a man of remarkable compassion. He seemed genuinely appalled at the savagery of the crime, and moved to do whatever he could to find out who was guilty. I'm not sure if I ever told him how much his support meant to me."

There was another murmur of approval around the gallery and a few of the jurors smiled.

Vespasia felt the bitterness of the irony, that Quixwood was thanking Narraway now, when Narraway was off trying to do every-thing in his power to help free Hythe.

"He spent a great deal of time at my home," Quixwood went on thoughtfully. "He read through Catherine's diaries, something I would find too painful to do, but which I was glad that he did." He looked at the jury. "The items are all in evidence, so he has not had to testify. I believe Catherine's maid authenticated them."

"Thank you, Mr. Quixwood," Bower said with a gracious gesture, an inclination of his head in respect.

Symington sat fidgeting, and Vespasia felt a wave of pity for him. It was clear he knew that Bower was asking such questions only to keep Quixwood on the stand and draw the jury's sympathy even more. There was no real evidence to give. But if Symington challenged him on it and won, then the trial would be virtually at an end. So he must drag it out as long as he could, to give Pitt and Narraway a chance to find the new evidence they were searching for. Bower had all the cards to play and Symington was desperate.

Bower was smiling now. It was a gentle, friendly smile, one of compassion. "Mr. Quixwood, was your wife a beautiful woman?"

Quixwood blinked hard several times before replying. "Yes, she was, in every way. Her face was uniquely lovely, full of life and wit and grace. She could be terribly funny, when she wanted to, and without unkindness. She loved beauty of every kind, and knowledge. She was interested in everything. You may think I say that now because I loved her, but ask anyone who knew her and they will say the same."

"Have you ever had instances before where another man craved her attention more than was appropriate?" Bower asked.

"Yes, but Catherine was well able to decline without ill feeling," Quixwood answered. "I suppose every truly lovely woman has to learn that art."

"So you had no cause to fear for her?"

"Of course not! For God's sake . . ." His voice broke. "She was in her own home with the doors locked and . . . and a full complement of servants!" Quixwood said in a sudden burst of anguish. "What should I fear? I was out at a reception my business required I attend. What sane man would imagine such a . . . a . . ." He struggled to regain his control, but failed. He bowed his head and quickly wiped at his cheeks.

For a moment Vespasia thought Pitt and

Narraway had to be wrong, at least in the assumption that Quixwood could have had anything to do with the crime. Perhaps it was Pelham Forsbrook, in revenge for Quixwood having been Eleanor's lover — if that was true. Yes, surely that made more sense? She would say so to Symington, when she had the chance.

"I have no further questions for this witness, my lord," Bower said. He looked at Symington with slightly raised eyebrows.

Symington rose to his feet, then seemed to hesitate. He looked at Quixwood, then at the jury. No one moved.

"Mr. Symington?" the judge asked courteously.

Symington smiled, a charming, almost luminous smile that Vespasia knew he could not possibly mean. The only chance he had was to win some sympathy from the jury, create some shred of doubt in their minds.

"Thank you, my lord," Symington said gracefully. He looked up at Quixwood. "I hate this. Heaven only knows how you have suffered already, Mr. Quixwood, and I cannot imagine what you have lost in this whole terrible tragedy. I do not believe that the accused was the man who did this thing, but I do not believe that putting you through any further agony will assist me in proving that.

494

I offer you my sincerest regrets over the fearful death of a woman who seems by every account to have been beautiful in all respects."

He sat down again, to the amazement of the gallery, the jury, and the judge. Even Bower looked momentarily wrong-footed.

Vespasia felt her heart sink. Pitt and Narraway could not possibly have found anything yet. Why on earth did Symington not think of something to give them time? Was the man a fool? Or did he know he was beaten, and could see no point in stretching out the pain?

Bower stood up again, victory flushing his cheeks, making his eyes bright.

"The prosecution rests, my lord."

Symington was pale as he stood again and asked the judge for an adjournment so he might speak privately with his client before beginning the defense.

Perhaps hoping that they could have a speedy end, the judge granted an adjournment until the following morning.

Vespasia stood up slowly, a little stiff, and waited a few minutes while the crowd pushed and jostled its way out. She did not want to linger, but she could not think of anywhere else to go. She had reached the main doors to the street and was hesitating there when she heard her name called. She turned to find Symington at her elbow.

"Lady Vespasia, may I speak with you, perhaps in half an hour or so? It is extremely pressing, or I wouldn't trouble you."

"Pressing is a magnificent piece of understatement, Mr. Symington," she replied. "If there is anything at all that I can do, I am entirely at your disposal."

"I'm afraid I must ask you to wait because now is the only chance I have to see Hythe again before tomorrow morning, although I have very little idea what I can say to him that will help, except a final plea to tell me the truth. I have nothing with which to defend him."

"Of course I will wait." She gave the only answer possible. "If you can show me where I may do so without being asked to leave?"

"I have the use of a room. Thank you."

She followed where he directed her; as soon as he left her alone in the small room, she rose to begin to pace the floor. Her mind went over and over the facts she knew, seeking for any escape whatever.

The minutes ticked by. She heard voices and footsteps outside, but no one disturbed her.

They were going to lose tomorrow. It seemed inevitable. And Narraway was so convinced that Hythe was not guilty. Perhaps he was capable of deeper emotion than she had considered, but he would never be a sentimental man, following wishes where his reason denied. The violence against Catherine Quixwood had appalled him. He had never known her in life, yet in her terrible death she had touched something in him deeper than anger or pity at a crime.

Assuming both Catherine and Hythe were innocent of any romantic or physical liaison and it was, as Pitt and Narraway had conjectured, a matter of his finding information for her regarding investment in the fiasco of the Jameson Raid, then why did Hythe not say so now? If he were the man he claimed to be, what could possibly be worse than the fate of conviction and hanging for a shocking crime you didn't even commit?

Lady Vespasia wondered what love or honor would make her willing to silently face such a hideous death.

Surely he was doing it for someone. And if so, it had to be Maris, whom he loved, and who had been loyal to him throughout. To save her from what, though? Destitution? But if he was prepared to remain silent about the truth to protect her, that could only mean that the truth would ruin someone else.

That in turn must be Quixwood. Or perhaps Pelham Forsbrook?

Would Hythe trust either of them, though? Not without something that committed them to keeping their word about caring for Maris. What could that be?

Vespasia was still pondering it all when Symington returned. The courage and grace he had shown in the courtroom had vanished. He looked totally beaten.

She did not ask if he had succeeded in getting information from Hythe; the answer was apparent.

"I don't know what else to do," he said, dropping into a chair and indicating with a weary gesture that she should sit opposite him.

She remained standing, unable to relax, but he appeared too exhausted to stand again.

"Mr. Symington, a reason for Mr. Hythe's refusal to defend himself has occurred to me," she said gravely. "He believes he cannot be saved, which in the circumstances is a reasonable assumption. However, if he is as noble a man as his wife believes, then he will not fight a hopeless battle for his own life or honor when to give in silently might preserve some measure of comfort and protection for her."

Symington looked up, frowning. "Narraway suggested much the same thing. We realized if he is hanged, as he well might be, then her life will be wretched, and unless she has family, she will probably also be destitute."

"So what if Quixwood has promised to look after her, even given Hythe some written commitment that cannot be broken?" she suggested. "On condition, of course, that Hythe does not reveal the financial information that he obtained for Catherine?"

"It's certainly possible. But how the devil do we prove all this?"

"I don't know," she admitted. "But for the sake of a man's life, we must spend all the time we have left trying. I intend to go to Thomas Pitt's home and wait for his return. He and Lord Narraway will solve this, if it can be done."

"I shall come with you," he insisted. "We have no time to waste in relaying messages to each other. Come."

CHAPTER 19

Charlotte was completely unprepared when Vespasia arrived, with Peter Symington immediately behind her. Vespasia looked magnificent, dressed in an exquisitely cut costume of dark blue-gray with flawless white silk at the neck and pearls on her ears. If the intent had been somberness appropriate for a trial, she had just missed it.

"I apologize, my dear," Vespasia said as a stammering Minnie Maude held the parlor door open for her. "But the situation is desperate. May I introduce Mr. Symington. As you know, he has undertaken the defense of Alban Hythe, for what I fear will be scant reward, and we are on the brink of defeat. We are beaten on every side and unless we can think of something tonight, tomorrow will deal us the coup de grâce. Although there will be little of grace about it. I do not like Mr. Bower, who represents the prosecution. There is a self-righteousness in the man, and a lack of imagination." The vitality and determination in her face seemed to reject the possibility of both tragedy and defeat. Symington was clearly weary and bruised from battle, but the warmth of his smile robbed Charlotte of complaint.

"How do you do, Mrs. Pitt?" Symington said quietly. "I am aware that we are intruding, and I apologize."

"You are most welcome," Charlotte said sincerely. "Have you come straight from court? It's early, isn't it?"

"Yes," he replied. "The judge allowed me time. I'm sure he assumes it's so that I can prepare myself for a strategic surrender. But we are not quite at the last ditch. Lady Vespasia hopes that Commander Pitt and Lord Narraway might yet be of assistance."

Charlotte's mind raced. She had no idea where either Pitt or Narraway might be. What should she do if they did not return until late? It was only just after three in the afternoon.

"Have you eaten?" she said practically. No one's mind was at its best when lacking nourishment.

"Yes, we have had luncheon, thank you," Vespasia said, still standing. "But perhaps Minnie Maude would be kind enough to make us tea. I remember in the past most profound conversations across the kitchen table. Might that be possible again?"

Charlotte did not bother to consult Symington. His easy smile as he stood suggested he would agree.

"Of course," she said quickly. "Minnie Maude will make us tea, and we'll have some cake as well. Neither hunger nor discomfort must mar our thoughts. I shall use the telephone to see if Mr. Stoker can help us get a message to Thomas. I also imagine Lord Narraway's manservant might be able to find him, if it is possible."

"Excellent." Vespasia nodded. She and Symington followed Charlotte to the kitchen, followed by a startled and uncomfortable Minnie Maude.

Around the kitchen table, with plenty of tea and some very good homemade cake, they brought Charlotte up to date with the day's happenings in the courtroom.

"What we lack is any kind of proof," Vespasia said unhappily.

Symington ate the last of his cake. "I would settle for a witness or two and a good deal of suggestions," he said. "You can scare people into admitting all kinds of things, if you get the balance exactly right. I would like to prove Hythe innocent, but at this point I'd be grateful for reasonable doubt."

Vespasia thought for several moments. "Let us consider what we know for certain," she said. "In the order of their happening, as far as is possible." She looked at Charlotte. "What does Thomas know?"

"That about four years ago Eleanor Forsbrook ran away from home," Charlotte said. "We don't know whether it was with a lover or not, nor do we know who that lover was, if there was one, may have been. Possibly she was beaten beforehand, but we have no evidence yet."

"No evidence yet? Then how do you know this?" Symington asked her.

"My husband found out from a man who works nearby in Bryanston Mews," she answered. "Thomas said he was intending to find the doctor who examined Eleanor's body after the accident, to see if any of the injuries inflicted were old.

"We also know that Neville Forsbrook beat a prostitute very badly, five or six years ago, when he was about sixteen," Charlotte continued. "And the woman's pimp beat Neville equally badly, in return. Apparently he scarred him with a knife." She pulled a slight face at the thought.

"And your husband knows this for certain?" Symington asked. "Or he believes it?"

"He believes," Charlotte answered reluctantly. "And he also believes that Neville raped Angeles Castelbranco, and so do I," she went on.

Symington looked puzzled. "Is this a Special Branch case, Mrs. Pitt?" His voice implied that he doubted it.

"There is no case," she told him. "It's just a tragedy we saw, one we care about very much."

"I heard about Angeles," Symington said thoughtfully, and there was a sudden sharp pain in his face. "I gather she was quite young."

"Yes." Charlotte kept her composure with difficulty. "About two years older than my own daughter. The problem is, Quixwood insists Neville was with him at the time of Angeles's rape. And we are here now to try to save Alban Hythe from being hanged for a crime he did not commit, not convict Neville Forsbrook for one that he did, unfortunately."

"They both involve rape," Symington thought aloud, his eyes unfocused, staring at the far wall. "Certainly that's the part of the Quixwood case that makes the least sense."

"Is it even imaginable that Neville Forsbrook raped Catherine Quixwood too?"

Charlotte asked in little more than a whisper.

Symington stared at her. "But why in God's name would her husband protect him from another charge of rape, then? Wouldn't that be the perfect answer? Neville could be convicted, without the shame and humiliation of a trial making the wretched details of Catherine's death public? It's what I would want, if it were my wife." He looked at Charlotte. "Are you sure he attacked Angeles? I mean, really sure that you are not assuming because it makes sense of other things we don't understand? And to be honest, because you don't like him, and you believe he's guilty?"

Charlotte hesitated a moment. "Do I know it? No. I can't prove it. But we know he raped Alice Townley . . ."

Symington looked confused. "Who is Alice Townley?"

"I'm sorry," she said. "Another young girl. Her father refused to bring charges against Neville, but Thomas went to see her, and she told him it was Neville Forsbrook who raped her. Her account was very similar to that which Angeles Castelbranco gave her mother, but with a lot of details filled in. And before you ask, no, the girls didn't know each other."

Symington clenched his teeth and breathed in and out slowly several times. "Then I think we may believe them," he said at last. "Let us take it that Neville Forsbrook raped Angeles, and this Alice Townley. Which means Quixwood lied to protect him. Why?"

"Because he does not wish Neville Forsbrook to be charged with rape," Vespasia answered.

"But why not, if he is guilty?" Charlotte said quickly.

"Because he wanted someone else convicted of it," Symington answered. His expression changed slowly. "Of course! What if Catherine was, in fact, murdered because she had discovered financial information that Quixwood could not afford to have made public." He stood up, his face eager. "Both Catherine and Hythe had to be silenced. Raping her was a convenient way to accomplish it. Everyone would presume she had committed suicide, and Hythe would be accused of the crime and hanged, going to the gallows in silence to protect his wife. God Almighty! It's diabolical."

Charlotte sat back, her gut twisting. "Can there be proof, then, that Hythe found any financial information for Catherine regarding investment in the British South Africa Company that would implicate Quixwood?" she asked.

"No," Symington answered miserably. "Most of his access to such records was probably illegal anyway, and even if we could prove it, there is nothing to say he obtained it for her. She seems to have kept no record of the information."

"That seems so peculiar," Vespasia interjected. "Why go through all the trouble to get the information if she wasn't going to document and use it somehow?" She turned to Symington. "And suppose what she found out was that Quixwood was ruining Pelham Forsbrook. Why would she care? Why would it matter enough to have one of them silence her in this brutal way?"

"Do we know that Quixwood was definitely trying to ruin Forsbrook for certain?" Symington asked.

"No. We need to know if Quixwood advised Forsbrook to invest, and then failed to warn him of the possible failure and consequent cost of the Jameson Raid," Vespasia answered. "And we have no time for that."

Symington turned to Charlotte. "Is there any way Commander Pitt could obtain, if not information on the major investors, then at least word-of-mouth reports? It would do

507

in a pinch. Quixwood won't know that I'm guessing."

Charlotte stood up. "I'll telephone Mr. Stoker again," she replied. "It is worth trying, at least."

She was back five minutes later. "I spoke to Mr. Stoker; he is going to look into it. I have no idea whether it will help or not. He will come here this evening with whatever he can find."

"So suppose Forsbrook and Quixwood both invested in Africa, only Quixwood withdrew his money in time, but did not warn Forsbrook to do the same." Vespasia picked up their conversation.

"He might've warned him, and Forsbrook might not have listened," Symington said.

Charlotte nodded her head in agreement. "Either way, that leads us to the Jameson Raid at the very end of last year, which has just now come to trial, and because Jameson is likely to be found guilty, the British South Africa Company will have to pay a fortune in damages to the Boers in the Transvaal. Some investors are going to be very badly damaged."

"Which, according to our suppositions, was of great concern to Catherine Quixwood," Vespasia remarked.

Symington sat up straighter. "But why?

We have all these theories, but no real reason for Catherine to act as she did."

Charlotte was struggling to make sense of it. "Could she have been a friend of Eleanor Forsbrook's? Or of Pelham Forsbrook's?"

"Has anyone investigated to find out?" Symington asked.

"Victor might know something," Vespasia said. "At the very least, he has learned enough about Catherine to have an informed opinion."

Symington studied the table for a few moments, then looked up again. "Anyway, Quixwood could claim that he advised Forsbrook to sell, and Forsbrook didn't take the advice. No one could prove otherwise. Quixwood might even have a letter to that effect. I would, if I were doing such a thing. I would say that I begged Forsbrook not to invest, and he was greedy and ignored me. That's quite believable. London is full of people who think Jameson is a hero."

"And without proof for at least one of these theories, or at least witnesses, we are merely slandering a man who already has the total sympathy and support of the Court, not to mention the jury." Vespasia's shoulders slumped slightly.

They were interrupted by Jemima and Daniel, just home from school. Both were greeted, and then politely but firmly dismissed to their own rooms. Charlotte rose from the table and went into the scullery to consult with Minnie Maude as to what they might serve for dinner, with at least three prospective guests. Vespasia and Symington returned to the parlor to wait for Pitt and Narraway, their discussion having come to a standstill.

A full hour later Narraway arrived, and within a few minutes Pitt came in also, in answer to Stoker's summons. Stoker himself was a step behind. They all looked weary and defeated, though each tried in his own way not to show it.

Pitt looked at Symington after no more than a glance at Charlotte, a meeting of the eyes, and then away again for an instant to Vespasia, as an acknowledgment.

"It went badly," he concluded.

Symington made a slight gesture with his hands. "We've still got tomorrow," he replied. "I have no way of stretching it any further than that, because although we have lots of ideas — we might even have the answer — we have no proof. We haven't even a witness to call that we can tie up in contradiction, or to raise doubts."

"Did you find out anything?" Charlotte asked Pitt, trying not to invest her voice with too much hope.

"I spoke to the surgeon who examined Mrs. Forsbrook's body after her accident," he replied. "He said there were old bruises, even a fractured rib that had healed, but it doesn't prove anything."

"It seems it could be true that Pelham Forsbrook beat her," Charlotte said quickly.

"Or not," he replied ruefully. "It could have been an earlier accident: riding, or even falling downstairs."

"Maybe." She would not give up. "We have been wondering . . . what if Quixwood deliberately advised Forsbrook to invest in the British South Africa Company, specifically the Jameson Raid, knowing it would fail, thus causing his ruin?" she suggested.

"Why?" Pitt asked reasonably.

"We don't know," she answered, frustrated. "Perhaps because of Eleanor, if he was her lover? Catherine seems to have been very involved. The whole crime centers on her after all. If Hythe is telling the truth, then he was looking for proof of that for her —"

"Again," Pitt interrupted, "why? Why would she care if Forsbrook was ruined?"

Symington blinked and frowned. "Maybe *that* was the affair? Pelham Forsbrook and Catherine, not Hythe at all."

Everyone turned to stare at him.

"Then who raped her?" Narraway asked. "It is difficult to believe Neville Forsbrook did it, in that case, isn't it?"

"Pelham Forsbrook maybe?" Charlotte replied, seizing the idea. "If he did beat Eleanor, he's a violent man. And she was supposedly running away from him when she was killed." She looked to Pitt.

"Yes," he agreed quickly. He turned to Narraway. "Was Pelham still at the Spanish Embassy when Catherine was raped?"

Narraway thought for a moment. "I saw Neville leave quite a while before ten. I think Pelham went around the same time. It would just have been possible. He would have known Quixwood was still there, and likely to remain at least another hour or more."

"How do we suggest that?" Symington asked, returning to the practical. "I've tried everything, but I can't persuade Hythe to admit that he was doing financial investigation for Catherine, even though it might offer the only defense he has."

Vespasia spoke for the first time in several minutes. "Realistically, Mr. Symington, what chance has that defense of succeeding, even in raising a doubt?"

He sighed. "Very little," he confessed.

"Then if Hythe's greatest concern is to keep someone safe, so he can provide care for his wife, dare he take the chance of trying what we are suggesting?"

"I wouldn't. Not if I loved my wife enough," Symington said.

Now Pitt was frowning. "Are we saying that Quixwood would look after Maris Hythe to keep Alban silent about his financial deceit, and in the process save Pelham Forsbrook, the man he hates enough to ruin, and who raped his wife? You can't convince me of that."

"And there is another question still to be answered," Vespasia continued. "Why did Quixwood lie to defend Neville Forsbrook in the case of Angeles Castelbranco? What was his purpose in that? We are still presuming he lied, aren't we?"

"Yes," Pitt said instantly. "Neville raped Alice Townley, and very possibly several other girls: one we know of, others we may not."

"Have we two rapists, father and son?" Narraway asked, frowning. "That might explain where Neville learned his behavior, from his father's violence and disregard for women, and why his father protected him when he beat the prostitute, and for all we know raped her too."

"We need to find something to prove that Hythe was getting financial information for Catherine, something concrete," Symington answered. "If we have proof, I know I can force him into admitting that was what he was doing for her, whether he wants to or not. Such evidence will throw doubt on the theory that they were having an affair, and will also help confirm whether Quixwood needed Hythe and Catherine dead."

There were several moments of frantic and miserable silence while each one of them struggled for a way to find any proof at all. Finally, it was Narraway who spoke, taking another tack and looking at Pitt.

"The Jameson Raid could provoke war with the Boers in Africa, which would be a very serious thing for Britain," he said, measuring his words. "Even if we win, it will cost lives, and at this distance be highly expensive. It could reasonably be within the remit of Special Branch, because the Boers will fight hard, and any country at war seeks to disturb the domestic life of its enemy. You can make an excuse to look into the cost of the Jameson Raid, and who was affected by it. You don't have to give reasons."

Pitt stared at him, understanding beginning to take a hazy shape in his mind.

"You have to start somewhere," Narraway

went on. "Begin with exactly what losses or gains Forsbrook and Quixwood made. You don't need to prove it, only justify what Hythe was looking for to give to Catherine, and show a cause for enmity between Forsbrook and Quixwood." He turned to Symington, who was now sitting upright, his eyes wide.

"Will that serve?" Narraway asked, although the answer was now obvious.

"Yes," Symington said firmly. "Yes, it will! It could be just enough."

"Good." Narraway nodded, then turned back to Pitt. "You'll need a little help. It might take us most of the night. If we get whatever we find to you in court by noon, will that be soon enough?" he asked Symington.

"Don't worry," Symington assured them. "I'll create enough of a display to keep it going until then. Thank you." He stood up. "Thank you very much. I'll go home and plan."

"Wouldn't you like supper first?" Charlotte invited him. "You need to eat in order to fight your best."

He grinned at her, a wide, charming expression full of warmth, and sat down again. "How wise you are," he accepted. "Of course I would."

■ ■ ■ ■

The trial of Alban Hythe resumed in the morning. Vespasia was again in attendance, this time aching with the double tensions of hope and dread. She watched Symington and was impressed with his air of confidence. Had she not known his anxiety from the previous evening, she would assume he had the perfect defense in his hands as he called Alban Hythe to the witness stand and listened to him take the oath.

Then, after a glance at Bower, he walked with grace into the center of the floor and looked up at Hythe's ashen face.

"You are an expert in banking and investment affairs, are you not, Mr. Hythe?" he began gravely. "Indeed, I hear you have remarkable skills for one so young. Modesty notwithstanding, is that not a fair assessment of your ability?"

"I have some skill, yes," Hythe replied. He looked puzzled.

Bower rose to his feet. "My lord, the prosecution will agree that Mr. Hythe has high intelligence, an excellent education, and is outstandingly good at his profession. There is no need for Mr. Symington to call evidence to that effect."

Symington's expression tightened so slightly, maybe no one other than Vespasia noticed.

Symington inclined his head toward Bower. "Thank you. I had not intended to call anyone, but you save me the anxiety of wondering if perhaps I should have."

A flicker of annoyance crossed Bower's face. "I fail to see the purpose of your observation."

"Patience, sir, patience." Symington smiled. "You have had several days to make your points. I am sure you have no quarrel with allowing me one day?" Before Bower could answer, Symington turned again to Hythe. "Are you acquainted with Mr. Rawdon Quixwood, sir?"

"Yes, slightly," Hythe answered. His voice was husky, as though his throat was dry.

"Socially or professionally?" Symington asked.

"Mostly professionally."

"You advised him on investments?" Symington raised his eyebrows as if he were interested.

Hythe tried to smile and failed. "No. That would be superfluous. Mr. Quixwood has great financial expertise himself. I doubt I could add anything to his knowledge."

"He is excellent also?" Symington asked.

Bower started to rise again.

Symington turned sharply, his face showing a flicker of temper. "Sir," he said irritably. "I afforded you the courtesy of letting you speak without unnecessary interruptions. Unless you are at your wits' end to keep your case together, please don't keep wasting everyone's time with pointless objections. His Lordship is perfectly capable of stopping me, should I wander all over the place without reaching a point. You do not have to keep leaping up and down like a jack-in-the-box."

There was a titter of laughter around the gallery and one of the jurors indulged in a fit of coughing, handkerchief up to obscure his face.

"Proceed, Mr. Symington," the judge directed.

"Thank you, my lord." Symington turned again to Alban Hythe, who stood rigid, his hands on the witness box rail as if he needed its support. "So you did not advise Mr. Quixwood as to his investments — say, for example, in the British South Africa Company?"

Bower sighed and put his head in his hands.

"No, sir," Hythe replied, his body suddenly more tense, his voice sharper.

"Would you have advised him to invest, for example, before the news came of the raid led by Dr. Leander Starr Jameson, into the Transvaal?"

The judge leaned forward. "Is this relevant to the crime for which Mr. Hythe is on trial, Mr. Symington?"

"Yes, my lord, it is," Symington assured him.

"Then please get to the point!" the judge said testily.

"Did you advise Sir Pelham Forsbrook to invest?" Symington asked, looking up at Hythe.

Hythe was, if anything, even paler. "No, sir, I did not. I did not advise anyone to invest in the British South Africa Company, either within a year before the Jameson Raid or since."

"Is Sir Pelham Forsbrook one of your clients?" Symington asked.

"No, sir."

"Are you quite sure?"

"Of course I am!"

Before Bower could stand up Symington raised his hand as if to silence him. "Let us leave that subject for a while," he said to Hythe. "Was Mrs. Catherine Quixwood a client of yours?"

"I have no knowledge that she had money

519

to invest," Hythe said, trying to look as if the question surprised him.

Bower turned one way then the other, appealing for sympathy and some respite.

"Mr. Symington," the judge said sharply, "I understand Mr. Bower's impatience. You do appear to be wasting the Court's time. The charge is rape, sir, not bad advice on investment."

"Yes, my lord," Symington said meekly. "Mr. Hythe, were you socially acquainted with Mrs. Catherine Quixwood?"

"Yes, sir," Hythe said almost inaudibly.

"How did you meet?"

Vespasia watched with unnecessary anxiety as Symington drew out the growing friendship of Hythe and Catherine Quixwood. It seemed to be moving so slowly she dreaded that any moment Bower would object again and the judge would sustain him, and demand that Symington move on. She knew he was delaying until the luncheon adjournment in the desperate hope that Pitt and Narraway would come with something he could use. But the chances seemed more and more remote as the morning wore on. There was no sympathy for Hythe in the gallery, and nothing but loathing in the faces of the jurors.

Symington must have been as aware of it

as Vespasia. Still, he plowed on. She could see no despair in his face, but his body was stiff, his left hand clenched by his side.

"Mr. Hythe," he continued, "all these encounters with Mrs. Quixwood, which you admit to, took place in public. What about in private? Did you meet her in a park, for instance, or in the countryside? Or at a hotel?"

"No!" Hythe said hotly. "Of course I didn't!"

"No wish to?" Symington asked, his eyes wide.

Hythe drew in his breath, stared desperately around at the walls above the heads of the gallery. The question seemed to trap him.

"Mr. Hythe?" the judge prompted. "Please answer your counsel's question."

Hythe stared at him. "What?"

"Did you not wish to meet Mrs. Quixwood in a more private place?" the judge repeated.

"No . . . I did not," Hythe whispered.

The judge looked surprised, and disbelieving.

"Was that in case your wife should find out?" Symington asked Hythe.

Again Hythe was at a loss to answer.

Vespasia watched and felt a desperate pity

for him. She believed that he had liked Catherine, but no more than that. It was Maris he loved, and he was trying now to protect her future. Symington was forcing him into a corner where he had either to admit that he had been seeking financial information for Catherine, or that it had been a love affair after all. He could not afford either answer.

Vespasia found that she was sitting with her hands clenched, nails digging into her palms. Her shoulders were stiff, even her neck was rigid, as if waiting for a physical blow to fall. Where was Narraway? Where was Pitt?

"Mr. Hythe?" Symington spoke just before the judge did.

"Yes . . ." Hythe said. His face was pinched with pain.

"Was your wife, then, unaware of your frequent meetings with Mrs. Quixwood?" Symington continued.

"No . . . yes . . ." Hythe was trembling. He could barely speak coherently.

"Which is it?" Symington was ruthless. "She knew, or she did not know?"

Hythe straightened. "She knew of some," he said between his teeth. He regarded Symington with loathing.

"You were afraid she would suspect an affair?" Symington went on.

Hythe had committed himself to a path. "Yes."

"And be jealous?" Symington added.

Hythe refused to answer.

"Is she a jealous woman?" Symington said clearly. "Has she had cause to be in the past?"

"No!" Now Hythe was angry. The color burned up his face and his eyes blazed. "I have never —" He stopped abruptly.

"Never deceived her?" Symington said incredulously. "Or were you going to say you have never allowed her to know of your affairs before?"

"I have had no affairs!" Hythe said furiously.

"Catherine was the first?" Symington asked.

Bower looked confused, unhappy because he did not understand what Symington was trying to do. Finally he rose to his feet.

"My lord, if my learned friend is attempting to cause a mistrial, or to give grounds for appeal because of his inadequate defense, I ask that —"

Symington swung round on him, glancing briefly at the clock, then launched into a denial.

"Not at all!" he said witheringly. "I am

523

trying to show the Court that there is someone with more motive to kill Catherine Quixwood, out of jealousy, than any cause Alban Hythe might have had to kill a woman with whom he was, as my learned friend for the prosecution has demonstrated, having a romantic affair! Albeit, one in which the two parties never met in private."

"That's preposterous!" Bower said, the color scarlet up his cheeks. "Mrs. Hythe may well have been jealous, and it seems she had more than just cause, but Mr. Symington surely cannot be suggesting she raped Mrs. Quixwood and beat her almost to death? That is farcical, and an insult to the intelligence, not to say the humanity, of this Court."

Symington steadied himself with an effort. "My lord, may I ask for an early adjournment in order to consult with my client?"

"I think you had better do so, Mr. Symington, and get your defense into some sort of order," the judge agreed. "I will not have the trial made into a mockery for the lack of skill or sincerity on your part. Do you understand me? If your client decides to plead guilty it will make little difference to the outcome, but it may be a more graceful and dignified way to shorten his ordeal. The court is adjourned until two o'clock."

It was half-past eleven.

Vespasia waited an agonizing half hour, watching the minute hand creep arthritically around the face of the clock in the hall. At five past midday she saw Pitt's tousled head an inch or two above the crowd, and with no thought for dignity at all, she pushed her way toward him.

"Thomas!" she said breathlessly as she reached him and clasped his arm to prevent herself from being buffeted by those eager to pass. "Thomas, what have you found? The situation is desperate."

He put his arm around her to protect her from the jostling of several large men forcing their way through, a thing he would never do in normal circumstances.

"I have papers," he replied. "If the judge asks to see them they may stand up to scrutiny, or they may not. But they will at least give Symington something to use to persuade Hythe he knows the truth . . . if that is the truth, and we are right as to what he and Catherine were doing."

"Thank God!" she said, not blasphemously but with the utmost gratitude. "Where is Victor?"

"I don't know," Pitt admitted. "He may arrive with more later. I thought you might not last much longer."

"No longer," she said. "This is our last stand. We had better find Mr. Symington."

The trial resumed at exactly two o'clock. Symington rose to continue the examination of his client. He moved with a new vitality as he walked across the open space, papers in his hand, and looked up at Hythe.

"Circumstances have placed you in a most unfortunate position, Mr. Hythe," he began smoothly. "You have an expertise that was sorely needed by a charming woman, with a conscience regarding financial honesty. I can call witnesses to testify to all that I am about to say, but let us begin by allowing you to testify to it first, and then if my learned friend, Mr. Bower, disagrees, we can proceed from there."

He looked up at Hythe with a sunny smile. "Catherine Quixwood knew of your financial reputation and sought you out, is that correct?"

Hythe hesitated.

"Do not oblige me to repeat the questions, Mr. Hythe," Symington said gently. "You know the answer, and so do I."

Hythe gulped. "Yes."

"Thank you. She sought you out and cultivated your acquaintance. She was a few years older than you, a beautiful woman of a slightly higher social rank, and she was troubled by a matter in which she very urgently wished for advice?" He held up the papers in his hand, still smiling. "Do not make me pull your teeth one by one, Mr. Hythe."

"Yes," Hythe admitted again, his eyes on the papers as Symington lowered them. Everyone in the court could see that they were covered on one side with writing.

Symington looked at the judge. "My lord, I shall put these papers into evidence, and give them to Mr. Bower, if it is necessary. But as they are financial papers of some very private nature, I would prefer not to do that, as long as my client cooperates, and at last we can get to the truth."

Bower stood up.

The judge held out his hand. "Mr. Symington, I am not going to allow you to dazzle the court with any of your parlor tricks. Show me what it is you have."

Symington passed them to him without a murmur.

The judge read them, his face darkening. He passed them back and Symington took them again.

"Where did you get these?" the judge demanded grimly. "And if you do not tell me the truth, Mr. Symington, you are likely to find your legal career at an end. Do you understand me, sir?"

"Yes, my lord. I have obtained them from Her Majesty's Special Branch, in the interests of justice."

The judge rolled his eyes, but held out one hand to require Bower to take his seat again.

"Very well. Do you intend to call Commander Pitt of Special Branch to testify?"

"Not unless absolutely necessary, my lord."

"Then get on with it. But I warn you, one toe over the line and I will stop you."

"Yes, my lord. Thank you." Symington turned again to Hythe.

From the front row of the gallery Vespasia could see that Symington's hands were shaking. Hythe looked gray-faced. The jurors stared at Symington as if mesmerized. There was absolute silence in the gallery, not a movement, not a breath.

Symington began again.

"Did Catherine Quixwood tell you why she wished this information, Mr. Hythe?"

Hythe looked as if he was about to faint.

Bower had a slight sneer on his face.

"It is not a pleasant thing to hang, Mr. Hythe!" Symington said with a hard edge to his voice. "Not pleasant for those who love you either. I ask you again, why did Catherine Quixwood wish for this information? If you don't answer, I can do it for you, and I will."

This time Bower did rise. "My lord, Mr. Symington is bullying his own witness, possibly asking him to condemn himself with words out of his own mouth."

The judge looked at Symington, his contempt clear.

Symington turned to Hythe.

Vespasia knew this was his last chance.

Hythe drew in a deep breath. "She believed that her husband had advised someone very badly on investments in Africa," he said with a catch in his voice. "She wanted to prove either that it was true, or that it was not. And if . . . if it was true, she thought he might repay some of the terrible loss."

"Voluntarily, or that he could be compelled to?" Symington asked.

Hythe gulped again. "That the damage to his reputation as a financial adviser would oblige him to . . . to keep the matter private," he said hoarsely.

Symington nodded. "And that was the reason she sought you out, and saw you increasingly frequently, and with a degree of privacy, at places your conversations would not be overheard, and where her husband would not know of it?"

"That is what she said," Hythe agreed.

"And have you any evidence that this is what she asked you to research for her?" Symington pressed.

"She was very knowledgeable in the matter," Hythe answered. "You have the papers in your hand. You know exactly what she wanted, and that it all makes sense. If you look at the dates you will see it is cumulative. After understanding one piece she then asked for more, based upon that knowledge. She was . . . she was most intelligent."

"Was she aware of the plans for the Jameson Raid before it took place?" Symington asked with interest.

There was a rustle of movement in the gallery. Several jurors looked startled, one leaned forward, his face tense.

"She was aware that something of that nature would happen, yes."

"But not that it would fail?" Symington continued. "Or did she know that too?"

"She believed it would," Hythe answered.

Symington looked surprised. "Really? Very perceptive indeed. Do you know why she believed that?"

Hythe hesitated again, glancing down.

"Mr. Hythe!" Symington said sharply. "What did she know?"

Hythe jerked up his head. "She observed the behavior of other people," he said so quietly even the judge was obliged to lean forward to hear him.

"What other people?" Symington asked. "Did she have access to plans?"

"No," Hythe said instantly. "She was aware of who was investing, and of who was not." He looked exasperated. "The raid cost a fortune, Mr. Symington. People pumped money into it: for men, guns, munitions, other equipment. She watched and listened." His voice caught suddenly. "She was a very intelligent woman and she cared deeply about the situation."

"Indeed," Symington said with sudden emotions thickening his voice. "Altogether a remarkable woman, and her violation and death is a tragedy that must not go unpunished." He hesitated a moment before going on.

One of the jurors had tears on his face. Another pulled out a large white handkerchief and mopped himself as if he was too hot.

Even Bower sat still.

Symington cleared his throat and went on. "So Catherine Quixwood had gathered a good deal of financial information regarding the Jameson Raid, and about various people who had made or lost money that had been invested in guns, munitions, and other speculations in Africa?" he asked Hythe.

"Yes," Hythe said simply.

"Could this have been damaging to anyone, financially or in reputation, had she made it public?" Symington was careful to avoid naming anybody.

Hythe stared at him. "Yes, of course it would."

"Very damaging?" Symington pressed.

"Yes."

"Financial reputations depend upon trust, discretion, word of mouth, is that correct?"

"Yes."

"Is it then possible, Mr. Hythe — indeed, probable — that there is someone named in these papers," Symington held them up, "who would be ruined if she were to have made them public . . . had she lived?"

"Yes." Hythe's voice was barely able to be heard, even in the silent courtroom.

At last Bower rose to his feet. "My lord, this is all supposition. If it were truly the case, why on earth would the accused not have said so in the first place?"

The judge looked at Symington.

Symington smiled. He turned back to Hythe. "Mr. Hythe, you have a young and lovely wife to whom you are devoted, do you not? If you are found guilty and hanged, she will be alone and defenseless, disgraced, and possibly penniless. Are you afraid for her? Are you specifically afraid that if you name the man Catherine Quixwood could have ruined, and whom her evidence could still ruin, that he will take out his vengeance on your wife?"

There was a gasp of horror around the gallery. Several of the jurors stiffened and looked appalled. Even the judge's face was grim.

Hythe stood frozen.

Symington was not yet finished. "Mr. Hythe, is that why I have been obliged to force this information from you, with the help of Special Branch, and financial papers that should have been confidential? Are you willing to be found guilty of a crime you did not commit, against a woman for whom you had the greatest admiration, because if you do not then your own beloved wife will be the next victim?"

It was a rhetorical question. He did not need or expect an answer.

He turned to the judge.

"My lord, I have no way of forcing Mr.

Hythe to reply, nor in any honorable way would I wish to. I hope were I in his situation, I would have the courage and the depth of loyalty and honor to die, even such a hideous death as judicial hanging, to save someone I loved." His face was devoid of all his confidence and easy charm; there was nothing in it but awe, as if he had seen something overwhelmingly beautiful, and it had robbed him of pretense. "I have no more questions for him."

Vespasia, watching him, hoped with an intensity that surprised her that all he'd said was true. And then with pain almost physical, she longed to love with that depth again herself. She dreaded sinking into a graceful and passionless old age. It would be far better to die all at once than inch by inch, knowing the heart of you was gone.

She forced the thought from her mind. This moment belonged to Alban Hythe. It was his life they must save. Where was Victor? Why had he not found something, or at least come here?

Someone in the gallery sobbed.

It was now Bower's turn. He walked forward into the center of the open floor space. For a moment he appeared confused. For the first time in the entire trial, the public tide was against him. If he criticized

Hythe he would seem boorish, a man close to brutality.

"Mr. Hythe," he began slowly, "my learned friend has suggested, but not proved, that you were seeking information for Mrs. Quixwood so that she could expose certain financial advice that was . . . shall we say, dishonest. You previously had been, for whatever reason, desperately reluctant to cooperate with him." He cleared his throat awkwardly. "Did you come by this information honestly, Mr. Hythe? Mr. Symington has said that his copies were provided by Special Branch. How, then, were you able to obtain them?"

Hythe looked wretched. "I don't know for certain what papers Mr. Symington has, sir," he replied, his voice hoarse. "I had bank papers from several different sources, which put together produced the conclusions you mention."

"I see. And you are suggesting that one of the men implicated in these dealings raped Mrs. Quixwood? If he feared her information so much, why on earth did he rape her? And did he leave her alive to testify against him? That appears unbelievably stupid, doesn't it?"

"I suppose, but I have no idea who raped her," Hythe said.

Symington stood up. "My lord, Mr. Bower is sabotaging his own case. Surely that is precisely what he is accusing Mr. Hythe of doing: raping Mrs. Quixwood, for no reason at all, and then leaving her alive to testify against him?"

The ghost of a smile lit the judge's face for an instant, then vanished again. "Mr. Bower, Mr. Symington seems to have made a distinct point. If no one else would do such a thing, then why do you wish us to suppose that Mr. Hythe would?"

"Because he was having an affair with Mrs. Quixwood, my lord," Bower said between his teeth. "And she refused him. It was not a natural thing to do, but men in the throes of passion and rejection do not always behave naturally. The suggestion that she was raped to silence her evidence would be presuming a totally cold and rational crime."

"Mr. Symington?" the judge inquired. "What do you say to that?"

Symington hid his chagrin well, but Vespasia saw it, and knew that at least one or two of the jurors would also.

"Mr. Hythe was not having an affair with Mrs. Quixwood, my lord," Symington said. "They met always in public places and no witness whatever has been called to testify to any behavior that would not be perfectly in keeping with simple friendship. If there were such witnesses, I'm sure Mr. Bower would have produced them, with pleasure."

At that moment there was a slight stir in the gallery. Vespasia half turned in her seat to see Victor Narraway walk down the center aisle and stop at Symington's table. He handed him a folded piece of paper, then moved back again to find a seat wherever anyone would make room for him.

Bower ignored the interruption and looked back again at Hythe.

"Mr. Hythe, do you seriously expect the Court, the jury of sensible men of business and professions themselves, to believe that some man, like themselves, unfortunately invested money in an African venture that went wrong — possibly about which he was badly advised — and that this man knew that an outwardly respectable, pretty young married woman had unearthed evidence that would be embarrassing to him? Then instead of stealing the evidence, or seeking to keep it confidential in some normal way, he went to her home, raped and beat her, but left her living? And all this was in order to hide his embarrassment at an unfortunate business venture? One in which, I might add, he is hardly alone? Sir, you strain credulity to the point of madness!"

Vespasia felt the wave of despair wash over her until she was drowning in it. Only minutes ago they had been winning — now, suddenly, it could be over.

Bower made an elaborate gesture of invitation to Symington, who was already on his feet.

Symington had no papers in his hands this time. He walked over to the stand and looked up at Hythe.

"That does sound rather absurd, doesn't it, Mr. Hythe?" he said, his charming smile back again. "Some stranger choosing such a course would have been an idiot. How could it possibly have succeeded? Why rape? That is an act of hate, of contempt, of overwhelming rage against women, but hardly one designed to rescue a financial reputation in trouble."

He looked at the jury. "But, gentlemen, that is what my learned friend suggested to you, not what I suggest. Imagine instead, if you will, an old hatred, centered on two men and one beautiful and willful woman, the wife of one of these men, and the mistress of the other. It is a story of high passion and hatred, the oldest jealousy in the world. It is woven out of the very fabric of human nature. Is this believable?"

"My lord!" Bower protested eagerly.

The judge held up his hand to silence Bower. "Mr. Symington, I presume you have some evidence for this? We are not off on a fairy story, are we?"

"No, my lord. I will call Lord Narraway to the stand to testify, if necessary. I am hoping to save the Court's time by asking Mr. Hythe himself. I am sure if we can reach a conclusion this afternoon, the Court would be better served."

"Get on with it, then," the judge directed. "Is Lord Narraway in court, should we require him? I presume we are speaking of Victor Narraway, who used to be head of Special Branch, until recently? I do not know him by sight."

"Yes, my lord, we are. And he is present in court. It was he who just passed me the information I now wish to offer."

"Proceed."

Symington thanked him and looked again at Hythe.

"To continue our story, Mr. Hythe. This beautiful woman was violently beaten by her jealous husband, justifiably jealous. She attempted to run away with her lover, but met with a tragic accident instead, and was killed. The lover never forgave the husband for beating her, and to his mind, causing her death. He planned a long and bitter revenge."

He glanced at the jury, then back at Hythe. There was not a sound in the room.

"But he was unaware that his own wife had learned of the affair," he continued. "And that she also learned of his revenge. She was an intelligent woman, observant, and she knew his nature. She was afraid of his rage succeeding, and all the destruction it would cause. She sought to prevent it."

Someone in the gallery coughed and the sound was like an explosion.

"But he realized what she was doing and needed to stop her," he went on. "Revelation of how he used his professional knowledge and power would ruin his reputation, and his career, even if it was too late to stop the plan from succeeding."

Hythe was ashen, seemed beyond the ability to speak.

But then, Symington gave him little chance.

"It so happens that the husband of the woman who died was a violent man, as we know. But what far fewer people were aware of is that this man's son is even more violent, that he is already guilty of several rapes, all with a consistent pattern of brutality. Are you following me, Mr. Hythe? No

540

matter, I am almost at the end. One husband who needs to protect his revenge from exposure by his wife, pays his enemy's son to rape this same wife, violently and terribly. He himself leaves her favorite wine laced with a deadly dose of laudanum, certain that in her extremity she will drink it."

No one stirred.

Symington continued.

"He also manages to conveniently place a love letter of his own from his wife, to make it seem that the man who provided her with evidence of his revenge will be blamed for her rape. Thus in one terrible night he has destroyed the wife who would have exposed his revenge, and the man who provided her with the information. And he has done one more thing to protect himself. He has befriended the wife of the man he has framed, and promised to look after her when the unfortunate man is hanged. No doubt he has also said that he will see her destroyed if this man does not take the blame, silently and bravely, without speaking a word of the truth.

"Do I have your attention now, Mr. Hythe?"

Hythe was hanging on to the railing of the witness stand — but even so, his knees crumpled and he all but collapsed.

Symington turned to the jury. "Gentlemen, was ever greater evil planned and all but succeeded in fulfilling its dreadful purpose? But you know now what is going on. You can prevent it. You can find justice for Catherine Quixwood. You can save the life of the young man who tried to help her prevent ruin and exploitation. You can save the wife he loves so much he will die to protect her. Leave it to others to find and punish the rapist. Already action is taking place to bring that about."

He turned a little with a gesture to include them all.

"The manipulators of money and investment will be punished. The wife who took a lover and was beaten for it is dead. Her husband has lost his fortune. We are almost at the end, gentlemen. Life and death, love and hate, greed and innocence are all in your hands. I beg you, act with the same mercy and forbearance we shall all need when we stand before the bar of judgment ourselves."

Symington bowed to the jury and returned to his seat.

It was Bower's turn to address the jury. He spoke little of fact, mostly of the brutality of the crime, repeating the worst details, his face twisted with rage and pity. He dismissed Symington's theories as a magic trick, a wealth of nothing, designed to mislead them. There was no substance, he insisted, only a desperate and self-seeking lawyer's castles in the air.

When the jury retired Vespasia was joined almost immediately by Narraway.

"Victor! What did you find?" she asked urgently.

"Catherine went to Bryanston Mews," he answered. "She knew that Quixwood was Eleanor Forsbrook's lover. A lot of what Symington said was guesswork, but it's actually the only thing that makes sense."

"Then it was Neville Forsbrook who raped Catherine?" she asked, still puzzled.

"I think it was Neville. Just as it was he who raped both Angeles Castelbranco and Alice Townley, and possibly others."

"And the laudanum?" she persisted.

"Quixwood surely put it there, knowing she would drink it. If she didn't he could always give it to her when he got home. It wouldn't have been as safe for him, but it could still have worked."

"What are we going to do about it?" she asked.

He smiled. "I hope we are going to get a verdict in Alban Hythe's favor. Then we will consider proving Quixwood lied to protect Neville Forsbrook from being prosecuted for Angeles's rape. I still want to see that young man pay for all he has done." His voice caught.

The jury returned after two long hours, every minute of which dragged by at a leaden pace.

The courtroom was packed. There were even people standing in the aisle and at the back.

The proceedings were enacted at the majestic pace of the law. No one stirred. No one coughed.

The foreman of the jury answered in a calm, level voice.

"We find the prisoner, Alban Hythe, guilty as charged, my lord."

In the dock Hythe bent forward, utterly beaten.

Maris Hythe looked as if she was about to faint.

Vespasia was stunned. She had truly hoped they had managed to cobble together enough information to create the required doubt, and the tide of despair that washed over her momentarily robbed her of thought. It was seconds, even a full minute before she could think of what to do next.

She took a long, slow breath and turned

to Narraway. "This is not right," she said quietly. "We have three weeks until he goes to the gallows. We must do something more."

CHAPTER 20

Pitt refused to accept defeat. It was intolerable. Alban Hythe had neither raped nor killed Catherine Quixwood, and yet he had sat in court and watched the judge put on a black cap and sentence him to death. As always, three Sundays were allowed before the hanging, a period of grace — hardly much time in which to mount an appeal, even if they could find new evidence.

They needed more time. The only way to get that would be to have the Home Secretary grant a reprieve, and there were no grounds for it. Pitt had spent long hours at his office, wanting to be alone, at least away from those closest to him. Their pain distracted his mind, and he needed to be absolutely undivided in his concentration. He had no emotional strength to spare for comfort.

He paced back and forth across his office floor, shoulders hunched, muscles knotted.

He went over it in his mind again and again, but there was nothing on which to appeal. Symington, crushed and miserable, had already said as much.

He was convinced that the answer they had found, and in part concocted out of fragments of evidence, was the truth. The unimaginative, pedestrian-minded jury had not believed them. Why not? What had they missed, done wrongly? Had it all rested on Bower's stirring of rage and fear in them so passionate they could not think? Did they simply not believe that Catherine could have been as intelligent or brave as they had shown her to be? Did they need so intensely to punish someone that they could not wait for the right man?

Surely Symington had stirred their pity and their anger with Hythe's willingness to sacrifice his own life to save Maris? But perhaps they were more taken in by Quixwood's feigned grief.

He pulled himself up abruptly. The reason didn't matter now. He needed to get Hythe a reprieve from the Home Secretary, a stay of execution long enough to find grounds for an appeal. They must not allow it to be over. Proof of Hythe's innocence after he was dead was of no use at all — and also once the execution had taken place it would be twice as hard to convince anyone that the Court had made an irretrievable mistake, judicially murdered a totally innocent man.

What argument did he have to take to the Home Secretary? It was there in the shadows at the back of his mind, knowledge crowding the darkness. That was the power of his position.

He snatched his hat off the rack at the door, jammed it on his head, and left his office.

On the street he hailed a hansom and gave the driver the Home Secretary's private address. He hated doing this, but there was no other way to save Alban Hythe's life.

He sat in the cab rattling over the cobbles, oblivious of the traffic.

Much interesting and highly confidential information came his way. As head of Special Branch there were potentially dangerous secrets that he knew about many people in power. He had to guard their vulnerability to blackmail, or any other kind of inappropriate pressures. The Home Secretary was a decent man, if a little pompous at times. Pitt did not personally like him. Their backgrounds, experience and cultural values were different. There was no natural sympathy between them, as there had been between Pitt and many of the men he had worked for in the past. They had been well bred, in many cases ex-military or navy, like Narraway, but not politicians, not used to keeping the favor of others by always seeking the art of the possible coupled with the confidence of the majority.

As a young man the Home Secretary had studied at Oxford and been an outstanding scholar, a man well liked by his friends. One friend in particular had been charming, ambitious but a trifle equivocal in some of his moral choices. He was not averse to cheating when he needed to pass an exam that was beyond his ability.

He had begged the Home Secretary to cover for him, necessitating a lie. In loyalty to his friend the Home Secretary had done so. He had learned afterward, painfully, that he had been used, made a complete fool of. He had paid for it bitterly in regret and had never done such a thing again.

The friend had fared well, progressing financially. That exam success had laid the foundation of his career. He had climbed higher in his chosen field, still using people at every step. The Home Secretary had never betrayed him, nor had he ever spoken with him again, except as was necessary. As far as Pitt was aware, very few other people had ever known of the incident, and most of those were long dead.

Unwillingly but without question, the Home Secretary could be persuaded to grant a stay of execution to Alban Hythe. Pitt could make his alternative far too painful for him to refuse. He had the upper hand.

But it was a terrible abuse of power. If he did this, would he no longer be capable of knowing where to draw the line? A little pressure, a little force, a little twisting of the fear. How was this so different from rape, in essence?

No, he acknowledged, there had to be another way.

He leaned forward and rapped on the partition to attract the driver's attention. "Changed my mind," he said. He gave the man Townley's address instead.

"Yes, sir," the driver agreed wearily, adding something else less courteous under his breath.

Pitt leaned back in the seat, Sweat was running over his skin, and yet he felt cold enough to shiver. Was it so easy to misuse power, and to let it misuse you?

Townley's footman permitted him in only

because he insisted.

"I'm sorry," Pitt said to the man. "Time is short and I am fighting for a man's life, otherwise I would not disturb you at this hour of the evening. I need to speak to Mr. Townley and very possibly the rest of his family. Please inform him so."

Townley came out of the sitting room to where Pitt was waiting in the hall. The man's face was grim and anger lay as close to the surface as good manners and a level of fear would allow it. He did not bother with a greeting.

Pitt was uncomfortable, wretchedly aware of how close he had come to exercising the power he possessed in a way he would ever after regret.

"I'm sorry to disturb you, Mr. Townley," Pitt said quietly. "I need your help —"

"I cannot give it to you, sir," Townley interrupted him. "I have a good idea of what it is you wish of me. My answer is the same as before. I don't know what can have made you imagine it would be different."

"The conviction of Alban Hythe of a crime he did not commit," Pitt said simply. "In three weeks they will hang him, then any evidence that proves his innocence will be of little use to him, or to his young widow. I shall pursue it, eventually I will prove our terrible mistake, and in so doing shake everyone's faith in our system of justice, and I daresay ruin a few men's careers in the process. Then I may also catch the man who is actually responsible, but not before he will have raped other young women and, unless they are very fortunate, ruined their lives as well — perhaps even taken them. I am sure you understand why I would very much prefer to correct it while I still can, rather than try to mitigate the disaster afterward."

"I cannot help you," Townley repeated. "Neville Forsbrook violated my daughter and there is nothing I can do about it, except protect her from public ruin. Now will you please leave my house, and allow my family to have what little peace we may."

Pitt clenched his fists by his sides, trying to control his voice.

"Will you come and watch the hanging?" he asked levelly, even though he was trembling. "Will you try to console the man's wife afterward? She is not so very much older than your daughter. And speaking of your daughter, how will you comfort her in the years to come, when she wakens in the night knowing that it was possible she could —"

"Get out of my house before I strike you,

sir!" Townsley said between his teeth. "I don't care a jot who you are, or what office you hold."

The sitting-room door opened and Mrs. Townley came out, her face stiff, eyes wide.

Townley swung around. "Mary! Go back to the withdrawing room. Commander Pitt is leaving."

Mrs. Townley looked past her husband, her eyes meeting Pitt's.

"I don't think he is, Frederick," she said quietly. "I think he will remain here until we act, because we are standing in the path of justice, and I do not choose to do that."

"Mary . . ." Townley began. "For heaven's sake, think of Alice!"

"I am," she said with gathering confidence. "I think she would rather speak to Mr. Pitt and gain some kind of justice than believe that her experience has so damaged her that she would see a man die wrongly rather than tell him the truth."

"You have no right to make that decision for her, Mary," Townley said quietly, struggling to be as gentle as possible.

"Neither have you, my dear," she pointed out. She turned to Pitt. "If you will be good enough to wait, sir, I shall ask my daughter whether she will hear you out or not."

"Thank you, ma'am," he said, the sudden

release of tension rippling through him like an easing warmth.

Five minutes later Pitt was in the withdrawing room facing Alice Townley, who was pale, clearly very apprehensive, but waiting with her hands folded in her lap, knuckles white.

"I am sorry to ask you again," Pitt began, sitting opposite her. "But events have not gone at all as I would have liked. Mr. Alban Hythe has been convicted of raping and beating Mrs. Quixwood and causing her to take her own life." He did not shrink from using the appropriate words. "I believe he is not guilty, and I have only three weeks in which to prove it —"

"Mama told me," Alice interrupted. "Do you think Mr. Forsbrook did it? He wasn't anything like so — violent with me. He did not . . . beat me. Although . . . although I did feel pretty dreadful." She moved her right hand off her lap, lifted it, then let it fall again. "It was revolting." She blushed scarlet. "It wasn't anything like love."

"No, he did not act out of love," Pitt said gently. "Can you tell me exactly what he did?"

She looked at the floor.

"Perhaps you would prefer to tell your

mother, and she could tell me?" he suggested.

She nodded, not raising her eyes.

Pitt stood up and left the room, Townley, still angry, on his heels.

They waited in silence in the morning room, chilly, fire unlit at this time of the year. After just over a quarter of an hour Mary Townley came in.

Pitt rose to his feet as a matter of courtesy.

"I think it would be a good idea if you were to go and sit with her," Mrs. Townley said to her husband. "I'm sure she would find your presence comforting. She doesn't want to feel that you disapprove of her decision, as if she has defied you. She is doing what she believes is right, and brave, Frederick."

"Of course . . . of course." He stood up and left without even glancing at Pitt.

Mary Townley sat down, inviting Pitt to do the same. She was very pale and clearly found the matter embarrassing. Hesitantly, in a voice so carefully controlled as to be almost expressionless, she told him exactly what had happened, in Alice's words, including that Forsbrook had bitten her painfully hard on the left breast.

That was it, the connection with Catherine Quixwood, and with Pamela O'Keefe, perhaps with Angeles Castelbranco too, although they would never know that now, unless Isaura knew and would testify to it. It might also prove to the Church that Angeles was a victim, not a sinner. Pitt would not rest until he had done that.

"Thank you, Mrs. Townley. Please tell Alice that her courage may have saved a man's life. Did you see the bite mark yourself?"

"Yes." She touched her own left breast lightly.

"If it should be necessary, would you swear to that? I ask because Mrs. Quixwood was bitten in exactly the same place, and so was another girl, one who was killed. I think perhaps he killed her accidentally, when he lost his temper, and was more violent with her than he meant to be. She might have fought with him, as Mrs. Quixwood did. That seems to enrage him beyond control."

"Yes. I would swear to it. Are you going to see that he is put in prison?" Mrs. Townley asked with fear in her voice.

"At the least," he replied. "At the very least." He was making a rash promise and he knew it, but in this quiet, modest home it seemed the only possible answer.

He thanked her again and went out into the silent street. Now it was time to go to the Home Secretary, and ask, respectfully, for a reprieve.

Narraway sat at the dining room table at Pitt's house the following day. Charlotte and Pitt were there, and Vespasia, and also Stoker, who was looking slightly uncomfortable. The Home Secretary had granted a temporary stay of execution, but that was all it was. Symington was working on an appeal. He had refused to accept any payment from Narraway, although Narraway had offered it again. He had said that victory itself would be enough reward.

Now the five of them sat around the table over a plain but excellent luncheon, for which Minnie Maude had been duly praised.

"We can't let it go," Charlotte insisted as the dessert was being served and the last of the main dishes removed. "They may arrest him in a month or two, but what if he gets wind of it and leaves the country again." She looked at Narraway. "Are you sure Quixwood himself killed Catherine?" Her face was troubled, bitterly aware of the unfinished nature of the case.

"I am," Pitt interjected gravely.

Charlotte looked at Pitt. "So it was all started by Eleanor Forsbrook having an affair with Rawdon Quixwood? Do we know that was true? I mean know it, not based on a deduction but a fact? Is there really anything to anchor it to reality?"

She turned to Narraway. "Is Rawdon Quixwood as terrible as Symington said? Did he deliberately create this whole appalling tragedy?"

"Yes," Narraway said with some embarrassment. "I've never made such a serious complete misjudgment of anyone in my life as I have of Quixwood."

Charlotte smiled at him. "We might respect you, but we wouldn't like you very much if you had withheld your compassion until he had proved himself innocent or guilty. You can't go through life always guarding against the most awful thing you can think of. You'd be miserable, and worse than that, you'd push away every possible good thing there is."

Narraway looked down at his plate. "It was not a slight error. I was rather seriously wrong."

"It was a magnificent one," Charlotte agreed, glancing at Vespasia, and seeing her smile. "I hate halfheartedness," she added.

Narraway smiled in spite of himself.

It was Pitt who brought them back to the business at hand.

"The affair between Eleanor and Quixwood is fact. We have witnesses to that now. And the surgeon who examined her body after the accident said some of the bruises predated her death, so Pelham did beat her. And I've heard from Rafael Castelbranco that Elmo Crask also added to the story about Neville Forsbrook and the prostitute he beat. Biting seems to be a weakness of Neville's. That story is also provable, and is even uglier than we first assumed. Neville Forsbrook is a very violent young man with an uncontrollable, and evidently increasing, disposition to rape women. Who knows what has caused him to be that way. I'm sure having a father like Pelham didn't help him much."

"What are we going to do?" Vespasia asked, looking from one to the other of them.

"I've been thinking," Pitt said to no one in particular. "We know of Eleanor's affair and can prove it beyond reasonable doubt. We know that Quixwood advised Forsbrook to invest in the British South Africa Company, with almost certain knowledge of the Jameson Raid, and that it would fail, and that reparations would be enormous. It was worth the risk because for him the worst that could happen would only be that the raid succeeded and Forsbrook made money.

Even then, he could always try something else in the future."

"Did he know of Neville Forsbrook's situation with the prostitute?" Narraway asked.

Stoker came to attention. "Yes, sir. He was friendly with Sir Pelham Forsbrook at that time, and he helped get Neville out of the country. Still can't find out exactly where the boy went, but he started out in Lisbon, then seems to have gone on by sea."

Narraway was surprised. "Lisbon? Not Paris?"

"Apparently not. Paris might have been the first place anyone would have looked for him. It was a pretty nasty business," Stoker replied. "And Quixwood had connections in Lisbon."

Narraway nodded slightly. "Interesting. So unquestionably Quixwood knew of Neville Forsbrook's nature. Isn't there a way we can hang him?" he asked, looking up at Pitt.

"Only if we can prove he poisoned his wife intentionally," Pitt replied. "In truth, I'd rather hang Forsbrook for raping her."

"Why?" Stoker demanded. "Quixwood murdered her."

"Because Forsbrook is as much a monster," Pitt answered. "I want him not just for Catherine, but for Angeles and Alice and Pamela."

"You can't get him for Angeles," Charlotte said miserably. "Quixwood swears he was with him, so unless we can prove he's lying . . . they're both protecting themselves by protecting each other!"

"That's it!" Pitt sat upright with a jolt.

"What's it?" Narraway was weary.

"That's the way to catch them!" Pitt said urgently, turning slightly to face him. "It's dangerous, very, but it might work." He went on without being prompted, leaning forward a little, his voice anxious. "Quixwood doesn't really need Neville anymore. But what if we could persuade Neville of that, tell him Quixwood is preparing to give him up now that Hythe's conviction isn't certain anymore and we are still desperately looking for the true attacker, in order to prove Hythe's innocence!"

Narraway was staring at him. "And what? Neville would go after Quixwood to silence him?"

"Wouldn't you?" Pitt said. "Persuade Neville that Quixwood now needs to protect himself, and he can only do it by giving Neville up."

"Dangerous," Narraway warned, but the light was back in his face and there was a keen edge to his voice. "Very dangerous." He did not look at either Charlotte or Vespasia, or even at Stoker. "How would we do it? If you tell him yourself he'll instantly suspect a trap."

Pitt's mind was leaping forward. "Crask," he answered. "Elmo Crask. Neville would believe him; he is impartial, and doesn't have anything to gain by lying. Can you think of a better way — or any other way at all, for that matter?"

"No, I can't," Narraway admitted. "But we must plan this very carefully indeed. We can't afford to have Neville succeed in killing Quixwood."

"Or the other way around," Pitt said with a twist of his mouth. "If Quixwood kills Neville he can legally, and morally, claim self-defense, and still walk away, and there'd be nothing we could do to touch him."

"Though his reputation would hardly be untouched, after the evidence in court," Vespasia pointed out.

"Neither name was mentioned," Narraway said, his face tight with anger. "And anyone who did name them could be sued for libel. Quixwood still has the vast weight of public sympathy."

"If we do this right, we'll get both of them," Pitt answered.

"If we do this right, we'll be damned lucky!" Narraway retorted with a shrug.

"But let's try."

"Are you sure?" Vespasia asked cautiously. "If we lose it would be a disaster."

"Of course it would," he agreed. "But if we don't try it's a disaster for certain — and one of cowardice, because we'd be giving up, to avoid taking a risk."

Vespasia smiled very, very slightly. "I thought you would say that."

The next evening Pitt and Narraway were together in Bryanston Square, waiting until Neville Forsbrook should appear. Stoker was in the Mews, just in case Neville left the house that way. Elmo Crask had already been and gone. They had agreed three men should be sufficient to follow Forsbrook, and they dared not trust anyone else with their plan, nor did they want to involve more men in something which was, at the very best, questionable.

They were in a hansom cab, slumped down so as to be all but invisible from the street. The cab driver was actually an agent from Special Branch, but he had no idea of the purpose they were pursuing.

Crask had been gone from Forsbrook's house for nearly half an hour. To Pitt it seemed like far longer.

He was wondering if Neville could have

gone out of the back into the Mews to take his father's carriage and Stoker had missed him, or been unable to get a message to them at the front of the house. He was about to suggest going to look when the front door opened and Neville Forsbrook came out onto the step, hesitated a moment, then walked down to the pavement.

Narraway sat up instantly. "Get Stoker," he told Pitt. "I'll meet you just beyond the corner."

Pitt was out on the road in a moment and going rapidly in the opposite direction from Neville, keeping the hansom between them for as long as possible so he would not be seen if Forsbrook glanced behind.

As soon as he reached the corner, he crossed the road and started to run along the distance of George Street to Bryanston Mews.

Stoker was looking back and forth, and saw him immediately. Together, they returned to Upper George Street. A glance told them that the hansom now faced the other way, and Neville Forsbrook was no longer in sight. They raced along the pavement and scrambled into the cab as it lurched forward and the horse broke into a trot.

They caught up with Neville on Great

Cumberland Place just as he hailed a cab. They had already assumed he was going to Quixwood's house in Lyall Street, and so were not surprised when his cab crossed Oxford Street and went south on Park Lane. They expected him to turn right on Piccadilly and then along Grosvenor Place, and then finally right again on any of the possible turns toward Eaton Square.

The light was fading and the traffic was growing heavier. They needed to follow him more closely. There were carriages and goods wagons in among the lighter, faster hansoms. Pitt found himself leaning forward. It was completely pointless, but it was instinctive, as if he could urge the horse himself.

They reached Piccadilly and there was a jam as two four-wheelers all but collided. In a matter of seconds everyone had stopped, but twenty yards ahead of them Forsbrook's cab was clear and racing toward Hyde Park Corner. Surely it would turn down Grosvenor Place, but what if it didn't?

Pitt clenched his hands and fidgeted with impatience. How long would it take for Forsbrook to face Quixwood and attack him, kill him, if that was what he intended? What if the whole tragedy played itself out before they got there? It would be a disaster, and they would be to blame. No, he would, not Narraway or Stoker. Narraway was a civilian, Stoker Pitt's subordinate. The responsibility was entirely his.

What could he do? It was too far to run . . . wasn't it? He glanced sideways at the street, considering it. Perhaps he should go on foot, and have Narraway and Stoker follow him in the cab?

Pitt tried to suggest it just as the carriages ahead unlocked and theirs lurched forward, picking up speed, weaving in and out dangerously. He broke out in a sweat of relief. He did not deserve the rescue, he thought. This was a totally irresponsible idea. But it was too late to back out now.

It was another full ten minutes before they pulled up outside Quixwood's house off Eaton Square. There was no hansom outside, and nothing on the street except one Brougham coming toward them with a man and woman in it, their outlines visible but without color in the fast-fading light.

Narraway swore and leaped onto the pavement. Pitt and Stoker were only a step behind him. It was the middle of summer and the air was still warm. His clothes stuck to his body with sweat.

Narraway tugged on the front door's bell-pull. Seconds later, he yanked it again.

Silence. Another cab rattled along the street.

The door opened and a footman stood there patiently, his face expressionless.

"Yes, sir. May I help you?"

"Lord Narraway. I need to see Mr. Quixwood immediately," he said.

"I'm sorry, sir, that won't be possible," the footman replied calmly. "I'm not asking you," Narraway snapped. "I'm telling you. This is business of state."

"My lord, Mr. Quixwood is not at home," the footman said. "He left about five minutes ago."

"Alone?" Narraway demanded.

"No, sir, there was a Mr. Forsbrook with him —"

"Where did they go?" Narraway cut across him. "Now, man! Quickly!"

The footman was trembling. He was the same man who had been there the night Catherine Quixwood had been killed.

Narraway controlled himself with an effort and spoke again, more gently. "I need to find them both, immediately. Mr. Quixwood's life is in danger."

The footman gulped. "He said to tell you, my lord, that he had gone to the house of Lady Vespasia Cumming-Gould. He said you would know where that was."

Narraway stood motionless, as if an icy wind had frozen him.

"And Forsbrook was with him?" Pitt whispered, horrified.

"Yes, sir."

Narraway whirled around, leaving Pitt and Stoker to follow him down the steps and into the hansom again, shouting Vespasia's address at the driver. They were barely seated when the cab lurched forward. It threw them hard backward and then swung them against the sides as it swept around the corner and picked up a crazy speed.

None of them spoke as they hurtled along the now lamplit streets. The horse's feet were loud on the stones; the wheels rattled. One moment they were almost at a gallop, the next veering around a corner and skidding to straighten up before pitching forward again.

Pitt's mind created all sorts of pictures of what might be happening, and what situation they would meet. What if the footman had lied to them, on Quixwood's orders, and the two men had not gone to Vespasia's house at all? Or what if they were actually at Pitt's own house, and it was Charlotte, Daniel and Jemima who were in danger? Might Neville Forsbrook this moment be raping Jemima? The thought was unbearable.

Instinctively Pitt leaned forward and shouted at the driver to go faster, but his voice was lost in the hiss and clatter of their progress.

Or what if Quixwood had murdered Forsbrook and left him in his own house, and was escaping now to who knows where?

They slowed to a stop outside Vespasia's house. Pitt all but fell onto the pavement. Once again there was no other vehicle in sight, but now it was fully dark. It must be an hour or so short of midnight.

Narraway was beside him and Stoker just behind as they moved silently up to the front door. What if no one was able to let them in? The maids might even be locked up by Forsbrook or Quixwood.

Who was the master anyway? Was Forsbrook Quixwood's hostage, or the other way around? Or were they truly allies?

Or was this a fool's errand and they were not here at all?

Pitt could feel hysteria welling up inside him.

Narraway shot out a hand and gripped Pitt's arm, his fingers like a vise. "Back," he whispered. "Garden door."

"Wait here," Pitt whispered to Stoker. "In

case they try to run." Then he turned and led the way. There was a brief, highly undignified scramble over the wall and down again, then they tiptoed through the garden, probably treading on all kinds of flowers.

The light from the sitting room streamed through the French doors and across the grass. The curtains were at least half-open; there seemed to be no one in the room, then Pitt saw a shadow move beyond the curtains, and then another. He froze. He looked at Narraway and observed that he too had seen.

Might it simply be Vespasia and her maid? He motioned Narraway to stand well to the side, and he himself moved out of clear sight of the windows. Feeling his way he took one step at a time until he was just outside the glass. Inch by inch he leaned forward and got a better look.

Inside, Vespasia was standing motionless in front of Neville Forsbrook, her face pale. On one side of her, between her and the door, Rawdon Quixwood was standing facing them. He had a revolver in his hand, held steady. It was pointing downward, but any second he could lift it and shoot Vespasia and, when she fell, Forsbrook.

Pitt stepped back slowly and motioned to

Narraway. When they were a couple of yards from the window he whispered urgently.

"Quixwood has a gun. Forsbrook appears unarmed. They have Vespasia. They're talking, but through the glass I couldn't hear what they're saying."

"Quixwood's playing for time until we get here," Narraway said softly. "Then he'll shoot Forsbrook, and claim it's self-defense, which I daresay it will be, by then."

"Why here?" Pitt asked. "Why not do it at his own house?"

"Because this way he comes out the hero. He can claim he was trying to prevent Neville from committing another hideous act," Narraway answered bitterly. "And I daresay both of us will be accidental deaths as well, blamed on Forsbrook."

"He'd never get away with that," Pitt said. "Vespasia would . . ." Then he stopped, realizing that Vespasia would be part of the tragedy as well. His brain seemed to be unable to think.

"I'll go in from the kitchen," Narraway whispered. "Give me time, and then you go in from this way. We might be able to surprise him that way."

"What about Forsbrook?"

"To hell with him," Narraway hissed.

"We've got to get Vespasia out of there. I'm going."

Pitt grasped his arm, holding him with all his power, but the older man was stronger than he had expected. "Stop it!" Pitt said savagely. "If you pull us off balance we'll alert them and will both be shot. I'll go round to the kitchen. I know my way, and I know how to break in without making a noise. Wait for me, then come in this way!"

Narraway drew in breath to argue.

"Do as you're damn well told!" Pitt said under his breath. "I'm head of Special Branch — you're a civilian. Stay here!" And without waiting for further argument he let go of Narraway and crept through the flower bed.

He found the scullery window and, after fishing in his pockets, came up with a piece of sticky paper and a small, very neat glass cutter. He put the paper on the window near where the catch was and quickly, carefully, cut out a circle, holding on to an edge of the paper. He removed the glass soundlessly and reached his hand through the opening.

A few moments later he had the window open and was inside. It was dark and he had to move very carefully. If he tripped over anything, upset a pile of boxes or

bumped into anything, he would alert Quixwood to his presence.

Step by step he went through the kitchen
and into the hall. Outside the sitting-room
door he stopped. He could now hear the
voices inside.

"You think Pitt will come?" Forsbrook
asked huskily, his voice laced with fear. "He
won't. Why should he?"

"Because he's following you, you fool!"
Quixwood snapped. "He told you I'd betray
you so you'd come and attack me."

"You *could* betray me," Forsbrook said
loudly, his voice wavering now. "They'll let
Hythe go and come after you. They know
you poisoned the wine. Why would you do
that if you didn't know she would be
raped?" It was clear panic was mounting in
him, and that he was close to losing control.

"That's what they want you to think, you
fool!" Quixwood said, his voice scalding
with contempt. "Get a grip on yourself.
They'll come here. I told the footman to
tell Narraway where I'd gone."

"Why should he care what happens to
me?" Forsbrook demanded. He was nearly
shouting now. "Pitt would see me hanged
for that Portuguese girl. He knows it was
me, he just can't prove it."

"No, he can't prove it," Quixwood agreed.

"Or any of the others."

"They don't know about the others!" Forsbrook yelled. "And if you tell them I raped Catherine, I'll tell them you paid me to."

"No you won't," Quixwood said levelly.

"If you shoot, you'll hit Lady Vespasia." Forsbrook's voice was almost falsetto, panic tearing through him. "How are you going to explain that? The bullet'll go through her and into me. You won't be able to say it was my fault!" Now he was crowing, high and shrill, sudden victory in sight.

Pitt chose that instant to open the door, pushing it hard and following straight in behind it.

Quixwood had moved a yard or two from where he had been when Pitt had seen him through the window. He was closer to Vespasia. He heard Pitt and swung around to face him, the gun in his hand. He smiled.

"At last! But slow, Commander. There's your rapist. Or perhaps I should say 'my rapist.' He's the one who raped and beat poor Catherine. But I daresay you know that. Though, I must admit, I hadn't expected you to work it out."

Forsbrook started to speak, then changed his mind. He held Vespasia, tight and hard in front of him. "Quixwood's mad. He

574

kidnapped me and now he's trying to kill me. I don't know who murdered his wife. She must have had some other lover, if it really wasn't Hythe."

"You know exactly who murdered her." Vespasia spoke for the first time. "You raped her and Angeles Castelbranco as well. Quixwood lied to protect you, probably the price for attacking Catherine for him."

Quixwood raised his revolver. His dark face was twisted with passion. It seemed hate and pain were all but tearing him apart.

At that moment, Narraway crashed through the French doors and charged Forsbrook just as the gun went off. Vespasia fell sideways onto her hands and knees. Neville Forsbrook pitched after her, his chest blossoming scarlet blood.

Quixwood reacted instantly. With his other hand out, he dived toward Vespasia and yanked her to her feet, wrenching her shoulder and tearing her gown. He still had the gun in the other hand. His eyes were wild. He backed toward the door, swiveling his glance from Pitt to Narraway and back again, pulling Vespasia with him.

Forsbrook lay motionless on the floor, the blood spreading wider and wider around him. There was no movement of his chest, no breathing. Pitt scrambled over to the

575

young man, checking for any sign of life.

The door was half-open where Pitt had pushed it. Quixwood groped for it with one hand, still holding the gun in the other, his arm around Vespasia.

Narraway seized his moment. He snatched up a letter opener from the desk and charged at Quixwood. He did not go for the man's gun arm, or for his heart, or even his throat.

Quixwood hurled Vespasia from him and raised the gun, but he was too slow. The letter opener pierced him through the eye, into his brain, and he buckled and collapsed to the floor, Narraway falling on top of him, still holding the letter opener. The gun roared uselessly, the bullet crashing into the ceiling, passing an inch to the side of Narraway's head.

Vespasia climbed to her knees and stared at Narraway. Her face was ashen, her hair half-undone. Her eyes were wide with terror and her whole body shuddered.

"Victor, you idiot!" she said, sobbing to get her breath. "You could have been killed!"

Narraway sat up very slowly, leaving the letter opener where it was, embedded in Quixwood's head. He swiveled around and looked at the tears on Vespasia's face.

"It was worth it," he said with a slow, beautiful smile. "Are you all right, my dear?"

Pitt rose to his feet, too full of exquisite relief even to look for words. He watched Vespasia move over to Narraway and very gently put her arms around him.

"I am very well indeed," she told him.

ABOUT THE AUTHOR

Anne Perry is the bestselling author of two acclaimed series set in Victorian England: the Charlotte and Thomas Pitt novels, including *Midnight at Marble Arch* and *Dorchester Terrace*, and the William Monk novels, including *A Sunless Sea* and *Acceptable Loss*. She is also the author of the World War I novels *No Graves As Yet*, *Shoulder the Sky*, *Angels in the Gloom*, *At Some Disputed Barricade*, and *We Shall Not Sleep*, as well as ten Christmas novels, most recently *A Christmas Garland*. She lives in Scotland.

www.AnnePerry.co.uk

The employees of Thorndike Press hope you have enjoyed this Large Print book. All our Thorndike, Wheeler, and Kennebec Large Print titles are designed for easy reading, and all our books are made to last. Other Thorndike Press Large Print books are available at your library, through selected bookstores, or directly from us.

For information about titles, please call:
  (800) 223-1244

or visit our Web site at:
  http://gale.cengage.com/thorndike

To share your comments, please write:
  Publisher
  Thorndike Press
  10 Water St., Suite 310
  Waterville, ME 04901